SAM HAWKEN is a writer of contemporary crime novels and other fiction, who makes his home near Washington, DC with his wife and son. Current events in Mexico are his preoccupation, and *Tequila Sunset* is his second novel set in the Ciudad Juárez/ El Paso area.

Praise for *The Dead Women of Juárez*

"Tense and gripping" *Sunday Times*

"Unusual and convincing" *The Times*

"Evokes the dust, decay and death" *Metro*

"Heartfelt" *Guardian*

"Haunting" *Irish Times*

"Powerful and shocking" Dreda Say Mitchell

TEQUILA SUNSET

SAM HAWKEN

A complete catalogue record for this book can be obtained
from the British Library on request

The right of Sam Hawken to be identified as the author of this work has been
asserted by him in accordance with the Copyright, Designs and Patents Act 1988

First published in 2012 by Serpent's Tail,
an imprint of Profile Books Ltd
3A Exmouth House
Pine Street
London EC1R 0JH
www.serpentstail.com

ISBN 978 1 84668 853 9
eISBN 978 1 84765 826 5

Designed and typeset by sue@lambledesign.demon.co.uk

Printed and bound by CPI Group (UK) Ltd, Croydon, CR0 4YY

10 9 8 7 6 5 4 3 2 1

For those who fight the good fight

The city of El Paso, Texas is the safest city in the United States. Across the border, in Mexico, Ciudad Juárez is one of the most violent cities in the world, with over 7,500 killed since 2006.

PART ONE

ONE

IN THE SUMMER IT WAS HOT, IN THE WINTER it was cold and all year round the halls and cells of Coffield Unit were busy with the business of incarceration. This day it was not so bad, teetering between two extremes. The ceiling-mounted fans did not turn and the big heating units that blew and blew, but did little to chase away the chill, were silent.

Flip lined up with the convicts, dressed in their white cotton uniforms, waiting for the COs to open the door and let them out onto the yard. Barred windows let in sunshine to compete with sallow fluorescents. It would be good to be outside.

When the door opened the COs counted them off. Already they had been counted before getting into line and they would be counted again when it was time to go back inside. Counting was a constant and if ever the numbers didn't jibe everything stopped.

They went out mixed, but as the cons distributed into the yard they broke into their component parts. White boys congregated by the weight pile, blacks by the half-court basketball blacktop and the Latinos by the handball court. Within each division were individual cliques, but the most important grouping was by race. The colors approached one another's domains only when certain dictates had been observed. In this way the facilities could be shared without it coming to blows.

Flip was not the youngest Latino on the yard. That honor went to Rafael Perez, eighteen years old, doing four for sexual assault on a child. He was shunned, and when anyone took notice of him it was bad news. The other Latinos didn't even let him find a corner to hide in; he was forced to stand away from the walls in the no man's land between handball and basketball courts, exposed to everyone. He seemed smaller now than when he came.

Today Flip stood with Javier who was doing thirty-five and Omar who wasn't ever getting out. Both men were old enough to be his father. They kept close and they let no one touch him, not on the yard or on the inside, because he was one of them. Flip was an Azteca. They called each other Indians.

Javier was tattooed from his navel to his collarbone and on his arms, too. The marks showed on his wrists where his cuffs pulled back. He had his initials over his left eyebrow. Many of his pieces he had done on himself. He did good work. Flip hadn't ever gotten anything from Javier, though Javier offered more than once. None of Javier's marks were a gang patch and he didn't do gang patches. They were Aztecas, but no one could prove it. That's how they all stayed out of Administrative Segregation, where gang members went and never surfaced again.

If anyone asked, they were all just good friends. Old-timers watched out for new fish and new fish did favors for the old-timers. There was nothing the COs could say about that. No Indian would give up another Indian. From time to time one of them would be picked off, sent to Ad Seg, but that was just bad luck.

In all there were two hundred and fifty men out of four thousand in Coffield on the yard. They were watched on the ground and from the towers. Double rows of thirty-foot cyclone fencing and yards and yards of densely coiled razor wire stood between them and a tall concrete wall. There were flatlands beyond. It was two hundred yards from the wall to the first tree and the COs in the tower were excellent shots.

Enrique Garcia was one of the last out. He'd been in the hole for sixty days and now he was free of the belly chain and ankle cuffs.

His size was intimidating though his waist was thick. The COs were careful watching him when he came on the yard because there was trouble before and there could be trouble again. In the time Flip had known him, Enrique spent more days in the hole than out.

The sun reflected off his bald head. When he came close to the others he smiled from under a mustache that made him look like a bandito. He rapped knuckles with Javier and Omar and Rafael and César and all the other Aztecas. And Flip, too. His fingers were tattooed. Under his shirt he had ink of an Aztec warrior in full headdress and a bare-breasted maiden beside him. Flip had seen it once. A scorpion crawled up his neck. That one didn't stand for anything.

"What's the word?" Enrique asked.

"*Nada, jefe*," Omar said. "It's good to see you."

"It's good to be seen. Flip, *¿cómo estás?*"

"I'm doing my time," Flip said.

"Not much longer, right?"

"Another week."

"A week? So soon." Enrique looked up at the sky and let the rays of the sun fall on his face. He breathed in the cool air like he was thirsty for it. Flip had never been in the hole, but he could understand.

A group of convicts took over the handball court and broke out in pairs. They did not mix with the Aztecas because they were La Eme. There was longtime peace between their cliques because Enrique had brokered it. Flip stepped off the corner of the court to give them all the space they needed. Before long they were playing, the echoes of the ball bouncing around their corner of the yard.

"How's that motherfucker Danbury?" Enrique asked.

"He got out of the infirmary, took protective custody," Javier said. "Ain't nobody seen him since."

Enrique showed his teeth. "Teach those *negros* to talk shit. He shows his face again, it'll be his ass. *¿Sabes lo que quiero decir?*"

Flip looked across the open ground to the basketball court where the blacks held together. They were watching Enrique and talking among themselves. There was no peace between the Aztecas and them. There could be no peace. They had Danbury to answer for and Danbury to avenge and there was no easy way to work that through. Flip was glad he would be out of it soon.

"Flip," Enrique said and his put his hand on Flip's shoulder. "The first thing I did when I got out, I made some calls for you. When you get home, you're gonna be looked after. Everybody will know your name."

"*Gracias, jefe*," Flip said.

"It's nothing. Blood don't stop at the gates. José, he's my boy, he'll watch over you like I would. You got no worries."

The blacks weren't looking their way anymore. Some of them shot hoops.

"No worries," Flip said.

Enrique squeezed Flip's shoulder, shook him gently. "No worries."

TWO

"**N**UMBER TEN!" THE CO CALLED. FLIP GOT out of his bunk. He had the top, Daniel the bottom. When Flip was gone, arrangements would change. Flip's things were in a white cloth bag with a string tie.

"Time's up," Daniel said.

"*Adiós*," Flip said. "See you on the outside."

"Not if I see you first."

They laughed.

The CO stopped at the cell door. He was one of the new ones and Flip didn't know his name. "Number ten, open up!" he yelled down the line and somewhere a buzzer went off. The CO put his key in the lock, turned and pulled. "Step out."

Outside the row of cells there was a yellow line painted on the concrete. Flip grabbed his bag and walked over the line, stood facing the wall while the cell was locked up again. When he felt the CO's touch on his elbow, he turned and marched, the CO at his back.

The convicts in their cells called out to him. *See you, man. Hasta la vista. Good luck, hermano.* Flip raised his hand to them until they came to the end of the line.

"One prisoner coming out," the CO said.

Danny Mascorro worked the gate. He buzzed the lock and the CO used his key to get them through. Now they were in a dead zone between gates, Mascorro behind reinforced glass. They were under the eye of closed-circuit cameras. Flip nodded to Mascorro and Mascorro nodded back.

After the second gate they proceeded down a long hall with no windows. At the end was a steel door. A CO peered through a slot at them and there were more buzzers and more locks.

They left Flip in a big cell with benches along three walls. He was in there for a long time, until finally another CO he didn't recognize came to get him. The CO took him down a passageway to another, smaller cell adjoining a large room with desks and computers. Women in TDCJ uniforms were at work there, clicking away on keyboards, and they ignored him. Flip sat down and waited.

There was a window in the room beyond his cell and through that window he could see a tree. He didn't know if he was looking at something beyond the walls or if there was a garden spot just past the glass. In his imagination it was a yard with concrete benches and flower beds and a flagpole flying the American and Texas banners. Maybe there was a little plaque dedicating the space to somebody or the other. Quiet and peaceful.

He was daydreaming when one of the women called his name. "Huh?" he said.

"Felipe Morales?"

"That's right."

"Let's get you out of there."

Flip waited until a CO could come and unlock the cell, and then the woman had him sit in a plastic chair by her desk. She was black and had extra long nails. Her hair was straightened and braided.

"I'm going to do your release processing," the woman said. "There are a lot of questions, but we'll do them just as quick as we can so you can be on your way."

"Okay."

"All right, let's get started…"

The whole interview took an hour and a half. The woman gave him an envelope with bus fare and a few extra dollars besides. He had to sign his parole certificates. After that Flip had to go back into the cell again for another hour. He could see a clock from where he sat. It made time go more slowly, the sweep hand going round and round, and the minute hand edging forward. His palms itched and he wanted to be out of there, but everything in prison took time, even getting out.

A CO brought him a bag and pushed it through the bars. When Flip opened it up, he saw the clothes he wore on the day he went inside. He hardly recognized them. No one looked as he changed out of his uniform. The clothes fit loosely on him because he was leaner now. He folded up the uniform and set it on the bench beside him. The CO did not come back to collect it.

"Felipe? It's time," the woman said at last. "Kurt, could you take him? The van's out there."

The CO, Kurt, let Flip out of the cell and walked him out of the room. They passed through two short hallways and into a broad area with rows and rows of plastic chairs locked together, lots of fake wood paneling and a big counter. On one side there was a security station set up with a metal detector and a table for searching bags. Two women were going through the process right then. In the plastic chairs there were more women and a few men and a bunch of kids, from babies on up.

On Flip's side there was just a velour rope like the kind that closed off the line at a movie theater. Kurt unhooked it from the stanchion and let Flip through.

They moved past the rows of plastic chairs into a relatively narrow foyer. When Kurt opened the door for Flip a blinding crash of sunlight rolled over him and it took a moment for his eyes to adjust. The sky was cloudless and pale blue and the sun was like an unblinking eye.

On the yard there was some grass, but it was patchy and mostly trod away to dirt. Out here there were two squares of neat green bracketing a concrete walk. Here was the flagpole with the banners waving and here was a wrought iron fence that could keep in no one and an open gate. A tan van with the TDCJ logo stamped on the passenger door waited on the asphalt roundabout.

The driver was an older man. He came around and hauled open the van's cargo door. The windows had metal mesh on the inside. "Hop on in," the driver said.

"Good luck," Kurt said and he offered Flip his hand. They shook.

Flip climbed in the back of the van. There was more metal mesh between the seats and the front of the cabin. The cargo door locked from the outside.

"Next stop, Palestine," the driver said.

"Where's that?" Flip asked.

"You don't know?"

"No."

"Doesn't matter. You won't be seeing much of it."

The van carried Flip fifteen minutes through greened country until they reached a scattering of houses along the little highway. They passed a sign that said TENNESSEE COLONY, POP. 300. They passed a simple white church with a mobile home next to it. The letter board out front read: PASTOR ON VACATION. GOD ON DUTY!

They found a bigger road and even some traffic. Flip just watched the miles slip by. Palestine seemed to grow up right out of the countryside, a busy small town with broad streets and clean buildings. The driver navigated without pause. He had done this a thousand times before.

"Bus station," the driver said and they slowed to the curb. The building was compact and had a Greyhound-logo sign on the front, benches for people to wait out of the sun and a snack machine.

The cargo door was pulled aside and Flip stepped out onto the sidewalk. The driver shut the van up behind him. "And that's it. Get your ticket inside. You're headed to El Paso?"

"That's right."

"Long haul."

"I'll be all right."

The driver produced a little clipboard the size of an open hand. "Just sign off. Here's a pen."

Flip put his signature to a green form and got a yellow receipt back. He crumpled it up and put it in his pocket.

"Stay out of trouble."

"No problem."

The driver got into the van and pulled away. Flip stood on the curb with his bag and watched him go. When the van was out of sight, he went into the ticket office. No one looked at him strangely at all.

THREE

THE SUN WAS DOWN AND THE STREETLIGHTS were on. El Paso after dark. Cristina Salas sat behind the wheel with Robinson in the passenger seat. Sodium light splashed across the windshield and reflected off the dash, making half-strength images in the glass. If anyone looked their way, the glare would make them invisible.

They looked along a row of detached houses with little fences and enclosed yards. Beside the car, a broad wall was painted with a mural depicting a group of children playing ball in a sunny green field. There was a dog, too.

A scattering of trucks and cars were parked along the curbs on both sides all the way down the street. People were coming home from work, gathering around tables, watching television. The border was just a few miles south.

Cristina's eye was on one house in particular, painted sky blue and fronted with hip-high hurricane fencing. There were two steps up from the street and a gate to the high yard. Five figures, Latino boys, clustered around the steps, one with a basketball that from time to time he bounced off the sidewalk and the side of a parked car. Thirty yards away, Cristina and Robinson let the clock tick.

"You want my permission to do something?" Robinson asked.

"Give it a minute."

Of the two of them, Robinson was the older by twenty years, his dark hair gone gray and his mustache, too. Cristina knew that sitting for a long time made his back sore and they'd been here half an hour. Two empty Big Gulps stood between them in the cup holders and Cristina wondered if maybe Robinson had to take a leak. Old guys were like that.

Cristina caught sight of herself in the rear view mirror and plucked at her hair.

"Jesus Christ," Robinson said.

"All right, if you want to go, let's go."

"I'm just saying they're not moving on, so if you want to bust 'em then let's bust 'em. If not, just call patrol and let them do it."

"Cokley will wonder what we were doing all this time," Cristina said.

Robinson frowned. "We were fooling around."

"Okay, come on."

Cristina got out of the car. Down the street, the boys were in their own world. She was too far away to hear them talking. Robinson clambered out of his seat and torqued his back. The night was cooling down fast from the seventies at the height of the day. Cristina thought of putting on her jacket.

Walking abreast Cristina only came up to Robinson's shoulder. They crossed the street and came up the sidewalk on the boys' side. Cristina had her badge on a chain around her neck. She pulled it out of her shirt, let it dangle onto her chest.

They were inside ten yards when the first boy noticed them. He didn't have to look a second time; he pushed the kid with the basketball hard on the shoulder and then ran. The basketball fell out into the street.

Cristina and Robinson rushed forward. They yelled "Police!" at the same time. Three of the boys put their hands up without taking a step.

Basketball made a move between cars to get his ball back. Robinson snared him by the back of his jersey and brought him around so hard the boy fell to the sidewalk. Cristina sprinted past the others, picking up speed after the runaway.

The boy made it to the corner and nearly tripped off the curb. Cristina closed the distance between them, spun hard on the balls of her feet at the end of the sidewalk and came up from behind.

He broke for the far side of the street but Cristina stepped on his heel. The runner's shoe went flying and he fell over, skinned his palms on the asphalt, lost his cap. Cristina caught him by the wrist and the elbow and levered him onto his feet. "What are you, an idiot?" Cristina asked. "You don't run from the cops."

"Damn, man, what did I do?"

"I'll tell you in a minute."

"Can I get my shoe?"

She marched him back to the others. Robinson had them sitting on the sidewalk with their hands on the backs of their heads and their legs crossed in front of them. He held the basketball. Cristina sat the runner down.

"How old are you?" she asked the first kid in line.

"Eighteen?"

"How about you?" she asked the next.

"Seventeen."

Cristina went down the line. One was underage and two were nineteen. She saw the basketball player's jersey had a 21 on it.

Cristina had a Mini Maglite in her back pocket. She twisted it on and played the beam over the boys on the ground. Robinson stepped up. "Let me see your arms. Front and back," he said.

"You," Cristina said to Basketball. "Let's see your arms. Lift up your shirts. What kind of ink do you have?"

"Cris, take a look at this," Robinson said. He had a nineteen-year-old by the wrist and shone his own light on the kid's hand.

Cristina looked. Inked between thumb and forefinger were the letters BA. "You're going to jail," she told the kid.

"For what?"

"For being obvious. You, too, 21," she said to the basketball player.

"What about us?" said one of the underagers.

"Go home."

Robinson stood over his kid and Cristina kept a hand on hers. They called for patrol to come pick up.

"I still don't understand what's going on," the basketball player said.

"You're gathering in a public place and displaying gang markers, stupid," Cristina said. "That's jail time and a fine. Didn't you hear? Segundo Barrio doesn't like your kind around anymore."

"Lady, I'm not in no gang."

"Your shirt tells me different. Now shut up."

In ten minutes there was a car on the scene and the kids were cuffed and stuffed into the back seat. Cristina saw them talk to each other for the first time, getting stories straight. By the time they were back at the house, they would be well-rehearsed.

The patrolman was named Alvarez. He took notes, got names. "You let the other ones walk?" he said.

"Didn't seem to be much point in keeping them," Robinson said.

"Your call."

They finished with Alvarez and waited until he drove off with their boys before heading back to their car. Cristina punched Robinson in the arm. "Two down," she said.

"It's getting harder to find them. Pretty soon they're not going to need us anymore."

"They're still plenty around. You just have to *listen* to your partner when she says she sees something she doesn't like."

"Yeah, I guess."

"What's the problem now?"

"I need to find a bathroom."

"Old man."

FOUR

Back at the house they wrote up the arrest sheets. They had Alvarez's booking forms in front of them, with pictures of the two kids staring into the camera. "Get this," Cristina said, "our 21 has priors for assault and misdemeanor possession. And then he goes around parading his number where he *knows* we're looking."

"Nobody said Aztecas were smart," Robinson said.

"Got that right."

Cristina saw Cokley first, emerging from his office at the far end of the room, cruising past empty desks to land right on the spot. He looked over Robinson's shoulder, then Cristina's. His face was sour. "I got two members of the gang unit sitting on a bunch of kids any patrol car could have rousted?" he asked. "Is that it?"

"It's my fault," Cristina said. "I spotted them, I thought we should bust them."

"Well, I didn't think it was Bob because he knows better."

"Thanks, boss," Robinson said.

"Not so fast. You're supposed to keep each other from fucking up."

"It's not so bad. We got two."

"Two. And you have how many cases pending?"

Cristina had nothing to say to that and Robinson was quiet. She turned back to the arrest sheet, tapped out the last two fields and clicked SUBMIT. The printout of Alvarez's booking form went into her out box. Cokley was still looking at her, but she didn't glance up.

Cokley sighed. "Next time just call a car and let them handle it," he said. "Okay?"

"Okay, boss," Robinson said.

"Now go home."

The captain went. Robinson and Cristina looked at each other from across their desks. "I'm sorry," Cristina said.

"Forget about it. It's done."

Cristina put on her jacket and gathered up her things. "I'm running late. My sitter's going to want to know what's up."

"I'm looking at cold dinner," Robinson said.

They rapped knuckles before they headed for the door. "Tomorrow," Cristina said.

"Tomorrow is another day."

In the parking lot they went separate ways. The temperature was down in the low fifties now. Cristina was glad when her car's heater warmed up and took the chill off. Winter was struggling with spring and they were still in a desert.

Robinson drove north, away from the border, to get home. Cristina turned south, back into Segundo Barrio. At this hour she was twenty minutes away in a little place on South Campbell Street across from a vacant lot. She found a place along the curb and walked a hundred yards to the house. The porch light was on and there was a yellow glow through drawn blinds in the front window.

Ashlee unlocked the door before Cristina could turn her key. The girl was twenty-one and she'd been waiting in the living room. Lamplight picked up strands of blonde hair and gave her a halo. "Hi, Ms. Salas," she said.

"Hi, Ashlee, sorry I'm late."

"It's okay. Freddie's doing his thing."

The house was small and the living room was small, but there was room enough for a couch, a TV and a compact desk. Freddie sat with his back to the door staring into a computer screen. The television was on and low. Freddie's computer game made little noise.

"Let me get my checkbook," Cristina said.

"You don't need to pay me tonight. Just wait until Friday."

"Oh? Okay. If that's all right."

"Sure."

Ashlee collected her things while Cristina waited. They said their good-byes at the door. Cristina closed and locked it behind the girl. She took off her jacket and hung it on a rack. "Hey, Freddie," she called.

Freddie didn't move. He was little for ten years old and the swivel chair he sat in was too big for him. Cristina came closer so she could see what he saw: little colored men made of virtual plastic bricks in a world made of more bricks. He was building something – a car, maybe – and the only sound he made was the click of the mouse.

Cristina kissed Freddie on the top of his head. "Hey, peanut. Mom's home."

"Hi, Mom," Freddie said without looking away from the screen.

"Did you eat your dinner?"

Nothing. Just clicking.

"Freddie," Cristina said more firmly, "did you eat your dinner?"

"Yes."

"Okay. You've got twenty more minutes and then it's time for bed. Hear me? Twenty minutes."

"Twenty minutes."

She went to the back bedroom where she slept. The bed was unmade and there were dirty clothes on the floor. She kicked those aside and sat down. On the second shelf of the nightstand was a metal box. Cristina wore the key on a cord around her neck.

The key went to the lock box and her pistol went inside. When she had the weapon secured, she went to the kitchen. Ashlee had set aside a plate of macaroni and cheese, corn and chicken tenders. A minute in the microwave and it was fit to eat. Cristina ate at the kitchen table, staring at nothing, until twenty minutes were up.

The dish went in the sink to be rinsed later. In the living room, Freddie was still playing his game. If she left him alone he would play it for hours, nonstop, with barely a break to visit the bathroom, until he could not keep his eyes open any longer. Interrupting him took work because the first try never took.

"Time for bed. Save your game."

"I'm doing something."

"It's bedtime. Save it and come on."

Freddie turned from the game reluctantly and left the desk. He allowed Cristina to escort him to his bedroom and help him get his clothes off. His pajamas he could put on without assistance.

"We need to brush your teeth," Cristina said.

"No toothpaste."

"Yes, toothpaste. I won't use very much."

She brought the Winnie the Pooh electric toothbrush into his room and brushed his teeth for him while he was in bed, taking special care to get the ones in the back. He had decay there before that took a hospital visit and dentistry under anesthetic to address. Cristina did not want to go through that again.

"Okay," she said when she came back. "Time for the lights to go out."

"Will you stay with me until I sleep?"

"Sure."

Cristina turned off the bedside lamp and the room went dark. She sat on the edge of his bed with her hand resting on top of the covers, feeling his little hip through the material, as he turned on his side to sleep. She did not have to wait long before she heard his breathing turn deep and regular and then she rose as carefully as she could. When she closed his door, she left it part of the way open so she could hear him in the night.

The dish was still waiting in the kitchen and she washed it off before putting it in the dishwasher. There was beer in the refrigerator. She took one to the television with her, switched the channel to something mindless and put her feet up.

She was more tired than she realized and the beer let her relax into it. The show changed to something else and she barely noticed, just letting the pictures and the sound wash over her in a continuous wave of babble. If she thought of anything, she thought of the two junior gang-bangers they had busted. That street was only four blocks away.

Cristina did not live in the Second Ward, El Segundo Barrio, just because she worked there. This house had been her parents' and when they moved to San Antonio it had become hers. Freddie's room was once her room, with the same bed and the same furniture. She changed the mattress, but she slept where her parents had slept.

There were newer, nicer places to live even in Segundo Barrio. The developers moved in five years before and put up condos, but most of the place remained the same. Moving didn't occur to her, and because she saw the changes on the street, she felt safer here than before. Today was an aberration; now the gangs were underground.

She let the clock mark the time until it was almost midnight and then she turned off the television and put the beer bottle in a recycling bin in the kitchen. She turned off all the lights, went to her bedroom in the dark to undress. Freddie had not stirred.

The alarm was set for six in the morning. Cristina crawled under the sheets and fell asleep before she realized it was happening.

FIVE

HIS PHONE WAS RINGING AND MATÍAS SEGURA struggled up from sleep. He saw from the bedside clock it was three in the morning. He had been asleep five hours.

"¿*Bueno?*" he answered.

"Matías? It's Felix."

"Felix, it's the middle of the night."

"I'm sorry, but we need you right now."

Matías sat up in the bed. Elvira was still asleep by some chance, but she stirred when he moved. He spoke on the phone in whispers. "What's the problem?"

"Shooting. Six bodies."

"Is there no one else?"

"You know better than to ask that."

He left the bed and went to the bathroom. After he closed the door he turned on the light. It was blinding. "Where?" Felix told him. "Give me thirty minutes. No, forty-five."

"We'll be waiting."

Matías washed his face and felt the bristles on his cheeks. In the mirror the skin under his eyes were heavy from lack of sleep. He brushed his hair to bring it under control and scrubbed his teeth. Then he shut off the light and crept back into the bedroom.

Elvira still did not wake as Matías put on his clothes. His gun was on the bed-stand. Again careful not to make a sound, he crept from the room and shut the door behind him.

He made a cup of coffee in a travel mug and took it with him out of the apartment. Down on the street it was deserted. When he got on the road he was only one of a few cars. Mostly there were trucks at this hour, trundling through the abandoned streets of Ciudad Juárez on their way north to the border.

The drive was not long and he got there ahead of his forty-five minute deadline. First he saw the blue and red lights flashing, then the spectacular white of portable floodlights, as if a star were giving birth. There were municipal and federal police vehicles present. An officer armed with an M4 carbine stopped him fifty meters away. Matías showed him his identification and drove on.

Matías looked around the neighborhood. There were no street-lights and it was inky black beyond the crime scene. He saw an auto shop across the street from a gaily painted brick building depicting a rising sun. There was a scrap yard a few meters beyond that and not a structure above a single story.

Felix Rivera met him at the perimeter. The man also looked tired, hunched down in his black jacket marked POLICÍA FEDERAL. He wore a .45 openly on his hip while other cops around him carried automatic weapons. Matías was even more underdressed, without body armor and his gun tucked away underneath his arm. "Welcome," Felix said.

The bodies were scattered in front of the sun-painted building as if tossed by a powerful storm. Blood streaked and pooled on the dirty asphalt and two of the corpses were soaked in it. There were weapons, too. A pair of dead men still had a hold on their pistols.

A shower of spent shell casings spread out across the street, but were thickest close to Matías' feet. Looking more closely at the building, he could see the façade was pockmarked in a dozen or more places. The steel door to the building was perforated.

"It's an after-hours club," Felix explained. "Salvadorans come here. There's drink, drugs, women... everything you need."

Matías stepped out into the ring of light, careful not to slip on the discarded brass. He approached the closest body, a thick-chested man with tattoos up and down both bare arms. A bullet had passed through his forearm. Another three crossed his stomach and chest.

Kneeling close, Matías examined the tattoos. A naked woman. A gun. Another gun. A fan of playing cards. "Any of the bodies have gang ink?"

"Two. There and there."

"MS?"

"*Sí.*"

"What about the rest?"

"We'll have to wait until the coroner examines them."

"Or maybe they were just unlucky."

"Maybe."

"Where is everyone?"

"We're keeping them inside. Most were already gone by the time the locals made it to the scene. We have a few girls and employees, some drunks too messed up to run."

Matías stood up. "Did anyone see the shooters?"

"One woman saw them roll up. A pick-up truck with four men in the back. They opened fire."

"Did they say anything?"

"Not that she told us."

"I want to talk to the witnesses."

"Let's step inside."

The club was meant to be dark, so it was a revelation with its overhead lights on. What seemed murkily inviting during business hours was stripped to the bare, black walls. All the spots on the pool table where the felt had worn through were exposed. The floor was filthy, as if it had not been swept in a year. On one wall was an undersized bar, chipped and scratched.

They had managed to round up an even dozen and they were corralled at the back of the bar in battered, used-up booths with torn vinyl upholstery. Stained foam stuffing bulged out here and there.

"Which one saw the shooters?" Matías asked.

"That one."

Matías found a fat woman in tight clothes sitting alone under the guard of two armed policemen. She had fake-blonde hair that would also look better under dark lighting. Her face was not pretty.

He slid into the booth across from her, put his notebook on the table. "My name is Matías Segura," he told the woman. "What's your name?"

"Elena," the woman said. "You are another policeman?"

"I am."

"I already told that one what I know," she said and pointed at Felix.

"I'd like you to tell me again."

"Why?"

"Because sometimes when we tell a story more than once, we remember more each time we tell it."

"I want to go home."

"I think we would all like that," Matías said softly. "Now... tell me what you saw."

SIX

CRISTINA WAS UP BEFORE THE SUN AND turned off her alarm before it had a chance to sound. The house was very still. When she moved, she moved lightly.

In the kitchen she got things ready for Freddie's breakfast. He liked chocolate-chip pancakes made in the microwave and drank chocolate milk. It was all bad for his teeth, but Cristina favored peace over battles in the early morning.

Then she packed his lunch bag. Lots of carbs, like fruit and pretzels and chicken for protein. He was always happy when she gave him Oreos, but she had to draw the line somewhere. Besides, when he ate them he spent the day with a circle of black crumbs around his mouth that he never thought to wipe away.

At the appointed time she went to his room and rapped on the door. "Freddie," she said softly. "Freddie, it's time to wake up."

She put on the bedside lamp and Freddie curled up into a tight ball under the covers. Cristina put her hand on his back and rubbed it. "It's time to get up now," she said.

The boy was slow to rouse and when he sat up his hair stuck up crazily on his head. Cristina helped him out of his pajamas and lay his clothes out for him at the foot of the bed, always in the same order: underpants, pants, shirt, socks.

"I'll be back in a minute," Cristina said. She would wait five and come back to see if he'd managed to dress himself. Sometimes he needed help with this, too.

Today he put on his clothes himself, though he left his pajamas on the floor. Cristina dropped them in the hamper without scolding him and followed him into the kitchen.

"Chocolate-chip pancakes?" he asked because he always asked.

"Of course. Sit down."

"I want to play Roblox."

"Food first, then game. And you have to take your capsule."

The pancakes came out first. Cristina cut them up for Freddie and gave him the plate at the table. She went back to make his milk. Along with the powder, he had a crushed pill mixed in. He drank through a bendy straw.

"Drink all that up."

She microwaved hot water for tea and toasted an English muffin. From time to time she checked the clock and Freddie's progress with his breakfast. He was quick this morning.

"Make sure you drink *all* your chocolate milk," Cristina reminded him.

When he was finished, Freddie got up from the table. "Can I play Roblox now?"

"Capsule first."

The capsule was small, yellow and white, and could not be crushed. Freddie did not know how to put a pill on his tongue and wash it down with water so this morning, as on all mornings, he opened his mouth wide and stuck out his tongue. Cristina put the capsule halfway back and then flicked it to the back of his throat. She didn't understand how he managed to swallow and not gag.

"Now?"

"Now."

Freddie went to the living room. Cristina steeped a tea bag in a cup and put butter and jelly on her English muffin. There was still plenty of time.

She ate her food and followed Freddie out. He was deeply

engrossed in the game, playing with virtual plastic bricks. Lots of other people played at the same time, making buildings and statues and everything else a person could make out of such things, showing off for each other. Freddie informed her that he was making an elevator.

"We have to get ready soon," Cristina said, though they had another fifteen minutes. "You have five minutes to play. Okay?"

"Okay."

Cristina gathered his things by the door. Shoes, book bag, lunch bag, jacket. She ran the checklist in her mind. Pills all taken? Yes. Breakfast all done? Yes. Was there anything special Freddie needed for school? She couldn't think of anything and it was probably too late already as it was.

She let ten minutes pass before she interceded at the computer. "The bus is coming," she said. "Come and get your jacket on."

Freddie was prepped to leave when Cristina realized she hadn't brushed his hair. She rushed to the bathroom for a brush and did her best to bring it under control. They had to hurry out the door and down to the corner, time used up to the last minute.

The bus was late. Freddie fidgeted by the STOP sign. "Is there no school today?" he asked.

"No, there's school today. The bus is just late."

"I don't want to ride the bus."

"Well, you're riding it." A patch of yellow appeared three blocks down and quickly sized up into a small bus. "See? There it is."

The bus pulled up to the corner and Cristina ushered him aboard. She said good morning to the bus driver and waved to Freddie when the bus pulled away. He did not wave back. He didn't even notice her.

SEVEN

THE BUS TRIP TOOK SIXTEEN HOURS AND passed through Abilene, Midland and Odessa on the way west. Flip spent most of that time dozing. There was little to see driving through the heart of Texas and the bus did not stop for sights, anyway. He had learned through long practice the art of sleeping when he wasn't tired, as a weapon against boredom. When Coffield was locked down and there was nothing to do, nothing to read, there was always sleep.

It was ten in the morning when the Greyhound bus reached the El Paso terminal. Flip unloaded with the other passengers and fetched his bag from underneath the belly of the bus. He went inside and bought a candy bar from a snack machine. It was the first thing he'd eaten since leaving Coffield.

He made a call from the pay phones but his mother wasn't at home. She knew to expect him, but not when, and he regretted not calling ahead once he learned the schedule. There was enough money left in his envelope to get him home, but he imagined himself sitting on the front step waiting. In the end he supposed it didn't matter; he could not hang out all day at the bus station.

A taxi carried him the rest of the way. Flip didn't have money enough to tip the driver and he knew the guy was mad, but all he could say was, "I'm sorry," and he got out of the car.

His mother's house was on a quiet street with other houses that looked exactly the same. Hers was a coral pink with white bars on all the windows and doors. The driveway was empty, a naked basketball hoop without a net hanging over the car park. Flip looked both ways up and down the street and there was no one around. At least no one would stare.

He put his bag on the front step by the door and circled around to the back yard. His dog, Nacho, was dead now four years but the yard still showed signs of the holes he'd dug. Flip peered through the windows into the house, knowing he wouldn't see anyone but doing it anyway. He saw empty rooms that looked the same as they had when he left: the same furniture, the same pictures on the walls, the same everything.

Flip returned to the front in time to see his mother's old Impala turning into the drive. She waved excitedly from behind the wheel and he raised a hand. He wanted to smile, but time inside had quashed that instinct.

"Felipe!" his mother exclaimed as she got out of the car. "Oh, Felipe, have you been here very long?"

"Not long, Mamá."

Flip's mother was short and very round and she had to raise her arms above her head to embrace him around the shoulders. She squeezed hard. "I'm so sorry you had to wait. You should have called!"

"I did call."

"Not the house, my cell phone! I would have hurried at the store! Help me with the bags."

They unloaded the trunk of the car and Flip's mother let them in. The house's smell returned to him immediately: the odor of cooking and scrupulous cleaning. The floors were hardwood and they shone. There was not a bit of dust in Silvia Morales' home.

Flip put the grocery bags on the kitchen table. At first he thought he should sit down while his mother put away her purchases, but then he felt strangely uncomfortable and chose to stand. If he had been back at Coffield, he would have retreated to his cell when this feeling came over him, or to some isolated table in the day room.

"I have everything you like," his mother told him. "We're going to have a big meal and your aunts and uncles are coming. We'll do it on Saturday. Tonight it's just you and me. Is that all right, Felipe?"

"It's fine, Mamá."

"Where are your things?"

"I left them outside."

"Bring them in! Your room is ready for you."

Flip gathered his bag from the front step and brought it to his room. It was the second largest of three bedrooms, the smallest a sewing room for his mother. He was glad to see that she had painted the walls and left them bare. The front rooms were an assault of family pictures and artwork. He was not ready for all of that in his space.

His bed awaited, neatly made with a quilt on top. Sunlight from the side of the house slanted through the window, cut into slices by the burglar bars.

He had a desk that was clear of objects except for a pad and pen. Maybe his mother expected him to write letters to his people back at Coffield, or maybe it was just an innocent thing. His red chest of drawers was the same.

His things were mostly books and he arranged them on top of the chest of drawers. He had notebooks filled with scribbles and thoughts. These he put away in the desk where no one would see. When he was done he sat on the edge of the bed and let the hush sink in. It was never quiet in prison.

"Felipe!" his mother called and broke the silence. "Do you want something to eat now?"

"Okay, Mamá," Flip yelled back.

"I will make you something. Did you have breakfast?"

"No, Mamá."

"Then you'll have breakfast now."

Before long there was the scent of browning chorizo, distinct even from here. Flip slipped off his shoes and lay down on the bed, watching the ceiling. Despite himself, his stomach rumbled.

He wished he could say that being here did not seem real, but it was real enough. The feel of the mattress underneath his body, the smells, the walls… all of these told him he was here now and not dreaming it. Soon he would sit down to eggs and sausage and a cup of dark coffee. His mother would ask him many questions and he would do his best to answer them without frightening her. Maybe to her the years in Coffield would be like something seen through a haze, but it was fresh in his mind and he did not foresee a time when it would not be.

Flip closed his eyes, listened until he could hear the clink of cooking utensils and his mother muttering to herself as she cooked. He felt the warmth of the sun falling on his leg. As he did on the bus, he zoned into another place, letting time compress and speed past him. It wasn't until his mother called to him again that he came back to this room, this bed, this body.

"Coffee is ready!"

"I'm coming, Mamá."

EIGHT

CRISTINA SPENT THE MORNING AT HOME reading an FBI document about cross-border trafficking and related gang activity. The language was clinically dry and made her eyes roll into the back of her head, but she forced herself through all one hundred and twenty pages. In the end she felt she could sum it up in one sentence: *business as usual along the border*.

In El Paso they had gangs and in Ciudad Juárez there were gangs. They traded with one other and helped one another and the common denominator was cash. On the US side they caught kids as young as eighteen with guns stashed in the dashboards of their cars. On the Mexican side it was the same, only it was marijuana and meth heading north.

These were small-time deals, just a few gang-bangers looking to earn some money. The big fish swam in deeper waters, where a hundred kilos could ship without anyone batting an eye and dozens of factory-fresh AK-47s shipped south into eager hands. In Texas it was hard to get dope, but easy to get guns. In Mexico it was just the opposite.

Cristina and Robinson did not handle the big fish. FBI and DEA were both in El Paso and they took care of the big-money deals, the heavy weight, the traffic in guns. Customs and Border Protection, too. Cristina had even met two agents of the ATF once, looking into weapons trafficking through the city. All eyes were focused on El Paso and its companion across the river, Juárez.

She had an early lunch and drove to work. Robinson was already at his desk reading the daily reports. He had a big cup of Dunkin Donuts coffee on hand. "Afternoon," he said.

"What's up?"

"Not much. We're the safest city in the US, you know."

"Are we?"

"That's what they say right here."

"Well, good for us."

Robinson passed the sheets over and Cristina scanned them. One of them touted the results of "an independent study" that showed El Paso's overall crime rate was down one percent. In Central Regional Command, which was their domain, it was down five percent.

"Safest city in the US," Cristina remarked.

"Yep."

"I guess I ought to just go home, then. No bad guys to catch."

"We should be so lucky."

Captain Cokley approached them with paperwork in hand. "How are the fearless crimebusters this morning?" he asked.

"Getting by," Robinson said.

"Well, I've got something for you. Grocery store on 4th. Gang tags and possible protection racket. I want you to go out there, talk to the guy, see what you can dig up."

"We're on it."

"And don't stop for any juvenile delinquents on the way. You have real work to do."

Robinson drove. They pulled up into a yellow zone and put a police placard in the front window. Cristina had a view of the long side wall of the little family-owned grocery and she could see the graffiti from the car. "You got the camera?" she asked.

"Right here."

First they took pictures of the gang tags. They were easy to read: the tagger's signature, the neighborhood and the gang stamp: 21.

"Aztecas," Cristina said. Robinson took pictures.

They went inside. The place had a peculiar aroma, of closeness and age, that wasn't totally off-putting. This grocery store had been in the neighborhood forty years and it lacked the stark, almost antiseptic feel of a chain store. Fresh produce was displayed just inside the front door, still smelling of the earth.

A teenaged girl stood at the register. Cristina showed her ID and asked for the manager.

"The owner is here."

"That'll work, too."

The girl disappeared for a while and returned with an old man in his late sixties, balding on top and widening in the middle. He nodded at their badges and shook both of their hands. "I am Ruben Delgado," he said. "*Mucho gusto.*"

"Do you have somewhere we can talk?" Cristina asked.

"Come back to my office."

The office was a cramped space at the far end of the grocery behind a door marked GERENTE. Somehow Delgado had found room enough for a desk and two chairs for visitors. The walls had cheap wood paneling on them and were covered with framed certificates and civic awards.

Robinson sat by the door and Cristina squeezed in next to the wall. Delgado settled behind his desk.

"We saw the gang tags outside," Robinson said. "What can you tell us about them?"

"There's nothing to tell. One day they aren't there, the next they are. Those kids, they come by in the night and do it. We can't afford security cameras outside. Not to watch a wall."

"Okay, then what is this about protection money?" Cristina asked.

Delgado sighed. "One day last week, a young kid comes in to buy a soda. He talks to my girl at the front, says the soda is free. Then he says he has friends who will come around and want free things, too. She told me right away."

"Did they ask for money directly?"

"No, just free things."

"Do you have a camera up front?"

"Yes."

"If you have tapes from that day, we'll need them. And we'll need your employee to come down and look at pictures."

"Does she have to go?"

"Well, no," Cristina said, "but if we can find out who's hassling your employees, we can put a stop to it."

"The policeman I spoke to, he said that they can keep an eye on my store, watch for trouble."

"A patrol car can't be here all the time," Robinson said.

"I just worry. My girl, she's young. She doesn't need no trouble."

"We're trying to keep her out of trouble," Cristina said.

"When does she have to go?"

"We won't take her now, but if she can come down sometime this week, that would be good."

Delgado stood up. "You think they'll come and wreck my store?"

"Probably not," Robinson said. "If these are just punk kids, they'll mark up your walls, try to cause a little trouble and then get out. They're not a serious problem."

"Good. I've been in business since 1972. We've seen some bad times down here in Segundo Barrio. We thought times had changed."

Cristina smiled for the old man. "Don't worry about it. We're on it."

They left their cards with Delgado and his cashier, then retreated outside. Robinson put on sunglasses against the glare. "That was a waste of goddamned time."

"I don't know about you, but I didn't sign up to be on free soda patrol," Cristina said.

"The tags and the kid probably aren't even related," Robinson said. "I don't know any member of Barrio Azteca who'd stop at stealing soft drinks from a *tienda*. Somebody shows a gun, then they can start to worry."

"Broken windows, Bob. We're chasing after broken windows. It starts with a spray can and ends up with an AK."

"You think that girl will even come down to look at mug shots?"

"Nope."

"Me, neither. Want to grab some lunch?"

"I already ate."

"Then you can watch me eat," Robinson said.

"Captain will want us on another call."

"We'll tell him this one took a while."

"Careful, or my bad habits are going to wear off on you."

"I think they already have."

NINE

AFTER BREAKFAST FLIP LINGERED AROUND the house, but his mother was always checking on him and after a while it started to get under his skin. He took a shower and put on fresh clothes and told her he was going out for a while.

"Where are you going to go?"

"Just out. Don't worry, Mamá."

"Stay out of trouble."

He walked the streets of his mother's neighborhood first, unconsciously making note of who was home and who was not. When he caught himself thinking that way, he pinched himself and forced his thoughts onto another track. He wandered far afield, down alleys marked with tags and along busy roads.

Flip wanted to be where people were and eventually he found them. These kinds of people didn't mind if he looked at them a little long, or if he met their gaze. And there were women. At a busy food truck he saw two young women in matching blue shirts and jeans getting lunch. They worked for a maid service. The younger one looked his way and he tried a smile. She turned her head.

For an hour he sat at an intersection as the cars went by. He heard snatches of music out of open windows, watched drivers when they weren't watching him, enjoyed the feeling of being somewhere things were happening. There was no standing around in the city, no endless waiting. It made him feel good to be a part of it, even if he wasn't doing anything himself.

The weather turned warmer as the afternoon wore on and eventually he found himself back in his mother's neighborhood, retracing his steps to the house. There was a pick-up truck in the driveway.

His mother was there, greeting him, when he came through the front door, hugging him as if he had only just appeared. She led him into the living room where a man Flip had never seen waited on the couch.

The man stood up when Flip entered and offered his hand. He was tall and rangy, his skin dark. When Flip shook with him, he felt hard calluses on the man's palms. "This is Alfredo, Felipe," his mother explained. "He came by to see you."

Alfredo sat down again and Flip took the chair across from him. The man had the sleeves of his denim shirt rolled up and Flip saw his tattoos. They were blurry, as if done cheaply. Flip could not figure out how old Alfredo was. Maybe as old as his mother.

"It's good to meet you finally, Felipe," Alfredo said.

"I didn't know anybody was interested," Flip replied.

"Silvia told me all about your… problem. She thought maybe I could help you out once you came home again. That is, if you'll let me."

"I don't understand."

"Alfredo's here to offer you a *job*, Felipe," his mother said. "You said you needed a job for your parole."

"Mamá—"

"Just listen to him, Felipe."

Alfredo smiled and showed nicotine-stained teeth. He clasped his hands in front of him. "I work at a warehouse. We handle groceries for local businesses. I'm the manager there. If you're interested, I can offer you part-time work. It's not easy work – a lot of loading and unloading trucks – but it's honest pay. I can start you right away."

"They'll let you hire a con?" Felipe asked.

"I get a choice of people to hire. If I choose you, nobody will complain. I can't say that about everybody out there."

"It's a good job, Felipe."

"You want it, it's yours," Alfredo said. "As a favor to your mother."

"As a favor to my mother?" Flip asked.

"Right."

Flip sat forward in his chair. "You know what I was in for?"

"I know. It's not a problem for me."

"What if I told you I stabbed someone? On the inside."

"Felipe!"

Flip saw a muscle in Alfredo's jaw working. Finally the man nodded slowly. His hands came apart and he gestured to the ceiling with them. "What can I do?" he said. "That was on the inside."

"How do you know I won't stab someone again?"

"Are you going to?"

"No."

"Then I don't have anything to worry about."

Flip tried to read Alfredo's eyes and failed. There was something in them that he recognized from prison: hesitation or the rudiments of fear. The man did not show it, and that was good, but he felt it.

"Do you want the job, Felipe?"

"Okay."

TEN

MATÍAS HEARD LOPEZ APPROACHING HIS desk from behind. There was a way the man walked, an unevenness to his step that was distinctive, as if he were deliberately walking out of time. Lopez clapped him on the shoulder then and leaned in. "How's it going, Matías?"

Carlos Lopez was entirely average, something that Matías thought might account for his rise through the ranks. There was nothing threatening about Lopez, which might cause someone to think twice about promoting him, and nothing exceptional, which might inspire jealousy. He was a perfect blank. His step was the only thing uncommon about him. He sat across Matías' desk from him.

"I'm working the shooting from this morning."

"The Salvadoran club?"

"That's right."

"Let me see if I remember: six bodies and no witnesses, right?"

"One witness. Next to useless. I could have pulled the details out of a hundred shootings just like it. The killers arrived in a pick-up and turned the street into a bloodbath. Six dead, just like you say."

"No identification possible, I suppose?"

"Of the shooters? No way."

"How about the victims?"

Matías shuffled through his papers to find his notepad. "Two victims with MS-13 tattoos visible, nothing on the rest."

"And the coroner won't be able to check for more ink for a week?"

"At least. They're piled up down there."

A telephone rang at another desk. It was swiftly answered. In all there were a dozen desks, all decorated with the same lamp and blotter, all equipped with identical computers. Some kept their spaces more neatly than others. Matías' desk was scattered with documents. Every responding officer to the shooting had an individual report and every person on the scene was interviewed regardless of whether they had anything to say or not. Matías had six open cases, all multiple homicides, and the paperwork for these filled a wire tray.

"Who do you like for the shooters?"

"Something like this? Definitely Los Aztecas."

"Not La Línea?"

"Too low-profile. Just like those," Matías said, waving a hand at the tray. "The Sinaloa hire MS-13 muscle to hit Juárez targets and Juárez hits back. If a few more Salvadorans get caught in the crossfire, so what? The way the Juárenses figure it, MS-13 shouldn't put its nose in. I can't say I disagree."

Matías shook his head. Sinaloa cartel, Juárez cartel, Mara Salvatrucha, Los Aztecas, they were all mixed up together in a bloody mess that no one man could hope to untangle. Every man in that room, every desk, was occupied with the same questions. Every desk had its tray of bodies. Only Carlos Lopez cruised above it all, supervising the men beneath him, never touching the ground. If he weren't so plain, he would be hateful.

"So what do you do now?" Lopez asked.

"I can try to match the slugs taken from the scene with previous hits, but that will take forever," Matías said. "I could reinterview our only witness and hope she makes up something that sounds like the truth or I can put it on my pile, kick it back to the locals or the PF."

"That sounds like you already have the answer."

"I wish I didn't. Goddamn it, Carlos!"

Lopez blinked. "You want to hear something that will make you happier?"

"Yes, very much."

"The locals got a tip on your shooters an hour ago. They passed it to the PF and they passed it to me. Now I give it to you."

Lopez handed over a folded piece of paper. Matías opened it. "Do they think this is legitimate?"

"Don't you think it's worth your time to find out? Or you can put it on your pile, whatever you choose."

"Very funny."

Lopez rose from his seat and twisted his back until there was a loud snapping noise. He exhaled sharply. "Call them and say you're on your way. The PF will be the tip of the spear, but they know it's your case. You have your vest?"

"In the trunk of my car."

"Make sure you wear it. Those Aztecas are crazy."

Lopez walked away. "Thank you, Carlos," Matías called after him.

"Thank me when you have your shooters."

Matías picked up the phone and dialed the number on the sheet of paper. It rang three times on the other end and was answered. "Matías Segura for David Muñoz," Matías said.

He was on hold for five minutes. When the line picked up again, Matías heard telephones ringing in the background and the hubbub of many voices talking over the noise. An old dot-matrix printer screeched away. "Muñoz."

"This is Matías Segura, PFM. Do you have a minute?"

"Segura? Yes, they told me you might be calling. What can I do for you?"

"I wanted to ask you about the tip that came in this morning, about the Salvadoran club shooting. How good do you think it is?"

"Good enough that I'm putting a team on it. We'll be ready to go in a few hours. Are you coming with us?"

"I've been cleared to."

"Then come on down. Some of my boys have never seen a PFM agent on a raid before."

"I hope I don't disappoint them."

"Wear a suit and tie."

"I'll see you in an hour."

Matías hung up the phone. He gathered up the papers from the shooting into one stack and shoved them off to one side. He left only the slip of paper on the blotter.

"Hey, Matías," said Francisco at the next desk. "Did I hear right? You're going through a door with the PF?"

"That's the idea."

"When was the last time you had tactical training?"

Matías shook his head. "I don't remember. I'm sure it will all come back to me."

"Well, be careful."

He put the slip of paper in his pocket and stood up from his desk. "You can count on it, Paco. Answer my phone for me, will you?"

"*Buena suerte.*"

ELEVEN

THE ASSAULT TEAM ASSEMBLED ON THE STREET
two doors down from the target house after spilling out of an
armored truck. Their black uniforms and armor were distinctive,
their faces masked, their heads helmeted. Matías went with them,
bringing up the rear. He was armored as well, though he did not
look as intimidating as the others. For a moment he wondered if
he should have borrowed a helmet of his own.

Dust blew in from between houses, carried on the wind. Matías
felt it grit between his teeth. He sweated underneath his vest.
No air circulated in the truck. The assault team must have been
sweltering.

The target house was two stories, taller than the houses around
it, with space on all four sides and a high chain-link fence squaring
it in. The front gate had a combination padlock and a chain on
it. The point man on the team carried a pair of large, red bolt-
cutters.

Matías saw a pair of black SUVs pull up to the far side of
the house to block the street, and more geared-up federal police
emerged. He was aware of another couple PF vehicles pulling up
behind the armored truck, completing the bracket.

All of the assault team members were armed with automatic
weapons. Matías just carried his pistol. The assault team leader,
Muñoz, told Matías ahead of time that he was to stay back, enter
only when the team called the all-clear, and keep his head down as

they made forcible entry. "I don't need the PFM coming down on me if something happens to you," he said.

The point man signaled the advance and the dozen men, plus one, crept up past the face of the neighboring house. Matías looked to see if anyone watched from the windows, but he saw no one. It was the middle of the afternoon and most people would be at work. A dog barked somewhere.

It was a matter of seconds for the bolt-cutter to do away with the lock. They passed through the gate unhindered. The windows of the target house were likewise blank, the curtains drawn. Suddenly Matías heard the throbbing of bass leaking through the walls of the place; the men inside would hear nothing even if the assault team was not moving in silence.

The space in front of the house was covered in cracked, uneven slabs of concrete. Weeds slithered up through the openings, wherever they could find purchase. A pair of cross-shaped uprights had clothesline strung between them, though there was no laundry out.

The assault team dipped under the line and then broke apart. The two men ahead of Matías headed right toward the corner of the house. One of them slung his weapon and produced an extensible rod that quickly opened to a length of ten feet. It had a loop on the end. The second man hooked a flash-bang grenade through the loop and then the pair of them were gone, headed to the rear of the house.

Men piled up on opposite sides of the front door. The door, like the windows, was barred with wrought iron. One man tested the bars, found them locked. He nodded to another, who produced a set of locksmith's tools and crouched down to work.

Matías tucked himself in behind one of the assault team members and watched the lockpicking progress. He was still sweating, this time from his brow, and he paused a moment to wipe his face with his shirtsleeve. The bass was powerful enough to be felt through the wall he leaned against, insistently thumping away.

He did not hear the click of the lock, but the man working the door stepped away and the entryway was unbarred. He was replaced by yet another member of the team, this one carrying a one-man battering ram made of steel pipe filled with concrete, handles welded on. Matías tensed.

Muñoz muttered something into his radio. From behind the house came a sharp blasting sound, a flash-bang going off. At the same time the battering ram smashed against the front door and tore the twin deadbolts out of the frame. A grenade was tossed into the room beyond. Another flat explosion and then the team poured in, man over man, with Matías behind them.

"*¡Policía! ¡Al suelo!*" came the shouts.

Matías plunged through the open door into a maelstrom of noise. Electronic music blared from big speakers on the far end of a large front room. Assault team members screamed to be heard. Matías saw three shirtless young men pushed to the floor, their protests swallowed up by the throbbing bass.

Federal police crashed through the open doorways leading from the room, returned with more young men and a pair of girls, all of them partially undressed. They were thrown to the ground. Muñoz kicked in the front of the stereo system and the music stopped abruptly. Everything was yelling and smashing as furniture was upended and loose pictures fell from the walls. Matías stood aside and let it all happen, his gun in his hand but not necessary.

They took control of the house in less than a minute, clearing the upstairs and downstairs. In the end they had ten men and six women in custody, lying on the floor of the main room with their hands behind their backs. Assault team members shoved furniture out of the way to make room for them all.

Muñoz vanished upstairs and returned after a short while. He signaled Matías over. "Come and see," he said.

Matías followed Muñoz up the stairs to a back room. It was

meant to be a small bedroom, but it had been converted into an armory. He saw shotguns, automatic rifles, pistols and boxes of ammunition.

"Three of them were armed," Muñoz told Matías. "The rest could have gotten to this and we'd be in a fight for sure. We win today."

The two men returned downstairs. The prisoners' wrists were secured with plastic zip ties. There was the noise of breaking glass from the kitchen as the cabinets were opened and cleared. A pair of assault team members kept watch over the prisoners, though they were not going anywhere.

"Right here!" someone called. A member of the team entered from another door carrying a gallon plastic bag half-full of white powder. He held it up for Muñoz and the others to see. "There's more in back."

Muñoz nudged one of the prisoners with his boot. "Guns and drugs, eh? You bunch know how to fuck up, don't you? I'll be right back."

Matías looked over the men and women on the floor. All of them were extensively tattooed, even the girls. He saw Indians and feathers, a full-back representation of the Aztec calendar, and another with the large numbers 21 marked on the back of his neck where no one could fail to see them. Another was less subtle, with a lower-back rocker that spelled out AZTECA. He guessed that not one of the prisoners was over twenty-three.

He knelt down by the first man in line and poked him in the shoulder. "Hey," he said, "you know something about a shooting this morning? Six Salvadorans dead? You know anything about that?"

"*Vete a la chingada*," the Azteca said.

Matías went to the next. "How about you? Feel like talking?"

"I got nothing to say."

"Okay," Matías said. He stood up. "You don't talk now, you talk later. Don't say I didn't try to make it easy on you."

Muñoz returned. "Anything?"

"They're going to be tough," Matías said.

"We'll see how tough they are. We have a wagon coming for them."

"I'll call ahead and make sure things are ready."

TWELVE

THE SUN WENT DOWN OVER EL PASO AND the night came on. Cristina parked their car across from a row of houses and killed the engine. She rolled down the window and let the cooling air in. Across the street and one door down there was a party going on, with lights out on the covered porch and rap music playing. The lyrics drifted her way, all in Spanish. Cristina thought she recognized it as a track from South Park Mexican.

"Friday night's all right," Robinson said.

"You know you didn't have to come."

"Naw, Penny's fine with me staying out. You're the one who has to pay a sitter."

Cristina shook her head. "She knows Fridays are late nights. I pay extra."

"You should spend more time with Freddie."

"We'll go to the park tomorrow. He'll like that."

"How's he doing?"

"Fine. Some rough days at school, but we get through it."

"He's a good kid."

"Thanks."

Robinson fished on the floor between his legs and produced a digital camera in a case. He handed it over. "Your turn to take the snaps."

The curb in front of the party house was lined with cars. The angle wasn't good for photographing license plates. They would have to crawl by, or approach on foot. Cristina didn't like the latter option; there were people crowded on the patio drinking beer and talking loudly over the music. A barbecue grill was going.

Cristina readied the camera and raised it up so it was just visible above the line of the open window. She used the zoom and watched the screen. When she had a clear face, she snapped a shot. Some she recognized, others she didn't. A new car approached slowly from the far end of the street. She got its license plate. It parked and two more faces joined the party.

"This is, what? His third party in a month?"

"Fourth, I think. There was that one a couple weeks ago."

"Right. He must go through a fortune in beer."

"He can afford it."

The neighborhood was working class, the houses all old, but they had decent-sized front lawns, or in the case of José Martinez's house, an extended patio. Cristina and Robinson had come to know the features of the neighborhood, who came and who went. Most of the people here were regular folks earning a wage. If they knew their neighbor, they didn't let on.

They sat. Robinson cracked a can of Full Throttle and sipped it slowly. Their main goal was to notice anything different – new people, new cars – and maybe catch a glimpse of the man himself. The photos they took were almost always of him at the grill. They had many, many pictures like that.

"I wish we could get in the house right across the street," Cristina said.

"What, you don't like parking with me?"

Cristina caught another girl she didn't know by sight. There were always girls at these things, sometimes more girls than men. Martinez brought them in to socialize, drink and eat with his boys. Sometimes they went home with them.

"You know, we could just bust the whole lot of them for congregating," Cristina said. "Book 'em and sort it out at the house."

"And then he'd never throw another party again."

Cristina sighed. She took more pictures.

"I figure a dozen Aztecas up there tonight," Robinson said after a while. "That sound right to you?"

"Yeah. I see Acosta, Solis, Ochoa. A couple I don't know. Might be new blood."

They watched as one of Martinez's boys came down to the street with a girl hanging from his arm. The both of them were unsteady and it took two tries for the Azteca to get his key in the door of his car. When the car pulled away from the curb, its headlights washed over Cristina and Robinson. Cristina made a note of the license plate. "Call in a drunk driver," she told Robinson. "We can put one of them in jail tonight."

She looked back to the party. A couple of the men were staring back.

"Oh, shit," Cristina said.

"What?"

"We've been made."

The pair came down to the street and advanced up the sidewalk, still carrying their beers. One of them called out, "What you doing? What you doing over there?"

Cristina started the engine. The two of them were halfway across the street, blocking her way. One of the men threw his beer down in their path, casting up foam. "Get out of the car!" he yelled.

She eased off the curb into the street, but the two didn't move out of the way. The one who threw his beer slammed his hands down on the hood of the car. The other came around the driver's side as Cristina put up the window. "Why don't you get out of the car?" he said. "Huh? Get out of the car!"

"*Pendejo,*" Cristina said under her breath. She put on some gas, and made to bump the man in front of the car. He skipped backward.

His partner banged his open palm on the driver's side window.

Cristina ignored him. She goosed the gas pedal again and a second time the man in front gave way. There was just enough room to move. "Punch it," Robinson said.

Cristina accelerated and left the two men behind. They whipped past the party house, saw others watching, then made the far corner. Cristina made the turn without slowing and the tires squealed. Then they were gone.

"That could have gone better," Robinson said.

"So much for using this car again."

"So much for using that *spot* again."

Cristina banged the heel of her palm on the steering wheel. "Fuck!"

"Just breathe."

"I'm telling you, we just bust the whole lot of them."

"Another time."

A light turned red and Cristina slowed to a stop. "I'm so sick of this shit," she said.

"You and me both, but it's one step at a time. You got some good shots?"

"Yeah."

"Then it wasn't a total waste. Take us back to the house. We'll pull the pictures, punch out and get home a little early tonight."

"We should bust 'em, Bob."

"I know."

The light turned green. They went.

THIRTEEN

FLIP SLEPT IN. IN COFFIELD IT WAS UP AT SIX
o'clock after a lights out at ten the night before. No one was allowed
to stay in their cell when it was time for chow. There was no snooze
button. This morning when Flip stirred at the habitual hour he just
turned over and put a pillow over his head.

The heat from the sun hitting the sheets finally stirred him.
He wandered to the bathroom, took a piss and had a shower. He
brushed his teeth with the same toothbrush he used at Coffield;
he'd brought it with him.

It was windy outside. He could hear the gusts buffeting the walls
of the house. His mother wasn't home and he remembered she had
a Saturday morning coffee klatch with some friends of hers. That
hadn't changed. Breakfast was cold cereal with milk and a glass of
orange juice.

He put on a sweatshirt, found his basketball in his closet and
brought it out onto the driveway. First he dribbled a bit, just
warming up, but then he took to shooting. He made standing shots
at first, then lay-ups. He wasn't tall enough or strong enough to
spring for a dunk. The wind made long shots difficult.

When he checked his watch it was about eleven. He thought about
going inside, watching some TV, when he saw the blue car creeping
up the street. The driver leaned over the steering wheel, peering at
each house number. The car coasted to a stop in front of the house
and the driver put it in park. The man put down the passenger side

window and leaned over. "Hey," he said, "are you Flip?"

"Who wants to know?"

"My name's Emilio. Come on over here."

Flip came down to the curb with his ball. If he had to, he could throw it in the guy's face and run the other way. He measured things that way because that was how it was done inside: what can he do to me, what can I do to him?

"You're Flip? Flip Morales?"

"Yeah, I'm Flip."

"There's somebody who wants to meet you. Why don't you come on with me?"

"Who am I supposed to meet?"

"Come on, don't be dumb. I come from José. You know José?"

"All right, give me a minute."

Flip brought the basketball inside and then locked up the house. He thought about leaving his mother a note, but he didn't. When he came back to the car, Emilio unlocked the door for him. "Get in," he said.

Emilio put the window back up. For some reason, he had the heater going, so it was hot and stuffy in the car. They pulled away from the curb and cruised to the end of the block before making a left-hand turn. Emilio seemed to know his way a little better now. "So you were inside?" he asked.

"That's right."

"How long?"

"Four years."

Emilio looked sidelong at Flip and Flip tried to guess his age. He was younger than Flip and he had a wispy mustache that reminded Flip of a teenager. Emilio was tattooed on his arm, just below the cuff of his short-sleeved shirt, with the pattern of a beaded armband, Indian-style.

"How was it? Inside, I mean."

"It was inside," Flip replied. "It's the same everywhere."

"I only got county jail time," Emilio said. "That's got to be different."

"I guess you're right. Where are we going?"

"You hungry?"

"Maybe a little."

"Good."

They drove out of Flip's neighborhood north until they were nearly out of Segundo Barrio, then made a sharp turn onto a street lined with businesses. Just past a used car lot was a taquería called El Cihualteco. Emilio pulled into the parking lot.

The taquería had a big, open patio with wooden picnic tables lined up underneath a long awning. There were a few people eating already, men in work shirts and uniforms. Another man sat apart from them, his white-collared sky-blue shirt standing out. He looked up from his basket as they arrived, lifted a hand in greeting.

Emilio pointed. "José," he said.

"I get out here?"

"You get out here."

"How do I get back home?"

"I'll wait for you. Just see José."

Flip got out and crossed the gravel parking lot. The wind whipped at the fringe of the taquería's awning and Flip saw a man in a green uniform grab his basket of food before it blew away.

José Martinez smiled. "Flip! Come over and sit down!"

José sat alone. Flip took the other side of the picnic table. Up close he could see that José was a young-looking thirties with just the merest touches of smile lines at the corners of his eyes. His goatee was closely barbered and his shirt pressed. He had chicken tacos in his basket.

"It's nice to meet you finally," José said and he offered his hand. Flip shook it. "I heard good things. Do you want something to eat? Lunch is on me."

Flip took the offered ten-dollar bill and got up from the table.

When he came back he had a basket of barbacoa tacos that oozed grease onto the wax paper. The man behind the counter drowned the tacos in cheese, diced tomatoes and shredded lettuce. The wind whipped the smell of them away, but the taste remained.

José nodded his head as Flip ate. "Good? I love this place."

"It's good," Flip said around a mouthful.

"Better than prison food for sure."

The two of them ate quietly. José licked his fingers when he was done and took a drink from a cup of soda. He waited for Flip to finish. "Get more if you want," he said at last. "I don't mind."

"That's okay."

José nodded again. "All right, then. We can talk now."

Flip looked at José and waited. The wind gusted again and disturbed José's hair. The man wore it a little long. Flip's head was almost shaved.

"I got the call on you," José said. "They say you're down for the cause. Is that so?"

"I earned my *huaraches*."

"That's what I heard. Stabbed a white boy?"

Flip shrugged a little. "No one could say I did."

"I like that," José said and showed his teeth. They were white and even. "You know how to keep your mouth shut. I know some guys, they'd be all about talking it up. 'Yeah, I stuck him.' You know what I'm saying?"

"That's a good way to go into the hole," Flip said.

"It's fucking stupid is what it is," José returned. "But you're not stupid. You seen your PO yet?"

"Not yet. I got a week before I have to report in."

"They're gonna try to bust your balls."

"I can deal with it."

"You got a job lined up?"

"Yeah. A guy my mother knows, he offered me work at a warehouse."

"What kind of warehouse?"

"Place that ships groceries, I guess. I don't know much about it."

José considered. "Good job?"

"Part time. Pays something. That's all my PO wants."

"Can't live on your own on what a part-time job pays," José said.

"I got my mother's place. My old room."

"That'll do for now, but you got to have some spending money," José said. "You come in under me, you'll get some. Maybe enough to move you out of there, into your own apartment. I can't make any guarantees, but you'll do all right."

"What do I have to do for it?"

José spread his hands just as another gust of wind hit the patio. The wax paper in his basket was whisked away, but he caught the basket before it could slip off the table. "*Mierda*," he said. "I don't like littering. Why don't you take this back up to the guy, okay? And throw your stuff out. We don't need paper flying all over the place."

Flip collected José's basket and took both to the counter. He emptied his basket into the trash, then passed them to the man at the register. His tacos made him thirsty. He bought a Coke with the leftover money from the ten.

When he sat down again, José was staring off at traffic going by. The man came back to him slowly, as if he were caught thinking. "That's better," he said. "Got to keep our city clean."

"I was asking you what I got to do for you," Flip said.

"Huh? Whatever needs doing, *mi hermano*. You're down, right?"

"I'm down."

"Then you got nothing to worry about. I got little pots all over the place and I got to keep my fingers in them. Whatever I can't take care of myself, I get other people to do. Like Emilio. I need you picked up, he makes sure you're picked up. He don't ask no questions and when it comes time to spread the wealth around he gets something for his trouble."

Flip didn't look at his watch, but he knew it was coming around to noon. New people were coming up to the counter to order and a small line formed. Cars started to slip into the parking lot. He glanced over and saw Emilio waiting behind the wheel, going nowhere. "I don't got a driver's license," he said.

"That's okay. I can find something you can do."

"When do you want me to get started?"

"Not so fast, okay. Let's take our time. I want you to get to know my crew, introduce you around. I had a party at my place last night, we're going clubbing tonight. You want to come?"

"To a club?"

"Sure. Do some dancing, have some drinks, meet some people. How's that sound?"

"Parole says I can't."

"You always do what you're told?"

"All right."

José smiled and offered his knuckles for a bump. "Yeah, now we're talking. It's your welcome back party! Everybody will know you after tonight."

"Okay."

"Listen, it's getting crowded here now. Why don't you have Emilio take you back to your place? He'll come back to get you around nine. You got clothes to dress up?"

"Yeah, I got some."

"Look sharp. There'll be ladies."

José stood up and Flip knew the interview was over. They shook hands again and José turned away without saying good-bye. He walked to a Lexus parked at the edge of the lot. Flip went back to Emilio.

"Good?" Emilio asked when Flip got in.

"Good."

"All right."

FOURTEEN

CRISTINA MADE FREDDIE WEAR A HAT BECAUSE of the wind, but he took it off before they got to the park. The day was a little cool, and at least he didn't take off his jacket, she reasoned, and that was a win. Freddie liked to run around in the dead of winter without gloves or even zipping up his coat. He would be frozen by the time he came inside and no matter how many times Cristina told him otherwise, he would do it again.

They parked near the playground. Freddie got out before Cristina set the brake and dashed off toward the monkey bars. He had a strange, stiff-armed way of running, like a high-speed waddle, that set him apart from other kids even at a distance. There were a few already playing and she saw him approach them right away.

It was good that he wasn't afraid, but Cristina knew the way it would go. He would ask them to play and then he would insist they play the only game he knew: tag. The first time someone told him he was It, he would give up in frustration. If he was well-behaved, he would just retreat into himself. If not, he would lash out.

Sometimes he would pretend to be inside an elevator and insist the other children stand with him, motionless, inside the invisible car as it went from floor to floor. That never lasted long. He did all the noises, the pings and chimes, and it was clear that the image was crystalline in his mind, but what he saw he could not communicate and even the most tolerant children got bored of it easily.

Cristina found a bench and sat down. There were other mothers here with their kids, some making idle chatter with each other, but Cristina could not be one of them; she had to watch Freddie every minute in case he had a fit of rage, or if he fell and hurt himself. She couldn't do that and hold a conversation at the same time.

She first knew there was something wrong when Freddie was three years old. He could not speak, or at least he could only say a few words. Evaluation cost a lot of money, but she had a temporary diagnosis of Pervasive Developmental Disorder. That was good enough to get him into a county-provided early-childhood intervention program that expanded his vocabulary, though he was still slow at other things.

They said he was smart and he played imaginatively. He communicated better after two years of intensive work and transitioned into special kindergarten. No one said he had autism, but the older he got, the more Cristina knew.

It was the obsession with elevators and escalators first. Freddie would draw pictures of them and talk about them and that was all he wanted to do. Cristina searched online and saw that children with autism sometimes had very narrow interests and would perseverate on whatever that interest was. In the back of her mind, the evidence file filled up.

After kindergarten he was still affected and the county paid for him to be transferred to a private school specializing in special needs education. When she first visited Cristina was put off by children in wheelchairs who could not sit up or children so severely autistic they barely moved under their own power. This was not her child, this was not where he belonged.

The school worked with him for three years before the diagnosis changed. He had Asperger's Syndrome, a kind of autism, and though the news was bad Cristina felt vindicated because all the research she'd done was right; she knew her own child best.

They wanted to know the medical history of the parents, but

Cristina could only give her side. Freddie's father did not answer letters or emails and eventually Cristina stopped trying. She suspected he didn't want to be held responsible for this, the way he hadn't wanted to be responsible for a child in the first place.

Her attention drifted and she didn't even realize she was daydreaming until one of the other mothers approached her. "Excuse me," the woman said. "Excuse me, miss?"

"I'm sorry, what?"

"I wouldn't bother you, but your son just hit my son twice."

Cristina stood up sharply. "I'm sorry. My son has autism. I'll get him right now."

She saw the expression change on the woman's face, from concern to repulsion. *Autism.* As if it were catching. As if it were deadly. "It's all right. I didn't know—"

"No, I'll get him. He needs to say he's sorry."

Cristina strode out to the monkey bars. Freddie was at the very top, hugging himself and rocking back and forth. His eyes were puffy with tears that hadn't yet come.

"Freddie?"

"I don't *like* those boys!"

"Freddie, come down here, okay? Mom needs to talk to you."

Now he cried and Cristina felt herself crumble a little. "I *don't like those boys!*"

"Come down from there. Come on, baby."

Freddie climbed down reluctantly until Cristina was on her knees, holding him. His shoulders hitched and he breathed hot in her ear. "They're mean to me."

"I know, but you can't hit. Now you have to say you're sorry."

It took time to cajole him and eventually he took her hand and let her lead him to the bench where the mother sat. She had a boy near her eating cheese crackers from a plastic bag. Again the look.

"Say you're sorry, Freddie," Cristina prompted.

Freddie did not look the boy in the eye. "Sorry," he said.

"Sorry for what?"

"Sorry for *hitting*."

"I'm really sorry," Cristina told the mother.

"It's all right, really. I didn't know."

I didn't know your son has autism.

"Come on, Freddie, let's go play somewhere else, just you and me."

Cristina guided him away and across the spotty grass to a toddler's playground with swings that had rubber seats with leg holes, a sandbox and a climber that was low to the ground. There was no one around.

"I want to play with my friends," Freddie said.

"I know, but let's play over here for a while. Let's make tunnels in the sand, okay? Or we can play spaceship. See, there's a steering wheel on the climber."

Freddie pulled away from her without speaking and mounted the climber. He put his hands on the spinning wheel and spun it, making a machine noise. "It's like an elevator motor," he said.

"Yeah, I guess it is," Cristina said.

FIFTEEN

FLIP DRESSED IN A PAIR OF DARK JEANS
and a white shirt from his closet. The shirt needed to be ironed
and though his mother offered, he did it himself. He wished he
had better shoes than the same sneakers he'd been wearing since
Coffield, but he did not have the money or the time to shop.

His mother insisted he sit down for a proper dinner. They ate
and sat in front of the television for a while. When nine o'clock
came around, Flip heard a car horn sound twice in the street. "Got
to go," he said.

"Don't stay out too late!"

Emilio was in the same car as before, only this time the stereo
was pumping Lil Rob. He'd changed from his t-shirt into something
more respectable and put gel in his hair. He pushed open the
passenger side door and beckoned to Flip. "Hey, man, get in!" he
said.

Flip put on his seatbelt as Emilio cruised away from the curb.
He saw the porch light in front of his mother's house go on. It was
possible she would be up when he came home, just waiting.

"Right on time, huh?" Emilio said.

"What?"

"I said we're right on time!"

"Yeah," Flip said. The music was punishingly loud inside the
car, especially with the windows up, trapping the sound. His first
instinct was to crank the volume down, but then Emilio would be

offended and that would be a problem. He suffered instead.

Emilio bobbed his head to the rap and when they stopped at lights he tapped the steering wheel in time. Flip wondered if maybe he was on something. He did not want to be caught in the same car with someone who was high. They drove west, parallel to the river, and passed near the airport. Incoming planes blinked in the sky.

"Where are we going?" Flip asked.

"A good place. You'll like it."

They left 180 and turned south, then angled off to the west. They were within blocks of the border now. For a moment Flip thought they were going to cross over and party in Juárez and his heart picked up a beat. Going to a club was risky enough, but crossing was something else altogether. If his parole officer found out about either, he would be going back to Coffield for sure.

"Almost there," Emilio said. He killed the music, but Flip's ears were still stunned. "There. See the sign?"

Flip looked and saw where Emilio pointed. The club's name was written large on a lighted sign: LA RAYA ANTRO. The parking lot was crowded with cars and there was a valet service by the door. Emilio drove up to the waiting men in white gloves, put the car into park and got out. Flip did the same.

"Don't bury it, okay?" Emilio told the valet and passed a folded bill in a handshake. He handed over his keys, then came to collect Flip. They went to the entrance together. A man held the door for them and they passed into darkness.

New music crashed over them and as they passed through the shadowed entryway the smells of fresh sweat, perfume, alcohol and cigarettes came to Flip. When they stepped out onto the main floor, the place opened up around them, mad with lights. The dance floor was crowded, the driving beat of Latin house moving their bodies. Flip saw the DJ lit from below, his face like a devil's, mirrored sunglasses shining.

"Come on," Emilio said. He led Flip through the throng of

bodies, past little tables and knots of people. There were lots of women, women everywhere Flip looked, and he was overwhelmed by them. He saw tight dresses and curves, styled hair and manicured fingernails. One girl threw her head back laughing, but the sound of it was swallowed up by the music.

Emilio brought them to a pair of booths positioned at right angles to each other near the far side of the club. Both were packed with new faces. Emilio started introducing him around, but the names were half-drowned and he couldn't remember them all anyway, though he tried. Emilio introduced a few of the girls. All of them seemed to be with someone and Flip could not help but be disappointed.

"Where's José?" Flip asked.

"José? He doesn't hang out here. He's in the VIP room." Emilio gestured vaguely toward the back of the club. "We'll go see him in a little while. Get something to drink, relax, okay? Just grab a spot anywhere."

It was impossible to sit in the booths, so Flip found a place to sit by one of the small tables. A waitress cruised through the press of bodies holding a tray of drinks over her head. Flip signaled to her and she came close. She had to lean down so he could speak directly into her ear. "Corona Extra," he said.

"A few minutes," the waitress told him and then she was gone.

Flip looked around. Emilio was deep in conversation with someone whose name Flip couldn't remember. He searched his memory. *Benicio*. He filed that away.

There were a few girls at tables nearby. Flip tried to catch their eye and when one turned her head this way he smiled at her. She smiled back before one of her friends caught her attention and she looked away. Flip hoped she'd glance over again, but she didn't. Finally his beer came.

The beer was cool and clean-tasting, straight from the bottle. Flip had never been a heavy drinker, but he appreciated a good beer. He finished half of it quickly and thought about Enrique and Javier and Omar and how much they would like to have a beer right now. Omar was not going to get out, not ever going to taste beer again. Flip drank some more for Omar, who was probably getting tattooed by Javier right now as a *fuck you* to the COs. That was his rebellion.

When the waitress came around again, Flip ordered another.

"Who's paying for this?" the waitress asked.

Flip pointed out Emilio. "My friend."

"Oh, I know him. Okay."

He was four bottles to the good by the time Emilio returned to him. The man clapped Flip on both shoulders. "Hey, man, why don't you get out there and dance? Anybody can sit and drink. Let's get you *circulating*."

"When do we see José?"

"You want to see José?"

"Yeah. Then I'll dance."

"Okay, come on."

Emilio conducted Flip through the crowds again, this time to a wide passageway in the very back of the club. They had to pass by the DJ booth where girls crowded around trying to get the man's attention. Some of them looked very good to Flip. They *all* looked good to Flip. He thought about touching one girl on the ass just to see what she would do, but Emilio tugged his arm and they were past temptation.

In a length of hallway there were four doors. Emilio went to the second on the left and knocked. Someone inside cracked the door, peeked out and then swung it wide to allow them in.

The room was semicircular and scattered with couches and tables. There was a private bar manned by a woman showing lots of cleavage in a black dress. Music from the front of the house played through speakers high on the walls.

José held court from a big couch that let him sprawl out almost completely. He sat with a man Flip didn't know on one hand and a girl on the other. There were other girls, too; more than Flip could keep track of.

"Flip!" José declared. He sat up and sloshed his drink onto his knee. "You made it!"

"I made it," Flip said.

"Good, good. Is Emilio taking care of you?"

"Sure."

"Get something from the bar, okay? Talk to some girls."

"I will."

Flip went to the bar where the woman bartender fixed him a strong margarita without being told. He sipped it, tasting salt, lime and tequila. All the girls scattered out in front of him, on couches and chairs, talking to each other or to their men. He didn't know where to begin.

Someone touched him lightly on the arm and he swung around fast, nearly toppling his drink. The girl beside him recoiled as if she was afraid he might hit her and immediately Flip felt bad. "Sorry," he said.

"It's okay. Buy me a drink?"

"Sure, but I think José is paying."

"José pays for everything."

The girl ordered some kind of pink and fruity-looking drink and Flip watched her. She was petite and dressed in red. Colored highlights in her hair shone dark auburn. She was light-skinned and had small breasts that her top emphasized. Her eyes were a golden brown.

"What's your name?" she asked him.

"Huh?"

"Your name. What is it?"

"They call me Flip."

"Flip?"

"My real name is Felipe. Felipe, Flip… you know."

The girl smiled. Flip thought she was the most beautiful girl in the room. "Flip, I'm Graciela."

"Graciela. Nice to meet you."

"I haven't seen you around before."

"No, I'm new. I just got in," Flip said. From prison, he thought, but didn't add. Graciela did not seem like the kind of girl who would be impressed by such a thing and suddenly Flip found it very important that she think well of him.

"Do you work with José?"

"Actually I just got a job at a warehouse."

"I thought everybody here worked with José."

Flip did not know how to answer that. He asked himself what he would tell a total stranger. "José is a friend of a friend," he said at last. "He's looking out for me."

"I understand."

"Good, because I don't," Flip joked. He laughed and she laughed and Flip wished they were somewhere else besides this loud, smoky room. She looked very good, but he thought she would look good in anything; she was that kind of woman.

"Do you want to sit down?"

"Sure, okay."

They found a table no one was using and sat across from each other. Flip drank from his margarita and wished he'd just gotten a beer instead. But then what would Graciela think of that? Too working-class, too ordinary? He felt stupid that he couldn't recognize what she was drinking, but he didn't know that stuff.

"Where are you from?" Graciela asked him.

"Oh, I'm from El Paso. My parents are from here, too. Well, my father was from Juárez, but my mother came from here."

"Ah. When you said you just got in, I thought you were from somewhere else."

There it was again. Flip did not want to lie to her. "I was away for a few years. Doing other things."

"Okay," Graciela said and Flip felt a great tension ease.

"Where are you from?"

"I come from here, too. I grew up in the Second Ward."

"Really? So did I."

"That's cool," Graciela said. "Maybe we were neighbors and didn't know it."

"Maybe."

It was easier to talk to her then. From time to time Flip looked over her shoulder and saw José with Emilio or somebody else, deep in conversation. Once Flip thought he caught José looking at him from across the room.

Flip learned that Graciela went to cosmetology school and worked at a craft store during the day. She had three sisters, all younger than her, and an older brother who died. About how she met José she was less candid, but Flip didn't care. He liked listening to her, even over the din of the house music, and watching her mouth form the words. Twice she asked him questions and he didn't realize it. He blushed.

He told her what he felt she should hear: about his family and growing up without brothers or sisters, but with plenty of cousins. About his father dying young. He did not tell her about shoplifting at eight and doing bicycle theft by thirteen. He did not tell her how he went to Coffield.

By the time he checked his watch it was after midnight. They had four drinks between them and Flip felt sluggish. He looked around for Emilio, saw him kissing a girl in the corner. José was still drinking and still talking. When he caught Emilio watching, he smiled and waved.

"I should probably get out of here," Flip said.

"You have to go?"

"My mother... I'm living with my mother right now. She worries. If I stay out too late, she'll never let me forget about it." Flip started to get up, jostled the little table and almost toppled their glasses.

Across the room Emilio looked over and Flip signaled to him.

"Hey, wait," Graciela said. "Let me give you my phone number. You can put it in your cell."

"I don't have a cell phone," Flip confessed. "Can you write it down?"

"You don't have a cell phone? Where have you been living?"

"I mean I had one, but it broke. I need to get a new one."

"Give me a minute. I think I have a pen in my purse."

Graciela went away and Emilio came over. "You been talking to that girl a long time," he said. "What's she like?"

"Nice," Flip said.

"'Nice'? What, are you kidding me? Is she good to go or what?"

"Not tonight, I don't think," Flip said.

"That's too bad, because she is fine."

"You think maybe you can take me home?" Flip asked.

"Take you home? The place doesn't close down until two!"

"I know, but I think I'm going to call it a night. I don't have money for cab fare."

Emilio rolled his eyes. "You don't need to take no cab. I'll do it. But you're cutting in on my time, man. Don't forget."

"I won't."

Graciela returned with a napkin and gave it to Flip. "Here you go," she said. "If you can't get hold of me, just leave a message."

Flip folded up the napkin and put it in his pocket. "Thanks. I'll give you my number when I have one."

"All right," Graciela said and she smiled. "It was good to meet you, Flip."

"Same here."

Emilio interposed himself between them. "I don't want to break you two up, but Flip says he has to go right now. So…"

"Good night, Flip."

"Good night."

"You want to say thank you to the boss," Emilio told Flip and jerked his thumb toward José.

"Yeah, right."

Flip went to José. The man's head bobbled and his eyes were glassy. The short table in front of the couch was crowded with empty glasses. Flip did not know how many were José's.

"How's it going, Flip?" José asked.

"I'm leaving now. I wanted to thank you for a nice night out."

"Leaving?!?"

"Yeah, I got to go, man."

"Well, if you got to go…" José finished the drink in his hand. Immediately the girl at his elbow got up and headed for the bar. "Sure I can't convince you to stay?"

"No, but thank you for everything."

"*De nada*. I hope you had a good time."

"I did."

"Then it was worth it."

Flip came away from José and found Emilio. They left together. Flip looked back once to see if Graciela was watching, but she was already talking to another girl. Then she was out of sight.

SIXTEEN

MATÍAS ARRANGED FOR SIX OF THE AZTECAS to be taken from their jail cells after dark and without warning. Flashlights were shined in their faces and then black bags were put over their heads. They were chained hand and foot and forced to shuffle their way barefoot along to the interrogation rooms where they were slotted away, one after the other.

He let them sit in the rooms for an hour without anyone coming to remove their hoods. In the meantime Matías gathered with his teammates and discussed what came next.

Sosa and Galvan were the muscle. They would go in first and Matías would follow after they had a chance to do their interview. Each man would be in the interrogation room for no more than twenty minutes. Some would be waiting a long time to see Matías, while others would see him right away. The goal was to keep them off-balance, never sure when the next interviewer would enter the room, and they would keep this up until dawn.

Matías found a straight-backed wooden chair and sat in the dingy hallway between interrogation rooms. The walls had not been painted for a long time and the floors were dirty enough that he would not want to touch them with his bare hands. He was impressed by the silence; even those prisoners who had been stirred awake were lying in the darkness hoping it was not their turn next and the others slept without any worry except what would be for breakfast in the morning.

He could not even hear Sosa and Galvan at work. The doors were thick, the rooms soundproofed. It was just as well because Matías did not have the constitution to do what they did. In times like these, he was content to let experts do their work without interference.

An officer brought a hot carafe of coffee and Matías indulged himself. It was going to be a long night and he needed to remain alert. There would be no going home until it was evening again. Already he missed having a morning shower.

After twenty minutes both men emerged into the hallway. Galvan had his shirtsleeves rolled up and was sweating heavily. Sosa had only loosened his tie. They helped themselves to coffee.

"Well?" Matías asked.

"I don't think we'll have to work very hard," Sosa said.

"Speak for yourself," Galvan said.

"You're just getting old."

"I'll tell you how it goes," Matías said. "I'll be in Interview One."

"We'll get started on the others," Galvan said.

Matías went to the first room. Harsh light cast down on the small space from a bulb inside a mesh cage on the ceiling. The table and the chairs were bolted to the bare concrete floor. A metal rail ran alongside one end of the table and the Azteca, named Meza, was cuffed to it.

There was surprisingly little blood, but Matías knew Sosa liked to work clean. Meza's ribs would be covered with bruises by the time they were done, but Sosa would not break a nose or split a lip. Galvan was another story and maybe Meza would not last the night when it was the big man's turn.

Matías put a notepad, a thick folder and a pen on the table and took a seat across from Meza. The Azteca observed him through lidded eyes, his face blank. Matías chose a look of concern that he knew seemed genuine. He did not give a shit about Meza.

"Eberto Meza," Matías said. "That's you."

Meza made no reply.

"You don't have to say anything. I know it's you. I have your records here." Matías put his hand on the folder. "Everything you've done, everywhere you've been."

"So what?" Meza said.

"Did you like your introduction to Señor Sosa?" Matías asked. "Because if you want, I can have him come in and interview you again. Or you can talk to me."

This time Meza was silent again, though Matías thought he saw the young man's cheek twitch.

"I have six dead Salvadorans shot dead outside a club and I have a tip saying you were involved. I believe the tip. All you Aztecas, you think you're too tough to snitch to the police, but some of you are talking."

"Who are you?" Meza asked.

"My name is Matías Segura. I work for the Ministerial Federal Police."

"What does the fucking PFM want with me?"

"I'm interested in anything to do with Los Aztecas."

"I'm not an Azteca."

"Do you want me to have you stripped so we can see your gang ink?"

"All you cops are *maricones*."

"If that makes you feel better."

Meza fell silent again and Matías let the minutes pass by. He checked his watch. Finally he said, "I don't have all night, Señor Meza. You can talk to me or you can talk to my colleagues."

"What's in it for me?" Meza said quickly.

"That depends on what you have to say. If you weren't a shooter, then that can mean a lot. But if you pulled a trigger, it will be more difficult for you. What do you think your friend is telling Señor Sosa right now? I only have so many deals to make before I run out of options."

"Who talked about me?"

"That would be telling."

"I want to know."

"I'm sure you do, but you'll never find out from me." Matías would have leaned back if the chair hadn't been fixed to the floor. Instead he put his hands behind his head and regarded Meza evenly. "I'm not the one who's going to spill his guts tonight."

"It won't be me. I won't," Meza said and his voice rose. He no longer looked at Matías with calculating eyes. "You can beat the shit out of me and I won't say a word."

Matías collected his things. "Then we have nothing else to talk about."

He rose from the table and went to the door. "Wait," Meza said. "Don't go."

Matías checked his watch again. "I told you: I don't have all night to do this. If you have something to say, say it now. Otherwise you'll see Señor Sosa very soon."

"Don't send him back in!"

"Then you have something for me?" Matías demanded. "Information? Names?"

"I can't say!"

"Then we're finished here."

"¡Por favor, espere!"

Matías had the door half open. His twenty minutes were almost up. There were five others to interview. He was torn between leaving and staying. Finally he shut the door and stood with his back to it. "Okay," he said. "Tell me what it is that you can't say."

"Will it come back on me? Will people know I talked?"

"That's not something that interests me. If you give good information and we can use it in court, then maybe some accommodations can be made. If you feed me a bunch of shit then you can go to hell. I'll tell everyone you snitched to me just for fun. How long will you last then? You won't even have to be on the streets to be killed. Los Aztecas will reach out for you and you will be gone."

Meza's face turned dark and he wrung his hands. Time was ticking past twenty minutes. Sosa and Galvan would be waiting.

"Talk to me, Eberto."

"Please…"

"Oh, this is bullshit," Matías said. He put his hand on the doorknob.

"All right," Meza said. "Just don't send the other one back in."

Matías came back to the table and put down his notepad. He sat and clicked his pen. "We'll start with the names of the shooters."

SEVENTEEN

On Sunday Flip went to Mass with his mother at El Segrado Corazón, the ancient church at the heart of Segundo Barrio. They met Alfredo there and afterward went to a restaurant to have Sunday lunch. It was only when he saw Alfredo and his mother holding hands that Flip realized they were more than just friends. Alfredo brought Flip a uniform shirt that he had to wear for work.

Afterward Flip asked his mother about a cell phone and they went to the store to find one. His mother picked out a cheap, simple phone and added it to her account. Flip thought about calling Graciela immediately but reconsidered; he did not want to scare her away and she might have her own Sunday business, too.

He spent the remainder of his afternoon shooting baskets in the driveway. From time to time he glanced up the street, half expecting to see Emilio coming down to carry him off, but he did not see anything of Emilio or anyone else that day.

Monday morning came early. He showered and shaved and put on the new uniform shirt. It was a little tight under the arms, but Flip thought he could get used to it. His mother made breakfast and he had only just finished when Alfredo honked his horn on the street. The sun wasn't yet up.

"Have a good day," Flip's mother said. She pressed a paper sack into his hands. "Here's some lunch for you. Make sure you eat to keep your strength up."

"I will, Mamá."

Alfredo drove a Ford pick-up truck that had been worked hard. The paint on the sides was scraped, the panels dented, and the toolbox mounted behind the cab was spotted with rust. A few loose boards and screws rattled around in the bed. Alfredo had the heater running because the morning was chill.

"Ready to put in some time?" Alfredo asked Flip.

Flip struggled with the seatbelt until finally it released. "Yeah," he said.

"You'll do fine."

"Okay," Flip said.

They drove in silence for a while. Flip looked around the inside of the cab. Compared to the rest of the truck it was well-kept. There was not even any trash on the floorboards and the ash tray had coins in it instead of butts.

"I wanted to ask you something," Alfredo said.

"Ask me what?"

"I wanted to know if you were all right with me and Silvia."

"What, that? No, it's fine."

"I didn't know. Sometimes it's hard for these things to change."

"My father's been dead a long time," Flip said. "I'm glad she found someone."

"She's a good woman."

"I know."

Alfredo had nothing else to say and they didn't talk the rest of the way. When they made the final turn, Flip saw the warehouse: a big, square building with several truck docks on the side. It was surrounded by a high chain-link fence with curling barbed wire on the top and Flip was reminded of Coffield, but only just. Any convict with ambition could scale a fence like that.

They parked with the other employees and went in. Alfredo took Flip to the main office where they filled out paperwork for most of an hour. At the end Flip got a time card and Alfredo showed him where to use it. Then he took Flip to meet his team.

There were four men assigned to Dock Three. Flip met Frank, Luis and Paul. All of the men were older than him and had the same sturdy look as Alfredo did. Frank showed Flip around their area: where to stand, what to do, when to do it. Their first truck arrived within minutes.

It was not difficult work and Flip found the rhythm quickly. The trucks rolled up and the driver brought around the manifest. Everything in the truck was unloaded quickly and sorted out into its warehouse area by number. The first truck had bananas, the next jars of tomato sauce. Many of the drivers were Mexican, their trucks and products from Mexico, making the short hop across the border in the early morning hours.

They worked hard until noon and then it was time for a break. Flip was sore from lifting and even the back support belt he wore could not completely stop the pain in his lower spine. He'd also managed to nick himself with a box cutter, though he wasn't sure how.

A shift was nine hours from start to finish and they were done in the afternoon. When the last truck had come and gone, Flip shook hands with his team and they parted ways.

Alfredo found him. "I talked to Frank," he said. "He says you did a good job."

"I tried."

"No, it's good," Alfredo said and he clapped Flip on the shoulder. "I'm proud of you. Silvia said you'd be a hard worker and she was right."

"I need to make some calls," Flip said.

"Sure, sure. Meet me outside when you're done."

Flip waited until Alfredo was gone before he took a folded paper from his pocket and spread it out on top of a stack of Pepsi twelve-packs. He picked out the phone number on his phone and waited for an answer.

"Parole and Probation," said a woman on the other end.

"Yes, can I talk to Mr. Rubio?"

"Who's calling?"

"My name is Felipe Morales. I'm supposed to report to him."

"One moment."

No one came on for a few minutes and Flip started to think they'd forgotten about him. After a long time a man picked up. "Rubio," he said.

"Mr. Rubio, my name is Felipe Morales."

"Yes, Mr. Morales, nice to hear from you."

"I need to make an appointment to see you."

"Yes, you do."

"Can we do that now?"

Rubio paused and Flip heard the click of a keyboard in the background. "How's Tuesday afternoon sound?"

"That's good. I work until four."

"The office is open until seven."

"Okay, I'll be there."

"Is there anything else I can do for you, Mr. Morales?"

Flip hesitated. His mouth ran dry and he checked in both directions. No one was watching. "Actually, there is," he said.

EIGHTEEN

CRISTINA WAS LOOKING AT A PICTURE OF Freddie when her desk phone rang. She answered: "Salas."

"Uh, yeah," said the voice on the other end. "I wanted to talk to someone in the gang unit?"

"You are."

Robinson was away from his desk and Cristina looked around for him. He wasn't in the squad room. She thought maybe he was swiping doughnuts from the box by the coffee machine in the hall. Robinson loved doughnuts.

"Yeah, okay. My name is Felipe Morales."

"Felipe?"

"That's right."

Cristina scrawled the name on the corner of her desk calendar. "What can I do for you, Felipe?"

"It's more what I can do for you. Look, can we meet somewhere?"

"You're going to have to be more specific. What can you do for me?"

"Look, call Lance Harcrow at Coffield Unit. He knows me. Then call me back at this number. You ready to write it down?"

Cristina frowned. "Ready," she said.

Felipe Morales gave her his phone number and then hung up without saying another word. Cristina held the phone for a moment, as if expecting him to come back on, but he was gone. She put the receiver in the cradle, then picked it up again.

Robinson returned. He had three doughnuts and a pair of little cocktail napkins. He put one of the doughnuts, a chocolate glazed one, on a napkin and placed it on her desk. The others he kept for himself. "What's up?" he asked.

"Nothing. I don't know. I just got a weird call. Give me a minute."

Cristina held the receiver between her shoulder and cheek as she looked up Coffield's number. She dialed and waited a long second before the line clicked and the phone at the other end started ringing.

"Texas Department of Criminal Justice – Coffield Unit," a woman answered.

"Yes, my name is Cristina Salas with the El Paso Police Department. I have an odd question: do you have someone there named Lance Harcrow?"

"Yes, ma'am. Assistant Warden Lance Harcrow."

Cristina flicked her gaze toward Robinson, but he was eating. Little crumbs fell on his desktop and he swept them away with his hand. "Would it be possible to speak with the Assistant Warden?"

"May I tell him what it's regarding?"

I don't know, Cristina thought. She said, "I wanted to ask about Felipe Morales."

"Hold on one moment."

It was more than a couple of minutes before someone picked up again. A man's voice came down the line, deep and unmistakably accented, Texas-style. "This is Assistant Warden Lance Harcrow. Who am I speaking with?"

"My name is Cristina Salas, I'm a detective with the El Paso Police Department. I was told to call you by someone named Felipe Morales. Do you know the name?"

"Before I say anything, Ms. Salas, I'd like to get your number there."

Cristina gave it to him.

"I'm going to hang up now and call you back. Wait for my call."

"Yes, sir."

Cristina put down the phone. A weird sensation passed through her, made of confusion and curiosity. She saw Robinson looking at her. "What is it?" he asked.

"I'm still not sure."

"Well, who's Lance Harcrow?"

"An administrator at Coffield Unit."

"The prison unit?"

"Yeah."

The phone rang and Cristina picked up. "Salas," she said.

"Detective Salas, it's Lance Harcrow. I hope you don't mind the runaround, but I had to make sure you were really calling from the El Paso Police Department."

"I understand, sir."

"Now, you were asking about Felipe Morales?"

"That's right. I got a phone call from him just a few minutes ago, wanting to meet with me. He gave your name as a reference. Do you know him?"

"Yes, I do," Harcrow said. "If you don't mind my asking, what do you do for the police department?"

"I'm a part of the gang unit."

"Well, that makes sense."

"How's that, sir?"

"Felipe Morales is a member of Barrio Azteca. He was also a confidential informant during his time here at Coffield."

"He was a CI?"

"Yes, and pretty darned good, too. We got a lot of useful information out of him. He helped us keep track of our Aztecas, even the ones that are hard to pick out."

Across from Cristina's desk, Robinson was interested now, listening. His second doughnut was uneaten. He made a questioning gesture with his hands. Well?

Cristina put her hand over the mouthpiece and said, "It's good."

"We let Felipe out on parole just last week," Harcrow continued. "Put him on a bus back to El Paso with his PO's name in his pocket."

"Do you have any idea why he'd want to contact me, sir?"

"I expect he's got something to share."

"How cozy was he with your Aztecas?"

"He was right in the heart of it. Got real close to our local Indian chieftain. We could have put Enrique Garcia in Ad Seg and let him rot there, but with Flip – that's Felipe's nickname, you understand – telling us his secrets, it made more sense to keep him out.

"I have to tell you, I was real sorry to see Flip go. We don't have anybody like him on the inside now. We're going to have to start cracking heads."

"So you're saying if Felipe Morales is reaching out to us, it's likely to be good?"

"That's exactly what I'm saying."

"Thanks, Mr. Harcrow, you've been a big help."

"That's *Reverend* Harcrow."

"I'm sorry?"

"I work at Coffield, but I'm also the pastor of the local church."

"How about that?" Cristina said.

"I appreciate you calling me, Detective. Say hello to Flip for me if you see him."

"I will."

Cristina pressed the switchhook on the phone and waited for a dial tone. She looked at her scribble and picked out Flip's telephone number. He answered right away.

NINETEEN

ROBINSON WAS BEHIND THE WHEEL AS THEY crept along the block. Cristina pointed Flip out. "There he is," she said. "Hurry up."

They pulled up fast by the corner where Flip waited. Cristina twisted around in the seat to get the back door open and Flip got in. Robinson immediately put the accelerator down and they were off, turning north away from the Segundo Barrio and toward the airport and Fort Bliss.

"Flip?" Cristina asked.

"Yes. Felipe."

"I'm Detective Salas. This is Detective Robinson."

Flip looked young, though Cristina had pulled his records and knew he was twenty-six. He had strong features and his eyes were quick. When he looked at her, she could see he was a thinker. She had dealt with dull-eyed gang-bangers with nothing behind them. He was not that way.

"How long until anyone notices you're gone?"

"I just have to be back to my house by dinnertime. A half hour? I have to walk back."

"Okay, we'll be quick."

"Where are we going?"

"Out of the neighborhood," Robinson replied. "We use this car when we work and someone might recognize it. Or us. Better if we take a little drive."

Flip nodded, but said nothing. Cristina thought he had learned that on the inside.

"I talked with Reverend Harcrow," Cristina said. "He told us what you did at Coffield. He vouched for you, but I still have to ask: why call us?"

"I can help you out."

"You were active with the Aztecas in prison?"

"Yeah. I met a dude named Javier. Javier Davila. He saw I was a stand-up guy, gave me an invite into the group."

"It couldn't have been that easy."

Flip cast his eyes down for a moment, looking at his hands. "I had to stab a dude. White boy giving one of the other Aztecas some trouble. I did it and they blooded me in."

"How'd you skate on the stabbing charge?"

"Nobody ratted me out. Must have been twenty people saw it, but nobody said nothing." He looked up again and whatever dark shadow had been there was gone. His eyes were clear.

"Harcrow said you were close to the boss at Coffield."

"Yeah. Enrique Garcia. He's the one in Coffield. One of the Originals. He's been inside thirty years or something. Aztecas come and go, but he stays. Everybody listens to him. He got me set up out here."

"Set up with the Aztecas in El Paso?"

"Yeah, that's right. He talked me up to one of the *capos* out here. His name is José Martinez. Don't you want to write this down?"

Cristina glanced at Robinson. She could tell he was listening. "We know José."

"Are you watching him?"

"Maybe. That's not important right now. Tell me: Garcia sponsored you, said you were okay. José took you in?"

"I think so."

"What do you mean, you think so?"

"I haven't done nothing for him yet. We just met up, did a club, that kind of thing. He hasn't set me up with a job or anything."

"But you're coming to us now?" Robinson put in.

"I want to make sure I'm covered."

"Why take the risk?" Cristina asked. "Nobody knew you were dealing information at Coffield. You could just go along and get along."

Flip took a deep breath. "Look, I got in with the Aztecas at Coffield because they could protect me, all right? I know you saw my rap sheet; I'm not some marijuana cowboy. I'm not going back to prison for nobody."

"Makes sense," Robinson said. "You're on the inside, so why not use that?"

"Right, man."

Cristina looked out the window and couldn't tell where they were. Robinson was making a lot of turns, speeding up and slowing down, checking the mirrors to see if anyone was following them. He was doing everything right. "You understand being a CI doesn't mean you get a free pass," Cristina said.

"I know that."

"If either one of us feels like you're playing games, we'll cut you loose."

"Okay."

"Okay," Cristina said.

"Swing back around?" Robinson asked.

"Yeah. We'll drop him off right where we found him."

"I need to get your numbers so I can contact you anytime," Flip said.

Cristina gave him her number and Robinson recited his. Flip did not enter them into his phone, but just nodded when they were done. There would be no record in his phonebook to compromise him and that was smart.

Robinson drove them back to the spot. Even as he slowed down, Flip was unbuckling himself and prepared to get out fast.

"We'll be in touch," Cristina told him.

"Me, too."

They rolled to a stop. Flip bailed out and started walking in the opposite direction as if nothing unusual was going on. Cristina watched him as they pulled away. He didn't look back, even when they reached the corner and turned out of sight.

"What do you think?" Cristina asked Robinson.

"I'm willing to try him out. The worst thing that happens is he doesn't give us any good tips, screws up on the outside and goes back to prison. Then he can start snitching on his boys inside again."

"He's got balls," Cristina said.

"Definitely. But if he can put us next to José, then I think we've got something. No more sitting on the street taking pictures."

"You think he's going to get that close? He's just off the bus."

"If we push him, maybe he can."

Cristina looked back, but there was nothing but city street to see. "I guess we'll see how it goes. I'll write up the paperwork."

PART TWO

ONE

FLIP WAS UP BEFORE DAWN AGAIN AND, clutching another bagged lunch made by his mother, took a ride with Alfredo. This time Alfredo had the radio on, the sound turned down so Flip could just hear the norteño playing. There were more commercials than music, anyway.

"I need to see my parole officer tonight," Flip told Alfredo. "Can you give me a ride?"

"Sure. Any problems with that?"

"No. Just got to do it before my week is up."

"You're going to stick to the rules, aren't you, Flip?"

"Yeah, of course."

"That's good."

At the warehouse they split up and Flip went to his loading dock and his team. The first truck came just a few minutes later and it was time for work and not thinking.

When lunchtime came, Flip sat outside in the sun at one of three picnic tables set up in a grassy area beside the warehouse. His meal was simple: a sandwich, a piece of fruit and a little bag of chips. If he found himself getting hungry again before the day was through, he could borrow a dollar from Alfredo and get something from the snack machine.

In prison the one thing they had was food. It was not the best food Flip had ever eaten, but it was hot and there was plenty of it. No one complained about not getting seconds because firsts were generous enough. Flip applied to get a job working in the kitchen, but he was funneled into the carpentry program instead.

He'd never worked with wood before they put him in those classes, but he found it surprisingly fun and more involved than he would have guessed going in. There were advanced training courses available, where workers could sculpt trim and even make cabinets, but they started Flip off small and he found he had an affinity for it. After a while he even imagined that he could make a career out of carpentry if he were given a chance, especially with his certificate in hand. Some places would give a convicted felon another chance.

Flip didn't know now. Alfredo had been kind enough to get him this job and looking for another might be an insult. Shifting pallets and unpacking great cubes and pyramids of boxes onto shelves was not what he had in mind when he left Coffield, but it was work and work would keep him out of trouble. At least until José came calling.

Thinking of José made Flip frown.

He was beaten up his first week at Coffield by a white boy named McClain. He hadn't done anything to start the fight; McClain just wanted someone to take his frustrations out on and Flip was a new fish. Flip had no friends then, knew no one's name except Daniel, his cellmate. Daniel stuck his neck out for no one.

Flip expected another beating when Javier Davila came for him. The man was hard with muscle and laced with tattoos and looked like everything people feared when they thought of a convict. They were in the chow hall where it all went down with McClain. "You got heart, *chico*," he said. "Why don't you come eat by me?"

They sat down at one of the hexagonal, stainless steel tables that had four seats, all molded into one big hunk of metal. Omar Cantu sat on the other side of him. Rafael Zúñiga joined them.

"How long you in for?" Javier asked. This was just making conversation. When Flip told him, Javier didn't bother asking what it was for.

The only thing that mattered was the time, not how you earned it.

"I haven't seen a fish with gills like yours for a long time," Omar remarked.

"He means you're a target," Javier said.

"Bang," Rafael added.

Flip had bruises on his arms and the backs of his hands where McClain stomped on them. He'd only looked at himself in the mirror once, but he knew his face was a mask of dark marks, including a blue-black blotch centered on his left eye. McClain punched hard with his right. As the men talked to him, he ate his food and kept his mouth shut.

"I hear you're from El Paso," Javier said.

Flip stiffened because he'd only told Daniel that on their first day in the cell. Daniel, who took no risks, would talk to people who were interested. At that moment Flip felt more exposed than ever before. "Yeah," he said finally.

"I'm from El Paso, too," Javier said. "And Omar there. We're both natives of Chuco Town."

"That's right," Omar said.

"Omar and me, we keep an eye out for guys who come from El Paso. Especially when they're new fish and they got nobody to watch their back. You got an outfit to watch your back?"

"No."

"That's what I thought. Nobody with a crew would take a beating like that. McClain, he's got the Aryan Circle watching over him. You know who they are?"

"No," Flip said.

"They're bad. They pick you out, they come back at you again and again until you can't fight back no more. Or you're dead."

"But I didn't do nothing."

"You don't have to do nothing," Javier said. "They'll come at you because you're brown, *hermano*. But they don't touch nobody who stands with us."

"Why would you want me?" Flip asked.

"I got a soft spot."

"What do I got to do?"

"First thing you do, you meet Enrique. If he says you're okay, then we go on to the next step, but *only* if he says it's okay."

"Who's Enrique?"

"*El jefe.*"

"Where is he?"

"He's in the hole."

"What did he do?"

"He kicked some white boy ass, is what," Javier said.

Across the table, Rafael giggled like a little girl. Omar was silent, just watching. Flip looked to each of them in turn, trying to think of what to say next. Way across the chow hall, he saw McClain and a bunch of other white boys gathered together at their tables. They didn't turn their heads his way. The bruise on his face hurt.

"Yeah, okay," Flip said.

TWO

He saw them when he emerged from the warehouse at the end of his shift. They were beyond the chain-link fencing, leaning up against a car Flip recognized. After a moment he placed one of the figures: Emilio, dressed in knee-length shorts and a t-shirt to go with the warm afternoon.

Emilio waved to Flip and Flip looked around to see if anyone else had noticed, but everyone was saying good-bye, splitting up, going to their cars. Then Emilio motioned Flip to come over.

Alfredo hadn't come out of the warehouse yet. Flip checked over his shoulder once and then half-jogged to the fence line, where Emilio met him. "Hey, *esé*," Emilio said. "What's up?"

"What do you want?" Flip asked.

Emilio put his hands up. "Hey, don't come at me like that, bro. I'm not trying to get up in your shit."

Flip glanced back toward the warehouse. Cars and trucks were easing their way out of the gate, one after another, but there was still no Alfredo. He imagined Alfredo coming out at any moment, spotting them together, and then the questions he would ask. "It's not a good time," Flip said.

"I understand, I understand. José just sent me out to have a look at your place of business, you know? Check in on you."

"Did I do something wrong?"

"Wrong? No. But José was talking about you. He wanted to know what kind of a place you worked."

"Why?"

"I don't know why. José tells me do something, I do it."

"I got to go," Flip said.

"See you around."

Flip left the fence and hurried back toward Alfredo's truck. They were the last ones left in the parking area. Alfredo stepped out and locked the door behind him. The big truck docks were sealed, the warehouse closed tight. He met Flip at the truck. "Ready?" he said.

"Yeah."

They got in the truck together and as they pulled out, Flip saw Emilio and his nameless friend get into Emilio's car. When they turned Flip looked in the side mirror to see if Emilio was following them, but he didn't see anything.

He saw no sign of them when they headed south toward downtown. Flip gave Alfredo the address of the Parole and Probation office and they found it easily; it was in the County Court Building and next to the El Paso County Jail. It cost two dollars to park.

"You want me to come in with you?" Alfredo asked.

"What? No, you don't have to do that."

"Your parole officer might like to talk to your boss."

"I'll ask him. Maybe next time."

"Okay. I'll be right here."

Flip left Alfredo with the truck and went around the building to get in through the front. The police manned a metal detector and an x-ray machine at the entrance and Flip had to empty his pockets. There wasn't much to put in the plastic tray.

He followed the signs to where he needed to go and found himself in a large room lined with rows of plastic seats, facing two glassed-in desks with little metal grilles to talk through. The women behind the glass looked bored. Flip didn't know which one to go to, so he chose the woman on the right.

"I'm here to see my PO, Mr. Rubio," Flip said through the grille.

"Sign the clipboard and have a seat."

Flip did what he was told. The chairs were slick and uncomfortable. Four more men waited, raggedly spaced along the rows, scrupulously avoiding looking at one another. Flip knew they had all done time; prison taught a man to keep himself to himself.

Nearly an hour passed. From time to time a door by the windows would open and a man would come out, check the clipboard and call a name. More people came in and signed up without having to be told. Flip waited.

At last the man called his name and Flip came over. "Are you Mr. Rubio?" he asked the man.

"No. Follow me."

They went back into the area beyond the windows, where lots of little offices clustered together in a honeycomb. The man led him to a door that looked no different from any of the others – there was no nametag, no number – and rapped on the frame. "Felipe Morales," the man said.

"Okay," came a voice from inside.

"Here you go," the man told Flip.

The office was barely large enough for a desk and another plastic chair just like the ones from outside. Rubio was a short, round man with a brush-like mustache and thinning hair cut military-short. His tie was loosened and he wore short sleeves. "Come in and have a seat, Mr. Morales."

Flip wedged himself into the chair between wall and desk. He had nowhere to put his elbows, so he sat with his arms extended out in front of him, tucked between his knees.

"The first thing we're going to do is get you fingerprinted, but let's get some basics down beforehand. Address and that kind of thing."

The question and answer session was short. Rubio asked for

Flip's home address, his telephone numbers and for the license plate number of his car, if he had one. After that he took Flip down the hall to a room where a big machine with a glass plate on the top squatted, humming, beside a computer monitor.

His fingerprints were taken by rolling his fingers across the glass plate so the machine could pick them up. They displayed on the computer monitor. The whole process happened without ink. Rubio had some trouble with Flip's right ring finger, but they got through it and went back to Rubio's office.

The man had photographs tacked to a cloth-covered cork board on the wall. None of them were of children, like Flip would expect, but all of dogs. Sometimes Rubio was in the picture with them, sometimes the dogs were alone. One dog was a pit bull, the other a German Shepherd.

Rubio noticed him looking. "My dogs," he said. "They're my babies. You like dogs?"

"They're okay. I don't have one."

"You should get one. Pet ownership is a good way to practice responsibility."

"Yeah, I guess so."

"Well, maybe not. It's not for everyone."

Rubio then asked questions about Flip's work. He got his supervisor's name, the address of the warehouse, the telephone number there. Flip didn't tell him that his supervisor was his mother's boyfriend. Maybe that would work against him. "I'll be calling to check up on you," Rubio told Flip. "So if you start missing work, I'll know."

"I understand."

"Now for the rest. You'll find I'm a pretty relaxed guy and I won't come down on you for little things. You stay out a little late or you take a sick day... these things happen. But part of the terms of your parole is that you stay clear of bars and clubs and you don't have any contact with felons. You're not allowed to possess a firearm.

You have to submit to random drug testing and home inspections. If you fail a test, or if you violate your terms, I *will* put you back where you came from. I'll do it in a heartbeat. You get me?"

"I get you."

"All right, then. Let's get the drug test over with so you can go home." Rubio got a plastic jar and a sealing bag out of the deepest drawer at his desk. He handed the jar over. "There's a temperature strip on the side, so if it's not warm piss, I'll know. Bathrooms are down the hall."

Flip left the office and took the jar with him.

THREE

Mατías watched the Azteca named Ramón Ayala through one-way glass.

Ayala was just a kid, twenty years old, but a longtime member of Los Aztecas. According to the records Matías requested and received, Ayala had first gotten into Aztecas-related trouble when he was twelve years old. He had already served time in jail.

There was no mistaking his affiliation: both of his arms were sleeved with tattoos that told the story. On one side, a profusion of images associated with the ancient Aztecs. On the other side, guns and women and the number 21. Matías hadn't yet had a look at the ink Ayala wore on his chest and back, but he was sure it would be more of the same.

Of the ten men they'd taken from the Azteca house in the raid led by Muñoz, two names had floated to the top consistently. Ramón Ayala's was one of them. At this point Ayala had been kept up for forty-eight hours, denied anything but water and then given no access to the bathroom. Both Sosa and Galvan had visited him at regular intervals.

Matías could see it in Ayala's eyes, though Ayala did not know anyone was watching. Desperation had its own particular look, a tightness in the facial muscles, a pallor of the skin that artificial light only made more pronounced. And Ayala was sweating heavily, such that the material of his shirt clung to his body.

He closed the shade and cut off the view, collected his things

from the interview table behind him and left the room. Out in
the hall he could hear jailhouse noise filtering down: snatches of
shouts, clanging metal and the general din of many conversations
happening at once, reflected off concrete.

At the next door he paused and made sure he was presentable,
then he let himself in.

Ayala was hunched over the table. Up close Matías could see
that perspiration had made it into his hair, matted it together. There
was a bucket in the corner of the room. Maybe it wasn't sweat at all.
Matías had not watched Sosa and Galvan at work.

It was all theater, what Matías did. As he had done with all the
interviewees up to this point, he made a careful show of laying out
his notepad, his pen, his folder of paperwork. He knew he looked
like Ayala's polar opposite: clean and well-tailored and most of all
rested. The illusion was that this could go on forever in an endless
cycle and no one in authority would be bothered enough to even
show a hair out of place.

Matías could smell the despair coming off Ayala. The young
man reeked of urine and stale body odor. When he looked at
Matías, he trembled in anticipation of the blow. It occurred to
Matías that maybe they'd been too hard on this one, or maybe he
was just letting sentiment obstruct his better judgment.

"Hello," Matías said when he sat down.

"H-hello," Ayala said.

"I don't know if you smoke. Would you like to smoke?"

"I smoke."

The pack came from inside Matías' jacket. He slipped one cigarette
free and offered it to Ayala. The man took it with his free hand. His
lower lip was split and distended and Matías feared the cigarette would
fall. Ayala barely kept the tip steady for Matías to light it.

Matías let Ayala smoke for a minute or two uninterrupted. The
trembling was less pronounced now, but the air of distress didn't
leave the man.

"I think you know why I'm here," Matías said at last.

Ayala exhaled smoke. "Someone snitched on me."

"Yes."

"And now I have to confess."

"Yes."

"How much do you have?"

"Five signed statements attesting to your role in the shooting of a half-dozen Salvadorans outside a social club. I could get more, but we've left the girls out of it for now. I'm sure you bragged to at least one of them."

The tremor was back as Ayala took another drag. Matías let the smoke curlicue up between them, catch in the beam of the overhead light and dissipate at the ceiling. The smell of tobacco made Matías want a cigarette, too, but he had quit three years before and would not risk starting again.

"How much will I get?"

"Most likely? Life. If you're willing to give me the names of the other shooters, then maybe concessions can be made. A better prison. Privileges. At the very least, you won't have to go to prison alone."

Ayala's face screwed up and he rubbed at one black eye. "I was just doing what they told me to do."

"You can give me the names of those who gave the orders. Then they can pay, too."

A tear fell down Ayala's cheek and Matías had to steel himself from wrinkling his nose in disgust. Men like Ayala did not deserve the luxury of tears. He wondered if there would be any tears at all if Sosa and Galvan had not made their case so strenuously.

"I'll tell you whatever you want," Ayala said.

Matías took up his pen. "You know, you're very lucky this didn't happen on the other side of the border. In the States they have the death penalty."

"You still get my life."

"But not fast enough, *mi amigo*. Not fast enough."

FOUR

FLIP WORKED ALL WEEK AND ON FRIDAY HE
was exhausted. Even working in the carpentry shop at Coffield had
not been so demanding. All of his muscles hurt. He took a handful
of ibuprofen and soaked himself in a hot shower for thirty minutes
before collapsing on the bed for a nap.

His sleep was dreamless. A chiming sound intruded and when
he opened his eyes it was after dark. On his bed-stand his phone
was vibrating and ringing. He'd already missed two calls.

He answered. "Hello?"

"Flip?" A man's voice.

Flip sat up in the dark. "Yes?"

"It's José."

"José, yeah. How did you get my number?"

"Everything's easy to get."

He rubbed his eyes and stifled a deep yawn that came up
from his diaphragm. His mouth didn't taste right. "What's up? Is
something happening?"

"Yeah, something's happening: I'm having a get-together at my
place. You want in?"

"What? Sure."

"You don't sound so sure."

"Oh, it's nothing. I just woke up, is all."

"Well get dressed and get over here."

Flip turned on his bedside lamp. He checked the clock. He'd been asleep two hours. "I don't know where you live. And I can't drive."

"I'll send Emilio around to pick you up. Can you be ready in twenty minutes?"

"Yeah, I can be ready."

"All right. See you soon."

Flip put the phone down and went to the closet. He rummaged around for something to wear. They were not going clubbing, but he did not want to be disrespectful and just put on a t-shirt. He found a button-up shirt with narrow stripes that he hadn't worn in a while, matched them with some jeans. Again he thought he needed to buy new sneakers. Maybe he would when his first paycheck came.

His mother was in the living room watching television with the light off. Flip leaned in and gave her a kiss on the head. "I'm going out," he said.

"Where are you going this time?"

"A friend's house."

"Does your friend have a name?"

"José."

"Is he good people?"

"Good enough."

"I don't want you hanging around with no hoodlums, Felipe!"

"Mamá, he's not a hoodlum."

"Don't stay out all night."

"I didn't stay out all night before, did I? And turn on a light, Mamá; you're going to ruin your eyes."

"My eyes are fine. You stay out of trouble."

"Yes, ma'am."

He waited out front of the house until he saw Emilio's headlights make the corner at the end of the block. Overhead the sky was painted by city lights, with barely a star able to break through. In Coffield Enrique once told him that it was so dark on the yard at night that you could see every star in the sky all at once, but he didn't tell Flip how he knew that.

Emilio wasn't dressed up and Flip felt better. He got in and they drove off.

"What kind of party is this?" Flip asked.

"Just José and a few other people. Barbecue. Beer. Relax."

They drove less than ten minutes before they reached a street of houses. Flip spotted José's right away. It wasn't bigger or grander than the houses around it, but it had orange party lights strung around a large patio that extended out into the space where a lawn would be. There were cars lining the street on both sides and when they drew close, Flip saw a crowd of people outside with red plastic cups in their hands, talking. Loud music drifted on the night air.

"I'm going to drop you off here and go park," Emilio said. "See you later."

Flip got out in front of the house and went up the driveway. The patio was surrounded by a little fence. Flip found the gate and came inside.

He thought he might recognize some of the faces here from his time at the club, but he couldn't be sure. Adrift at the edge of the crowd, he cast around for José and finally spotted him through a gap in the press of bodies, working a large brick grill.

It took a minute to navigate the patio until Flip was close enough to tap José on the arm. Intense heat radiated from a mesquite fire. Meat spat on the grill. Jose wore a funny-looking white apron and brandished a pair of spring-loaded tongs in his hand. "Hey, Flip," he said. "Glad you could make it!"

"It smells good," Flip said.

"Thanks, man. I use my father's recipe for the rub. You want chicken or beef?"

"Chicken's fine."

"Grab a plate there." José put a dripping leg quarter of chicken on a paper plate for Flip and gestured with the tongs toward the house. "The door's open. Get some beer inside."

"Okay," Flip said. "I'll see you."

"No, I'll see you. Have fun. Meet some people."

Flip made his way to the house. The front door stood open. There were more people in the living room talking, eating and drinking. A big flatscreen television was turned to a music channel with the volume down. A stereo pumped out the music everyone was listening to.

The house was not what Flip expected. The TV and the stereo looked expensive, but the furniture was simple and there were photographs of family on the wall along with a few pieces of art. Flip expected bigger, fancier, but the house looked as old as his mother's house and had the same wrought iron bars on the windows.

He found the kitchen. The sink was filled with ice and bottles of beer stuck out of it, sweating condensation. A broad-mouthed punchbowl on the kitchen table served up a bright red mixture into plastic cups. Two bottles of tequila, almost empty, stood nearby. Flip chose beer.

It was hard to find a place to sit and eventually Flip went out the side door under the car park and put his plate on the roof of the parked Lexus. His chicken was hot and greasy and he licked his fingers to keep them clean. After that, the beer was the perfect complement.

A woman's voice brought him around: "Flip?"

Graciela was dressed differently than she had been at the club. Gone were the form-fitting clothes, replaced with jeans and an off-the-shoulder top that exposed a bra strap. Her hair was let down.

"Hey," Flip said. "Graciela. How are you?"

"I've been waiting all week for you to call me. Did you lose my number?"

Flip felt color in his face and took a swig of beer to cover. "No, I didn't. I just started a job and I've been real busy. I'm sorry."

Graciela raised an eyebrow at him. "Are you too busy to talk now?"

"No. It's fine."

"I was hoping you would call so we could go out," Graciela said. "But if your job keeps you so busy…"

"It's not that," Flip said. "I start work real early and by the time I get home I'm done. They've been working me hard, you know? And my mother, she wants me to stay in. But I promise I'll call you next week. Maybe we can get something to eat."

"That would be nice. Where are you working?"

Flip told her and then he told her other things, like how Alfredo had given him the job and what he had to do all day. It was not exciting stuff, but she listened and Flip was grateful. He caught himself almost mentioning that he'd been in prison. He decided to shut up for a while. "How is school?" he asked.

"It's good. At the school we get people who come in for manicures and we get to practice on them, but only when we're good enough. The people don't pay that much, but they want to have a professional nail job done, you know?"

"I've never had my nails done."

"Maybe I can do yours sometime. Men get it done, too."

"They do?"

"Sure. Men don't like to get all painted up, but the rest is nice."

"Okay, I'll try it."

"After you take me out," Graciela said. "I don't want you to think you can get a manicure for nothing."

A silence started to fall between them and Flip thought quickly for some way to keep going. He did not want her walking away. "Listen," he said, "José told me to meet some people. You know a lot of people here?"

"I know some. You want me to introduce you around?"

"Yeah. Just let me get another beer."

"Get one for me."

She led him through the crowd from kitchen to living room to patio, stopping here and there to introduce Flip to the people she found there. As he had at the club he tried hard to remember names and put them to faces, but he only had a moment or two to talk before Graciela whisked him away to the next group. From time to time Flip caught sight of José at the grill, cooking and talking and sometimes having a beer. They passed through his orbit once and then again and finally they were there.

José smiled when he saw them. "Flip! You met Graciela. She's a good girl to know because she knows everybody."

"I just found out," Flip said.

"Graciela, are you making sure Flip has a good time?"

"What do you think?" Graciela said.

"I think you're going to get Flip in trouble," José said. He laughed and touched her on the back familiarly. Flip felt a pang of something, but he wouldn't call it jealousy; he didn't know what it was.

"I'm going to take Flip away now," Graciela said.

"Good. You don't want to stand here all night talking to me."

Graciela took Flip by the hand and pulled him away from José, back toward the house. They entered through the front door, but she angled away from the kitchen and down an unlit hallway.

"Where are we going?" Flip asked.

Graciela put her finger to her lips.

They reached the end of the hall and turned left. Graciela found a door in the dark and opened it, tugged Flip to bring him along behind her. When he was inside, she pushed the door closed.

She stood on her toes and kissed him on the lips softly, then harder. He put his hands on her body, felt her slender waist and then her hips. He tasted her tongue.

There was a bed in the room and Graciela pushed Flip toward it until the mattress hit the back of his legs and he sat down. They kissed again. Her fingers were on the buttons of his shirt.

Flip helped her get his shirt off. She put her hands on his chest and eased him onto his back. They struggled together to climb farther onto the bed and then she was straddling him. Her top went up over her head. Flip's eyes were growing used to the darkness and he saw her slender body hovering above him as she unhooked her bra. He touched her little breasts, the erect nipples. She leaned over him so he could take one into his mouth.

They stripped each other. Flip was aching when she reached down between them and guided him into her. She was heat and wetness and she groaned when he pushed in.

She made love to him slowly, but with urgency. Flip wanted to put his hands everywhere at once, to feel her skin under his touch. When she kissed him again he couldn't hold back and he finished inside of her.

For a while she lay atop him and they breathed together. Eventually she slipped free of his embrace and he heard her dressing in the dark. "Do you have to go?" he asked.

"It's not our bedroom," Graciela whispered. "We can't stay here forever."

He got up and fished for his clothes, but she was already dressed. "Just a minute," he said.

Graciela kissed him. "Don't forget to call me this time," she said.

She opened the door and the sounds of the party poured in. Then she closed it and was gone.

FIVE

CRISTINA OVERSLEPT ON MONDAY MORNING and nearly didn't get Freddie to the bus on time. Traffic to the command center was bad because of a road accident. She got to the squad room a half an hour late.

"Nice of you to join us," Robinson said.

"Can it, Bob. Not this morning."

"Rough day at the office?"

"I need a new alarm clock. Christ, I didn't even get to have breakfast yet."

"I think there's doughnuts by the coffee machine."

"Okay."

Cristina sorted through her messages and checked her email, but it was hard to focus. A wrong start to the day could put her into a tight spot all day and she couldn't allow that. When Robinson returned with doughnuts she ate two almost without tasting them and then went for coffee.

The door to Captain Cokley's office was closed. When it opened, Cokley cocked a finger at Cristina. "Salas, Robinson, come on in here."

Cokley's office was not grand, but it was large enough for a small meeting table to fit in with his desk. He pointed them toward chairs and Cristina saw the woman in the black suit for the first time: she sat with her back to the wall, a laptop open in front of her and a scattering of printouts at hand. She looked tall even sitting down and her hair was perfectly straight to her shoulders.

"Special Agent McPeek, these are my detectives, Cristina Salas and Bob Robinson," Cokley said. "You two have a seat."

McPeek got up to shake their hands and Cristina saw that she was maybe as tall as Robinson. Her suit looked expensive. "Pleased to meet you both," McPeek said. "You can call me Jamie if you want, I don't mind."

"Salas and Robinson are my go-to people when it comes to Barrio Azteca," Cokley said.

"Is that so? Then I'm definitely talking to the right folks."

"What's going on?" Cristina asked.

"I'm with the Safe Streets Gang Task Force," McPeek said. "I'm new, so I'm still getting to know everybody. I've only been in the El Paso office for three months. From what I understand, your unit has coordinated with the task force before."

"Sure," Robinson said. "Special Agent Gorden was our last FBI guy."

"I've met Special Agent Gorden. He did a very nice job here, made it easy for me to get up to speed. He's out in California now."

Cokley sat on the edge of his desk. Cristina felt him hovering over her shoulder. "Special Agent McPeek is here to talk about something new that's coming down the pipeline. As soon as she told me all about it, I knew you'd have to be brought in."

"What is it?" Cristina asked.

"Well, I should start out by saying that this is an operation that's only affiliated with the task force and isn't actually part of its usual function. This particular undertaking involves the FBI, DEA, ATF and the federal police in Mexico."

"That's a lot of alphabet soup," Robinson said.

"It's a delicate balance," McPeek replied. "And now we're looking to draw in some members of the El Paso Police Department. Specifically: you."

Cristina leaned forward in her seat. "Why us?"

"Your captain tells me that you've been regularly surveilling a *capo* in the Barrio Azteca power structure by the name of José Martinez. Is that correct?"

"We like to keep tabs on him."

"So do we."

"We've been trying to keep track of José's lieutenants, sergeants and soldiers," Robinson added. "Guys on that level have been easier to bust and sometimes they'll roll on other Aztecas, but it's never José."

"What would you say if I told you that we're building a case against José Martinez that he won't be able to wriggle his way out of?"

"I'm interested," Robinson said. "Cris, you interested?"

"Yeah," Cristina said. "Tell me more."

McPeek closed her laptop firmly. "That can wait until tomorrow," she said. "I'd like to invite the both of you down to our offices for a full briefing on what we're doing."

"What, that's all you're going to tell us?" Cristina asked.

"I wouldn't want to spoil the surprise."

"But—" Cristina said.

"They'll be there," Cokley interjected.

"Ten o'clock tomorrow," McPeek said. "You know where to find us. Don't be late."

SIX

THE EL PASO FEDERAL JUSTICE CENTER WAS
on the northwest side of town not far from the mall. Cristina and
Robinson arrived by nine-thirty and spent a half hour waiting in
the hall outside a conference room. A secretary came to unlock the
door and let them in. They were the first ones at the table.

As people began to file in, they saw familiar faces. The Safe
Streets Gang Task Force pulled in some of the same people from
the same agencies. Cristina nodded hello to Michael Staff from
Department of Public Safety and Madge Crompton from the
DEA.

McPeek was five minutes late and by then the table was full.
She took a spot at the head and plugged her laptop into a projector
set-up. A picture of her desktop flashed on a broad screen on the
wall. "Good morning, everyone," she said.

The same secretary returned, this time with a rolling tray
topped with a carafe of coffee and a plate full of danishes. There
was a general shuffle to collect food and drink before everyone
settled down again. The secretary sat down at a side table where a
laptop was already set up. McPeek was ready then.

"I guess we should start by going around the table," McPeek
said. "We have two new people with us this morning: Detectives
Cristina Salas and Bob Robinson from the El Paso Police Department's Central Tactical Gang Operations Unit. I know some of you
know each other already, but let's make it official for the record."

They went one by one around the long conference table introducing themselves. As McPeek had promised, there was complete representation by all the major federal agencies – DEA, FBI, ATF – as well as the state. The only people missing were the Texas Rangers. Cristina took notes in a little book, jotting down names. Robinson did the same.

When they were finished, McPeek brought up a PowerPoint slide that depicted the interlocking agencies in graphical form. "I've explained to Detectives Salas and Robinson that what we do here overlaps somewhat with the Safe Streets Gang Task Force. Where there's deviation it has to do with our international cooperation with law enforcement agencies in Mexico. This is a true cross-border operation coordinated between this group and the Ministerial Federal Police of Mexico. They're not represented here today, but all of the minutes of our meetings are transmitted to the point man in Ciudad Juárez. We're also scheduled to have bi-monthly contact meetings in Juárez with a core from this group meeting with our opposite numbers.

"I called this meeting today because I wanted to bring local law enforcement up to speed with what we're doing at the state and federal levels. It's overdue. I want to apologize to the representatives of the El Paso Police Department for not including them until now."

Cristina raised her hand. "How long has this… operation been underway?"

"About six weeks. We're still putting things together on the ground floor, but we're moving fast."

"And this is gang-related?"

"We're just coming to that." A new slide came up. "The people in this room were selected because of their involvement in anti-gang law enforcement or because their agency has a vested interest in some aspect of the operation. The initial push for a new operation came from the Mexican side of the border. They brought their case to the FBI and the DEA and that got the ball rolling.

"We have one focus: Barrio Azteca, both on our side of the river and the Mexican side. In some respect this group resembles the one that coordinated Operation Knockdown, which pulled in fifty-four Aztecas, and the operation that reeled in the US Consulate murderers. We're after big game."

Another slide. Cristina noted José Martinez's name at the top of a pyramid of other names, all linked by different-colored arrows.

"Barrio Azteca in El Paso and Los Aztecas in Juárez are the same entity, trading across the border in guns and drugs. This is nothing new. What we want this time is to roll up a whole section of Azteca operations from top to bottom. The guys on the streets and the man at the top."

"How do agencies like ATF get involved?" Robinson asked.

"I can answer that," the ATF rep said. Cristina checked her notes: his name was Gerald Muir. "We've been picking up noises of increased gun trafficking by members of Barrio Azteca. Preliminary investigation ties that trafficking to the Martinez outfit. We're just not sure how it all fits together. Part of our job is to start feeding his people firearms that we can document and track."

"But in the end this is just laying the groundwork for RICO charges, right?" Cristina asked.

"That's the idea," McPeek said. "But we're taking things a step further by involving the PFM the way we did last year on the consulate operation. Guns smuggled into Mexico by Barrio Azteca on our end will be snapped up by federal police forces in-country. We'll be able to draw a direct line from the US to Mexico."

"And the DEA?" Robison inquired.

"The same thing, only in reverse. When the Aztecas send drugs north in exchange for guns and money, police forces in Mexico will track them as they can and build cases on their end." McPeek shuffled through a couple slides. "We get both ends working against the middle."

"Who's the capo you're targeting in Mexico?" asked Cristina.

"His name is Julio Guerra. He does all his dirty work through his lieutenants. With luck, we'll be able to put both men and their outfits out of commission at the same time."

"We've been putting together a picture of what José's outfit looks like," Cristina said. "We've run surveillance on him, kept track of known associates, put pressure on low-level Aztecas when we bring them in."

"So you're as close to the ground level as we're going to get," McPeek said. "Every piece of intelligence feeds the operation. To get José Martinez we need you, and you can use us. Coordinated right, this could be the single biggest bust of Barrio Azteca members we've ever had. Think about that when you think about safe streets."

Cristina glanced at Robinson. "Okay," she said. "Tell us more."

SEVEN

MATÍAS SLEPT UNTIL THE SUN FELL THROUGH the open curtains directly onto his face. He covered up with a second pillow for a little while, but the heat made him itch. Out of bed, he went to the bathroom and had a shower. Shaved and with fresh deodorant on, he felt new.

Elvira came into the bedroom while he was getting dressed. She still wore her robe, which looked as good on her as any dress. "It's about time you got up," she said. "I thought you were dead in here."

"How long were you going to wait to check?"

"Only a little while longer. You want breakfast?"

"Okay."

It felt strange, not wearing a tie, but it was his first day off in four weeks and he was not going to spend it stitched up. He put on a short-sleeved shirt and left the collar open, but he didn't wear shorts. Barefoot he went down the hallway to the kitchen where Elvira was already frying eggs. He pulled her hair back and kissed her on the ear.

"What was that for?"

"No reason."

They had been married three years. Matías met her at a *fútbol* match with a bunch of other members of the PF and PFM. At the time she was with another man, but that soon ended and she began seeing Matías. They married after six months together.

Their apartment was small, but it worked for two people and the rent was well within their means, with his salary from the PFM and hers from a law firm in the city. From time to time they discussed finding someplace bigger, making room for a family, but the discussions went nowhere and they stayed right where they were.

He found the paper in the living room on the coffee table. *El Diario*. He was still reading it when Elvira brought him the eggs, larded with tomato-chili salsa. "Eat up," she said.

The eggs were gone in a few minutes. Matías put the paper down long enough to go to the kitchen and pour himself a glass of grapefruit juice. He stood at the sink drinking it. Elvira entered, still wearing her robe. "Aren't you going to get dressed?" Matías asked.

"What should I get dressed for? We're taking the day off together, but what are we doing? We haven't even talked it over."

"What do you feel like doing?"

"We could ride bikes at the park. Pack lunch. Eat under a tree."

Matías put his arms around her and inhaled her smell. "That sounds like a good day," he said.

"Well, you're not dressed for it. Change into some shorts."

"You know I hate shorts."

"I'm not going to be seen cycling with you if you don't dress properly." Elvira squirmed in his embrace and her robe came off her shoulders. She was naked underneath. "And now you have a reason to get undressed."

They made love in the bedroom on top of the sheets. Matías could not remember the last time they had been together and he went too fast. Elvira kissed him on the chest and held him back from her so they wouldn't finish too soon. The sun fell across them both and made them perspire.

"*Me encanta*," Elvira whispered in his ear. "*Te amo*."

This time she let him fulfill himself and they lay side by side under the sun and let the thin film of sweat evaporate. Matías let his hand roam up and down Elvira's body, touching her breast, touching her hip.

"I didn't get my turn," Elvira said.

"I'm sorry."

"It's all right. But you owe me for next time."

Matías soured. "Whenever that is," he said.

"What do you mean?"

"Nothing. I'm only being bitter."

Elvira tousled Matías' hair. She smiled at him. "You let them work you too hard. You don't even have time to get a decent haircut."

"I knew what I was getting into," Matías said. "Long days. Long nights. Los Aztecas don't keep a regular schedule."

"Don't talk about them here," Elvira said. "Right now it's just you and me."

"I love you," Matías said. "You do know that, don't you?"

"Of course. Don't be silly."

"It's just sometimes when we're apart for so long, I wonder if…"

"If I will fall out of love with you?"

"Something like that."

"You don't have to worry," Elvira said and she kissed softly him on the forehead. "I'll never love another man. I promised you."

"And if I were gone?"

"Don't say things like that!"

"I'm sorry."

Elvira caught his gaze with her own and held it. "The truth is that you aren't going anywhere and neither am I. We're in this together. For life. If you wanted a wife who would leave when things got tough, you should have married someone else."

"I worry about you. This city."

"This city has survived. I will survive."

Down on the street three stories below, a car horn suddenly blared and there was the shriek of tires. Matías braced for the sound of a collision, but there was none. Tension formed in his shoulders. He tried to shrug it away.

"So," Elvira said, "are we going to go to the park?"

"Yes."

"Then smile for me and say we're going to the park."

Matías smiled and hoped it was real enough to fool her. "We're going to the park."

"Now… make love to me again."

"I thought we had to leave. The park is waiting."

"The park will still be there. You wanted to know the next time we would be together and this is it."

Matías touched her and felt the skin tighten beneath his fingers. He roved lower, between parted legs, and felt the heat there. "I do love you," he said.

"I know. You said. *Oh*, that's it."

EIGHT

ALFREDO BROUGHT FLIP HOME FROM WORK and parked his truck out on the street. Flip looked at him. "I'm coming to see your mother," Alfredo explained.

Flip thought it was strange, seeing her mother hug and kiss a man. All of his life she had never seemed interested in such things, but now she had Alfredo and everything had changed. He let the two of them settle down in the kitchen and went to his room.

The walls were still bare. He hadn't thought of anything to hang on them yet. It had been the same way in prison. Daniel liked to put up pictures of girls in bikinis because nothing more explicit was allowed within prison walls. Flip did not like the reminder of what he was missing on the outside. It was worse when he heard Daniel masturbating at night in his lower bunk. That was when Flip knew he had fallen as far as he could go.

He heard his mother laugh. Alfredo was good to her. Neither of them had explained where or how they met and he hadn't thought to pry by asking. Maybe they simply used the same grocery store. Stranger things had happened.

Flip changed out of his uniform shirt. He felt sore and sweaty and opted for a shower. With a fresh t-shirt on he felt much better. On the inside a convict only got a shower every other day and time was limited. The COs locked the convicts into their stalls so there was no fear of "dropping the soap." It got so that Flip looked forward to showering more than anything else, even going outside, because it was his only alone time. On the yard he was with Javier and Enrique and the others. In the cell there was Daniel and his paper harem.

Tying his shoelaces he got an idea and went to the kitchen. His mother looked up. "Felipe, do you want something to drink? I just made fresh iced tea."

"No, Mamá. I was wondering if I could borrow some money to buy some new shoes. I'll pay you back when I get my check. If that's okay."

His mother looked at his sneakers and nodded. "It's okay. Bring me my purse."

Flip did what he was told and she gave him fifty dollars in return. "Thank you, Mamá," Flip said. "I won't waste it."

"You need a ride to the store?" Alfredo asked.

"I don't know. Maybe. I'll let you know."

He went back to his room and sat on the bed. His phone was on the bed-stand, along with the napkin with Graciela's number on it. He dialed.

At first he thought she wasn't there, but she answered on the fifth ring. "Hello, it's Flip," Flip said. "Graciela?"

"*Hola*, Flip! You didn't forget to call me this time."

"No, I didn't. I wondered… are you busy right now?"

"Right now? No. You want to go do something?"

"Yes, but I don't have a car. I wondered if you—"

"I can pick you up," Graciela interrupted. "What's your address?"

Flip gave it to her and thought he could hear her writing it down. "If it's too much trouble, it's all right if you don't want to come," he said.

"Don't be stupid. It'll take me half an hour; I have to get ready."

"You don't have to dress up."

"Listen, Flip: I'll dress up if I want to. I'll see you in thirty minutes."

Flip put the phone in his pocket after first saving Graciela's name and number to the memory. It said something in the instruction booklet about making personalized ring tones for people, but that was too confusing for him and he left the function alone. He went back to the kitchen. "I don't need a ride," he told Alfredo. "I have someone picking me up."

"A friend?" his mother asked.

"Yes. A girl I met the other night. Her name is Graciela."

"That's a pretty name," Alfredo said.

"I hope she's a *good* girl," Flip's mother said.

"I think she is. She's from the *barrio*. She's studying to do nails," Flip said. He wanted to make Graciela sound good to his mother, for his mother to say he was doing a right thing. Suddenly it seemed very important.

"It's good she's going to school. You should think about that."

"I told you, I got my carpentry certificate."

"Oh?" Alfredo said. "I didn't know about that."

"It didn't seem important."

"I hope I don't lose you to a better job. Everybody says you're great."

"I think we're okay for now," Flip said.

"When is this girl coming?" his mother asked.

"Any minute."

"I want to meet her."

"Uh, okay."

Flip sat on the front step and waited for Graciela to arrive. Eventually he saw her approaching in a green Hyundai with a missing hubcap. She parked at the curb and he went down to see her.

She was smiling and looked good in a t-shirt that was not too tight. His mother would be watching for things like that. "Hey," she said. "Get in."

"Wait," Flip said and he felt himself blush. "My mother... my mother wants to meet you first."

Graciela laughed. "Sure, it's okay!"

She put her hand in his as they went up the walk. Flip held the door for her. "Mamá," he called, "she's here."

Alfredo and Flip's mother came from the kitchen. Flip introduced them.

"Hello, *señora*," Graciela said. "I'm Flip's friend. It's good to meet you."

His mother looked Graciela up and down as if she was appraising a horse. "You seem like a nice girl," she said at last. Flip let out a breath he didn't know he was holding.

"I promise not to keep him out too late," Graciela said.

"Good, because he has work tomorrow," Alfredo said. "Have a good time."

"Where will you have dinner?" Flip's mother asked.

"We'll get something while we're out," Flip said.

"Be careful!"

"We will," said Graciela.

They went down to the car and Graciela let him in. Behind the wheel, she carefully put on her seatbelt before turning the key in the ignition. Flip watched her. "What?" she asked.

"Safety first," Flip said. "My mother always told me."

"Your mother is smart. She likes me, after all."

"I need to get some new shoes," Flip said.

"So where do you want to go?"

"Sunland Park?"

"Sure."

They drove and Flip noticed how she always used her signals and came to a complete stop at signs and lights. She never sped. The little Hyundai was clean inside and a strawberry air freshener dangled from the rear view mirror. They got on the highway. Traffic was stacking up at rush hour.

Flip wasn't sure what to say. He thought he should say something about the party, about the way they said good-bye, but there were no good approaches that way. If the radio was on then he could make some comment about the music, but it was turned off. Talking about the traffic seemed stupid.

He caught her look at him out of the corner of her eye. "You nervous?" she asked.

"No, no."

"Because you seem nervous. You keep rubbing your hands on your pants."

Flip immediately made fists with his hands. "It's good to see you again," he tried.

"If you're nervous because of what happened the other night—"

"No, that was good," Flip said.

"It was good," Graciela said and she took one hand off the wheel to reach over and touch him. Flip thought her fingertips were electric. "And I don't want you thinking I do that with a lot of guys, because I don't."

"I didn't think that."

"Okay. Just so you know."

After a while they left the freeway and got off on a feeder road. The mall came into view with its acres of parking lot filled halfway with cars glittering in the sun. "The mall," Flip said, and immediately felt like an idiot.

"What kind of shoes do you want?" Graciela asked.

"Oh, just shoes. Some sneakers. Nothing special. Mine are… you know."

"Don't be picky!" Graciela remarked and flashed him a smile.

They parked and entered next to Sears. Together they checked the mall directory and found the shoe stores. Flip picked Payless because he did not want to spend all of his mother's money on shoes. There was food to think about. He wondered how Graciela would feel about fast food and wished he could afford something better.

"Are you going to stay this quiet?" Graciela asked. "Talk to me about your day or something."

"Why don't you tell me about your day? Mine's boring. Moving boxes."

"Okay, but now you're going to get all the gossip!"

Graciela told him about the school and the salon where advanced students worked and all the details about the girls she went to classes with. Rosenda and Eva were her closest friends; they'd all entered together. Leticia was the common enemy: ready to graduate, full of herself but, Graciela had to admit, very talented. Flip listened to all of this while trying on shoes, glad because the longer she talked the fewer opportunities she would have to ask him where he'd been the last four years and the awkward turn the conversation would take then.

He settled on a pair of white and red sneakers that looked more expensive than they were. Flip put his old shoes in the box and wore the new shoes out. After that they wandered along the stores. Graciela linked hands with him.

When the question came he wasn't ready for it. "What?" he asked.

"I asked if you were in jail."

"Why would you ask me that?"

"I just have a feeling about it, is all. A lot of José's friends have been in jail. It doesn't mean anything."

Flip looked at her and tried to tell if she was saying what she really felt. He felt the earth opening up beneath his feet. He stopped by a planter and let a mother and her children go by. "Yeah," he said. "I was."

He watched her face when he said it, but he saw no disappointment or anger there. She didn't let go of his hand.

"How long were you in?" Graciela asked finally.

"Four years."

"That's a long time. You're on parole?"

"Yeah."

"It's okay. Let's walk some more."

"I thought maybe you wouldn't want to be with me if you knew," Flip admitted.

"Why did you think that?"

"I don't know. I just did."

"I'm a big girl. I know how things work."

"Don't you want to know why I went in?"

"Do you want to tell me?"

"Not right now."

"Then you don't have to."

NINE

Robinson's desk was empty. He was due in court to testify and would not be back until the afternoon at the earliest. Cristina caught up on paperwork. There was always paperwork. She had just gotten approval to add Felipe Morales as a confidential informant. Now he could be paid for the information he brought in.

She'd checked with Flip's parole officer and found out most of what she needed to know. He was drug-free and at the time of his test hadn't had alcohol in twenty-four hours. He had a full-time job working at a grocery store's delivery hub. He lived with his mother at a stable address. He was scheduled for visits every three weeks from now until the end of time, or close enough.

The phone rang. Cristina answered.

"Detective Salas, it's Jamie McPeek. Am I calling at a bad time?"

"No, Agent McPeek, I wasn't doing anything in particular."

"I was wondering if you had some free time this morning."

"What do you have in mind?"

"Well, if you're free, I'd like to take you to Juárez."

"Juárez?"

"Yes. I thought you might want to see what's happening from the other side of the fence."

Cristina checked her watch and then her desk calendar. "Okay," she said. "I can do that. When do you want to pick me up?"

"Give me an hour to get things squared away here."

"All right, then."

"See you soon, Detective."

Cristina rose from her desk and went to Captain Cokley's office. She knocked on the open door. "Hey, boss, I'm going to be off the board for a few hours this afternoon. Reynolds and Trevino are here, so they can pick up the slack."

Cokley wore little granny half-glasses when he read. He peered over them at Cristina. "Where are you headed off to?"

"Special Agent McPeek wants to take me to Juárez."

"Juárez? What's in Juárez?"

"I guess it's part of getting to know you."

"Will they even let you carry your piece over there?"

"I don't know."

Cokley put down the sheaf of papers he was reading and turned to his computer. "Let me look into it, unless you're out the door right now. I don't like the idea of you going over there with nothing but harsh language."

"Maybe McPeek will cover for me."

"We'll see."

It took half an hour for Cokley to come up with an answer. He came by her desk still wearing his granny glasses.

"What do you got?" Cristina asked.

"According to what I found out, you're not allowed to carry, but I think this is one of those times where it's better to ask for forgiveness than for permission. You got me?"

"I get you."

Cokley started to walk away and then stopped. "It's just that I worry."

"I'm sure I'll be all right."

"Keep an eye out, is what I'm saying."

"I will."

McPeek called Cristina at her desk when she was downstairs

and Cristina left her desk. She found McPeek idling in a red zone. When she got in the car it was freezing; the air conditioner was turned up full blast. Cristina wished for a sweater.

"I'm glad you could find the time," McPeek told Cristina. "Too cold?"

"No, it's fine," Cristina lied. "Where are we headed?"

"To see our point man in Juárez. He's my opposite number. Matías Segura with the PFM."

Driving to Mexico from Central Regional Command was a question of minutes. Less than a mile separated then from the other side of the river. They took the bridge from South Stanton Street, an El Paso thoroughfare that flowed directly into a Juárez street without interruption. At the border checkpoint, McPeek showed her federal ID to the men on duty and spoke Spanish to them. They asked for Cristina's ID and she gave it to them.

If she expected to be relieved of her service pistol, Cristina was disappointed. After examining the women's IDs closely, the men waved McPeek's car through without need for inspection. They were in Juárez.

People said that Segundo Barrio in El Paso was just Juárez continued north of the river, but they were wrong. There was an immediate shift that took place once a person passed over the bridge and it was obvious to anyone who could see. The buildings were closer, the streets narrower and less well maintained. It was not like this everywhere in Juárez, but here it was. They saw an army vehicle within two minutes of crossing over.

Cristina did not visit Ciudad Juárez anymore. There was a time, in high school and in college, when she spent much of her free time in the neighborhoods along the border, especially the marketplaces and the tourist strip called Avenida Juárez. Near where McPeek crossed over there was the bridal district, where Cristina bought her wedding dress.

Things were different now, of course. That was the

understatement. The reality was far more frightening. Bullets from Juárez sometimes landed in El Paso. There were thousands of police and military everywhere and at any moment whole neighborhoods could be shut down for police action. Cristina knew no one who crossed, even for a few hours, unless they had family in the city. There were still some hardy leftovers who would go anywhere without regard to the consequences, but the tourist industry in Juárez was functionally dead.

McPeek knew which way to go. They headed downtown where the streets opened up and the traffic thickened. Cristina started counting police vehicles she saw, but stopped at thirty. Once they passed a roadblock where cars were being checked one at a time, packing an entire avenue tight with trapped automobiles.

Cristina found herself bracing for something, then relaxing and then bracing again. She realized it was her unconscious expecting the bullet to come. Everyone knew the stories about pitched gun battles transforming a quiet block into a war zone. It could happen anywhere. She had to unclench her fingers from the armrest.

McPeek glanced down at Cristina's hand. "Jitters?" she asked.

"Something like that."

"I get them, too."

"Tell me we're almost there."

"We're almost there."

Cristina had no idea where they were now. McPeek had taken them well away from the areas where tourists went and deep downtown. Cristina noted that she was seeing more and more heavily armed trucks passing and then they passed a sandbagged machine gun emplacement on a street corner manned by uniformed soldiers.

"And we're here."

There was no way to tell what the building had looked like before. With its small windows and high sides it would have looked like a fortress anyway, but the concrete car barriers, barbed wire and huge metal roadblocks welded together to make giant jacks transformed the structure utterly. Two pick up trucks with mounted weapons in the bed blocked the way and a half-dozen armed police occupied the traffic stop.

McPeek put down the driver's side window and readied her ID. Cristina did the same.

TEN

FTER THEY PASSED THROUGH THE CHECK-
point they were guided into an underground parking structure.
Another policeman armed with a shotgun put a paper ticket under
the car's windshield wiper and waved them on. They parked in a
spot marked VISITANTES.

When they got out of the car, Cristina felt exposed though there
were nothing but rows and rows of parked vehicles around them.
The gun under her arm was heavy and she was certain everyone
could see it. She wanted to clamp down on the weapon, but she
knew that would only call more attention to it.

"Come on," McPeek said.

Elevator access to the building above was also secured by an
armed policeman. This man wore a simple uniform and a pistol in
a holster. McPeek greeted him as if they had met before. Cristina
nodded to the man. She wasn't sure whether to smile.

They went up four floors and came out in a hallway lined with
identical doors. McPeek went left, Cristina tagging behind, until
they reached a large room full of desks, some empty and some
occupied. McPeek waved. "Matías!"

A man rose from his desk and waved back. He met them
halfway.

Matías Segura was in his thirties, clean shaven and neat. He
wore a charcoal-gray suit and a red tie. Next to him and McPeek,
Cristina felt underdressed. She saw that most of the other men in

the room were in suits or shirtsleeves and ties. Anyone whose idea of a Mexican policeman came from a movie or a TV show would be totally disoriented by the view.

"Matías, ¿cómo estás?" McPeek asked.

"*Estoy bien. ¿Y tú?*"

"*Muy bien, gracias.*"

The Mexican policeman turned to Cristina. "*¿Quién es este?*"

"Matías, this is Cristina Salas of the El Paso Police Department."

"*Mucho gusto,*" Matías said and he switched to English. "How are you?"

"I'm fine, thanks. You don't need to speak English on my account. *Yo hablo español.*"

"No, no, I am happy to speak English for my American visitors. Please, won't you come into our conference room? It's the only place where we can sit down."

Matías led them across the room to a side door and opened it for them. A motion detector flicked the lights on for them when they entered. Cristina saw a big table surrounded by chairs, a projector set up on the far end. It could easily have doubled for the conference room at the Federal Justice Center, except the seal on the wall was the federal seal of the United Mexican States.

"Can I get either of you coffee? Something to eat? Options are limited, but we can try," Matías said.

"I'm fine, thanks," Cristina said.

"A cup of coffee would be good," McPeek said.

"I'll be right back."

Matías vanished and McPeek took a seat. "What do you think?" she asked.

"Of what?"

"Of Matías. He is some kind of handsome. He's married, though."

"Yes, he looks nice," Cristina said.

"He's also a damned solid cop. Don't let the good looks fool you.

Last year he cleared fifty-eight cases against Los Aztecas."

"Just the Aztecas?"

"I'll let him explain."

Matías returned with a cup of steaming coffee and a fistful of creamers and sugar packets. "There you are," he said. "Anything else?"

"Oh, no. Thank you."

"I live to serve," Matías said and he made a little bow.

"Agent McPeek says you make a lot of cases against Los Aztecas," Cristina said.

"Los Aztecas, yes," Matías replied. "They are my constant companions. Everything that goes through my desk is related to them. Everything. It's why Jamie and I are working together on this *operación*. Are you aware of what we're doing?"

"Cristina and her partner were just brought in to provide support on the street," McPeek said. She stirred her coffee with a small plastic stick. "They've been on the tail of José Martinez for a while now."

"Ah, José. We know him well. Please, Detective Salas, have a seat. Make yourself comfortable."

Cristina sat down and Matías took the seat facing her from across the table. His hair was so black that it shone beneath the fluorescent lighting. McPeek was right that he was striking. She put it out of her mind. "So you have something on José?" she asked.

"We see José once every couple of weeks in Juárez," Matías said. "He comes to meet with Julio Guerra's people. José comes to stay the night, usually parties with one of Guerra's people. Cocaine parties with lots of women."

"You've never busted him?"

"They've passed their information on José back to us in the States," McPeek said. "José gets a free pass, gets comfortable, does more business and we get to learn who he's dealing with and what for."

"Meanwhile he's making deals that affect my city," Cristina said.

"My city, as well," Matías said quickly. "Believe me, I would like nothing better than to send him to El Cereso to rot with his Azteca friends, but he's more valuable this way. We're finding out so much about Julio Guerra's dealings. It will be very satisfying when we finally go in for the kill."

"So what are you learning, exactly?" Cristina asked.

"José is very interested in trucks," Matías said.

"Trucks?"

"Transportation is a serious issue for *narcotraficantes*. It's the reason they do business in Juárez in the first place: easy access to trade routes that they can use to move their product. A cheap, safe, reliable source of transport across the border is the Holy Grail for people like José. You have to remember, the street gangs do not have the power of the cartels and they do things at a much smaller level. To them, a few kilos of marijuana is a big deal. José wants more. And so does Julio Guerra."

"The Juárez cartel controls the Aztecas on this side of the border," McPeek explained. "Los Aztecas are the street soldiers for the cartel. What drug- and arms-dealing they do on the side is purely of their own devising; they don't get access to cartel funds or cartel resources in any significant way. So when our Aztecas and their Aztecas start thinking bigger, I get interested."

"So do we," Matías added.

"You said 'José wants more,'" Cristina said.

She saw McPeek and Matías share a glance. Matías spoke first. "It is a theory of Jamie's and myself that José Martinez is no longer simply doing the Juárez cartel's bidding. We think that José has designs of his own."

"Based on what?"

"Increased frequency of meetings, for one," McPeek said. "Also it's *who* he's meeting. Julio Guerra doesn't do face-to-face with many people. According to Matías and his people, José has met with Guerra no fewer than four times."

Cristina sat up straighter in her chair. Both McPeek and Matías were watching her. "This operation has to have been going on for longer than six weeks," she said at last. "There's no way you could have this level of information on such short notice."

"I'll admit there was some groundwork laid as far back as Special Agent Gorden's tenure in El Paso. But you have to remember, Matías has been working cases against Los Aztecas for years. In fact it was intelligence passed from the PFM to the DEA that first got the FBI's attention."

"Los Aztecas are my life," Matías said. "Every day, I come to work and deal with them. Nothing else."

"I think you see now why this operation was put together," McPeek said.

"Our Aztecas and their Aztecas want to become major players," Cristina said.

"Exactly."

"How will this fly with the Juárez cartel?"

"The Juárez cartel is losing the war against the Sinaloa cartel," Matías said. "At this point, anything that makes their street presence stronger is a good thing. More money. More guns."

Cristina ran her hands through her hair. She could feel tension riding high at the back of her neck. "I see now why you wanted me and Bob. We're all over José; who he meets and what he does."

"The more pressure we put on José Martinez on our side of the border, the more he's going to want to close deals on the Mexican side," McPeek said. "We'll push him until he puts himself and Julio Guerra in a compromising position. Then we roll them all up."

"It's a good plan," Matías said.

"It's thinking big."

"But now you see where we're coming from," McPeek said.

"I can. I just wonder if we can make it all stick."

McPeek nodded. "We'll worry about that at the top. If you do your part, we can take care of the rest."

Matías checked his watch. "Ladies, I apologize, but I must be present for a meeting in fifteen minutes. Don't feel you have to leave in a hurry; please, take your time."

They rose from the table and hands were shaken all around. "It was good to meet you," Cristina said.

"Likewise. I can tell you have reservations about what we're doing, but rest assured that we'll make it work. Next time I will be better prepared to receive you and you can meet the whole team. I think you'll find we have more than adequate resources to manage."

"I don't doubt it."

"Yes. If you'll excuse me…" Matías said and he left the conference room.

"And that's Matías Segura," McPeek said. "You have been introduced. Let's see ourselves out."

In the big room scattered with desks no one looked up as McPeek led the way back to the elevator. Cristina noted that from the inside the building did not seem so different from any other kind she'd been in; judging from the exterior she might have expected every window to be covered with a blast shield and every hallway equipped with barricades made out of sandbags. It was almost peaceful, though men were hard at work.

The uniformed cop in the parking garage nodded to them as they went past and mumbled a good-bye. Once they were in the car, McPeek paused at the gate and then pulled out onto the street. Armored vehicles moved aside to allow her to make way. Cristina found she was happy to leave the building behind; being in it made her feel like a target.

"Do you have another hour?" McPeek asked. "I know a good restaurant on the Avenida Juárez. We could get an early lunch."

Cristina looked in the side mirror. The fortress was nearly out of sight. "Sure," she said. "Lunch would be fine."

ELEVEN

LUNCH FOR MCPEEK CONSISTED OF A LARGE, rare steak with a baked potato and green beans. She asked for a glass of red wine. Cristina decided on a salad topped with grilled chicken and peppers. When she asked, the server brought her a bottle of water.

"You'll have to fill your partner in when you see him again," McPeek said. When she cut into her steak, it bled red. The meat looked as thought it had been seared, but barely cooked. "Get him up to speed."

"I will," Cristina said.

"I'm going to make sure you get all relevant documents we've collected so far pertaining to the operation. You'll be given everything new as intelligence comes in. I want you completely in the loop."

"That sounds fine."

McPeek took another bite, followed it with wine, and looked at Cristina over the rim of the glass. "What is it?"

"What do you mean?"

"I mean what's the problem? I could tell you had concerns before, so tell me what they are. Don't worry about me; I won't break."

"It's not that," Cristina said. "I guess maybe it's a little too cloak-and-dagger. I'm a cop, Agent McPeek. I bust bad guys and send them to jail. There's a reason I don't do espionage."

"We're not talking about being international spies here. You're not going to be called upon to do anything that you haven't already done in the course of your work. I brought you here so you could get a sense of the scale we're working on, the bigger picture. It helps."

The salad was good and Cristina was suddenly aware she'd eaten half of it without realizing it. She picked at it now, thinking. "What's the bigger picture for you?" she asked. "How does this play out at the federal level?"

"There's concern that Juárez violence could spill over into El Paso. That's nothing new. But the President has to look like he's tough on the issue of border security and that means he leans on the Director, who leans on the Deputy Director, who leans on the Associate Deputy Director, all the way down the line. We put one in the win column, everybody gets a little praise and maybe some extra funding when it comes time for that."

"Promotions?"

"Maybe. I try not to look that far ahead."

"I get the feeling you're always at least five moves ahead of the game, Agent McPeek," Cristina said.

"Please, call me Jamie."

Cristina drank from her water bottle. Even now, after years on the border, she would not drink of Juárez's tap. "Where were you before this?"

"I was in Virginia with the Criminal Investigative Division, doing pretty much what I'm doing now."

"So is this a step up or a step down for you?"

"I like to think of it as a step up. There's a lot of action happening here. Like I said, border security is a hot topic and Juárez is the hottest spot there is."

Cristina looked around the restaurant. It was a tourist place, not meant for locals, but there were only Mexicans eating there and very few of those. The festive paint looked as though it could use a touch-up and there was dust on some of the decorations on the walls. Everywhere there were cutbacks. She turned back to McPeek. "Why don't you come clean with me, Jamie?"

"About what, Cristina?"

"You're only in town three months and you already have a favorite restaurant in Juárez. Your task force—"

"Our operation," McPeek corrected.

"Your *operation* is only six weeks old, but you have Mexican intelligence reaching back I don't know how far. You know Matías Segura well enough that he brings you coffee. How long have you been on this? For real, this time."

McPeek forked another bloody hunk of meat into her mouth and chewed thoughtfully. She touched a napkin to her lips. "A year," she said.

"Why all the misdirection?"

"It's been a year since we got our first tip from the DEA. The rest of the time was spent laying the groundwork for the Mexicans' cooperation. Plus there was getting all the ducks in a row on our side. I started working with Mark – Special Agent Gorden – last fall as his unofficial replacement. As soon as everything was set up, he went to California and I took over. Then it was just a matter of turning the ignition and seeing if the engine would start."

McPeek hadn't answered the question, but Cristina didn't pursue it. If McPeek wanted to play things close to the chest then that was her prerogative. Cristina moved on to other things: "And did it?"

"Well enough. There are still some wrinkles to iron out, but overall I'm pleased."

"And El Paso PD, are we one of the wrinkles?"

"Oh, come on, you're not upset that we didn't bring you in right away, are you? Because it was only a matter of time. This whole thing operates from the top down and, like it or not, local law enforcement is on the bottom of the totem pole."

"At least I know where we stand."

"What you should know is that we came to your captain asking for the best detectives he had to offer and your name came up, along with your partner's. You ought to be proud of yourselves."

"I am. I just want to know we're full partners."

"I wouldn't ask you here if you weren't." McPeek held Cristina's gaze from across the table. She offered her hand. "Partners?"

Cristina shook it. "Partners."

"Now let's enjoy the rest of our lunch and get out of here."

TWELVE

FLIP HAD JUST TAKEN HIS SHOES OFF AFTER work when his phone rang. It was not Graciela. "Hello?" he said.

"Flip, it's José."

"Hey, José, what's up?"

"I want to send Emilio around to pick you up, bring you to my place."

"Is this another party? Because I have work tomorrow and I can't be out late."

"No party. I want to talk, but not on the phone."

"Okay, I'm here. Tell Emilio he can pick me up anytime."

"Keep an eye out for him."

There would be no time for a soothing shower or even a quick rest on the bed. Flip put his new shoes back on. He found his mother in the kitchen. "I'm going out, Mamá," he said.

"Again? You're never home!"

"Come on, Mamá, it's not so bad. I'm just going to chill at a friend's house for a little while. I'll be back in time for dinner."

"Are you going to see that girl, Graciela?"

"Not today, I don't think so."

"Too bad. She seems like a good girl."

Flip went outside with his basketball and had time to shoot a few hoops before Emilio's car arrived. He put the ball away and went down to Emilio. "Hey, what's up?" he asked.

"Nothing," Emilio said. "Get in. Let's go."

This time Flip paid attention to where they drove and he realized that he could probably make the walk to José's place without too much difficulty. He was still unsure what José was doing living in a house in Segundo Barrio when there were better places to go with bigger houses and broad, green lawns. It wasn't up to him to understand.

"You coming in?" Flip asked when they got there.

"No, not right now. I got some errands to run. I'll swing by to pick you up after."

"Okay. See you."

The patio was empty of partyers and the grill was cold. All the party lights had been taken down. José's Lexus waited under the shelter of the car park. Flip went to the front door and rang the bell.

The door was answered by a tall man Flip hadn't seen before. The guy wore his shirt untucked, but Flip saw the bulge of a pistol in the front of his pants. When Flip came into the front room there was a second man, also carrying. The television was on.

"I'm here to see José," Flip said.

"He's in the kitchen," the tall man said. "Go through there."

"I know the way."

The house seemed bigger without so many people crowded into it. The kitchen table was cleared of punch bowl and tequila bottles. José sat with his back to Flip, playing with a tablet computer. Flip saw cartoon birds being slingshotted into teetering buildings filled with green-faced pigs.

"You goddamned bird!" José exclaimed. He put the computer down, flipped its cover closed, and looked over his shoulder at Flip. "Come and sit down."

Flip took a seat at the table.

"You want something to drink? Something to eat? I've got beer if you want it," José said.

"No, thanks."

"It's not a problem."

"No, I'm fine."

José shrugged. "Suit yourself. Maybe next time."

"Next time, sure."

"Did you like the party the other night?" José asked.

"Yeah, it was good. Your barbecue is quality."

"I don't think the barbecue was your favorite part of the night."

"What do you mean?"

"What do you mean, what do I mean? I'm talking about Graciela. You hooked up with her, am I right? A little bird told me."

Flip blushed and looked down to hide it. He remembered José's familiar touch on Graciela's back, the easy way he spoke to her. If she had told José, Flip didn't know how to feel about that. His time with her had been strange and special. "Did she say something?" he asked.

"Graciela? No. She's not the type to kiss and tell. But a party has a lot of eyes and they see things."

Flip tried not to blush again. "I like her."

"Hey, of course you do! She's a likable girl." José clapped a hand on Flip's shoulder. "And don't worry, it's not like you have to stop seeing her or anything. If she makes you happy, I say go for it. A man like you, spending time inside, you need a good woman."

"Yeah, okay," Flip said.

José leaned back in his chair so he could reach the refrigerator. He fished around with his fingertips and snared a bottle of Dos Equis from the door. The bottle went between them. José twisted the cap off. "Anyway, it isn't Graciela I wanted to talk to you about," he said. "I wanted to ask you about something else."

"Sure, whatever."

"That warehouse where you work, it gets about how many trucks a day?"

"A couple dozen at least."

"A lot of them come up from Mexico, is that right?"

"Yeah."

José took a drink, swished the beer around in his mouth, swallowed. "Any of them stay overnight?"

"No, they come and then they go."

"Where do the night shipments go?"

"Another warehouse, I guess. We only work days."

"Okay," José said. "Okay."

"Why you want to know for?" Flip asked. "It's just a job I do."

"Be patient with me, Flip. I get curious about things and today I'm curious about this. I heard you go to work with the boss."

"Yeah, he's my mother's boyfriend."

"What's his name?"

"Alfredo."

"What's he like?"

"I don't know. Nice. Works hard. People like him."

"Does he make a lot of money?"

Flip shrugged. "What's a lot of money? It's not like he's rich or nothing."

"I'm just asking, that's all."

"He does all right, as far as I can tell."

José nodded and took another drink. "So he's an honest kind of guy."

"I guess. Hey, listen: you got to be careful if you send around people to see me," Flip said. "My PO, he can visit my work anytime and if he sees me talking to some Indians he could violate me."

"Are you worried about that? Getting violated?"

"I don't want to go back to Coffield."

"I don't blame you. I tell you what: I'll make sure if Emilio comes around, he doesn't bother you any. How's that?"

"That's good."

"You sure I can't fix something up for you? A plate of anything? I'm not just good at the grill; I can handle myself in this kitchen."

"No," Flip said.

"All right," José said. "I guess that's all we need to talk about right now. Why don't you go watch some TV with Angel and Fernando, wait for Emilio to come back?"

Flip stood up. José shook his hand.

THIRTEEN

MATÍAS FILLED OUT THE LAST FIELD ON AN electronic form and clicked SAVE. He waited until his email pinged with a confirmation notice and then got up from his desk. His back was stiff and he rocked back and forth to make it pop.

"Matías." Lopez was coming, a slip of paper in his hand, his step still uneven.

"I'm quit for the day," Matías said. "Everything's done."

"Felix called. He wants you."

"Carlos, I just want to go home."

Lopez handed over the paper. It had an address scrawled on it in red pen. "You go home after you go here. You're the one Felix wants."

"What is it?"

"A fire."

Matías winced inwardly and thought about handing the paper back to Lopez. "I hate those," he said instead. "Is there nobody else?"

"Of course there are others, but Felix wants *you*. How many times do I have to tell you? So get out there and get it done."

"All right, but I want credit for this time. Extra hours *at home*."

"You get paid for overtime just like anyone else," Lopez replied. "Now get going before the ashes get cold."

Matías drove southwest to where the city thinned out into scattered buildings and shanties and houses that had never seen better days. Despite the dust he drove with the windows open. He caught the smell of the fire long before he got there.

It was in the back yard of a rundown, two-story home that looked abandoned. There was an empty pen for animals that were long since gone and a shed. Underneath the lengthening shadow of a live oak tree, a fire-pit had been dug twelve feet long and four feet wide.

Two PF vehicles were there and Matías saw six PF agents, including the figure of Felix Rivera. Matías parked away from the PF trucks. The wind shifted as he got out of the car and he was buffeted with another invisible cloud of stench. It was enough to make him want to retch.

There were no longer any open flames, but the mesquite logs in the fire-pit glowed white with heat. Two of the PF agents were working with long-handled shovels, fishing out large black hunks of what looked like charcoal. It was not charcoal.

Felix shook Matías' hand. "Thanks for coming," he said.

Someone had laid out white sheets on the dirt and spotty grass and the black hunks went onto the sheets. Matías saw three and assorted pieces. Still more were coming out of the pit.

"Where is forensics?" Matías asked.

"Coming. They're probably lost."

"It's not easy to find. I almost got lost myself."

"Well, now you're here."

"Let's have a look," Matías said.

They rounded the fire-pit. The heat coming from it was substantial and Matías felt for the PF agents in their black uniforms, digging in the ashes for more cooked bits. Near the pit were three discarded plastic gasoline cans and a box of matches that had hit the ground and spilled. Away from the property, perhaps ten meters off, there was a thick stand of mesquite trees.

"How many?" Matías asked.

"You can see the three. I think that's a fourth one there."

"Who called it in?"

"Anonymous. There's not a public phone within five kilometers of this place, so it was probably someone on their mobile. We'll trace the number, but I don't have high hopes."

"They probably called it in themselves," Matías said.

"Most likely."

Matías watched as one of the PF men dislodged a heavy chunk of blackened flesh from underneath a bed of roasting mesquite. This one still had a head attached, though the features were burnt into obscurity. When he circled completely around to the sheet, he saw the remains of three torsos and most of five legs. The heads came separately, severed through the neck. One section of arm was only elbow and the flesh immediately above and below the joint.

"They were dismembered first," Matías remarked.

"At least they didn't go into the fire alive," Felix said.

"I'm sure they were very thankful. Goddamn it, where are our forensic people? This whole area should be cordoned off and picked apart centimeter by centimeter. Look for cigarette butts, discarded brass, footprints, anything."

"They'll get here."

"I *hate* fires," Matías said.

A crosswind blew and the blistering hot coals were fanned into life again. Now that Matías had gotten a chance to grow used to the smell, he was able to pick out the gasoline stink from the over-powering odor of burned human flesh. "I'm sorry I called you out," Felix said, "but I knew you'd take it seriously. Not like some of the others."

"Of course I take it seriously," Matías said. "What other way is there? *Madre de Dios*, it's the worst goddamned thing in the world. I can almost stand the bodies even when they're in pieces, but when they burn them…"

"So you'll look into it?" Felix asked. "Try to identify them?"

"For whatever good it will do. We got lucky on the Salvadoran thing, but you know how it is with fires."

"I know."

The fourth torso was dropped onto the sheet. It still smoldered.

FOURTEEN

CRISTINA SIGNED OUT EARLY AND WENT home. She paid Ashlee for a full night's work and made dinner herself. It was just things she could thaw out in the oven or the microwave, though she made macaroni and cheese from a box.

Freddie was at his computer, building in Roblox. When Cristina came home he said nothing until Cristina came over and kissed him on the forehead. "Hi, Mom," he said.

"Hello, peanut."

She put his plate on the desk beside the computer. Freddie would eat bites between clicks, his eyes hardly flickering from the screen. Cristina thought about putting on something Freddie might enjoy, like the show that showed how factories made different things, but he was engrossed and she didn't want to disturb him.

From time to time she felt guilty for letting him play and not insisting that they do something together. Once they had put together a simple jigsaw puzzle on the coffee table and he seemed to like it, but when she bought another he was no longer interested. Now it was just Roblox and only Roblox and nothing could deter him. Even when he played with real plastic bricks he called it "playing Roblox for real."

There were three sheets of homework in Freddie's folder from school. They would go undone. This was something else Cristina felt guilty for. She reasoned it away by thinking Freddie worked hard all day at school to follow the rules and do his work and the last thing he needed was for that atmosphere to come into his home. Sometimes she would fill out the answers to the worksheets herself, but most of the time they went straight into the trash, as they did tonight.

He had a point sheet that reviewed his day, period by period. If he consistently raised his hand before talking he would earn a point. If he managed to go a period without having a fit of anger or frustration, he earned a point. Today he had earned almost all his points with just a few rough spots. Cristina signed the bottom and put the sheet back in his folder.

The phone rang and it was Robinson. Cristina turned the sound down on the television.

"You left before I had a chance to get back to my desk," Robinson said.

"Yeah, I know. Busy day."

"I heard you went to Juárez."

"I did. Met with their guy in the PFM. He seems all right."

"Just all right?"

"We'll call it 'all right' for now."

"You're going to tell me all about it, aren't you?"

"Sure, tomorrow. You don't want me to lay it out for you on the phone."

Robinson paused and Cristina could almost hear him nod. "I was thinking. About that kid, Flip. We need to set up regular contacts, especially if he's close to José. Anything he tells us we can feed up the pipe."

"We don't want to push it. They might be watching him."

"I know, but we can't let him go to waste, either."

Cristina looked at Freddie's back. His left hand twitched on the keyboard and his right hand worked the mouse, steering his virtual plastic avatar through a fanciful land of houses made of multicolored bricks. He passed a flowerbed someone had made. Cristina wondered if it was possible to water them.

"Still there?" Robinson asked.

"What? Oh, yeah. Sorry, my mind was wandering. If you want, we can give Flip a call tomorrow and tell him what to keep his ear out for. Now that we know the target is José, he should be on the lookout for anything he can give us on him."

"I like it. How's Freddie?"

"He's being Freddie. Playing his game."

"I showed Louise how to play it the other day. Maybe they can be buddies online."

"He'd like that. He said he wanted to put some people on his friends list, but you never know who's a kid and who's a pervert."

"I make Louise play on the computer in the kitchen so we can see what she's doing."

Cristina looked back to Freddie. At the bottom of the screen was a constantly scrolling bar of text, the inhabitants of Roblox communicating with each other. She had the game set to "safe chat," so Freddie could only communicate through sentences constructed from a drop-down menu. He wanted to have it the other way, but there were the perverts to consider. It was better like this.

"I don't want to be rude, but I'm probably going to go to bed early tonight," Cristina said.

"Don't let me keep you up."

"I'll see you tomorrow. I'll tell Freddie about Louise."

"Good night."

Cristina dropped the phone on the couch beside her. The TV was showing a commercial about a glove that peeled potatoes. She shut it off. "Hey, peanut," she said, "let's wrap it up. I want you to take a bath tonight. And we have to brush your teeth."

He didn't answer, but she knew he heard. After five minutes she got up and stood behind him. "Let's go. Save and quit now."

"Can I play some more?"

"Not tonight. It's bath time."

She left him alone to start the bathwater, knowing that he would use every extra minute to play the game until it was *really* time to move. Cristina put bubbles in the bath to make it more fun. When it was just the right temperature she called him and he came.

When he was naked he looked like all arms and legs, gangly and skinny. He still did not know how to bathe himself, so it was up to Cristina to use a washcloth and scrub him down. She washed his hair and for her own amusement spiked it up into devil's horns. After the washing was done, Freddie liked to wait until the water was completely drained before hopping out of the tub to be dried.

There was pajamas and tooth-brushing and Freddie snuggled into his blanket while Cristina made up a story about a hamster who went to school. Freddie wanted a hamster of his very own. Before she was finished, he was asleep.

Cristina put out the lights in the house and undressed in the dark. Though she was tired, she didn't fall asleep right away. She stared at the ceiling, thinking of nothing except what dreams she might have. Her last thought was of Freddie playing in the bubble bath, making an elevator out of bubbles.

FIFTEEN

THEY TOLD HIM WHAT TO LISTEN FOR AND when to call them. They gave him their personal phone numbers with instructions to contact them day or night if he had something useful. Flip did not call for three weeks.

On most weekdays he worked in the warehouse and things were good. He got his first paycheck and repaid his mother for the shoes with enough money left over to open a checking account. He made arrangements with Alfredo for his check to be direct-deposited.

On weekends he saw Graciela. She was close to finishing her time at the cosmetology school and she told him stories about all the job opportunities there were in the nail business and how she'd be able to save up fast for her own place. Her nail salon would be in Segundo Barrio "for all the local girls," and she would be able to walk to work. She even had the spot picked out: an empty space in a little strip mall next to a liquor store.

Flip and Graciela made love in the back of her Hyundai at the end of a dead-end street near the cosmetology school. It was cramped and uncomfortable, but when Flip was with her he didn't mind the difficulty. He asked her when he could go to her place or meet her folks. She always said "soon."

They went twice to the club and danced. Graciela got to mingle with her girlfriends and Flip spent time talking with Emilio. Flip did not think they were friends, but they were close enough to talk frankly and that was close enough for him.

"You see that girl?" Emilio said one night. He pointed to a slightly chunky girl in a tight dress with a wide bottom. She danced with the enthusiasm of a much lighter girl and when she caught sight of Emilio watching, she blew him a kiss.

"I see her," Flip said.

"I'm going to marry her."

Emilio was six beers into his drinking, the empties on the table of their booth. Flip was closed in by a couple on his left side and pushed up close to Emilio such that he could smell the alcohol on his breath when he talked.

"Aren't you too young to get married?" Flip asked.

"I'm twenty-four," Emilio said. "That's plenty old."

"I guess so. Does she want to get married?"

"You kidding? That's all she ever wants to talk about. When am I going to get her a ring? How big is the ring going to be? And all that. We could get married tomorrow and she would be thrilled."

Flip looked around for Graciela, but he didn't see her. He wondered if she'd retreated to the VIP room where José held court and brushed away the twinge of jealousy that gave him. "Graciela never talks about that," he said.

"She's in no hurry to settle down," Emilio said.

"What do you mean?"

"I mean she likes to party. Know what I mean?"

"No, I don't know what you mean."

Emilio waved Flip away. "Alicia likes to party, too, but she's been looking for a husband all her life. Suits me fine. If I say I'm going to marry her, she lets me get away with anything."

Flip swallowed the question he wanted to ask. "Like what?"

"Like when I keep my weight at her place."

"The weight you move for José?"

"Yeah. I don't keep it at *my* place. I got a record and it's the first place the cops would look. But her, she doesn't even have a parking ticket. I move everything through her."

"What are you going to do when you get married?"

"I guess I'll have to keep it at my girlfriend's place then," Emilio said and he laughed. "Hey, tell the waitress I want another beer."

Flip got the couple on his left to move and he slid out of the booth. He found a waitress and pointed her toward Emilio, then went back to the VIP area. Tonight there was a bouncer in place with a clipboard. He asked for Flip's name.

"You're not on the list," the bouncer said.

"I know José," Flip said. "I just want to see if my girlfriend's back there."

"I can't let you go in."

"Come on, man, I don't want to stay. I just want to get my girlfriend."

"You're not getting through. Sorry."

Flip thought about trying to rush around the man, but it was useless. He found a table near the VIP entrance and waited until a waitress came by to take his order. His shoulders felt tense and they would not relax. Graciela did not come out until three beers later and his mind was working. "Hey, Flip," she said. "What are you doing out here alone?"

"I was waiting for you."

"I wish I knew. I was just talking to my girls."

"Let's get out of here," Flip said.

"What? Sure."

Flip herded her toward the exit, his hand on her elbow. They rushed through the front doors and Graciela almost tripped. "Hey, slow down," she said.

There was a wait while the valet went to fetch her car. Flip looked back into the club. No one followed them out. "You were just talking to your girls?" he asked.

"Yeah."

"What about José?"

"I said hi to him. Why? What's wrong?"

"Nothing."

"Don't tell me 'nothing.' What's wrong?"

"It's something Emilio said."

A dark look passed over Graciela's face. "What did that *idiota* say?"

The doorman and the valets weren't paying attention to them. Flip felt the muscle in his jaw working. "He just said some things about how you like to party."

"Sure, I like to party. Everybody knows I like to party."

"He said you liked to *party*."

"*What?* Did he call me a whore?"

The doorman looked their way. Flip put himself between the man and Graciela. "He said you weren't in no hurry to settle down."

"That's what he said?"

"Yeah," Flip said and he began to feel stupid for saying anything at all.

"I'm *twenty-one years old*, Flip! Of course I'm not looking to settle down!"

"I just thought—"

"You thought that means I like to fuck around? I don't believe this! Is that why you asked me about José? You think I fucked José in front of everybody, or what?"

Flip put his hands up, but he wanted to beat his own head in. "Forget I said anything. I'm being crazy."

"There's crazy and then there's being a *pendejo*, Flip. How much did you drink tonight?"

"I'm not drunk. I'm just an asshole."

"You got that right."

Graciela's car came. Everyone was staring now. Flip took the passenger seat, though he expected her to drive away without him.

She spent the drive muttering to herself and striking the steering wheel with the palm of her hand. Flip heard her say Emilio's name more than once.

"I want to say—" Flip started.

"Don't say nothing! You're not talking."

"Okay."

"I should dump your dumb ass at your mamá's house and say good-bye for good, you know that? After I treated you right, you listen to *Emilio*? Emilio is a dumbass. His girl had more boyfriends than *anybody*. Calling *me* a whore? I'm going to tear his balls off."

"Hey—"

Graciela put up a hand. "You're still not talking. You don't talk 'til I say so. No, wait: you answer me something. If I'm some kind of *puta*, what does that make you?"

"I don't know. Listen, I'm sorry."

"I introduce you around, I tell you it's okay that you were in prison and the first time someone says something bad about me, you believe it?"

"I said I was sorry."

"I don't know if sorry's going to cut it, Flip."

Flip didn't say anything. He let her drive and from time to time she took her eyes off the road to glare at him.

"I like you, Flip. I like you a lot," she said finally.

"I like you, too."

"Then why did you listen to Emilio? Don't you know he's a fool?"

"He was just saying and you weren't around and I..." Flip didn't know how to continue.

"It's because I slept with you too soon," Graciela said. "That's the problem. Guys always think it's because a girl's easy. I'm *not* easy, Flip. I could have been with plenty of guys and I wasn't."

"I believe you."

They were on Flip's street and Graciela slowed. Flip did not want to get out of the car.

"Here's your house," Graciela said. They came to a stop.

"Graciela, I'm sorry," Flip said. "I don't want you to go away angry."

"It's a little late for that, Flip," Graciela said and he heard her sadness.

"Can I kiss you at least?"

"Yeah, okay."

He leaned over and kissed her, but didn't pull away. Her breath feathered across his face and he thought he could see her trembling. He kissed her again, softly. "I'm sorry," he whispered to her.

Graciela put her hand on his cheek. Her eyes shimmered and then Flip knew for certain how much he'd hurt her. "I'm not a whore, Flip," she said. "Don't ever call me that again. Don't even *think* it."

"I won't. I'm sorry."

"Don't say 'I'm sorry' again. I know you're sorry." Her eyes overfilled and tears trickled down. She blinked hard to make them go away, but they came on anyway and her mascara started to streak.

"What can I do?" Flip asked.

"Wait a few days. Call me. Take me out somewhere. Treat me good."

"I can do that."

"You don't know how much I like you, Flip."

"Graciela—"

"Go. Get out. Go home." Graciela took up her purse and looked in it for a tissue. She used it to dab at her eyes, but the damage was done. "I said *go*. Remember what I told you."

"I'll call you."

"Okay. Go."

Flip got out of the car and waited while she pulled away. He watched her all the way to the end of the block until her taillights vanished around the corner. His eyes itched and he rubbed them rather than letting himself cry. He willed the tears away.

He didn't go inside. He sat down on the front step and watched the house across the street. All the lights were off, but a flickering blue illumination in the front room was the telltale of a television. Inside his house his mother would be fast asleep. He would have to be careful not to wake her.

If he felt anything it was sadness and regret mixed together and a touch of anger. Anger with Emilio for planting the seed and anger with himself for believing it. He hadn't known a girl like Graciela before and he didn't know how to treat her or what to expect. It occurred to him to send her flowers. Girls liked flowers.

A car cruised by without slowing and made the same turn as Graciela had. Someone coming home late to a wife or a husband, he imagined. Maybe the kids were sleeping in their beds. He wondered what that would be like. He could not imagine.

"Graciela," he said out loud. "Graciela, Graciela."

He should go inside. He should go to sleep. Flip told himself this, but he stayed on the front step, anyway. He brought out his phone and dialed a number he had committed to memory.

SIXTEEN

CRISTINA AND ROBINSON SAT AT THE LEAD OF four vehicles, all parked against the curb: two cars and two SUVs. They'd been in place since noon, counting off the hours as the sun canted westward and grew shadows on the street. The houses nearby were still; no one had so much as moved a curtain in the whole time they were there. From time to time a car approached and there was tension until it passed.

Empty snack bags of chips were between Cristina and Robinson. Neither of them had anything to drink because there was nowhere to use the restroom if the urge struck. If it came to that, they had to leave the line or come up with improvised solutions that weren't great.

Both Cristina and Robinson wore their vests, the word POLICE printed out in block letters front and back. Cristina was sweating under hers, the temperature outside the car climbing into the mid-eighties and inside the car ten degrees hotter. Today she wore her gun in a hip holster and it pressed against the emergency brake handle.

The radio tucked into the door pocket squelched and Matt Guillemette from Narcotics spoke up: "Hey, you said it was a blue Civic?"

Cristina picked up the radio. "Yeah, a blue Civic, tag number BMV1738."

"I can't see the plate yet, but it looks like a blue Civic's coming up from behind."

"Hang on." Cristina looked into the side mirror. She saw the car approaching, but the reflection and the sun conspired to make identification difficult. "Okay, I see it. This could be her. Stand by."

The car drew closer and Cristina could make out the H-logo on the nose of the car. Then it was moving by and she saw it was a Civic. The license plate matched. She hit Robinson on the arm.

"Let her go inside first," Cristina said over the radio. "Then we move."

She watched as the car pulled into the short driveway outside one of the still houses. The girl, Alicia Gonzalez, got out with her purse and went to the front door. She dropped her keys, picked them up, went inside.

"Okay," Cristina said to Robinson.

They got out of the car and behind them more officers stepped out of their vehicles. All were openly armed and wearing light vests. One carried a stubby, handheld battering ram.

Guillemette approached. "I still think we should take the lead on this. A drug bust makes it ours."

"Our informant," Cristina said.

"There's plenty to go around," added Robinson. "The drug collar is all yours."

"All right, let's do this," Guillemette said.

There were ten of them altogether and they crossed the street in a ragged line. Somewhere nearby a piece of heavy machinery started backing up, making high-pitched beeps.

Cristina opened the gate and entered the yard with everyone behind her. She was first to the house and tested the barred door. It was unlocked. She swung it wide and rapped hard on the front door itself. "Police," she announced loudly.

To her right Robinson drifted to the front window and tried to see through the drawn curtains. Some of Guillemette's men watched the sides of the house, and one climbed the fence into the back yard.

"Anything?" Cristina asked Robinson. He shook his head.

Guillemette stepped forward and pounded on the door with his fist. "Police," he said. "Open the door."

"Somebody's moving in the front room," Robinson said, and then the curtains parted right in front of him. Cristina was able to catch only a glimpse of a face before they were drawn again.

"Police! Open the door!"

"I don't see her anymore," Robinson said.

Guillemette spat into the flowers by the front door. "Fuck this," he said. "Carns, bring the ram."

Cristina tried one more time: "Open the door or we're going to break it down!"

Carns hefted the ram and stepped in front of Cristina. "Watch out," he said.

It took two sharp blows to splinter the frame and knock the door wide open. Carns stepped back and Cristina went through with her weapon out, Guillemette right behind. "Police, executing a search warrant," Cristina called out.

She was in a modest living room with a couch and a couple wing-backed chairs. The TV wasn't large. A throw rug on the wooden floor was pink and white and the walls were painted coral.

The girl appeared in the adjoining hallway. Cristina put her weapon on her. "Police! Put your hands in the air!"

The rest of the team spilled into the room. The girl stretched her arms up over her head and Guillemette stepped forward to put her in cuffs. Within a matter of seconds the others were headed through down the hall, deeper into the house.

"Search warrant," Cristina told the girl. She presented the paperwork, but the girl's hands were behind her back. "We have permission to search the house for illegal drugs and drug paraphernalia."

"This is my mother's house," the girl said. Her face was taut with panic. "There's nothing here."

"That's not what we heard," Guillemette said. "Come on and sit on the couch where you're out of everyone's way."

Guillemette sat the girl down. He turned to Cristina: "I'm going to knock some things over, see what I find. You can babysit."

"Thanks," Cristina said.

When Cristina looked at the girl, she saw the girl was crying. She had a round face and wore too much makeup. Tears cut grooves on her cheeks. "I didn't do anything," the girl said.

"You're Alicia Gonzalez, right?" Cristina asked.

"Yes, but—"

"We have reason to believe there are narcotics on the premises. You can save us all a lot of time and trouble if you tell us where they are right now. We don't even have to mess the place up."

"There aren't any drugs here!"

"Okay," Cristina said. "If that's how you want to be, we'll turn the house upside down."

A voice came from farther back in the house: "Here!"

Cristina looked to Robinson. "Watch her a minute?"

"Sure."

She went down the hallway and followed Guillemette to a small bedroom at the rear of the house. It was a girly room, complete with a frilled bedspread. The furniture was all white and there was an open jewelry box on the top of a chest of drawers, a tiny ballerina balanced inside.

"Here," said one Guillemette's men. He knelt by the bed.

They dragged out a half of a cardboard box, cut down so it could slide easily beneath the bed. Inside was a bag of weed and a bag of white powder and a collection of smaller bags, each loaded with a small amount. A few dozen empty baggies were tossed on top of an electronic scale.

"Under the bed?" Guillemette said. "That's original."

"Looks like meth here."

"There could be more," Cristina said.

"Right. Keep looking. But this is distribution weight right here. Looks like your informant has good ears, Salas."

"I want to talk to the girl when we bring her in."

"Be my guest. She doesn't have to say a word for me to make my case."

Cristina left them and went back to the front room. The girl was still crying. Robinson stood over her impassively. Cristina nodded to him.

"We found the dope," Robinson told the girl. "You have anything to say?"

"It's not mine!" the girl exclaimed.

"We'll talk about that later," Cristina said. "Just think about this right now: there's enough weed and meth back there to send you away for *years*."

The girl collapsed into tears as Guillemette's men took the house apart.

SEVENTEEN

THEY HAD ONE INTERVIEW ROOM AND IT WAS not large, just big enough for two people. A camera high on one wall recorded everything and transmitted to any computer with access, so there could be many eyes watching. Cristina had the interview room in a window on her desktop and kept her eye on the girl's body language as she sat alone, waiting.

"When are you going in there?" Robinson asked.

"Give it a minute."

"She's been waiting an hour."

"I don't think she's ready."

Cristina let another fifteen minutes slide by. The girl put her head down on the interview table. Cristina got up from her desk and put on a light jacket; it was always cold in the little room.

"Now?" Robinson asked.

"Now. Be ready in case we need to switch off."

"We won't need to after you sweet-talk her."

Cristina went down the hall and around the corner to the interview room. It wasn't locked, but there was no way out of the area without passing a cop. She let herself in.

The girl straightened up sharply when Cristina entered. Her tears were dried and now there were just the tracks they left behind. She wiped at her cheeks trying to fix the damage.

Cristina took the only other chair. "Hello again," she said.

"Hello."

"I'm Detective Cristina Salas. I'm going to be talking with you today."

"I'd like to call my mother."

"In a little while. First let's chat. Can I call you Alicia? You can call me Cristina if you want."

"Cristina," the girl said.

"That's right. I don't mind."

Cristina took a small notebook from her jacket pocket and opened it on the table. She had a mechanical pencil and on a fresh page she wrote the girl's name and the date.

"Am I going to jail?"

"Probably. We found a lot of drugs in your room, Alicia."

"I told you they aren't mine."

"You know what? I believe you."

"You do?"

"Yes," Cristina said. "And what I'd like to talk to you about first is who they do belong to and how they got under your bed."

Cristina saw the girl's eyes dart to the side. The girl was no longer handcuffed, but she kept her hands together underneath the table. She shifted in her seat.

"I'm not asking for much," Cristina said.

"I don't know if I should talk to you."

"Well, you don't have to, but I think you'd rather tell me the truth now than have me find it out on my own. And I *will* find out on my own. If that happens, there's no chance for any deals or special consideration."

The girl did not look up.

"Okay, let's start with some easy questions and work our way up to the hard stuff. Who owns the house where you live?"

"My mother."

"You live there alone together?"

"Yes. My brother moved away last year."

"Is it lonely without him?"

"Sometimes."

"Do you have a boyfriend?"

The girl waited a long beat, and then she said, "Yes."

"What's his name?"

"I don't think I should say."

"Why's that?"

"I don't want to get him into any trouble."

"Is there some reason he would be? Does he know about the drugs you keep in your room?"

"I can't say."

"You can't say, or you won't say?"

"I don't know."

Cristina put her pencil down and reached across to touch the girl on the arm. "Hey, look at me. Come on, lift your head up. That's better. Just tell me this: does he know about your drugs?"

The girl nodded.

"Does he know where they came from?"

"I really want to call my mother."

"You can call her when we're finished. Does your boyfriend know where the drugs come from?"

Another long pause. So long that Cristina thought she'd lost the girl completely. "Yes," she said at last.

"Where do they come from?"

"Should I ask for a lawyer?"

"Do you want a lawyer?"

"I don't know."

"I tell you what: you want something to drink? I'll bring you something from the machine. Then we can talk some more."

"Okay."

Cristina closed up her notebook and tucked it back in her pocket. She left the room, careful not to slam the door. Robinson came from the squad room. "I don't need you yet," Cristina said.

"It's not that. Someone's here."

They went back to the squad room. Cristina saw McPeek from

behind, watching Robinson's monitor and the video feed from the interview room. The woman turned when they came close. "Cristina," she said. "How are you?"

"Working," Cristina said.

"Bob was just telling me this girl's a known Azteca *esquina*."

"That's right. We have a confidential informant that puts her with Emilio Esperanza, one of José Martinez's *carnales*. He also tipped us off to some drugs being held at her house."

"If you know whose drugs they are, why don't you just go after this Esperanza?"

"We want to keep the integrity of the CI," Robinson said. "We arrest the girl, get her to give us her boyfriend's name and then it looks like we connected to him through her."

"And then you lean on him to give you something on José."

"That's right."

"She doesn't sound like she's talking much."

"I just got started with her," Cristina said. "If the soft touch doesn't work, Bob will take over for a little while."

"Put a scare into her," Robinson said.

"Sounds like a plan."

"Is there something we can do for you?" Cristina asked.

"Not really. I stopped in to talk with your captain, thank him for allowing your cooperation. That's all."

Cristina searched her pockets. "Bob, do you have a dollar for the machine? I can't go back without a Coke."

"Here."

"You can feel free to stay and watch if you want, Agent McPeek," Cristina said. "I can't guarantee it'll be exciting."

"I always like to watch professionals work."

"Yeah, okay," Cristina said. She left Robinson and McPeek in the squad room and went to the soda machine for a bottle of Coke. She gave the girl twenty minutes and then she would tell everything. Cristina was willing to set her watch by it.

EIGHTEEN

"**H**OW'D YOU GET MY NAME?"

"I told you, Emilio: your girlfriend, Alicia."

"Alicia wouldn't rat on me."

"Looks like she just did."

"I'd smack that fat bitch if she said anything."

"Are you threatening her?"

"No, I'm just saying. Hey, man, what about my car? You just left my car by the side of the road."

"It's been impounded. You can pay to get it when you get out. If you get out."

"I'm getting out. My lawyer'll have me out tomorrow."

"What lawyer?"

"The one I get assigned by the Public Defender."

"Let's not get ahead of ourselves."

"No, you get ahead of *this*: I'm not saying nothing 'til I talk to a lawyer."

"If that's how you want to do it."

"That's how I want to do it."

Cristina left Emilio Esperanza in the interview room and came back to Robinson. She checked the clock. "I'm going to be late. I need to call my sitter. Can you deal with getting asshole a lawyer?"

"Sure."

Cristina called Ashlee and explained that she would be running into some overtime tonight and could she stay longer than usual? It was all right, but Cristina felt badly not being there for Freddie. Ashlee could handle most things, but Freddie could be very particular without meaning to be and he might not get to sleep like he should.

"Oh, hey," Robinson said with his hand over the phone, "McPeek asked if you'd call once you reeled in Esperanza. Her number's on your desk."

She called and McPeek picked up right away, as if she had just been waiting for the call. "You wanted to know when we got him," Cristina said. "We've got him."

"What's he charged with?"

"Possession of a controlled substance with intent to distribute, illegal possession of the firearm we found in his car, conspiracy to distribute a controlled substance and generally being a *pinche cabrón*. The DA's office may want to pile on with more charges, but that's more than enough to hold him for now."

"So you're going to hold him?"

"We can't lean on him otherwise."

Robinson was talking in the background, his voice a comforting bass mumble. There was no way anyone from the PD's office would have someone for Esperanza until morning and maybe not even until the afternoon. In the meanwhile they would sit on the man and let him wonder what they knew.

"I'd like to bring in Madge Crompton from the DEA for this," McPeek said.

"What for?"

"Just to see if we can work the federal angle a little bit. Esperanza might not feel the heat from the locals that much, but he'll definitely know he's in trouble if we scale up our offensive."

Cristina pushed a pen around on her desk with the tip of her finger. "With all due respect, I'd like to keep this in-house. Our informant, our bust."

McPeek was quiet, then she said, "All right, we'll let it play out. I just want to make sure we're all on the same page, working for the same thing."

"If it's José Martinez you want, that's what we want. Everybody wins."

"Keep me posted, Cristina."

"I will. Good night."

She got off the phone at the same time Robinson hung up. The live feed from the interview room was on her screen and Esperanza had his feet up on the other chair, relaxing. The urge to punch the image came and went. "Well?" she asked.

"He'll have a lawyer tomorrow," Robinson said.

"Good for him. Meanwhile we get to sit on our thumbs. I should have let you go in with him first."

"He was going to clam up no matter what," Robinson said. "You, me, it wouldn't make a difference."

Cristina watched Esperanza. He could have been sleeping. "I dropped the girl's name on him and he didn't miss a beat. I hope Flip is covered just in case this comes back at him."

"Esperanza talked when he was drinking. He could have told a lot of people."

"Yeah, you're right. Listen, why don't you go home? I'll do up the reports and we'll meet back here tomorrow fresh," Cristina said.

"You sure? I know you have Freddie to think about."

"He's covered for right now. Go ahead."

"All right," Robinson said. "Knock yourself out."

He got his things and left and Cristina was alone in the squad room. The door to Captain Cokley's office was closed, the lights out. Cristina cracked her knuckles and turned to the picture of Esperanza. A uniformed cop was in the room now, hooking Esperanza up for an overnight trip to jail. The lockup was right across the street.

She closed the window.

NINETEEN

FLIP WAS FINISHED WITH WORK AND HEADED out to Alfredo's truck when he saw them parked in the same spot outside the fence as Emilio had used. They waved to him and Flip felt more irritation than concern. They were watching him, but they were doing it so openly that anyone could see.

He went to the fence and one of the Aztecas came over. "I told José I couldn't have you guys hanging around here," Flip said.

"I'm Nasario."

"Nasario, you need to get the fuck out of here."

"No, you need to come with me," Nasario said.

Alfredo was always the last to the leave the building and there were still workers filing out. There was still time. "I can't come with you," Flip said. "I got to go with my boss."

"José says you come with me and César. Now."

"I can't—"

"It's not a request."

Nasario's expression was flat, his eyes invisible behind sunglasses. Flip thought about saying to hell with it and just walking away, but they would not leave and there would be trouble he was not ready to deal with. "Give me a minute," he said.

Flip stopped Alfredo at the door as the older man locked up. "Hey, Flip," Alfredo said. "Ready to go?"

"Listen, Alfredo: some friends just came by and want to take me out for some drinks."

Alfredo looked past Flip to the fence line and beyond. His expression creased into a frown and Flip saw the disapproval there. But he couldn't know. "What friends are these?" he asked.

"Some guys, you know. I met them at a party."

"Your mother expects you at home."

"Tell her I won't be too late."

"Okay, Flip. Whatever you say."

Flip left Alfredo in the lot and crossed the street to where Nasario waited. They opened the back door for him and he got in. As they pulled away, he saw Alfredo talking on his cell phone and he felt remorse. He did not like lying to Alfredo.

They drove downtown to an apartment complex in a neighborhood Flip didn't know. He thought they couldn't be too far from the border here and maybe he could walk home if they'd let him. Nasario led him into the complex with César in tow.

On the second floor of one of the buildings, facing a courtyard with a pool, they found the right apartment. Nasario knocked twice and the door was opened. Nasario stood aside to let Flip enter ahead of him.

The apartment was dark, with just the light filtering in through drawn curtains. Flip took one step inside and he knew they were going to kill him. He stopped abruptly, moved back and bumped into Nasario.

"Hey, what the fuck?" Nasario said.

"I got to go," Flip said.

"Get your ass in there."

Nasario pushed him forward and the fear came swelling up again. They would cut his throat or just shoot him in the back of the head with a .22-caliber pistol. They *knew* and if he did not run, no one would ever find his body.

There were others in the front room, sitting on a couch and some chairs. All of them were looking at him, looking through him, seeing him dial the cops and tell what he knew. Seeing him snitch.

The front door was closed. Nasario and César were at his back. Flip's breathing was shallow and he was sweating. They had to smell it on him, the panic. Nasario bumped him again and he stepped out into the ring of staring eyes.

"Flip."

José's voice brought him around. José stood at the entrance to the kitchen, a bottle of beer in his hand. He was loose-jointed and relaxed and he smiled. This was the worst part.

"What's the matter, Flip, you sick or something?"

"Huh?"

"You're pale as shit, man."

"I am? I am."

"Let me get you a beer."

Flip looked around at the others. Some of them had beers of their own and now they went back to talking amongst themselves. There was no more circle of accusation, just Indians talking to other Indians. Flip could breathe again.

José gave Flip a cold beer with the cap off. "Have a drink. You look like you need it. They must work you extra hard at that warehouse."

"Yeah," Flip said stupidly.

"Find a seat. We'll get started in a minute."

There was a spot at the end of the couch and Flip squeezed into it. The guy next to him gave him a little nod and some room. Nasario and César stood by the door like they were guarding it. José lingered at the kitchen, nursing his beer.

After a while there was another knock at the door and Nasario opened it up. Flip saw Emilio step across the threshold with two more Aztecas at his back. Evening light shafted in and dazzled Flip's eyes.

"Here he is," José said.

The door was closed and the shadows descended again. Flip wondered why they didn't turn on the lights.

They pushed Emilio to the center of the room and this time Flip saw what he only imagined before: the probing gazes and the sudden stillness and quiet. Emilio stood up straight, but Flip saw himself standing there and being found out.

"Okay," José said. "Time for business."

The beer bottles were put away. Flip put his empty hands in his lap. His palms were sweating.

"Emilio, you know why we're all here, right?" José asked.

"Yeah, I know."

"For those of you guys who didn't hear: Emilio got popped. They found his stash at his girlfriend's place. He's lucky they didn't remand his ass. Guess the free lawyer worked out this time."

Flip found himself chewing his lip. He forced himself to stop.

"I don't ask much," José said, "but you blew it, Emilio. Big time. I got people on the street who *depend* on you, man. I depended on you."

"José, I—"

"Don't talk. Listen. The only reason you aren't taking a ride to Juárez right now is because you kept your mouth shut when the cops asked you questions. You're dangerous to me, Emilio. You're dangerous to all of us. You know things."

Emilio's leg trembled. It was only a moment, but Flip saw it. He wondered if any of the others had. If it had been Flip standing there, he didn't think he could hold it all in like that. His respect for Emilio increased.

"You've been loyal and strong, Emilio, and I honor that about you. That's why I called this trial. I want you to explain to everybody how you fucked up and how it won't happen again. Go ahead."

Flip waited. Emilio swallowed hard and licked his lips. He caught Flip's eye in the darkness. "Okay," he said. "I fucked up. I trusted that bitch Alicia to keep our stuff safe. She must have opened her mouth to somebody because the police didn't know it was me until she told them. I was real careful, I thought. And I won't make the same mistakes. I'm gonna teach that bitch to keep her mouth shut and then I'm not gonna let anybody carry my weight for me. From now on I'm watching my own stuff. That way I'll *know* who knows what and if they snitch, I'll kill them myself. I'll take them down to Juárez and see them burn."

Emilio fell silent and José allowed the hush to continue uninterrupted for a long time. Flip fidgeted in his seat. Finally José said, "I want everybody here to make a decision. Does Emilio stay, or does he go?"

The verdict started at the door and worked its way around the room, every Indian rendering judgment in turn. *Stay. Stay.* Flip felt the pressure bearing down on him until it was his turn to say something and his mouth was too dry to form words.

"What do you say, Flip?" José asked.

Emilio watched him.

"He should stay," Flip croaked out.

"Then the decision is made," José said. "It's unanimous. He stays."

Flip saw all the stiffness go out of Emilio's spine and Emilio drew a ragged breath. He smiled a little at some of the brothers who congratulated him. There was the sense of something dark having passed over and when José put on the lights even the shadows were chased out of the room.

When Flip picked up his beer again, his hand shook. He hoped no one would see.

The gathering turned social and more drinks were brought from the kitchen. Flip didn't know whose apartment they were in and it didn't seem to matter. Someone ordered pizza. Emilio fell into conversation with two men Flip thought he might have recognized from the club. It was all so casual. Flip wanted to flee.

He got up to use the bathroom and found José in his way. "Hey, Flip," José said, "how's it going?"

"Fine, José. How are you?"

"Better now. Emilio's one of my best guys. I don't like to see him in this kind of mess."

"He'll beat the rap."

"Maybe. Like you beat the rap?"

"Some guys aren't lucky."

"Your luck has changed, I think," José said.

"You think?"

"I think." Flip started to go. José stopped him. "Listen, Flip: I wonder if maybe you and your boss could meet with me sometime. Sometime soon. I'd like to have a word with him."

"What about?"

"Oh, this and that. You think you can set it up?"

"I don't want to get him into any trouble."

"No trouble, Flip. We're just going to talk. What, you worried about your job?"

"Something like that."

"Don't be. I'll take care of you. Just remember: sometime soon. When you have it all worked out, you call me."

"Okay, José."

"That's a good boy."

"I got to take a leak."

"So go take a leak! Nobody's stopping you."

Flip locked himself into the bathroom and a wave of tremors came crashing over him. His eyes were tearing up. He thought he might be sick. In the end he could barely piss, though he thought it would let go when he first stepped into the apartment. He sat on the edge of the bathtub clutching his hands together trying to will them to be still. Outside in the apartment there was laughter now, as if nothing had happened.

His phone was in his pocket but he didn't know who to call. He wished he could speak to Graciela, but now was not the time to call her. How could he explain that he was in the toilet of a strange apartment, hiding from everyone there? It was not something he could do.

He flushed the toilet and washed his hands in very hot water. When he came out again the pizzas were almost all gone and the beers, too. Some were getting ready to leave.

Flip found Nasario. "I need a ride back to my place."

"Yeah, we'll take you, just chill a little while."

In his corner of the room, perched at the edge of the couch, Flip watched Emilio talking to a few others, his face animated, his hands in motion. Flip tried to imagine what Emilio was like when the police brought him in, and whether he had been nonchalant then, as well. Maybe he had been. Maybe Emilio was just that cool.

Flip remembered when the police grabbed him in the last time, the time that sent him to Coffield. He hadn't been cool. The detective talked to him for what seemed like hours and when he was done Flip told the man everything he knew. They promised him a deal and they made good on their promise, but there were still four years he would not get back.

More left and then Flip knew it was time to go. Nasario gave him the signal. He went with Nasario and César without the fear hanging over him, the dread of the apartment fading away with every step farther away. By the time they got to the car he felt all right, not twisted up inside. He did not want to go through that again.

TWENTY

"ARE YOU READY?" MATÍAS ASKED. "OUR reservations are for nine."

"I'm coming."

Elvira emerged from the bathroom, fixing an earring into place. She was dressed in slacks and a blouse, not too extravagant, and her makeup was done just right. Matías still wore his suit from work, though he considered changing. In the end he thought it was good enough.

"You look wonderful," Matías said.

"You look like you're ready to go back to the office."

The question occurred to Matías again. "Do you think I should change?"

"No, just be yourself," Elvira said and kissed him on the cheek.

They left the apartment and went down to the street. The street-lights were on, and one cast sodium illumination directly onto the roof of Matías' car like it was on stage. Matías went around to the passenger side to open the door for Elvira. "*Señora*," he said.

"Thank you, *señor*."

He got them on the road and then put on the radio to something soft. The evening traffic jams were gone, the streets open, and they made good time. Only once did he see an army vehicle guarding a lonely corner and there were no roadblocks. Matías hummed to the music, his hands light on the wheel.

Frida's was their destination. The restaurant was not far from the border and its façade was meant to evoke classic Mexican adobe architecture. There was valet parking and a man with white gloves held the door first for Elvira and then for Matías. Matías tipped the man more than he probably should, but the drive and the night made him feel generous.

Inside guitar music and gentle singing came through speakers close to the ceiling. A short line of people waited at the maître d's podium. The walls of the foyer were decorated with rustic paintings. In the restaurant itself there would be reproductions of Frida Kahlo work all around, so that it was impossible to look anywhere without seeing her eyes staring back. Matías put his arm around Elvira and pulled her close to him.

When it was their turn, Matías gave their names. "Yes, *señor*, your table is ready now," the maître d' said and a waiter hurried up to escort them. He brought them to the main dining room, where softly lit metal stars were suspended from wires and the round stage was surmounted with a stylized depiction of the sun. A *guitarrista* all in black played and sang.

It was dim, but light enough to read the wooden-framed menus. Not far from their table was a shrine to Frida, lit with flickering candles. A photograph of Frida looked idly on, as if distracted.

Elvira reached across the table for Matías' hand. "It's good to go out," she said.

"I'm glad," Matías said.

"What should we start with?"

They ordered and the food came quickly. Matías ate shrimp ceviche and carne asada and drank beer to cool the peppers. Elvira had a salad and chicken mole with wine. Matías had never liked wine. They shared a slice of cinnamon and vanilla cheesecake as the *guitarrista* finished for the night, bidding everyone in the dining room a fond farewell and leaving the stage bare except for an empty stool and a microphone stand.

"He was good," Elvira remarked.

"Yes. More wine?"

"You don't have to get me drunk, you know," Elvira said and touched his leg with her foot beneath the table.

"I was only asking."

"No, I'm ready to go home."

Matías paid the check and they left the darkened restaurant. Out on the street the temperature had dipped. Matías would have given Elvira his jacket, but then everyone would see his weapon. He put his arm around her instead.

"I'll get your car," the valet said, and stepped away.

Elvira turned Matías' face toward her and kissed him on the lips. "Thank you," she said. "We needed this."

"I'm sorry you had to wait so long."

The valet came with their car and left the engine running as he jogged around to the entrance. Later Matías would not remember exactly when he sensed it. The recognition came to him suddenly as a pair of headlights washed over the three of them on the sidewalk. He pushed Elvira back toward the door as the long side of a dark blue SUV came to a stop facing them from across the narrow street. The windows were already down and the weapons sticking out.

The first volley shattered the windows of Matías' car and punctured the hood in a dozen places. The windshield exploded into mad white spiderwebs. Matías felt the bullets passing him, heard them strike the front of the building.

Elvira stumbled over her own feet and fell hard to the ground. Matías looked at her and in that second another fusillade of bullets raked the restaurant. One of the doors collapsed into fragments. The valet was on the sidewalk bleeding from the neck. Somehow they did not find Matías.

He drew his gun and ducked behind the front wheel of his car. The engine block absorbed more rounds and Matías heard the left front tire explosively deflate. "Elvira!" Matías shouted. "Elvira, come to me!"

There was a pause. They were reloading. Elvira lay almost prone on the glass-scattered concrete, her face twisted up in naked fright. She heard his voice and crawled to him. Matías put his arm around her and pressed her hard against the side of the car. He could feel her trembling.

Gunfire split the night and the car shuddered. The engine died. Matías felt his palm slick against the grip of his pistol. He did not want to raise his head to fire.

The SUV abruptly gunned its engine. Its wheels shrieked and then it was accelerating down the street. Matías rose to his feet in time to see the taillights shining at the end of the block before the truck veered around the corner. His ears were full of the sound of his heartbeat and he almost didn't hear the approaching sirens.

"Elvira, ¿estás bien?"

"I'm all right."

Matías went to the valet. The blood was everywhere and the valet was pallid. He holstered his weapon and pressed his hands to the wound that still leaked freely over the man's collar and onto the concrete. "Someone call an ambulance!" Matías shouted. "¡Ambulancia!"

People crowded into the entryway, but Matías did not take his eyes off the valet's face. Blood oozed between his fingers. The valet's pulse was thready and weakening.

"Matías…"

"Not now, Elvira! Use your phone, call an ambulance!"

He heard more tires squealing and then the front of the restaurant was awash in flashing colored lights. Elvira was on her phone, calling 066, pleading for an ambulance. The valet's eyes glazed over. His heartbeat stopped.

PART THREE

ONE

FLIP LET THE DAYS SLIP BY AND THEN HE called Graciela on his lunch break. He stepped away from the picnic tables so no one could hear. "Hi," he said. "It's me."

"Flip."

"I want to apologize again."

"Is that all you want to say?"

"No. I wanted to know if we could go out. Get something to eat."

"When?"

"How is tonight?"

"Maybe I'm busy tonight."

"Are you?"

Quiet. "No."

"Then we can go out?"

"What time do you get off work?"

"Four o'clock."

"Tell me how to get there."

Flip gave her directions and waited while she wrote them down. "You sure you want to pick me up here?" he asked.

"You embarrassed to be seen with me?"

"It's not that."

"Then I'll see you at four," Graciela said and hung up.

Flip went back to the tables. He sat down by Alfredo and opened his lunch.

"You look like someone spit in your eggs, Flip," Alfredo said.

"It's nothing. Girl trouble."

"I know all about it, son."

They ate without talking about it anymore and then it was time to go back to work. Flip did not spend time chatting with the other men on his team; he did the job and waited for four o'clock to come around. Whenever he checked the clock, it barely seemed to move.

At quitting time he gathered his things and went outside. Graciela was by the gate.

Alfredo came to lock the doors. Flip saw him spot Graciela, but there was no look of disapproval. "Are you going with her?" Alfredo asked.

"Yeah."

"Go on, then. I'll make excuses to your mother."

Flip went down to the gate. Graciela was not dressed up, but he thought she might have done something with her hair. He didn't know whether to compliment her or not. Instead he said, "Hi."

"Hi."

"You ready?"

"Let's go."

They went to her car and Graciela got behind the wheel. She didn't look at him and he didn't look at her. He wanted to touch her hand or hug her or give her a kiss, but he could not breach the space between them.

"Where are we going?" Graciela asked.

"How about El Pasito?"

"Okay."

She drove him in silence and Flip contained himself until he couldn't do it anymore. "Are we still together?" he asked.

"Do you want to be?"

"Yes. You have no idea."

"I think I do," Graciela said and she touched her cheek, though he saw no tear there. For the first time she looked over and Flip felt the thaw happening. Impulsively he reached out and took her hand from the wheel, squeezed it in his.

"If I could take it all back, I would," Flip said.

"Let's not talk about it."

"What do you want to talk about?"

"What we want to eat."

They had their meal together in the little storefront restaurant between a tool shop and a hair salon and afterward they walked the street. When Flip held Graciela's hand she did not pull away. At the next block there was a fruit store and Flip bought a bunch of apples for his lunches and an orange that he split with Graciela.

"I missed you," Graciela said.

"I didn't know what to do."

"You listened to what I said. That was the best thing to do."

"There's just one thing I got to know," Flip said.

"Flip…"

"It's not like that. I just want to know: did José tell you to talk to me that first night?"

Graciela watched her feet as they strolled the block. They passed a mother leading a small child while pushing a baby in a stroller. Flip stepped out of the woman's way. "Why do you want to know that?" Graciela asked finally.

"Just tell me. Please?"

Graciela stopped in front of the barred windows of an appliance store and looked through the dirty glass at a line of refrigerators facing a row of washing machines. Flip watched her. She hadn't dropped his hand.

"If I say yes, will you think I'm a bad person?"

"What? No way."

She nodded and then shrugged and then looked at Flip guiltily. "He told me to make you feel welcome. But he didn't tell me to do nothing else. I did that on my own."

"It was real," Flip said.

"It is real," Graciela said and she came to him and kissed him as hard as she could. Flip let his arms settle around her narrow waist and kissed her back. When a big truck rumbled by and kicked up a cloud of dust over them, they didn't notice.

TWO

THEY SPENT THE FIRST PART OF THE AFTER-
noon in a training seminar on gang violence that was utterly boring
and completely irrelevant. There was not an officer in the conference hall that hadn't learned the same things from working the
street as the expert speakers put on their PowerPoint slides. It had
been all Cristina could do to keep from falling asleep. Robinson
nudged her when her head began to nod.

When they returned to the squad room their desks were laden
with reports, the fruits of several shifts' worth of uniform patrols
and 911 calls. If the uniforms deemed it "gang related," it went to
the gang unit for a follow-up. Most of it was nothing, sometimes it
was something, all of it was tedious.

Cristina was glad when her phone rang. "Salas," she said.

"Cristina, it's Jamie McPeek."

"Hello, Agent McPeek."

Robinson looked up from his work.

"I'm calling everyone who should know to tell them: Matías
Segura was almost hit last night."

"Hit? What happened?"

"There aren't a lot of details right now. He was out and a
truckload of shooters tried to kill him on the street. His wife was
with him."

"Are they thinking it's the Aztecas?"

"It would make sense."

"Is his wife okay?"

"She's fine. They're both fine. They were lucky."

"Thanks for keeping me in the loop."

"Not a problem. Is there anything more on the Esperanza case?"

"He's out on bail. Probably already back in business."

"In Mexico he'd be dead on the side of the road by now."

"Let's be glad this isn't Mexico."

Cristina hung up the phone. She turned to her computer and called up the file on Emilio Esperanza. His picture flashed on the screen. Even in his mug shot he was smirking.

"You going to tell me what that was all about?" Robinson asked.

"That Mexican cop, the one I told you about? The Aztecas tried to kill him last night."

"No shit. What's that have to do with Esperanza?"

Cristina shook her head. "Nothing."

"You worried he'll put a green light out on you?"

"You think he'd do that?"

"I don't know," Robinson said. "Anything's possible. You live right in the middle of Azteca territory, you busted his balls in interrogation."

"You're not making me feel any better."

"Sorry. Just thinking out loud."

Cristina scrolled through Esperanza's record trying to will something new to appear, but it was all the same things. There was not even something she could pull him in on and sweat him for.

The judge set the bail too low. In the courtroom at Esperanza's arraignment there had been a half dozen or more rangy, tattooed young men watching the proceedings. Any one of them could have substituted for Esperanza; they were the same person, essentially, and in the end they were all interchangeable. That's why the gangs never went away no matter how many went into the system: there were all the identical soldiers ready to pick up where the fallen ones left off.

She thought of Matías Segura. They had only met for a little while, but she thought she could understand him. How many Emilio Esperanzas had crossed his path in the years he had been working? How many José Martinezes? In Mexico it was worse than the worst day in El Paso. At least Cristina and Robinson did not have to deal with bodies lying in the streets, or in back alleys with their heads and arms hacked off. They did not have to live with the knowledge that Los Aztecas owned the city and they were just living in it.

Cristina called home. "Hi, Ashlee, it's me," she said. "Can I talk to Freddie?"

Freddie came on. "Hello?" he said.

"Hi, Freddie, it's Mom."

"Hi."

"How was your day at school?"

"I didn't have a good day."

"No? What happened?"

"I can't know," Freddie said.

"You can't know? Why not?"

"I said I can't know."

"Well, I'm not mad. Are you being good for Ashlee?"

"Yes."

"Okay. I'll be home in time for you to go to bed."

"I'm going to play Roblox now."

"You do that, peanut. I love you."

"Bye."

When she put down the phone she wanted to be home so she could hold Freddie and squeeze him tightly until he told her that was enough, just like she wanted to be home to make a real dinner for him and spend time with him. And maybe if she did those things she wouldn't be afraid for him anymore, sitting at his computer in a little house in the Segundo Barrio, not knowing anything about what went on beyond those walls.

"Freddie good?" Robinson asked.

"Yeah."

"What's wrong?"

"It's nothing. Whenever somebody takes a shot at a cop, I get nerves. And you're not helping."

"What did I do?"

"Emilio Esperanza isn't going to his capo to put a green light on an El Paso cop. Even he wouldn't be that stupid. You've got me thinking Freddie's going to be an orphan by the time he's eleven."

"I'm sorry, I didn't know it bothered you so much."

Cristina cleared Esperanza's record from her computer screen. She didn't want to look at his face anymore. It was bad enough that she was still thinking about it and the way he looked when the judge announced his bail. He knew right then he was going to walk, and if the inclination struck him, he could take one step across the border and just disappear into Juárez. Los Aztecas would take care of him; he was their family.

"I've got to get out of here," Cristina said.

"I'll go with you."

"All this paperwork's going to be here tomorrow."

"Then it can wait. I'll walk you to your car, make sure nobody tries to take you out."

"Thanks, Bob."

"Don't mention it."

THREE

Matías had never been inside Carlos Lopez's office before. He had come to the door a few times and he'd glimpsed it from his desk, but he had never set foot across the threshold. It was an alien feeling, being in there, and he wanted to go.

The blinds were half-drawn and the office was dim. Lopez had a broad desk and his chairs were all upholstered with black leather. There was a couch. A neat stack of reports stood on one side of his blotter, an arrangement of pens on the other. In many ways it was exactly what Matías might have expected: orderly, clean and utterly ordinary.

The door was closed so he did not hear Lopez's steps approaching. Suddenly it was opened and Lopez came in with another man Matías had never met. The man wore a suit that made Matías' seem cheap and if he carried a weapon it wasn't obvious. His hair was flat against his scalp and had a sheen to it. Matías got to his feet.

"Matías Segura, this is Hector Romero," Lopez said. "He's from the Attorney General's office. Up special from Mexico City."

"*Mucho gusto*," Matías said and he offered Romero his hand. The man's shake was surprisingly firm and his hands weren't soft. Matías wondered what Hector Romero was before he became a lawyer.

"Please, Sr. Romero, have a seat," Lopez said. "Can I offer you something to drink? I have Scotch whisky."

"That would be fine," Romero replied. He took the chair next to Matías and crossed his legs. Matías saw that he had very shiny black wingtip shoes without a trace of dust on them. He resisted looking at his own shoes.

"Matías? Will you join us?"

"Sure."

Lopez poured three glasses and gave Romero his first. "*Salud*," he said.

Matías thought the Scotch tasted like rubbing alcohol. If he had a drink, he preferred beer. Maybe that made him less refined. Romero seemed to like his.

"Sr. Romero is here because of the incident that occurred last night. He flew up right away at the specific request of the Attorney General," Lopez said. "They are very concerned in Mexico City."

"We're concerned in Ciudad Juárez, too," Matías joked, but Romero didn't smile.

"I understand your wife was with you at the time."

"She was."

"Is she all right?"

"Yes. In shock, but all right."

Romero considered this with his fingertips on his chin. He tapped his lips, and then said, "I am here not because this is an unusual happening in Juárez, but because it is so common. For a time we were losing officers every week. But now they have come after you, a prominent member of the PFM."

"I'm not that prominent," Matías said. "I'm just a man doing his job, like everyone else here."

"You are part of the joint American and Mexican operation against Los Aztecas," Romero said. "A very important part. Our concern at the PGR is that Los Aztecas have found out your vital role in all of this and have conspired to rid themselves of you."

"Every policeman in Juárez is a target."

"But not every policeman is an agent with the PFM with

connections across the border. How many people know of your position?"

Matías thought for a moment. "A few dozen. We'll call it fifty people on both sides of the border. You know about me in Mexico City."

"And a leak could have come from anywhere."

"Are you saying I've been sold out by someone on the inside?" Matías asked.

"There has never been a police unit assembled in Mexico that hasn't succumbed to corruption or co-option by the cartels," Romero said. "That means the locals, the state police, the PF, the PFM… anyone. And I don't know how it is in the United States, but their security can be suspect."

Matías shook his head. "I don't see someone on the American side giving my name to the Aztecas. No."

"Then you admit it must have happened here."

A sense of melancholy settled over Matías, and he looked away from Romero toward the windows. In the hours after the attack he had almost managed to convince himself that it had been nothing more than a random assault perpetrated by one of the armed factions in the city. These things happened all the time and for no reason that could be fathomed. Sometimes Matías thought they killed just because they could.

If Matías was the target, then a pall of suspicion fell on everyone, even the men in this office. He did not like the sensation of suspecting the whole world, of having to watch what he did and said every moment of every day. But of course that was what he had been doing anyway. Who was he trying to fool?

"The Aztecas have marked you," Romero said. "What do they call it? A 'green light.' You're now directly in their sights."

"What do you suggest I do about that?" Matías asked.

"One thing that has been recommended is removing you from your position in the American thing. That was certainly what caught the Aztecas' attention in the first place."

"It could have been anything," Matías protested. "I've been working inquiries involving Los Aztecas for two years now. I've made cases against them. I've testified in court."

"But never have they openly tried to kill you in a public place," Romero said. "That is the difference."

"Then what do you want to do?"

"We could rearrange your duties."

"What do you mean, 'rearrange' my duties? So you are removing me!"

"No, no, no," Lopez said. "It's only something that's been proposed. People high up are concerned."

"I'm concerned. It's me they were shooting at," Matías said.

"You won't be reassigned," Romero said.

"Good, because that would be a foolish thing to do. It would send a message that we can be swayed by violence. That can't be allowed."

"I agree completely," Romero said flatly.

Matías blinked. "You do?"

"Yes. But now we must tread carefully. Someone passed on information about you, and we have to know who that is. My office has opened an official inquiry into the matter. We'll find the one who talked."

"When you do," Matías said, "I want to thank them personally for all that they've done."

"I'll see to it that you get that chance."

FOUR

THE FINAL TRUCK WAS UNLOADED AND THE work gloves came off. Back support belts were stripped off. Men made for their lockers and the time clock. Flip went with them.

He was slow to put together his things and slower still to leave the building. What came next, he wanted nothing to do with, but he was bound to it. Flip felt the expectations smothering him.

At first he thought he'd see Emilio or one of the others – Nasario, maybe – waiting outside the fence ready to tail the truck, but there was no one around. Flip stopped at Alfredo's pick-up and leaned against the dented side, staring at his feet. It was coming.

Alfredo came along after a little while, carrying his black plastic lunch pail. He put it in the bed of the truck. "Ready?" he asked.

"Sure."

Flip waited until they were on the road before he asked. He wanted it to seem natural, but he did not like the sound of his own voice. Clearing his throat helped. "Hey, Alfredo, why don't we stop somewhere on the way back? Get a couple of beers."

"Beers? I thought guys on parole couldn't go to bars."

Flip tried a smile. Alfredo wasn't even looking. "What he doesn't know won't hurt him. Besides, I'm not talking about getting loaded. Just a couple of beers before you drop me off."

Alfredo looked straight ahead and for a moment Flip was afraid he would say no and the whole thing would go straight into the garbage. Finally he shrugged and said, "Sure, why not?

Where do you want to stop?"

"There's a place on Stanton. Rafa's Bar. I saw it the other day when I was with Graciela. Seems like an okay spot."

"I don't know it. But I'll find it."

They drove and Flip found himself clutching the vinyl armrest. He felt like he was sweating all over. His teeth ground and he forced them apart. Street passed street, and every mile they went he felt his tension surge.

Eventually Alfredo turned on Stanton and they found the bar: a little brick-faced place just a few doors down from El Pasito Restaurante. Alfredo parked by the curb. In one window red neon letters advertised BEER and WINE. In the other, RAFA'S BAR. Both windows were heavily barred.

Inside it was dark and Flip saw nothing but black until his eyes adjusted. The place was not large, with a scattering of tables, a few booths and a short bar. Taps for Corona and Dos Equis stood up beside Budweiser and Bud Light. There were at least six different types of tequila behind the bar.

Flip did not see José at first, tucked into one of the booths alone with a half-finished beer in front of him, but he heard him call his name. "Over here, Flip! Hey, come and sit down."

Flip went to José but Alfredo did not follow right away. Suddenly Flip was afraid Alfredo would rather sit at the bar and how that might change things. He touched Alfredo on the arm. "Come on," he said. "He's one of my friends."

Alfredo went into the booth first and Flip second, so that he was bracketed between them. José was dressed in a denim shirt and had a gold chain with a crucifix dangling from the open collar. He looked like a workingman and Flip wondered if that was somehow his way of putting Alfredo at ease. Alfredo did not look at ease.

"I'm José," José introduced himself. He stuck out his hand for Alfredo to shake. They did.

"Alfredo."

"Oh, so *you're* Alfredo. Flip's told me all about you. You're Flip's boss, right?"

"That's right."

"Let me buy you something to drink. How about Corona? You like Corona?"

"Corona's fine," Alfredo said.

José hollered the order and then relaxed into his seat. Flip was uncomfortable, but he did not know if it was because of the cheap cushions or because he did not want to be there. Alfredo was still.

"How is Flip working out?" José asked Alfredo. "Doing good work?"

"Yes. He works hard."

"I'll bet. Flip is solid. That's why I want him doing things for me."

Alfredo looked sharply at José then, as if taking his measure for the first time. "Are you a carpenter?"

"Me? No. I'm a businessman."

"Then how is Flip supposed to work for you?"

"I have things that need doing, Flip can do them."

Alfredo glanced back at Flip. "What kinds of things?"

"Like I said: things that need doing."

Alfredo put his hand down flat on the table and turned on José. "You're some kind of hoodlum, aren't you? You think just because Flip was in prison that he's going to take up with your type?"

"Haven't you heard? Flip's already part of the family."

"Flip? What's he talking about?"

A waiter brought Alfredo his beer, but it went ignored. José put a bill on the table and the waiter swept it up. Flip wished for a beer just so he could have something in his hands, something he could look at. He did not want to meet Alfredo's glare.

"José… he's tight with some people I knew back in Coffield," Flip said.

"'Some people'? Gang members!"

"Hey, man, relax," José said.

"Don't you tell me to relax! I've spent my life staying away from people like you. And now you're trying to pull in Flip."

"Actually I wanted to talk about how you could make some extra money."

"Screw your extra money. Flip, move over. We're getting out of here."

Flip let Alfredo push him from the booth. He looked to José and held up his hands in surrender. What else could he do? He couldn't hold Alfredo down. José just shook his head.

"You're making a mistake, man," José called after Alfredo. "It's good money."

"*Vete a la chingada*," Alfredo said and he caught Flip by the arm. "Let's go."

Flip allowed himself to be led out through the front door into dazzling sunlight that left him blind. By the time they reached the truck again he could see Alfredo climbing behind the wheel, slamming the door, but he didn't get in.

"In the truck, Flip!"

He looked back toward the bar, but José did not emerge.

"Get in the truck!"

Flip took the passenger seat, still watching to see if José would pursue them. Alfredo put the truck in gear and wrenched the wheel so that they pulled an illegal u-turn in the middle of the street. Then he stomped the accelerator.

"What a bunch of bullshit," Alfredo said. "I thought we were going to get a drink and be friendly, but you had one of your gangster friends waiting for us! 'Make some extra money.' Who the hell does he think he is?"

"I'm sorry," Flip said.

"Your mother told me you were a *good boy*, Flip! That all that mess you got into wasn't your fault. Now you're out, you have a chance to do things right, and who do you fall in with? More criminals!"

"It's not like that."

"How is it, then? Explain to me how you just happened to run across a *matón* like that. It doesn't happen by accident. You have to want to walk on the right side of the law."

Flip still couldn't look at Alfredo. He stared out the window instead. "Inside the gang did me favors. I owe them."

"They're in *prison*, Flip. You're in the real world. Everybody has choices."

"So what am I supposed to do?"

"Do what I do," Alfredo said, "and tell them to fuck off."

"It's not so easy."

"Have you tried it?"

Flip had nothing to say to that. They were close to home now and Alfredo was driving too fast. Anger came off the man like heat. He gripped the steering wheel so hard that his knuckles were white.

Alfredo brought him to the front of his mother's house and pulled over. Flip felt Alfredo's eyes drilling into the side of his head. "I'm not going to tell your mother about this, Flip, but I want you to know that things are going to be different between us. You betrayed my trust. It's going to take some work to earn it back."

"So you're not going to fire me, either?"

"No. You can stay on."

"Thanks," Flip said and he risked a look in Alfredo's direction. Alfredo's face was stone.

"Just tell me you're going to fly right from now on. If you won't do it for yourself, you can at least do it for your mother."

"I'll do what I can."

"That better be good enough."

He left Flip on the curb and drove away fast. Flip came up the walk slowly and opened the front door as quietly as he could, but his mother still heard him. She came from the kitchen, chased by the smell of spicy meat. "Felipe, you're late!"

"Only a few minutes, Mamá."

"When you're late, I wonder if there's been an accident."

"No accident. Alfredo and me, we just stopped for a drink."

"It's good that you two are getting along. We're having early dinner tonight, so no running off."

Flip went to his room. The shakes were coming more often and now he had them again. He barely got the door closed before he began trembling all over and he sat down hard on the bed.

His phone vibrated in his pocket. He answered. "Hello?"

"Hey, it's me."

Graciela. All at once the shivering stopped. Flip held the phone tightly, the way he'd hold her tightly. "Hi," he said. "I'm glad you called."

"I was just finishing up. I wanted to know if you wanted to do something."

"I don't know. My mother has dinner on the stove and she wants me to eat with her."

"I understand. Maybe tomorrow?"

"Maybe. I really want to see you."

"How badly do you want to see me?" Graciela asked and he heard her teasing him.

"You know."

"Are you all right, Flip? You sound a little funny."

Flip kicked his shoes off and lay back on the bed. His back was hurting, he realized, though he hadn't felt it before. Whether it was from work or worry, he didn't know. "It's... I just... I had some trouble with my boss today."

"Oh, no."

He weighed how much to tell her, though he wanted to share everything. Nothing would give him more relief, he knew it. Then he said, "He found out about José and me. He wasn't too happy about it."

"Is he going to fire you? Because that would be bad for your parole."

"No, he's not going to fire me. He just doesn't understand it's for life, you know? I made a promise on my blood to stick with the family and now it's all messed up. I got to do for José, but…"

Graciela was quiet. Then she said, "You got to do what's right, too, Flip."

"That's what he said."

"I know about Aztecas," Graciela said. "I been around them all my life. My brother was an Azteca before he got killed in that car crash. I'm an Azteca girl. But I don't let them run my life. I got my own thing."

Flip felt the plastic case of the phone creak in his grip. He relaxed his hand. "I want to have my own thing, too."

"You can. You just got to be strong, Flip. Do what you got to do for José, but don't let them take you over," Graciela said. "I wouldn't like you so much if you did."

"I wish I could see you now."

"You'll see me soon."

"Not soon enough," Flip said, and from the other room he heard his mother calling him to dinner.

FIVE

ALFREDO DID NOT TALK TO FLIP WHEN THEY
went to work the next day. They rode together to the warehouse
and went their separate ways, not even meeting at lunchtime which
had become their habit. Flip ate by himself, resisting being drawn
in by the conversations of his co-workers. He put in his hours and
when it was time to go home he was glad.

"I'm taking your mother out tonight," Alfredo said when they
were almost there. "Just so you know."

"Where are you going?"

"To a nice restaurant," Alfredo replied, and that was all he
offered for the rest of the ride.

Flip found his mother already dressed for the evening in black
with heels. It was the first time he had seen her this way, reaching
all the way back into his childhood. She even wore makeup.

"I put a plate in the refrigerator for you," his mother told him.
"All you have to do is heat it up."

"What time will you be back?"

"I don't know. Alfredo said he wants to take me dancing, so it
will be late. Don't wait up for me."

"I won't, Mamá."

"Good boy."

An hour later Alfredo was back to pick up Flip's mother. He had
changed into a nice shirt and pants and his hair was slicked back.
A bouquet of flowers was her gift. Flip watched his mother kiss

Alfredo and he felt strangely distant from all of it. Alfredo took her away without saying anything to Flip.

At first he tried watching television, but he couldn't stop switching channels. He called Graciela and left a message for her. What was she doing? Maybe it was better if he didn't know.

The sun was down before he went to the kitchen and brought out his plate. Chicken and rice with beans on the side. He nuked them and ate alone at the kitchen table. The idea of going to bed early and trying to sleep the rest the evening away occurred to him, but he resisted, still hoping that Graciela would call.

It was another hour before his phone rang. He saw Graciela's number on the display. "Graciela," he answered. "I'm glad you called."

"Are you all right? I didn't like your message."

"My mother and Alfredo went out. I'm by myself. Do you want to come over?"

"Sure. Wait for me."

Flip put on the front light and went to the bedroom to change shirts. If he had time he would have showered, but it was too late now. He watched out the front window for Graciela's car. When she arrived he opened the front door for her and resisted rushing out to meet her.

She took his hands and smiled and kissed him. It was good to kiss her again, as though a long time had passed and her kiss was something he needed to live. "Hi," she said.

"Hi."

"Let me in."

"Okay."

Graciela came in and looked around the front room as if she had never seen it before. Flip thought it felt strange to have her here without his mother somewhere in the house, but he was too glad to see her to worry about that for long.

"I could come to see you sometime," Flip said. "I've never seen your apartment. What's it like?"

"Small. I'd rather have a little house like this one, but it's too expensive for one person to rent."

"And you have to cut the grass," Flip said.

"That's what I have you for!"

He came to her in the middle of the room and kissed her again. When they broke their faces stayed close together and they breathed each other's breath. "Do you want to see the rest of the house?" Flip asked.

"Show me your room," Graciela answered.

Flip did not turn on the lamp by his bed and in the dark he stripped off Graciela's shirt while she helped him with his buttons. She took off her bra and when they embraced he felt her nipples drifting against his skin. He lifted her and she put her legs around his waist and they kissed, tongues and lips, before they went to the narrow bed.

He loved the way her jeans slipped away from her body as he tugged them, revealing soft flesh beneath. Graciela raised her hips to let him take her panties. Flip kissed the insides of her thighs, then lower, kneeling by the edge of the bed with her leg resting on his shoulder.

She was quiet, but he felt her and when she came she let out a whispery, shuddering breath that was as delicate as she was. Flip struggled out of his pants and went to her gently, mindful of the way she touched him, the way she told him what to do without saying anything.

Flip wanted to take his time, but his body got ahead of him and he was inside her and shuddering as she kissed his chest.

There was barely room enough on the bed for them to lie side by side, facing each other. Flip stroked her hair and she touched his face. His eyes were used to the shadows now and he could see her clearly, watching him back.

"Thank you," Flip said after a while had passed.

"You don't need to thank me for anything," Graciela whispered back.

"I do," Flip insisted. "I need to thank you every time."

"No, you don't. I wanted to."

"Why? Why with me?"

"You don't know?"

"No."

Graciela smiled. "Because you're a good guy."

"I'm not such a good guy."

"Yes, you are. I could tell right away. You talked to me with respect. You didn't expect me to put out just because we were in a club. You treated me like a lady. You still do."

"I didn't want you to think you I was some kind of bum."

"That's the thing, Flip: you aren't. That's why I tell you it's all right when you worry, because you got a good heart. The way you make love to me, I *know*."

"I don't feel it sometimes," Flip said.

"Sooner or later it's gonna get through."

Graciela kissed him on the point of his chin, then on his lips. She put one leg over his, drawing him closer to her. Flip felt like he could break her if he held on too tightly, but he did not want to let her go.

"What time is your mom getting home?" Graciela asked.

"I don't know. Late."

"I'm gonna use your shower."

She left him on the bed and he saw her slim figure framed in the doorway as she slipped away. The water started. Flip turned onto his back and listened to the tinkle of the spray as it carried to his ears, imagining her there.

Sooner or later it's gonna get through, she said. Flip still didn't feel it. He wanted to call Alfredo on the phone and beg his forgiveness for being such a fool. This man who took his mother dancing, who gave him a job, and was paid back with José Martinez. The thought made him feel ill.

The shower stopped and there was a long quiet as Graciela dried herself. He heard her leave the bathroom and come down the hall to his room. She reappeared with a towel around her. "I got to go," she said.

"Where do you got to go?"

"Just home. I got to get up early."

"Can't you stay a while?" Flip asked.

"I don't want to be here when your mom gets home."

"Don't worry about that."

Graciela kissed him on the forehead. "You worry about other stuff. I worry about this."

"When can I see you again?"

"Call me tomorrow."

She gathered up her clothes and got dressed by the closet. Flip put on shorts to take her to the door. He held her close and this time he was sure he'd break her, but she didn't.

"Call me tomorrow," she said again and then she left.

SIX

THINGS CONTINUED THAT WAY FOR A WHILE. Alfredo still drove Flip to work and brought him home without inquiring into his evenings or weekends, when Flip would go to the club or visit José's house for one of his barbecue gatherings. Graciela was always with him during those weeks, visiting him after his day was done or accompanying him to the parties. When they were together at the club she didn't vanish into the VIP rooms without him anymore; her friends came to her.

José introduced Flip to other Indians on those warming nights at his house. Flip kept a mental record of their names and faces and anything else about them that he could glean from talking to them. He passed these things on to the detectives, who promised him payment the next time they met. Flip asked José when he could expect to have some action sent his way, and whenever he asked José would tell him not to worry about it. He worried anyway.

The warehouse job paid every two weeks. Flip gave his mother money to help with food, though she swore she didn't need it. He would have offered to pay for his room, but he was still saving for his own place. Flip thought maybe he would be able to settle somewhere close to Graciela. Segundo Barrio was not large.

On Wednesdays Graciela had a short day at school and she came to pick him up at work. This Wednesday was no different; she waited by the gate for him to come down to her and they went off together. Alfredo had nothing to say about that.

"Where are we going today?" Flip asked.

"I thought you might like to see my apartment."

She drove him to a building that couldn't be more than five minutes away from his mother's house. There was no off-street parking, so they left Graciela's car by the curb. Graciela unlocked the door on the ground floor and let them into a narrow hallway with stairs leading up at one end. Flip followed her up the steps.

There was another hall with three doors. Graciela opened the closest. "Here it is," she said.

It was dark inside, and warm, with the only light creeping in through closed blinds. Then Graciela found a lamp and turned it on, illuminating a small room. After a moment Flip realized that the room was almost the entire apartment.

Graciela's bed was a mattress on the floor, made up with black sheets and a comforter. She had a petite sofa against one wall and a tiny television set in the corner opposite it. The kitchen was basically a niche with enough space for a miniature table with two chairs. Another door must have been the bathroom.

She turned on a window-unit air conditioner and cool air started to creep into the room. When she looked at Flip she made a gesture with her hands as if to say this is it. "My place," she said.

Flip noticed that she had nothing on her walls, too. Her mattress was lain in front of a closet with sliding doors, one half open to reveal a compact book shelf with a few volumes on it. She had her alarm clock there, too. Everything was laid out to save maximum space, and in this way Flip was reminded of what it was like to be in prison, when room was an issue and everything a convict owned had to be compressed into as small an area as possible.

"It's nice," Flip said.

"I've never had a guy back here before," she said, and she shifted from foot to foot with nerves. "You're the first."

"I'm glad you brought me," Flip said.

"You want something to drink? I've got sodas."

"Soda is good."

He stood in the center of the room because he did not want to sit down without her permission. Graciela had allowed him into her personal space, so it was up to her what Flip could do in it. It had been the same when she came into his house, his room.

Graciela came back with orange soda in bottles and gave Flip one. They stood there drinking and saying nothing. From time to time it seemed as though Graciela was about to speak, but then the silence went on.

After a long time she said, "You want to sit on the couch with me?"

"Sure."

It was not a large couch and even sitting at opposite ends they were close enough to touch. Flip finished his soda, but there was nowhere to put the bottle. He held onto it.

"You really like it?" Graciela asked.

"Yeah. You keep it neat."

"I have to, otherwise I can't get around, you know?"

Flip nodded. He understood this, too.

"I don't know why I didn't bring you here sooner," Graciela continued. "I guess I… I don't know. Maybe I'm being stupid."

"You like to have your own space," Flip said. "I get it."

"It's nothing against you."

"I'm not upset."

"I moved in here when I was eighteen, just to get out of my parents' house. I couldn't be there anymore; it was crazy with all us kids. *Mis padres*, they helped me pay the rest for a little while until I could get on my feet. I worked at a grocery store for a while. I was a cashier."

Flip listened. There was something coming, he could tell, but he could not guess what. It was in the way she spoke, the way she held her body on the couch. He had learned to pay attention to these things. He was patient.

"You want me to throw that bottle out for you?" Graciela asked.

"If you want. I'm okay."

"I'll take care of it," Graciela said and she rose from the couch to do that. She came back empty-handed. Before she sat down she rubbed her palms on the seat of her jeans.

Flip reached across to touch her on the arm. "Are you okay?" he asked.

"I got something to say."

"All right."

"I don't want you to think bad things about me because of anything I've done," Graciela said. "Not the way you did when Emilio told you that stuff."

"I won't."

"Okay," Graciela said and she looked away from him. "Okay."

"You don't have to tell me if you don't want."

"I want to."

Flip touched her again and she moved closer so he could press his palm against her shoulder. Maybe it was the air conditioning, but she felt warm to him. There might have been color in her cheeks.

"When I needed money I did some things for José," Graciela blurted out. "And don't ask me what because I don't want to say. He paid my way for a while, until I could get into school."

He bided his time until it seemed there was nothing else coming. Flip didn't take his hand away. He wished she would look at him. "It's all right," he said.

"I told you I was an Azteca girl."

"You did. I don't care."

"You don't?"

"No. You told me you got your own thing now. José don't run your life."

"No, he doesn't."

"Then you got no reason to worry," Flip said.

Graciela leaned over then and Flip put his arms around her. They stayed like that, just together. Flip couldn't be sure if she was crying, and maybe she was. All he knew was that he would hang onto her no matter what.

His phone rang. Flip ignored it, but then Graciela pulled away from him and he knew their moment was over. He dug the phone out of his pocket and answered it.

"Flip, it's José."

Flip felt a stab of anger at the interruption, but he kept it to himself. "Hey, José," he said. "What's up?"

"You free? I want to take you for a drive."

"Where do you want to go?"

"Don't worry about that. You got your ID on you?"

"Sure."

"Where are you? I'll pick you up."

Flip looked around. He did not know the address and he did not want José coming here. Graciela was watching him now. Her expression was guarded. "I'm on the road with Graciela," he said. "How about I meet you at that taquería, El Cihualteco?"

"Okay. Twenty minutes."

"I'll be there."

He put his phone away. Graciela said, "You have to go?"

"It's José. He wants me for something."

"José always wants something."

"Can I get you to drop me off?"

"Sure, Flip. Let's go," Graciela said, and Flip thought it was the bitterest thing she'd ever said.

SEVEN

THEY WERE AT THE TAQUERÍA IN TEN MINUTES. Flip kissed Graciela good-bye, but she was distant. He wished they'd had time together, but José stepped into the middle of all that and ruined it. Flip wondered if he'd ever see Graciela's apartment again, or if that would be the only time she'd let him in. He tried to push the thought from his mind.

José came not long after. Flip got in the car.

"Where are we going?" Flip tried again.

"Juárez."

"I'm not allowed to leave the country, José. My parole—"

"Your PO won't know you were gone, Flip. We go in, we come out, no problem."

"I don't have a passport."

"Let me worry about that."

Flip held his tongue as José turned them toward the border. They were there in minutes, crossing the bridge with the weak flow of traffic headed southward. At the customs check they showed their Texas IDs and the bored officer waved them through.

José drove familiarly through the streets and didn't seem to notice when Flip tensed every time a police vehicle or one of the big army trucks rolled out in front of them. He changed the radio to a Juárez station and listened to the traffic reports and news interspersed with a little music. They could have been anywhere.

Without conversation to distract him, Flip's mind chewed over the last few weeks: the calls he'd made, the people he'd met. There was no reason he should end up in a fire, or dumped at the side of the road. And even if there was, José would not do the killing himself. If Nasario or Emilio had been with him, then he would have been in real danger, but not with the boss alone. Flip almost had himself convinced.

They kept heading south until at last they reached an overpass that cleared a section of railroad five tracks wide. José pulled up to the curb in the middle of the bridge and stopped the engine. "Get out," he said.

Flip exited onto the narrow sidewalk that mounted the overpass. No trains were going by, so the tracks were bare and rusting except where they were worn smooth from the passage of metal wheels. They were out in the open. José would not kill him here.

José joined him. He put his hand on Flip's shoulder. "Take a look," he said, and he pointed.

Flip followed José's finger. On the far side of the tracks there was a fenced-in compound and a big warehouse that could have been the oversized twin of the one where he worked. There were a dozen loading docks and most of them were full, with more trucks parked in the open yard waiting for their turn. The name of the ware-housing company was spray-painted in huge letters on the wall of the structure, but the sun had almost blasted them away.

"It's a shipping depot," José explained. "Food suppliers from all around Juárez bring their stuff here to get loaded onto trucks. Those trucks go into the United States. Now, take a look at those trucks there. You see them?"

"Yeah, I see them," Flip said.

"Recognize the logo?"

Flip did recognize the logo. It was one he'd seen many times before on trucks stopping at the warehouse to unload. Not all the trucks down there had the design, but there were several and they stood out because they were red with bright orange letters. Flip had the inkling of an idea.

"*Productos Frescos de Granja*," José said. "I know the man who tells those trucks where to go, what to pick up, what to drop off. He's a good friend. He likes money. But don't we all, right?"

"Right."

"The thing is, Flip, some of those trucks go to your work. You get what I'm saying?"

"No, I don't," Flip said.

"*¡No seas estúpido!* Think about it!"

"You got something on those trucks?"

"Not yet, but it can be arranged. Only those trucks got to be unloaded somewhere. You following me?"

Flip looked at José. "Nobody's going to let you unload that stuff at my work."

José drew Flip close. "Your boys don't have to do the unloading. *We* do it. The truck just has to have someplace to sit for a few hours. That's where your mamá's boyfriend comes in. The truck shows up, he sets it aside where no one touches it. We wait until closing time and then we take what belongs to us."

"What if the truck doesn't make it through?"

"That's a risk we got to take."

"I don't know. You heard what Alfredo said: he's not interested in taking your money."

"Then you have to change his mind. You know how to do that, don't you, Flip?"

"I can't put a gun to his head."

José let Flip go and smiled. "I don't think you have to go so far. But you let him know that if he doesn't come through for us then I *will* send somebody to put a gun to his fucking head and then he won't be so goddamned smart! I put a lot of thought into this, Flip. We got people lined up in Juárez ready to make deliveries."

Flip watched as a truck inched away from its loading dock and headed for the open gates of the depot's compound. He saw the place had security and even from this distance he could tell they were armed. In Juárez even food had to be defended with a gun.

"I need to know you're down for the cause, Flip. You wanted to know when I was going to throw you some action? This is it. Are you gonna do what you need to do?"

"Yeah," Flip said and he nodded. "I can do it, José."

"That's what I wanted to hear! Come on, let's go get something to eat."

They got back in the car and José got them moving again. Flip caught a glimpse of the depot as they came down off the overpass, but then it was gone. José turned down a nameless street, following some internal map of the city that only he knew. Flip was lost already, and now he was only more lost.

"José," Flip said.

"What?"

"Why are you trusting me with all of this?"

"What?"

"I said, why—"

"I heard what you said." José turned down the radio. "I just don't know why you're asking, that's all."

"Because this is big time. I'm just some guy, you know? I've been inside for four years, I don't know nothing about shipping stuff across the border. I know how to cut wood and make cabinets. I lift boxes for a living."

"You don't know?"

"No, I don't know."

"You *really* don't know?"

"For serious, José, I got no idea."

"Holy shit, Flip, I thought you knew."

Flip felt his face reddening and he looked out the windshield. They were passing through a densely packed neighborhood of paint-peeling apartments and little storefronts. It could have been a street in Segundo Barrio.

José laughed. "I guess old Enrique didn't tell you everything," he said. "But let me lay some knowledge down on you, okay?"

"Okay."

"The Indians in Coffield are the true blood, Flip. That's where it all got started. Enrique, he's one of the Originals."

"Yeah, I know that."

"Then you got to know that Enrique's word is like gold in Chuco Town. He lays his hand on somebody, that somebody's going to have a lot of juice when they get out."

"I don't have any juice," Flip said.

"But you ain't just some cherry, neither. You earned your *huaraches* inside and that means something on the street. When Enrique talked to me, he said you were reliable and smart and you know how to keep yourself clean. I need all those things, Flip. I'm surrounded by *idiotas* like Emilio who do stupid shit and fuck up. I'm thinking about my place in the world, what I got to do to move *up*."

"You're already on top, José."

"There's always room for improvement, Flip. Always. And if I'm gonna break through, it's gonna be because I picked the right people to make it happen."

"I didn't know Enrique thought I was so good," Flip said.

"He don't say that about just anybody, and I should know better than anyone."

"What do you mean?"

"I mean Enrique Garcia's my father-in-law," José said. "And when he talks, I listen."

EIGHT

THE PARK WAS BUSY TODAY, WITH MORE THAN the usual number of children milling around the monkey bars and climbers, and playing on the swings. It took a half an hour before a bench cleared for Cristina to sit, but when she did she had a good view of the playground and of Freddie.

He was doing all right today, moving from cluster to cluster, never settling, but not disrupting the other children's games. Freddie did better with children much smaller than himself because he could convince them to play his simple games, though even they were turned off when the games turned strange.

There had been trouble at school. When he was away from his computer and the demands of the day were on him, Freddie's temper could become a problem. No warnings would come before he was in an inconsolable state, throwing things and kicking school staff and saying things he never said to Cristina. They told her that he'd been screaming the word *fuck* when they had to put him in the quiet room. It was so unlike the Freddie of home that Cristina could not put the two images together.

Cristina went to regular meetings at the school where a psychiatrist saw him once a month. This time they recommended a medication change. They said the medicine might make Freddie sleepy, but that it would regulate his mood.

Freddie had been on a parade of drugs since the beginning. Some worked well and others seemed to have no effect at all.

Cristina was not afraid of the new medicine, but only of what came next if the medicine didn't work. When that happened, she fell back on questions. *What did I do wrong? How can I make it better?* She did not like the medication meetings.

He was playing with a little boy about half his size, chasing around the monkey bars in erratic loops with the boy behind him. The sun was out and he was in a short-sleeved shirt that exposed his skinny arms. He wore new pants because he'd torn a hole in his last new pair after wearing them one time.

After a while Cristina felt safe enough to take her eyes off Freddie and scan the street that ran alongside the park. A woman walked her dog with a plastic bag in her hand. A car passed. She did not see who she was looking for.

A half hour passed and Freddie was still doing well. He'd fallen back into the pattern of playing by himself, imagining an elevator. The other children ignored him. Cristina did not have to hear him making the noises; she could imagine them.

Flip came from the opposite direction she had expected and she jumped a little despite herself. "Sorry," he said.

"It's okay," Cristina said. "Sit down."

They sat on the bench together but didn't look at each other. Flip kept an eye out one way, while Cristina watched over the other. After a few minutes had gone by, Cristina was assured that no one was watching them. Even so, they could not be together for very long.

"You said you had something important," Cristina said.

"I do. I think maybe it's just what you were hoping for."

Flip told her about his trip into Juárez and the things he'd seen. He was meticulous in the details, which was something Cristina liked about him. Though he could not tell her exactly where the shipping depot was, he gave her enough hints that someone might recognize it if they knew Juárez well enough. Maybe McPeek. Maybe Matías Segura.

He finished by telling her about Enrique Garcia and his relation to José. "I didn't know he was even married," he said.

"I didn't, either. But it accounts for some things," Cristina said. She fished in her back pocket for a slender notebook and a pen and passed these to Flip. "I want you to write down the names of everything you remember, starting with that grocery company. How did you get back into the States?"

"José took care of it. He knew someone at the bridge."

"Of course he did," Cristina said. "Tell me: did he ever mention somebody named Julio Guerra to you?"

"Who?"

"Did he say if he was going to bring you back to Juárez again?"

"No, but I don't think so. He needs me here, putting pressure on Alfredo. Listen, I don't want to do anything to Alfredo; he's good for my mother."

"We'll figure something out, but you have to stay on José's good side. That might mean doing things that you don't want to do. Until we can pull you out and put you under protective custody—"

"Wait a minute," Flip said, "what are you talking about, 'protective custody'?"

"Well, eventually you're going to have to testify to what you've seen and heard, Flip. That means making statements in open court."

"I never agreed to nothing like that!"

Cristina glanced back toward the monkey bars. Freddie was near the top, clambering arm over arm in pursuit of another child. He was smiling. She forced herself to look back to Flip. "I don't know what to tell you, Flip. There are people involved now that have pay grades a lot higher than me and Bob. They're going to want you to testify against the Aztecas."

Flip pushed the notebook back at Cristina. He hadn't written a word. "You tell them I won't do it."

"Flip, you don't understand."

"No, *you* don't understand: I do this without nobody knowing my name, or I don't do it at all. I'm not going to put my mother or Graciela or Alfredo in danger because you need somebody to talk in court. If you don't like it, I'll walk away right now."

His eyes were steely and black. Cristina stared back at him. "I could tell your PO you've been in Mexico. He'd violate you back to Coffield."

"You won't do that."

"What makes you so sure?"

"Because you need me."

Cristina couldn't argue with him. She offered the notebook again. "Okay," she said. "Just write it all down."

NINE

"THERE THEY ARE," ROBINSON SAID.

Cristina looked. She saw Flip and Alfredo Rodriguez leaving the warehouse and walking down to the older man's truck. Neither of them looked up the street where Robinson sat behind the wheel of the unmarked police unit they'd learned to call their second home. Robinson started the engine.

"They're going to come right in front of us," Cristina said.

"Just act inconspicuous."

The truck pulled out onto the street and moved toward them. Neither Flip nor Rodriguez looked their way as they drove past. Robinson made a u-turn in the street behind them and fell in three or four car-lengths back, driving slowly. When they stopped for a signal, Robinson simply coasted up. Cristina thought he was good at this.

Robinson and Cristina trailed the truck all the way back to the South Side, turned on Flip's street and kept a careful distance as Flip was dropped off. Cristina watched Flip walk to the house without glancing back and then they were on their way again, pursuing Rodriguez's truck to the end of the block and around the corner and beyond.

"Where does he live again?" Cristina asked.

"Not far. About fifteen minutes, tops."

"When we stop him, you want me to make the first move?"

"Maybe you should let me. He's a working-class kind of guy. I figure he'll open up faster to another fella."

"I'll follow your lead, then."

They drove ten minutes, always keeping their distance, though Rodriguez hadn't seemed to notice their tail. Eventually Rodriguez came to an apartment building and turned into the lot. Robinson followed and parked a few spaces down. They got out of the car.

Robinson caught Rodriguez on the steps going up and flashed his badge. "Detective Robinson, El Paso Police Department," Robinson said. "This is Detective Salas. Can I get a word with you, Mr. Rodriguez?"

"What? How do you know my name?"

"Can we talk inside?"

Rodriguez looked from Robinson to Cristina and back again. "Sure. What's this all about?"

"We'll talk inside."

Rodriguez led them to a second-floor apartment and let them in. It was dark inside until Rodriguez put on the lights and then it was yellow and underlit. The place smelled faintly of Pine-Sol. "Come in," Rodriguez said.

Cristina was the last through the door and she closed it behind her. Rodriguez stood in the center of the living room with his arms at his sides, his confusion warring with the need to be polite. Cristina could see uncertainty in his eyes.

"Am I in trouble?" Rodriguez said. "Because I don't think I've done anything."

"No, you haven't done anything," Robinson replied. "Why don't you go ahead and have a seat? Mind if we sit down?"

"Go ahead."

Robinson sat on the couch with Rodriguez and Cristina took a chair. Now Rodriguez couldn't look at both of them without turning his head, and so he fixed his attention on Robinson. He licked his upper lip.

They would start with the easy questions. Robinson took out

his notebook even though he didn't need it and made a show of flipping the pages. "Mr. Rodriguez," he said, "are you familiar with a young man by the name of Felipe Morales?"

Cristina saw Rodriguez's lip twitch at the mention of Flip's name and the man's eyes went immediately dark. "Yeah, I know him," Rodriguez said. "He's the son of my girlfriend, Silvia Morales."

"Mr. Morales works for you, doesn't he?"

"He does. Listen, if he—"

"Hold up a minute, Mr. Rodriguez. Let me ask the questions for right now."

"Okay."

"Mr. Rodriguez, you're aware that Mr. Morales is a convicted felon, are you not?"

"Yes. He was in prison until a little while ago."

"Do you know what he was in for?"

"I don't know the details."

"That's okay, it doesn't matter. But did you know that while he was in prison he joined a gang called Barrio Azteca?"

Cristina saw an eyebrow rise for just an instant. Rodriguez hadn't known.

"I knew he was in a gang. I didn't know he was an Azteca."

"Well, he was. He is. Gang membership in Barrio Azteca is for life."

"I've never been involved with any gangs."

"I know, Mr. Rodriguez, don't worry. Now, I have to ask you: has Mr. Morales or anyone else approached you about doing something for the gang? Anything at all. A little favor?"

Rodriguez glanced at Cristina. "No," he said.

"I think maybe you're lying, Mr. Rodriguez."

"I'm not lying. Nobody told me anything."

"What if I said that I knew for a fact that you were approached by a man by the name of José Martinez? That he offered you money to do a favor for him?"

Rodriguez made fists and shifted his position on the couch. He was only half-turned to Robinson now. Cristina had seen the same body language a hundred times in the interview room.

"Mr. Rodriguez?"

"Okay, someone came to me and offered me money. I don't know what for. And I didn't ask! I don't want anything to do with any gangs."

"But you didn't fire Morales," Cristina said.

"No, I didn't fire him. I hired him because of Silvia. She would want to know why I fired him and I couldn't tell her the truth: that her son is still a crook."

"Mr. Rodriguez, we have a pretty good idea what José Martinez wants with you," Robinson said. "And we know you're a solid citizen. That's why we're here. We need to ask you for something."

"Like what?"

"We need you to reach out to Morales," Cristina said. "Tell him that you've changed your mind about earning a little extra cash. He'll put you in touch with José Martinez and Martinez will ask you to do what he wants you to do."

"Why would I do that?"

"Because we want to put Martinez away," Robinson said. "We can do it without your help, but it would be a whole lot easier if we could get your cooperation."

"I don't want to get involved in that."

"Please, Mr. Rodriguez," Cristina said. "I know it seems like a lot to ask, but it's really very simple. I doubt your contact with José Martinez would extend beyond one meeting. And if we could get you to wear a wire at that meeting, it'll mean that much more evidence to use against him."

"A wire?!?" Rodriguez exclaimed. "You want me to wear a microphone? These thugs *kill people*. What will they do to me if they find out I'm helping the police spy on them?"

"You'd be under our protection the whole time," Robinson said.

"No! Absolutely no!" Rodriguez came off the couch and gestured emphatically with his hands. "I work very hard to stay out of situations like this and I'm not going to get into one now. I'm sorry."

Robinson stood up. "Mr. Rodriguez, just give us a chance."

"No. I'm sorry. No. Now I have to ask you to leave. Please."

Cristina and Robinson let Rodriguez herd them to the door. She wanted to say more, but she knew it would fall on deaf ears. Even Robinson had nothing to say. Rodriguez got the door open and almost pushed them out.

"Please don't come back," Rodriguez said, and then he closed the door.

TEN

THE BIG ROOM WAS QUIET AND ALL THE DESKS empty. Matías and Paco retired to the conference room and Matías waited while Paco struggled to load images from a flash drive to the room's computer. The projector was on, showing a huge blue square where pictures should have been.

"Fucking thing!" Paco cursed. "How does this work?"

"Do you want me to show you?"

"No, damn it, I can do it myself."

Lopez had put Matías and Paco together after Matías' meeting with Romero. Matías was told it was because they wanted to reduce his workload, but Matías thought perhaps they wanted another man fluent in the Azteca situation if something should befall him. He did not blame them, and in truth he enjoyed having someone he could share his knowledge with. Paco was anxious to know everything and Matías was willing to tell all.

In the end the change had affected the amount of work Matías had to do himself. He was able to go home earlier, knowing Paco was there to pick up the slack. Some of the little things Matías would have handled himself he passed on. It was good.

Another few minutes of wrangling and the blue square changed to a picture of the computer's desktop. Paco fiddled with the cursor until the right window opened. He clicked and the frame expanded to fill the whole screen.

The photographs were in high-definition color, a series of busy street scenes that were instantly identifiable as Ciudad Juárez. Matías could almost narrow the images down to a single street just from what he could see, and at the center of the snapshots, two men he knew equally well.

"There's José Martinez," Paco declared. "I don't know the other guy."

"Víctor Barrios," Matías said. "Víctor is one of Guerra's *capos*. He meets with José Martinez a lot."

"How often is a lot?"

"Once every ten days or so. José slips across the border, has lunch or dinner with Víctor, and then heads back to the States. Víctor likes the ladies, so he and José party together."

"I have a lot of pictures here with the two of them."

"Any audio?"

"No. You can see they're eating on the street. It's too noisy to pick anything up, even with the new microphones."

Matías frowned. "Show me something I haven't seen before."

"Okay. How about this?"

They were looking at a substantial warehouse from street level, trucks in motion all around, with others loading in the background. José was caught through the chain-link fence talking with a man Matías did not recognize. There were several of these, and the series concluded with José shaking the man's hand.

"Where is this place?"

"A shipping depot off Vial Juan Gabriel. On the same day José met with Guerra's man, he went here. Talked to this guy for a long time."

"No audio there, either?"

"Sorry."

Matías pounded the arm of his chair. "It's no good if we don't know what he's talking about! It's all about those damned trucks!"

"What should we do?" Paco asked.

"I'm thinking on it."

Paco clicked through more photos showing the depot at large, the entrance and the armed guards. The men with their shotguns paid no mind when José passed through them, as if they knew him by sight, and perhaps they did.

"The first thing we have to do is increase surveillance on the depot," Matías said at last. "And we need to find out the name of the man José talked to. Once we have that information, we can start digging through his life: who he is, where he lives, how much he makes. Does this place show up in any reports as a known way-station for drugs? Are the cartels using it? Do we have any information at all that would allow us to make a raid?"

"I'm working on it. Tomorrow I'll start calling around and we'll get this depot covered. José wants trucks? We can let him have some trucks."

"That's good," Matías said.

"What about Guerra?"

"Guerra will put his head out," Matías said. "Sooner or later he has to step into this and then we'll have him. We'll have all of them."

Matías got up. It was late, but he wasn't tired. He could make his calls right now, wake up some people and put them to work, but he had to be home for Elvira.

Paco clasped him by the shoulder. "It's going to work, isn't it?"

"If it doesn't, then you had better start sharpening your own pencil. There's always lots of paperwork to be done, and we'll be doing it together."

ELEVEN

MATÍAS KNEW SOMETHING WAS WRONG AS soon as he turned the key in the door. There was a sense of stillness on the other side that bled through the wood into the hallway. When he opened the door it was dark, all the lights out.

He didn't call out. He stepped inside and closed the door quietly, thinking for a moment that maybe Elvira was sleeping, having gone to bed early. Once she would have waited up for him to all hours, but things had changed.

There was no sound. She was not sleeping.

Matías switched on the living room lights and went down the hall to the bedroom. He put on the lights in there and saw the bed was empty, still made. The closet door was half-open.

In the closet he saw the missing clothes, the empty spaces on the shoe rack where she'd taken away her favorite pairs. His things were undisturbed.

She had left no note in the kitchen or anywhere else in the apartment. She was simply gone.

They had a bottle of brandy from Spain that they had barely touched in the year since it was given to them as a present. Matías found the right glass in the cabinet and poured himself two fingers. He sat on the couch in the empty living room and stared at the picture on the opposite wall. The brandy burnt, but it had a fruity taste he had never noticed before. He would have mentioned this to Elvira.

After an hour he brought out his phone and called her number. It rang five times and went to voicemail. "It's Matías," he said. "I'm not angry. Please, just call me when you get this message."

He put his jacket and tie away and rolled up his shirtsleeves. He took off his shoes and put his sockfeet on the coffee table while he had another glass of brandy. It was close to eleven o'clock and she did not call back.

"It's Matías again," he told her voicemail. "If you get this you can call me anytime, no matter how late. I'm going to stay up until I hear from you."

It was not his drink, but another brandy would be good. He did not want to be drunk when she called, so Matías put it away. He rummaged in the freezer for something to thaw out and eat and settled on a pasta meal that only needed a few minutes in the microwave. When it was ready he ate at the kitchen table not looking at anything, waiting for the phone to ring.

Midnight came and went. The energy he felt at the office with Paco had faded, but he knew he would not be able to sleep even if he tried. He did not like watching television very much and all the shows at this hour were pointless and stupid. There was a mystery novel in the bedroom that he'd been trying to finish for a month. Reading it now helped a little, though he immediately forgot everything he read as soon as he turned each page.

It was two o'clock in the morning when his phone vibrated and then chimed. He put down the book and cleared his throat and answered. "*Bueno*," he said.

"Matías," said Elvira. Her voice sounded far away, Matías thought, but then it could just be his imagination. "Matías, I'm sorry."

"Where did you go?" Matías asked.

"I'm in Monterrey with my sister."

Matías closed his eyes. He had been to Elvira's sister's home several times and stayed in the spare bedroom, which was made up like a sun-dappled field of yellow flowers. Imagining Elvira there made her feel closer. "Why did you leave?"

"It's not you, Matías. It was never you."

"I'm glad."

"I can't be in Juárez right now. I arranged for a leave of absence from work."

"And then you flew to Monterrey. How long have you been planning this?"

"Not long. Or maybe that's not true. I knew as soon as that night that I had to leave, only I didn't want to go without you."

"You know I can't go."

"I've thought about that. You can go. You said yourself that they want you to keep a low profile. Why not take some time off and come away with me? You have it coming to you, so why keep saving it? You can use it now."

Matías thought of his meeting with Paco, of the things they discussed, of what would happen. Trying to explain all of this to Elvira was pointless; she wouldn't want to hear it, but he would have to do it anyway.

"Matías, are you there?"

"I'm here."

"Will you come?"

Matías felt a pain inside. "No."

"Why not?"

"Because I have work to do here. If I go now…"

"If you go now someone else can deal with it."

"I wish I could make you understand, Elvira."

"So you won't come. Even though I'm asking you."

"I would if I could, but I can't," Matías said. "That's all you need to know: that I can't. The work *won't* be done without me. They need me here."

"I need you!"

Matías sighed. "I have to get up early tomorrow, Elvira."

"You're hanging up on me?"

"There's nothing to be gained by continuing this discussion. You've told me what you want, I've told you what I can do. We could go on forever like this. I'm happy to know that you're safe somewhere. That's the most important thing."

Elvira's tone shifted and Matías knew she was crying. "I only want for both of us to be safe!"

"I know. Please don't cry."

"Come with me, Matías. I'm begging you."

"Don't do this to me, Elvira."

"You won't be happy until they get you!"

"Elvira, you know that's not true."

"Do you love me, Matías?"

"Yes, I love you."

"And still you can't do this for me?"

"No, I can't."

"To hell with your work!"

"We'll talk again tomorrow. Get some sleep."

Matías keyed off the phone and put it on the coffee table. Elvira did not call back.

TWELVE

CRISTINA SPENT THE MORNING LECTURING junior high students on the dangers of gangs. They called it the "speaking tour" and at different schools she talked to children as young as ten and as old as eighteen. Some were already in the life and nothing she said would turn them away. Those kids she would see again, locked in the back of a patrol car or in a cell.

Freddie's school was not one of the ones she visited. The children there were not targets for recruitment. Cristina worried about them mostly because they could become targets – for bullying, for robbery, for assault – and they were unable to defend themselves. Freddie was not in a wheelchair, at least, and he didn't need a walker. Cristina told him that if someone scared him on the street, he was to run away as fast as he could and keep running until he could find a police officer. She hoped he would never have to do that.

Because of the speaking tour she had the afternoon off and she went to pick up Freddie from school. She parked in the small lot and went in through the main entrance. The door was electronically locked from the inside and a guard had to buzz her in. At the front desk she was obliged to sign her name in return for a sticker that declared VISITOR in big, red letters. The stickers were dated so they could only be used on the same day they were issued.

The office was downstairs, below street level. Cristina signed her name again and scribbled down her reason for picking Freddie up. Bureaucracy was the same everywhere.

The secretary called to Freddie's classroom. "Ms. Salas?" she asked after a moment.

"Yes?"

"Ms. Gillies wants to know if you'd come down. Freddie's in the quiet room."

"Okay."

"Right down that hallway. She'll meet you."

Cristina followed the secretary's finger down a corridor she hadn't been allowed in before. She saw Ms. Gillies, Freddie's teacher, waiting almost at the far end and she faintly heard the sound of screaming.

The screaming grew louder and more vehement the farther she went. She felt her breath catch in her throat because she knew what Ms. Gillies would tell her when she got there, but she didn't want to know.

"Hi, Ms. Salas," Ms. Gillies said. She was an elfin woman who looked far too young to be a teacher. Maybe a teacher's assistant. Her expression was sympathetic. The screaming was very insistent now. "Freddie's right through here."

She was brought into a room with white walls and a few desks. A pair of offices branched off from the central hub, but two other doors were closed. They were marked ROOM 1 and ROOM 2. The screaming came from Room 1. Two staff were on hand, looking sober.

"We have the door closed and locked because Freddie is out of control," Ms. Gillies told Cristina. "Since you're here, maybe you can talk to him?"

Cristina nodded. She didn't trust herself to speak. The noises coming from behind the door were brutish and animalistic. No child should make sounds like that.

Ms. Gillies went to the door. She spoke through it. "Freddie? Freddie, your mom is here. We're going to open the door, okay?"

Something slammed violently against the door, shaking it in

its frame. Cristina almost jumped. "He kicks the door," said one of the staff members.

"Freddie, the door is opening now!"

Ms. Gillies unlocked the door and cracked it slowly open. It was dim inside the room, which was no bigger than a walk-in closet. A small bench was built into the wall.

Freddie was flush-faced and sweating, his hair stuck together. His eyes rolled in their sockets. He opened his mouth to scream again, but he saw Cristina and rushed forward instead. Cristina was caught around the waist, Freddie's face buried in her stomach, and he was crying.

Cristina looked at Ms. Gillies and the others looking at her. They were watching her for some lead, some clue. All she could do was shush him and pat his head and neck. "It's okay, peanut. It's okay."

"I'll get his things for you," Ms. Gillies said, and left the room.

She got Freddie to loosen his grip on her and Cristina knelt down to brush the hair away from Freddie's face. His eyes were swollen with tears now and his cheeks were still ruddy. Breath came in hiccups and spurts. "It's okay," Cristina said again. "I'm here. It's all over."

"One of the other students took a toy from him," one of the staffers said. "He hit the student and we had to separate them. He wouldn't walk to the quiet room so we had to transport him."

"I w-want to go h-home," Freddie said.

"We're going to go home," Cristina told him. "Let's just get your book-bag."

Ms. Gillies returned with the backpack. "His homework is inside and his point sheet."

"Thank you," Cristina said.

"Freddie, I'll see you tomorrow," Ms. Gillies said brightly. "Okay?"

Freddie put his head down and didn't answer.

"Oh, well," Ms. Gillies said. "He'll feel better in a little while."

THIRTEEN

GRACIELA DROVE THEM TO JOSÉ'S HOUSE. They were forced to park a block away. It was a big party tonight. Cinco de Mayo.

"Do you think José's wife will be there?" Flip asked.

"Her?" Graciela answered. "Never. She doesn't even live with him."

"Huh," Flip said. "Where does she live?"

"I don't know. Somewhere."

Coming to these get-togethers had become a ritual of a kind. The club was one place where the Indians gathered, but it was at the house that they really bonded. They were all under José's watchful eye when they ate his barbecue and drank his beer. And Flip was always aware that this was the place where he had first been with Graciela. Conflicting feelings came to him with that memory.

Walking up the sidewalk toward José's place, Flip looked for some sign of the detectives watching. Detective Salas told him they kept an eye on José, but he never saw anyone on the streets. A few of the other Aztecas said once they rousted a pair of cops who were taking pictures of a party, but Flip wasn't sure if they were telling the truth or lies.

Graciela held Flip's hand until they were almost upon the house, and then she spotted her friend Rosenda standing in the driveway. She kissed Flip on the cheek and said, "Got to go. Have fun."

"Bye," Flip said.

As he headed into the crowded house, Flip realized that he was not ready for all of this tonight. He would have preferred to spend the evening at Graciela's at her apartment, watching TV or doing other things. The noise and the music and heady clouds of smoke were too much and he could already feel himself getting a headache.

He grabbed a beer to try and quash the pain before it had a chance to take root, but it was already too late. Flip circulated to the very edge of the party, tucked away in one corner of the car park with the Lexus as a shield against the crush of bodies. The music could still get to him and the nauseating smell of cooking barbecue.

Flip wondered how long he would have to stay before he could make his excuses and get out of there. Graciela would be in no hurry to leave; she was in her element at these gatherings, always mingling, always talking. Everywhere there was someone glad to see her, even if it had only been a week since they last spoke together. Flip didn't really understand it.

At one point he spotted Emilio, looking glum with his girlfriend Alicia on his arm. Flip knew Emilio's court date was coming up, but nothing more than that. The less he knew about what the police did with his information, the less he could let slip if he was careless. Emilio spotted him watching and raised his bottle halfheartedly. Flip did the same for him.

After a while enough time had passed that Flip began to feel like he could make it the rest of the way without knuckling under completely to the pressure of the night. He was three beers in and finally they were starting to make a dent in the headache, but he was aware he hadn't eaten. The barbecue smelled no better to him.

Nasario appeared out of the partygoers spilling out of the kitchen onto the driveway. Flip saw himself be spotted. Nasario zeroed in on him.

"Hey," Nasario said when he came close.

"Hey," Flip said. His bottle of beer was empty and he had the sudden, insane urge to smash it over Nasario's head and run. He knew if he did that he would never get away.

"José's been looking for you. He wants to talk."

"Right now?"

"Right now. Come on."

Flip allowed himself to be led back into the house and down the back hallway where Graciela had taken him what seemed like forever ago. They didn't go to the bedroom, but found a door that opened onto a rear patio and a small yard. It seemed strange that no one would be there when everywhere else was packed, but when Nasario shut the door and closed the party out, Flip understood that the back yard was José's place and his alone.

José offered Flip his hand and they shook. The odor of mesquite smoke clung to José. He probably didn't even smell it anymore. "Flip," he said. "Glad you could make it."

"I never miss one of your parties, José."

"I know. And I like that."

Nasario stayed by the door, his back against it so no one else could come through. Moths fluttered around the light above him. It was still spring, but the mosquitoes were out. Flip could hear them buzzing his ears.

"How is Graciela?"

"She's good, thanks."

"When she graduates from school, I'm going to have something for her. Just a little gift. To get her started, you know?"

"Sure."

José looked left and right into the adjoining yards. They were both dark and no one stirred. He turned to Flip. "I've got something I want you to do for me, Flip."

"What do you need?"

"It's Emilio. He's been snitching."

"Emilio? No way."

"Yes way! Those *pendejos* at the District Attorney's office, they got to be sweating him pretty good on that drug beef. And a lot of Indians are getting busted right now. I can hardly put a *carnale* on a corner somewhere without the police snapping him up. Somebody's snitching. It has to be Emilio. He's trying to buy his way out of doing real time."

Flip shook his head. "I can't believe it."

"Well, start believing it. He's been coasting for a long time, anyway. Now he's snitching on the family? When's he going to turn on me?"

"What do you want me to do?"

"I want you to go to Juárez with Nasario and César. Tonight."

"José, I can't be going in and out of Juárez, I told you."

José stiffened. "You saying no to me?"

"No, I'm not, it's just—"

"You go to Juárez with Nasario and César. You take Emilio. I'll square it so you can get back to our side of the border with no problem. I'm telling Emilio it's to pick up some weed and bring it back. He's done it before. Only this time you get him over there and you pop him."

Flip's headache was gone. He could not turn away from José though he wanted to, and he could feel Nasario's eyes on him. The tiny, glass sounds of moths hitting the cover of the patio light were loud to him. "I don't know if I can do that," he said.

José took something from his pocket and pressed it into Flip's palm: a stainless-steel pistol not even as long as his hand. "It's loaded," José said. "You down?"

"You know I'm down. What about Graciela?"

"I'll tell her you had to do something for me. She doesn't need to know what."

Flip put the gun in his pocket. It couldn't weigh much more than a pound. His heart beat against his chest so that it hurt. He wished for another beer.

José clapped Flip on the shoulder. "You'll do all right."

FOURTEEN

NASARIO PUT ON THE RADIO AS THEY DROVE to Juárez. Flip sat in the back seat next to Emilio, with Nasario and César in the front. The Mexican police at the border barely even glanced at them, though Flip felt the gun in his pocket weighing him down and so cold. He wondered if Emilio was carrying and what Nasario would do if Emilio pulled his own gun.

The car wound down dark streets with little lighting, past closed businesses secured with iron. Emilio seemed to know where they were going, or if he didn't he didn't seem to mind one way or the other. Flip was afraid Emilio would catch the look on his face and the whole thing would be blown. Emilio barely glanced at him.

"Hey, man, why you driving so slow?" Emilio demanded of Nasario. "I want to get back before the party's all over."

"We're almost there," Nasario replied. Flip clenched his hands until he thought his knuckles would burst.

They drove slower and slower until they were barely crawling along. Nasario peered into the empty spaces between buildings where there were no lights at all. Finally they stopped before a broad vacant lot. Nasario killed the engine.

"¿Que carajo?" Emilio asked. "This isn't Octavio's place."

"We're gonna wait for him here," Nasario said. "Let's get out."

Flip was the last one out of the car. Emilio was already complaining about the stop, about the delay. Flip saw Nasario had his gun out and by his side as he rounded the car.

"I'm telling you, *esé—*" Emilio said.

Nasario shot Emilio through the neck and Emilio danced sideways. César drew his pistol from the waistband of his pants and put two rounds into Emilio's chest. Flip fumbled with his pocket, trying for the pistol there, as Emilio staggered out into the lot. His mouth was working and blood was coming out.

Nasario and César shot Emilio six more times before Emilio fell. Flip finally had the little gun in his hand, but he was trembling so hard he nearly dropped it. He watched from the side of the road as Nasario came close to Emilio and shot him twice more in the head.

They came back to the car. "*Gracias por tu ayuda,*" Nasario said. "You want to take a shot now?"

Flip shook his head. He was breathing shallowly and words wouldn't come. The pistol was gripped in his hand as if he were ready to throw it, not shoot it. Already Nasario and César had put their weapons away.

"Get in the car, man," Nasario told Flip.

He thought to drop the gun right where he stood, but his finger-prints were all over it and surely the police weren't so stupid that they wouldn't be able to find him. Flip stuffed the gun back into his pocket and climbed into the back seat, sitting right where Emilio had.

Nasario turned the engine over and gunned down the road with his high beams on, making for a bend up ahead and then a sharp turn north. They were within a mile of the border. If Flip looked toward the United States, he could see bright lights coming from El Paso.

The car crisscrossed its path several times and then they drove on a road parallel to the border fence. Flip couldn't make his hands be still. The bridge wasn't far.

"Here," Nasario said and they turned into the lot beside an auto shop. Cars were parked haphazardly, butting up against each other like insects in a hive. They came up alongside a long dumpster piled high with metal scrap. Nasario stopped. "Give me your piece, man."

Flip was happy to be rid of it. He pushed the gun away from himself as if it were a diseased thing and Nasario took it out of the car to the scrap loader. César went with him. Flip watched them use a red mechanic's rag to wipe the guns down and then toss them in with the metal. They came back to the car in a hurry. Within a minute they were back on the road.

He could still feel the gun in his pocket, only now it was a void where the weapon had been. Anyone who looked at him would know he had just seen a man die, he was sure of it. "Pull over," he told Nasario.

"What? We're almost there."

"Pull over!"

Nasario turned the car onto the shoulder. Flip barely got his door open before the beer in his stomach came boiling up and he vomited into the dust. He spat to clear his mouth, heaved again on an empty stomach and then closed himself in again.

César laughed and Nasario cast a smile over his shoulder. "You didn't even do anything, dumbass," César said.

"Don't tell José," Flip managed.

"Don't worry, we won't tell José nothing."

Nasario turned up the volume on a song by MC Crimen and they went on. Flip leaned his head against the window and felt the cold glass against his skin. He was not sick again.

FIFTEEN

THE FIRST THING CRISTINA THOUGHT WHEN she woke was that the ringing phone on her bed stand would wake Freddie. She smothered the phone with her hand and answered without checking the incoming number. It was four o'clock in the morning.

"Hello? Who is it?"

"It's Flip."

"Flip, it's awfully early to be calling me."

"I got to talk to you."

Cristina sat up in bed. With one ear she listened out for the sound of Freddie's feet hitting the floor, walking the short distance down the hall to her room, but it was quiet. If she was lucky, he was still deeply asleep. "What do you want to talk about?"

"I saw something tonight. I saw a guy get killed."

Now Cristina was fully awake. It was not chill in the bedroom, but her skin prickled. She slipped out of bed and found her robe. The little bit of light coming through the bedroom window was enough to see by. "Who? Where did this happen?"

"In Juárez."

"You were in Juárez again? You can't keep crossing like that, Flip."

"I didn't have a choice!"

"Tell me everything from the beginning."

She listened as Flip told the tale. The party. The order. The killing. Cristina could hear his voice quavering as he spoke and knew it was all the truth. He had never lied to her or Robinson, and this was assuredly the truth.

"Are you sure Emilio is dead?" Cristina asked. She sat in a rocking chair in the corner, and set it to moving with her foot. It did not relax her. "Absolutely sure?"

"There's no way he's still alive," Flip said. "They shot him too many times."

"And you didn't pull the trigger?"

"I never did."

"People are going to ask me what you were doing there. Whether or not you took a shot. Only one bullet and it's enough to nail you."

"I know, but I never shot him."

"They're going to say this is a lot like last time. When you went up."

"It is the same."

"Only this time you knew there was going to be a murder."

Flip was quiet. Cristina rocked the chair quickly. This is the chair she sat in when she nursed Freddie and when he would take long rests as a baby. Now the movement was as nervous as she was.

"Flip," Cristina said, "what do you want to do?"

A sigh. "José suspects me."

"No, he doesn't. José wouldn't bring you in on something like this if he didn't trust you. You're on the inside, Flip. All the way. And now that you've done this for him, he's going to trust you even more because he thinks he's got his hooks into you for a killing. Don't you see, Flip? He's blooded you, just like Enrique Garcia blooded you at Coffield."

"That time it was a stabbing. I wasn't out to kill nobody."

"The stakes are higher now."

"What happens when I keep telling you stuff and you keep

hassling José's people? He's going to know it wasn't Emilio and he's going to start looking again."

"We'll back off," Cristina said. "We'll wait a few weeks and let things cool down. If José thinks he's got the right guy, he's not going to turn his eye on you or anybody else. We can afford to give him some breathing room."

Flip paused, and then he said, "Sooner or later, it's going to come back on me."

"I don't believe that. But if you really want to put a stop to it, then I'll revoke your CI status and you can go back to being one of José's Indians. That means no more cover from the police department. You'll be on the hook for everything you do."

"You would do that?"

"I'd have to. But it's up to you, Flip. I can't make that decision for you."

"I want to do the right thing."

"Sure, I understand," Cristina said. "We all want to do the right thing."

"But…"

"Just say the word and I cut you loose."

Flip sighed again. "You don't make it easy."

"It's not my job to make it easy. My goal is to put José Martinez in prison and I'll do that sooner or later. With your help it'll be sooner, but I can wait. Right now we're talking about how you can do for yourself."

Cristina turned on a lamp and lit the corner. The sudden light hurt her eyes. She concentrated on the phone, listening to Flip's breathing, trying to divine his thoughts out of the silence. What she wanted him to say was that he would go on and the case against José would keep building, but she knew that Flip was on a knife's edge.

"You'll talk to your people about Emilio?" Flip said after a long while.

"I'll tell them exactly what you told me: that you didn't have a hand in it, that you saw it all go down. But there are going to be questions when the time comes. I'm not going to lie to you about that."

"Okay. Okay," Flip said.

"Does that mean we're still in this together?" Cristina asked.

"Yeah. I'll do it."

Cristina could hear the reservation in his voice, in the way he dragged the words out. She could not know what he was feeling, not really. Anything she thought would be speculation. "Are you going to be okay?" she asked.

"I guess I have to be."

"I'm here if you need to talk. Anytime."

"Yeah, all right," Flip said and killed the connection.

Cristina sat a while in the rocking chair, her mind working, and thought of Flip wherever he was, with the weight of death pressing on his shoulders.

SIXTEEN

Matías picked up the phone almost before it finished its first ring. "Segura," he said.

"Matías. It's Felix. I've got a body for you."

He looked around. "Felix, I'm not doing bodies right now. I have things going on."

"Oh, right, you're not interested in Los Aztecas anymore."

"I didn't say that."

"Then come out and see this body. You'll find it interesting."

"Okay. Where?"

Felix told him and Matías wrote it down. When he hung up, he gathered his jacket from the back of his chair and headed toward the elevators.

It took twenty minutes for Matías to reach the neighborhood Felix had called from. He made note of how few houses there were here and how many little businesses with chain-link fences or corrugated tin walls. The broad vacant lot where the body lay looked like it used to be something before the building there had been cleared. Lines of concrete still showed in the dirt.

The body was worth only a handful of police. Felix was the lone federal presence, the other cops part of the local force. Stakes had been driven into the ground and police tape strung between them. A white van from the city stood by to take the corpse away.

Matías shielded his eyes from the sun when he left his car. The day was dry, tending toward hot. Summer crept further and further into spring every year. The scientists called it global warming. What would it be like when he was old? Would they ever see a winter?

"Matías," Felix said when Matías came near. "Man of mystery. What do you have cooking in those offices of yours?"

"Show me the body."

"Over here."

The corpse was dressed in jeans and a t-shirt heavily stained with blood. Its face was deformed by a pair of bullets put through the center of the skull. Matías tried to estimate the number of entry wounds, but it was such a mess he couldn't tell for sure. "Expensive shoes," he said at last. "Nikes."

"He still has his jewelry and his wallet was in his pocket," Felix said. "You'll like this: he's an American."

"Really?"

"Emilio Esperanza. Address in El Paso. And look here—" Felix bent down to push the dead man's head to one side, exposing a tattoo with the stylized numbers 21.

"Azteca. One of theirs," Matías said.

"They say he's been out here three days."

"Three days? He's right by the roadside. Anyone could see him."

Felix shrugged. "I guess no one thought it was worth reporting until now."

"I can't say that's it really worth our time, either," Matías said. "So the Aztecas from the American side lose one of theirs in Juárez. It's happened before a hundred times. Two hundred times."

"This one was under indictment in El Paso," Felix said. "Come on with me."

They went to Felix's car, which squatted hot and black under the sun. Felix brought out a thick folder full of papers from the passenger seat and pulled out a thin sheet of fax paper. He handed it to Matías.

"Emilio Esperanza, out on bail," Felix said. "They put a warrant out on him when he didn't show up for his court date and faxed us just in case he crossed the border. Looks like he did, but I'm thinking maybe he didn't go willingly."

"They killed one of their own."

"Like you said, it wouldn't be the first time."

"So why bring me in?"

"You're in tight with the Americans on the Azteca thing. I thought maybe there might be a connection."

Matías touched Felix on the arm and smiled. "There may be. May I keep this?"

"Sure. You need the stiff for anything?"

"No."

Matías went back to his car. On the lot the technicians were coming for the body with a black, rubberized canvas bag. Behind the wheel he started the engine and turned on the air conditioning to chase off the heat. His jacket was too heavy for standing out in the sun.

He called a number in El Paso. The face of Emilio Esperanza stared out at him from the fax paper, obviously a booking photo. There was nothing of that face left on the corpse.

The phone was answered. "McPeek."

"Jamie, it's Matías."

"Matías. I was going to call you."

"I have a body here," Matías said. "I'd like to find out where it came from."

"Tell me everything."

SEVENTEEN

Enough time had passed that Flip had begun to think things were improving between himself and Alfredo. For one, they had started eating lunch together again, though their conversations were very short and to the point. For another, Alfredo put on the radio when they drove to and from the warehouse, which was better than the stony silence of their drives before.

When Flip had been sick from seeing Emilio killed and stayed up all night, he almost thought Alfredo was going to ask him what was wrong, but he hadn't and they went to work as usual. Alfredo didn't even reprimand him when he made a mistake that day and almost crushed one of his workmate's hands.

Alfredo hadn't said anything about what transpired between them to Flip's mother, and for that Flip was glad. He was also glad when Alfredo took his mother out for dinners and dancing because she always seemed lighter and brighter the following day, as if illuminated from the inside. Never in his life had he seen his mother that way. When Flip and Alfredo treated Flip's mother to a Mother's Day meal, she was overjoyed.

Now they sat opposite each other at one of the picnic tables, Flip eating cold cucumber soup his mother had made, Alfredo with a sandwich. Not much had passed between them that day.

"Payday today," Alfredo said.

"Yeah."

"What are you going to do with your money?"

"Same as always," said Flip. "Save some. Take Graciela out."

"You like that girl a lot, don't you?"

"Yeah, I do."

Alfredo nodded sagely and tore off another bite of sandwich. He chewed thoughtfully and then he said, "Flip, I want you to know something about me and your mother. It's important."

Flip waited.

"I was going to let your mother tell you when it was done, but I wanted you to know first so it wasn't a surprise."

"What?"

Alfredo put his sandwich down and fixed Flip with his gaze. "I'm going to ask your mother to marry me. This weekend."

Flip blinked. He heard the words, but they weren't connecting to something real that he could grasp. "Married?" he said.

"Yes. We've been seeing each other three years and I think it's time I did the right thing. I'm not going to ask if it's all right with you. I just want to know that you understand what I'm doing and why."

"No," Flip said. "I mean, yeah. I get it. You waited long enough, right?"

"That's right," Alfredo said firmly.

"Does that mean you'd be moving into our house?"

"That's up to Silvia, but if that's what she wants, then I will."

"Well, that's okay."

"You can stay," Alfredo said. "Until you've saved up enough for a place of your own. I know you want to find some work away from here. Maybe that will come through."

"Congratulations, I guess," Flip said.

"Don't say anything to your mother. And when she tells you, act surprised."

"I will."

"Okay."

Alfredo fell silent again and they finished their lunches. Flip went back to work. On that afternoon they got two trucks with the red and orange markings, the kind José had pointed out to him. One was loaded with jars of jalapeños, the other with boxes filled with corn meal. Flip wondered what the ones carrying dope would have in them. He tried to put it from his mind. José had not asked again, and Flip did not want to remind him.

The day ended and Flip met Alfredo down by the truck. Alfredo put on Tejano music and rolled his window down to let the wind in. Flip did the same. He almost smiled.

Flip didn't see the car slot in behind them, or even notice it was there until they came to a stop in front of his mother's house. There was the sound of slamming car doors from behind the truck and Flip caught movement in the side mirror.

Alfredo's door was wrenched open and two young men – kids, from Flip's point of view – dragged the man out of the truck. They started beating him before he was even clear of the cab. He went down quickly.

"No!" Flip cried and flung his door open. He rounded the nose of the truck, but two more bodies intercepted him and pushed him back. There were four around Alfredo, kicking and stomping him, and the worst part of it was their silence; they didn't shout or taunt Alfredo at all.

Flip fought to get away from the two boys holding him. He put his elbow hard into the side of one and wrenched free of the grip on his arm. They grabbed him again and put their weight on him and Flip felt himself being pulled down to the hot asphalt. He yelled Alfredo's name. "Help! Help!" he shouted.

The front door of the house opened and Flip's mother burst out. She was halfway down the walk when she started shrieking their names, Alfredo's and Flip's. One of the boys holding Flip down straightened up as if to go after her and Flip grabbed for the boy's crotch. He got a kick in the head. Blood hit the blacktop.

"Mamá, get back in the house!" Flip yelled.

"I'm calling the police!" his mother shouted back and she went for the front door.

Flip couldn't catch a glimpse of Alfredo. The boys were all over him. He tried to get a purchase on the street with his shoes and push out of the hold he was in, but it was no good.

He gathered his strength for another try when suddenly the whole crowd of boys backed off. Flip collapsed onto his face as they let him go, and saw Alfredo through a forest of moving legs. The man wasn't moving and his face was washed with red.

"Alfredo!" Flip crawled to Alfredo's side. He was still breathing. Flip cradled the man's bloody head in his hands. "No, no, no, no," he said. "Alfredo."

EIGHTEEN

THE LOBBY OF THE UNIVERSITY MEDICAL Center was oddly quiet when Cristina and Robinson stopped there to wait for Agent McPeek. An elderly woman in a wheelchair sat near the front doors, attended by a much younger lady who could have been her granddaughter. The only sound was the occasional click of footsteps, the soft ringing of a phone from time to time and the whoosh of electric doors opening and closing as people entered or left.

A row of chairs fixed together between a pair of broad-leafed, green plants provided a good view of the entrance and Cristina and Robinson sat there. It was fairly early in the morning. Bright sunlight shafted through the glass entryway and glared off the polished floors.

McPeek arrived fifteen minutes later, carrying a briefcase and dressed in another dark suit. Cristina waved her over.

"Have you been in to see him?" McPeek asked.

"Not yet. We're not even sure the doctor will give us the okay. She turned us away last night."

"Let's not wait to find out."

Alfredo Rodriguez was on an upper floor and all three of them had to show their IDs before the nurse would even summon the doctor. Cristina saw it was the same doctor who'd forbidden them access to Rodriguez the evening before. "Hello, Dr. Capra," Cristina said. "We're back."

Dr. Capra was a small woman with tense features and she looked at each of them with the same sharp expression. "Mr. Rodriguez is better this morning. I can allow you a few minutes."

"Thank you."

The doctor led them down a side hallway to a room with an open door. Inside was a single bed, no doubles here, partly shielded from the bright window by a drawn curtain. Alfredo Rodriguez was there.

Cristina knew from her last visit the extent of the damage: the broken arm and ribs, the head trauma, the smashed fingers. Looking at Rodriguez now she thought he looked terribly diminished, as though his insides had been drained away. His skin was sallow.

One eye was uncovered. Cristina saw it dart toward them as they entered.

"Mr. Rodriguez," Cristina said. "Do you remember me? I'm Detective Salas. This is my partner, Detective Robinson. And this is Special Agent Jamie McPeek of the FBI. How are you?"

Only part of Rodriguez's mouth was free to move. The jaw, Dr. Capra said, had been dislocated. Rodriguez was clear enough: "Go away."

Robinson stepped forward. "Mr. Rodriguez, we're here to help. We already know who did this to you. We just have to hear it from your lips."

"I have nothing to say."

Now it was McPeek's turn: "Mr. Rodriguez, like the detectives say, I'm from the FBI. I want you to know that we're involved in an aggressive operation against the same gang that attacked you. We can move forward without your testimony or your assistance, but it adds to the weight of the prosecution if you give us both."

"What are you going to do?"

"Everything in our power."

Rodriguez's eye flashed and Cristina thought she saw some

new attentiveness in his sour mien. "There was no one to help me before."

"We're here now," Cristina put in. "Just give us a chance to help you help yourself."

The man was quiet for a while, and if his eye hadn't stayed open, Cristina would have thought he'd gone to sleep. Then he said, "It was that bastard Flip. Felipe Morales. Him and his gang buddies."

"You're saying Morales was involved in the beating?" Cristina asked. "He called it in?"

"He was there. He was in on it."

Cristina spared a glance toward Robinson. Robinson quirked an eyebrow.

"Who's Felipe Morales?" McPeek asked.

"Mr. Rodriguez's employee," Robinson said quickly. "He's involved with the Aztecas."

"How involved are we talking about?"

"Let's hold off on that for now," Cristina said. She turned to Rodriguez. "Mr. Rodriguez, we think this beating was retaliation from José Martinez because you turned him down. I personally think he's still going to try and get your help with what he has planned."

"I wouldn't help that *hijo de puta* for any amount of money!" Rodriguez exclaimed, and then he stiffened and fell back into himself. He was still in pain, despite what the doctor was giving him.

"If you help him, you're helping us," McPeek said. "It's evidence we can use against him. We'll put him away for a long time."

"And Flip, too?"

McPeek looked confused. "Felipe Morales," Cristina explained.

"If he's a part of it, then yes," McPeek said.

Now Rodriguez did close his eye and Cristina feared he was drifting, but he opened it again and said, "If it will get them all…"

"It will."

"I can't do anything now."

"Wait until you're better," Cristina said. "They'll come to you and we'll be ready."

Dr. Capra appeared at the door. "That's enough for now," she said. "If you'll step out, Mr. Rodriguez can get some rest."

"Thank you, Mr. Rodriguez," Cristina said, and then she followed Robinson and McPeek out of the room. Dr. Capra closed the door.

"When will he be released?" Robinson asked the doctor.

"We'll hold him another day, but then he can go home."

"How long will it take him to heal?" Cristina asked.

"Six weeks. Eight at the most. He avoided serious internal damage and he managed to escape with just a concussion. He was very lucky."

"Thank you, Doctor," McPeek said. "We'll go now."

"Yes, thank you," Cristina said.

"Good-bye."

They left the floor and went down to the lobby. Cristina could sense questions bubbling up inside of McPeek. Before they reached the door, McPeek boiled over. "Who is this Felipe Morales?"

"He's our informant," Cristina said. "Very close to José. Rodriguez is dating Flip's mother. When José originally brought his offer to Rodriguez, he did it through Flip."

"When were you planning on sharing this information with me?" McPeek asked.

"When we knew we had something," Robinson said.

"Flip's the one who gave us Emilio Esperanza," Cristina said.

"Emilio Esperanza. One of José's *carnales*?"

"Right."

"Emilio was found shot to death in Juárez a few days ago."

Cristina hesitated. Then she said, "We know."

"How did you know that?"

"Our informant was… aware of the killing."

McPeek's face crossed up and she put a hand on her hip. "You're not giving up very much to the group," she said. "This operation is supposed to be about sharing information among all the involved agencies so we can work *together*. I want to meet this informant of yours."

"We promised him we'd keep him from being exposed," Cristina said. "That includes to other members of the operation."

"I know his name and where he works now. It wouldn't be that difficult to get the rest. Arrange for a meeting."

"I'll do what I can."

"No, you'll do what you're *told*," McPeek said sharply.

Cristina was silent. There was something simmering inside of her now and she did not want to give it voice.

Robinson spoke instead: "We'll work it out."

"Good."

Without saying good-bye, McPeek turned on her heel and went out through the automatic doors into the sun. Cristina remained where she was, flexing and unflexing her fingers slowly, chewing the inside of her cheek.

Robinson turned to her. "We can't fight the power," he said.

"I don't want Flip out of our control."

"We may not have that choice."

NINETEEN

Flip's mother left the house early to visit Alfredo in the hospital. She asked if Flip wanted to come, but he begged off and called in sick to work, too. Clayton, Alfredo's second in command, said he understood and told Flip to take as much time as he needed.

A long shower did nothing to relieve his tension and Flip lay on his bed naked with a towel around his waist until he felt he would bore a hole in the ceiling with his eyes. He called Graciela once, left a message, and then called again an hour later. This time she answered.

"It's me," Flip said.

"Flip! I heard what happened. Are you okay?"

"How did you hear?"

"Are you kidding? It's all over. They even had it on the news."

"They came out of nowhere," Flip said. He touched the scab on his forehead. "I couldn't do nothing."

"How is Alfredo?"

"Mamá says he's going to be all right. They busted him up good, though."

"It was José?" Graciela asked.

"Yeah."

"Listen, I'll cut classes today and come see you. You're at home?"

"I am."

"Don't go nowhere."

Flip put his phone on the stand by the bed and sat very still. Inside he was in constant motion, but his body did not react. He supposed that was how he was able to lie to the people who trusted him and betray their confidences without giving himself away; he was blank.

Eventually he got dressed and took himself to the kitchen. He dragged together the makings of a sandwich and stood at the window looking out over the back yard while he ate it. Part of him was waiting for José to call, but then he knew José didn't have to call, because his message was sent and already received. This was true of Flip and Alfredo both.

He wasn't sure what to do with himself and he was already contemplating an empty afternoon with silence and stillness for company when there was a knock on the door. Graciela waited on the step. Flip hugged her and kissed her and smelled the delicate floral scent of her perfume.

"You don't look so good, baby," Graciela said when she saw him better.

"It's the lights in here," Flip said.

"No, you really look bad. And your head!"

"It's nothing."

Flip sat on the couch and Graciela came with him, her arm around his waist and her hands on his body. He was taken with the sudden urge to shake her off, but he was glad she was here and he wouldn't do that.

"Did they hurt you bad?" Graciela asked.

"No, I said it was nothing. Alfredo is the one that got hurt. Because of me."

"How because of you?"

He would have kept it all from her, but Flip did not want to tell another lie. The story began with José's first questions about the warehouse and followed through to José's confrontation with Alfredo and the trip to Juárez. The *other* trip to Juárez. Flip would not tell her about Emilio, not ever.

"I didn't do it right," Flip said. "If I helped talk Alfredo into it, he'd be okay now."

"Baby, that's not your fault. José is the one who scared Alfredo off. What were you supposed to do? Hold him down? You did what José told you."

"I guess."

"No 'I guess'! You did what he said, even when it was your mamá's boyfriend. José should never have asked you to do that. It's not right, messing with family."

The feeling of Graciela close to him didn't bother Flip so much anymore. He pulled her closer to him, as if he could absorb her energy and make himself stronger. Flip found he didn't want her body, but just her presence. That was novel, and he tried to understand it.

"What are you going to do now?" Graciela asked.

"I don't know. Whatever José tells me to."

"Just like that?"

"How else should I be?"

"You got to tell him you won't go against your own."

"José won't listen."

"Maybe not, but you got to try."

Flip kissed Graciela on the forehead. "I'll think about it."

"Think about it *hard*."

"I'll think about it hard."

They sat together for a while, just being, and Flip found he liked this, too. It was easy to imagine, together like this, that they were in their own home. Again Flip wasn't sure where the thought came from. It didn't displease him.

PART FOUR

ONE

AFTER THE ATTACK, FLIP WAS ACUTELY AWARE of anything that happened on his street. Clayton gave him rides to and from work while Alfredo recovered, and always Flip watched for another carload of Indians following them. There never was.

Flip's mother split her time between Alfredo's place and her own, so Flip was alone more often than not. Some nights he called Graciela over and they made love on his small bed or watched television. Occasionally she would have him over to her apartment and would make them dinner in the tiny kitchen. She was not a very good cook.

They came for him in the middle of the third week, trailing behind Clayton's SUV and parking one house away when he dropped Flip off. The car came cruising up slowly after Clayton was gone and Detective Salas opened her window and waved him over. "Get in," she said. He obeyed.

"What's happening?" Flip asked, because in the pit of his stomach he knew that some change was taking place and that it was beyond his control.

"You're meeting someone new," Detective Salas said.

"Who?"

"Her name is McPeek. She's with the FBI."

Flip felt cold. "FBI?"

"She's working with us on bringing José down," Detective Robinson said.

"What does she want to see me for?"

"It's just a meeting. Nothing to worry about."

Detective Robinson drove them to a motel off I-10. Flip looked around when they got out of the car, but if anyone was watching, he didn't see them. On the second floor they knocked at a door at the end of the row. Someone on the inside let them in.

"Special Agent McPeek," Detective Salas said, "this is Felipe Morales."

Flip thought Agent McPeek was very pretty, even in her suit, but her looks weren't important. The woman had an open briefcase on one of two queen-sized beds and there were photographs spread around. She offered her hand for Flip to shake. She had a firm grip. "Felipe," she said.

"Call me Flip."

"Okay, Flip. Have a seat. Right there on the bed. Good."

Detective Salas and Detective Robinson remained standing. Flip wondered if they would sit down, but they looked as uncomfortable being there as he was. He was curious what their relationship to Agent McPeek was. Was she like José was to him?

McPeek sat on the other bed next to the photographs. "I've heard a lot about you, Flip," she said. "You're giving Detectives Salas and Robinson good information. That's very helpful. Thank you."

"Sure," Flip said.

"Flip, I don't know if you realize this, but you're in the middle of a pretty high-stakes game. We're out to get José Martinez and his whole crew."

"Does that include me?"

"It can, but the detectives tell me you're too valuable to waste. I happen to agree, otherwise we wouldn't be talking right now."

"What can I do?"

McPeek smiled. Flip wasn't sure if it was for real. "For starters, you can keep doing what you're doing: informing on local Aztecas and telling us when big deals go down."

"I don't know anything about big deals."

"That's not what I heard. I heard that you're in the middle of one of those big deals. It involves your work and some trucks headed up from Mexico."

Flip looked toward Salas and Robinson. They were stony-faced. "José doesn't tell me everything."

"He told you enough. He showed you where the trucks are coming from, even which trucks to watch out for. And I hear he trusts you with other things: like when someone has a green light put on them." McPeek picked up one of the photos and showed it to Flip. The man in the picture was all but unrecognizable. "Do you know who this is?"

Flip nodded.

"Who is it?"

"Emilio."

"Emilio Esperanza?"

"Yeah."

"José personally ordered a green light on Esperanza?"

"Yeah, he did."

"And he ordered your boss beaten, too," McPeek said. It was not a question.

"I didn't know about that."

"But it was him."

"It had to be."

"Flip, I'd like to show you some more pictures and if you can, I'd like you to tell me who they are. Can you do that for me?"

"Sure."

McPeek took up the photographs one by one and held them for Flip to see. Some were local Indians, guys whose names he'd picked up from parties and the club. Some he didn't know. McPeek said it was all right that he didn't. "I don't expect you to know the Mexican side of the operation."

Whenever Flip gave McPeek a name, she used a Sharpie to

make a note on the back of the picture. Flip guessed it was half an hour before she was done showing him photos. She gathered them up and stacked them neatly into a folder. The folder went into her briefcase.

"That was very helpful, Flip," McPeek said.

Flip now recognized the tone she used: it was the way a teacher would talk to little kids, only it was a grown woman talking to a grown man. He decided then that he didn't like McPeek. Detective Salas and Detective Robinson didn't seem to, either.

"Do you think José will approach your boss again?" McPeek asked.

"I don't know. Maybe. Now that he knows Alfredo's scared."

McPeek nodded. "Flip, I'd like you to step things up a little bit. The detectives tell me you have access to José. I'd like you to use it. And I'd also like you to wear a wire."

"A wire?"

"Yes. If José's willing to talk to you about what he's doing with those trucks, I want to get it recorded. You'd wear a wire and a digital device that stores everything. It's smaller than a pack of cigarettes. The wire is very light."

"I haven't seen José in weeks."

"But he's going to come to you eventually."

"I guess."

"This would be a big help to us, Flip. You record José, you record any Azteca you have contact with. All the information you can provide is valuable. And if you testify—"

"I already told Detective Salas I won't testify."

"Flip, you don't have a choice. You're at least an accessory to one murder we know of and you're right on the inside of a conspiracy to smuggle drugs into the United States. If you don't work for us – and I mean *work* for us – that means you go down with the rest of them when the time comes. The time for cutting deals is now."

Flip looked to Detective Salas. "I tried to tell you," she said.

"If I testify, what about my family, my girl?" Flip demanded. His heartbeat picked up.

"We can offer protection if it becomes necessary," McPeek replied.

"José already had Alfredo beat all to shit," Flip said. "What's he going to do to me?"

"Better you be on the outside under our care than on the inside with the people you turned on," McPeek said.

Flip's hands were shaking. He made fists of them. "You don't understand."

"I've done plenty of these cases," McPeek said. "Believe me, I understand. And the detectives understand. We *all* understand. Do you understand that we have no choice? We have to use you. There is nobody else."

Flip gripped his hands until the knuckles bled white. "Okay."

McPeek let out a sigh, as if she had been holding her breath. "Good. The detectives will be in touch with you. They'll provide you with the wire and how to use it. In the meantime, get as close to José Martinez as you can. Anything you hear, no matter how trivial, you pass it on."

"Okay," Flip said lifelessly.

"Don't be afraid, Flip. We're going to be right behind you."

TWO

MATÍAS RECEIVED A CALL FROM JAMIE McPeek that lasted almost an hour. He took extensive notes, drawing circles around names and connecting them with arrows and lines. Large blocks of the flowchart were missing: the Mexican parts. Paco was doing what he could to fill them in, but the rest was up to Matías.

"They're going to move soon," McPeek told him.

"Weeks? Months?"

"Once they get the warehouse manager roped in, it'll just be a matter of time before they're ready to start shipping. ATF's already tracked three separate shipments of weapons from Texas into Mexico. I'll have all the serial numbers and information faxed to you. You'll have them by tomorrow."

"Good-bye, Jamie."

"*Adiós*, Matías."

Matías hung up the phone and looked over his notes again. They were lucky on the American side to have a voice on the inside of José Martinez's operation. No member of Los Aztecas was lining up to give information to the police in Ciudad Juárez, though Matías would have paid dearly for the source.

Paco looked up from his desk. "Good news?" he asked.

"There'll be some faxes coming in from Agent McPeek. About guns the Aztecas are taking in."

"I don't like it when they let guns across the border," Paco said.

"It's too dangerous. We might not get them all."

"Try not to think about it," Matías said. He stretched and looked at his watch. It was time to be gone from here. "Anyway, I'll see you tomorrow."

"Oh, I put a dedicated team on Víctor Barrios," Paco said.

"And?"

"Nothing so far. If he goes to the depot, we'll know right away."

"What about José's contact there?"

"Oh, yes! I have that. One second. Here it is: Gonzalo Flores."

"Do we know anything about him yet?"

"The depot is locally owned, so we can't get his work records without alerting the whole place to what we're up to. I made an official request for his financial records as soon as we got the name. They tell me it'll take forty-eight hours."

"All right."

Matías stood up and put on his jacket. It was home to another microwaved meal eaten in front of the television set and then a night spent sleeping alone. Elvira hadn't come back from her sister's and talking seemed to do no good. Matías didn't know how long she could stay away from her firm and keep her job.

He left Paco behind and took the elevator down to the basement level. It was nighttime when he drove onto the street, though the guards around the building were no less vigilant. He took the long way home, watching the few brave pedestrians that ventured onto the streets after dark, ghosting buses from the *maquiladoras* that trundled through the city on the way to rundown neighborhoods and *colonias* alike.

His key stuck in the lock of the inner door of the vestibule at his apartment building, but some wrangling got it to turn and he was inside and up the stairs. The apartment itself was as dark and neglected as it had been when he left. Dishes had begun to accumulate in the sink and something unpleasant was rotting in the kitchen trash.

It took a half-hour to wash the dishes and the garbage went into the chute. Matías found he was ravenous and consumed two microwaved meals instead of one, electing to eat them out of their plastic trays rather than dirty the dishes all over again. There was a recorded *fútbol* match on the television and though he was a fan of neither team, he watched the whole thing.

He noted the time and thought about going to sleep, but he wasn't ready yet. Unbidden, his phone was in his hand and he was speed-dialing. Elvira answered right away.

"Good evening, my love," Matías said, and he muted the television.

"It's late, Matías."

"Were you sleeping?"

"No."

"Then there's no harm in me calling."

"What do you want, Matías?"

"I want you to come home."

There was the murmur of a sigh from Elvira's end, and then she said, "I don't know. I still haven't made up my mind."

Matías flicked through voiceless channels as he talked. Finding nothing, he snapped off the television. "If you won't come home, then at least talk to me when I call. I miss the sound of your voice."

"I miss yours."

"You can hear it all the time if you come home."

"Don't keep pushing."

"I will. I will until you give this up and come back to where you belong."

"My sister says I could get legal work in Monterrey. We could move here."

"And what would I do?" Matías asked.

"You could do private security."

Matías thought about everything that had happened, everything that was going to happen. The depot. The trucks. He shook his head, though Elvira couldn't see. "I'd be no good at it."

"Won't you think about it?"

"All right, I'll think about it."

"Thank you."

"Now tell me about your day. Don't leave anything out."

"Won't you be bored?"

"I'll never be bored with you."

THREE

ALFREDO CAME TO FLIP'S MOTHER'S HOUSE
for a quiet celebration of the Fourth of July. Graciela was there
to make four and they cooked hot dogs and hamburgers on the
grill and set off fireworks in the back yard. The entire time Alfredo
didn't say a word to Flip, nor would he look in Flip's direction.

Flip thought his mother must have seen what was happening,
but she said nothing and neither did he. After a long, uncomfortable quiet where both men drank beers nearly side by side without
speaking, Flip finally made his excuses and left with Graciela.

She took him to her apartment and they made quiet love on her
mattress on the floor. Afterward they lay together with the sheet
pulled over them as the air conditioner in the window rumbled
away. Flip thought he heard something dripping inside.

"Party at José's tonight," Graciela said.

"I guess we have to go," Flip said.

"Have you talked to José since... you know, since?"

"No."

There had been no calls, no visits, no sign of any Indian. Some
days coming home from work Flip almost felt like the storm had
passed him over and he was still whole. The wire and recorder the
detectives gave him was in his pocket. He had put it there that
morning, perhaps unconsciously knowing that he would need it.

"What will you say to him? Will you tell him to leave Alfredo
alone?"

"I don't know."

"You said you would think about it."

"I have thought about it, and I don't know."

Quiet, and in the silence the sound of water. The air conditioner was definitely leaking. Flip wished he knew how to fix stuff like that. He liked to do things for Graciela, the way a guy should do for his girl. Like Alfredo did for his mother.

"Flip, I have to tell you something," Graciela said after a while.

"What?"

"I'm pregnant."

Flip started and looked at Graciela where she was settled against his body. "What did you say?" he asked, though he knew.

Graciela sat up and pulled the sheets around her to cover her breasts. "Don't be mad! I promise I didn't do it on purpose!"

"How can you be pregnant?"

"Well, you haven't used nothing all the times we've been together."

"I thought you were taking the pill or something!"

"No, I wasn't. Oh, now you're mad."

Flip's head whirled. He climbed up off the mattress and took two uneven steps to the couch before sitting down heavily. The couch was scratchy against his bare skin. "Are you sure?" he asked.

"I've missed a couple of times now, so I took one of those home pregnancy test things. It was positive," Graciela said. Her face was screwed up and she looked as though she was about to cry. Flip felt the urge to go to her.

"I don't believe it," Flip said.

"Do you hate me?"

"No, I don't hate you! Just give me a minute to think, okay?"

Flip had too many thoughts clamoring for attention at once. He flashed on Alfredo and his mother and the men at work and even his PO, Mr. Rubio. What would they say about this? What would they do? And there was José in the middle of it and he was laughing at Flip for being a fool.

After he had been quiet for a long time, Graciela said, "I don't have to have it."

"What?" Flip said. "No way! We're not doing that!"

Graciela sniffed and now she was crying, wiping away tears as fast as they could course down her cheeks. The sheets were still clutched around her, a dark pool holding her body unseen. "I didn't know. Some guys—"

"I'm not some guys!" Flip declared. "And I say you're not going to do that. You hear? It's not gonna happen."

"Flip, I love you."

Flip pressed his hands to the sides of his head. He got up and stalked the room. "No, no, this is all wrong! It's not supposed to happen like this!"

"I'm sorry! I promise I didn't mean to!" Graciela said and the tears came faster than before. She was breathing erratically and her shoulders shook. Flip couldn't stand it any longer and he went to her on the mattress and put his arms around her and pulled her close to him.

"You don't have to be sorry," Flip said, and he said it calmly though his heart was hammering and he felt as though his head might float away. "It's not your fault. I should have been more careful. I was stupid."

"Do you love me, Flip?"

Flip closed his eyes. "Yes, I love you. I love you both."

"You love our baby?"

"Of course I do. And you're gonna be the best mamá there is."

"You'll be a good father, Flip. I know it."

Flip shushed her and held her and rocked her gently back and forth. She cried freely, but he did not let go. A father. He would be a father. That was not something to hide from, to run away from. He was a father and Graciela was the mother.

When there were no more tears, Flip lifted Graciela's head and kissed her softly on the lips. Her face was flushed and her eyes red-rimmed. It did not make her look beautiful, but Flip didn't care. He kissed her again. "I want to marry you," he said. "I don't want our baby to be born without a mamá and a papá. I want it the way it should be."

"Do you mean it, Flip?"

"Yeah, I mean it," Flip said and he held her again.

FOUR

FLIP WANTED TO KEEP GRACIELA WITH HIM when they went to the party, but she went to circulate and he could not stop her. For the baby's sake, he hoped she wouldn't drink. Graciela was smart. She wouldn't.

There was nothing to stop him from drinking and he set to it without any prompting, liberating two bottles of beer from a cooler and drinking them quickly, one after the other. When they were gone, he got more. One Indian, a kid named Oscar, cheered him on as he had a fourth and then a fifth.

Alcohol coursed through his veins and his head felt lifted before he finally headed toward the flaming heart of the party that was José's grill. Flip armed himself with a paper plate and stood in line as José doled out servings of chicken and beef. It was difficult for Flip to remember a time when he wasn't here, begging for food off José's table; it seemed like it had gone on forever. He resolved to drink more beer.

"Flip!" José said when it was Flip's turn. "Chicken for you!"

"Thanks," Flip said without enthusiasm.

"I want to talk to you later. Out back."

Flip felt sick to his stomach, the beers curdling. Out back. Where José ordered Emilio killed. A tremor started in his right hand, his gun hand. "Okay," he said thickly. "I'll be there."

"Nasario will get you."

Eating something quelled the sick feeling, but there was still nervous pressure in his guts that did not go away. He cornered himself in the kitchen and found that his enthusiasm for further drinking was dampened. The taste of beer wouldn't leave his mouth, despite the barbecue sauce and the spice.

He saw Nasario cruising through the partygoers like a barracuda. When Nasario spotted him, he jerked his head for Flip to follow and Flip did follow because to do nothing was to invite José's displeasure. Emilio had died because of José's displeasure.

Like before, the back yard was a place of peace, with the sounds of the party closed off, muted. Flip expected to see César, but instead it was one of the big men that served as José's bodyguard. This man's name was Angel, or maybe it was Fernando. Flip wasn't sure who was who.

José shook Flip's hand. "All right," he said. "The man."

"What's up, José?" Flip asked. His words were relaxed, but he was not. All he could see was the way Emilio jogged to one side when the bullets started to hit him, the final barks of the pistol in Nasario's hand as he shot Emilio in the face. The weight of the gun in his hand. The gun he never fired.

"Your boss, Alfredo, is coming back to work soon, huh?" José asked.

"Yeah. This week."

"I want you to take my offer to him again, see what he says."

"About the trucks coming in?" Flip asked.

"About the trucks coming in. The ones with our stuff on them. We make a call, tell him which truck to watch out for and he sets it aside. I'll pay him a thousand dollars a truck, which is more than he ought to get. *Cabrón.*"

Flip nodded, but didn't say anything else.

"You okay, Flip? You look a little sideways."

"I'm okay. I think I drank too much."

"At least you're not driving. And listen, Flip: when this is over I want you to get your patch and come work for me for real. We'll have a lot of stuff to move and I need people I can trust."

"But my job at the—"

"Hey, they can keep you on the books," José said, "but you're going to be a full-time *sargento*. You got to step up for the family now, *entiende*? I got faith in you, man. Don't let me down."

"Okay, José."

"Now go back to the party. We'll talk after you see your boss."

"All right, José."

"Oh, hey, Flip: keep an eye out for cops. I got my ear out and I hear there's a couple of cops in the gang unit pushing all these busts on our people. We're gonna deal with them, too, when the time comes."

Nasario held the door for Flip and Flip went back to the noise and the bustle. The tremor in his hand was back, but making a fist made it go away. He went down a side hallway to the bathroom and locked himself in.

The bathroom was small and the mirror had painted filigree around the edges so Flip looked like he was framed in a picture. He saw that he was sweating and had circles under his eyes. How could they not know? How could José talk to him and not suspect? Flip didn't understand.

He lifted his shirt and exposed the white wire underneath. He peeled the sticky tape that held it to his body and pulled the recorder itself out of his pants. The wire wrapped around the little black box and he shoved both into his pocket. Anything else that was said tonight would have to be off the record.

Flip closed the toilet lid and sat down on it, his head in his hands. If he concentrated, his breathing was steady and even. Alfredo's face materialized out of darkness and sat squarely in his mind's eye, staring at him with judgment in his eyes. His mother would be ashamed of him for this and so much more, and compromising the man she loved was yet another betrayal.

Graciela. He thought of her and the burden lightened. This girl, this woman, would be his wife and only good things would come from her. When Flip turned in his recordings and said his bit in court, she would still be there for him and all of this would have been worthwhile.

Someone pounded on the door and jarred Flip out of his thoughts. "Hey, hurry up in there!" a man's voice said. "I got to take a leak, man!"

He washed his hands in the sink and dried them on a little green towel. A stranger waited in the darkened hallway when he opened the door. "Sorry," Flip said.

"Yeah, okay, man. I got to go!"

I've got to go, too, Flip thought. He needed to find Graciela and leave this place. They could find a restaurant open and have something to eat that didn't taste of José's mesquite grill. And most of all it would be quiet, inside and out.

FIVE

Robinson was on Cristina's phone when she returned to her desk. He murmured a good-bye and hung up. His mouth was a flat line underneath his mustache. Cristina said, "What?"

"I just heard from our boy, Flip. He was at a party with José last night."

"Good," Cristina said. "McPeek told me that the DEA got access to a house across the street and have José's place under twenty-four-hour surveillance. Better than we ever got. They're pulling every plate and face going into or out of there."

Robinson did not look pleased. "Cris, he said José's talking about green-lighting cops."

Cristina sat down. "What did he say?" she asked. "What did he say *exactly*?"

"Flip says José's got his eye on a couple of cops in the gang unit. It doesn't take a lot of brainpower to figure out who he means. José's talking about dealing with the problem."

"He wouldn't," Cristina said.

"Wouldn't he? This guy's moving up in the world: he's opening up a goddamned expressway for moving dope into the city, for Christ's sake."

"It's a big jump from trafficking to killing cops," Cristina said. "This isn't Juárez."

"Maybe he'll bring in outside talent. The Aztecas from Juárez won't have a problem doing it. He could pay them off with money and guns, and they'd just disappear back over the border like they were never here."

"He's got to know we'd come down on him like nobody's business."

"Except he'd be clean. All his people would be clean."

The idea settled in Cristina's mind. She remembered the call from McPeek telling her that Matías Segura had been targeted and how she reflexively thought, *it can't happen here*. But it *could* happen here.

Los Aztecas were used to having their own way on the streets of Juárez, accountable to no one but the cartel. Barrio Azteca was the original, but now they were like the shadow cast by their Mexican brethren, aping what happened across the border. Killing innocents. Killing their own. Killing cops.

"Flip," Cristina said. "We've got to get him together with José again and he's got to figure out how to get José to say he wants us dead in so many words."

Robinson shook his head. "I wouldn't count on that."

"Why *not*? José's trusted him this far."

"The kid is scared, Cris. I could hear it in his voice. He's already watched somebody get killed. Who's to say he won't be the next body?"

Cristina grabbed for her phone. "I'll talk to him. He listens to *me*."

"Give him a break! He doesn't need you talking in his ear right now."

"He called me."

"And he heard from me. I say you back off and let him get his head together. He's risking his ass every time he uses his phone."

She let go of the receiver and let it fall back into place. "So we do nothing."

"No, we just take a different approach. We can't lay it all on the back of one informant. The first thing we do, we report the threat to Cokley and arrange for some extra patrols near my house and yours. Then we call McPeek and let her know what's happening. She'll spread the word to everybody else in the chain. I promise you: everybody's going to take this seriously."

"Bob, I live less than a mile from José Martinez's place. If somebody's got a target on their back, it's going to be me," Cristina said. She checked her watch. "Freddie's going to be home soon. I should be there."

"You want me to tell Cokley?" Robinson asked.

"He doesn't need to hear it from both of us. I'd feel better if I was there at the bus stop."

"You can't be there all the time."

"Just for today. We'll work something out for after."

"Meet back here?" Robinson asked.

"Okay. Thanks, Bob."

"Be careful out there."

Cristina left the building and by the time she reached her car she was walking fast. The clock was ticking too quickly, though it was only a matter of minutes to drive from Central Regional Command to her home. On the road every stop sign was an imposition and everyone seemed to be driving too slowly.

Ashlee wasn't answering her phone. Cristina passed Nachita's, a little meat market and grocery where she and her mother used to shop when Cristina was little. There was relief when she saw the house with Ashlee's car parked in front of it. Cristina's tires rubbed the curb when she stopped.

Down at the end of the block she saw a familiar figure. She did not run, but she walked fast until she was close enough to shout, "Hey, Ashlee!"

The girl turned away from the street and waved. When Cristina was closer, she said, "Hello, Ms. Salas. What are you doing here?"

"Why aren't you answering your phone?" Cristina demanded.

"What? Oh, I must have shut the ringer off. Is everything okay?"

Cristina looked up and down the street. If there were strangers around, she would have seen them. "I thought I'd come by," Cristina answered, too rapidly. "Make sure everything was all right. Check on Freddie."

"Here comes his bus now."

The little yellow bus came up the street and stopped at the corner, red lights flashing. Cristina saw Freddie's outline moving on the other side of the windows and then he was coming down the steps with his book bag in one hand and a papier-mâché cat painted blue in the other. "Mom," he said.

"Hey, peanut," Cristina said and she knelt down to hug him. He accepted this passively. "How are you?"

"Fine," Freddie said. "Are you home?"

"I'll be home for a little while, but then I have to go back to work," Cristina said.

"I want to play Roblox."

"Okay," Cristina said.

"Are you sure you're all right, Ms. Salas?" Ashlee asked. "You look flushed."

"It's nothing," Cristina said. "The weather. It's hot."

"Yeah, I know what you mean."

"Freddie, let's get inside," Cristina said and she let Freddie lead the way. She did not stop watching the street.

SIX

THOUGH ALFREDO WAS BACK ON THE JOB, Clayton drove Flip home and the first thing he did was take a shower. He wiped the steam off the mirror and lathered his face for a shave. One cheek was clean when he heard a rap on the bathroom door. His mother was there.

Flip looked from her face to the battered shoebox she held in her hands. It was obvious she had been crying. "What's wrong, Mamá?" he asked.

"I don't want to interrupt," his mother said. "When you're finished, I want to talk to you."

"Sure."

He hurried through the rest of his work and dried his face with a clean towel. After he dressed in new clothes he went looking for his mother. She was in the living room, the shoebox balanced on her knees. As he came in, she wiped her eyes with the back of her hand. "Come on in, Felipe," she said.

"Why are you crying, Mamá?" Flip asked.

"Sit here. Next to me."

Flip sat. His mother wrapped one small arm around his shoulder and found it hard to do. Flip's eyes fell on the shoebox, which was plain and brown with no brand name on it.

"Flip, I want you to know that I love your father. I have always loved him and I won't stop ever. Do you believe me?"

"Yes."

"Alfredo asked me to marry him. Yesterday, after you left. Here is the ring."

Flip didn't know how he'd managed to miss the ring. It was a pretty gold one with a diamond that was not small. Flip wondered just how much Alfredo had saved to buy it. "That's great, Mamá," he said. "I'm really glad for you."

"I went into the closet and found some of your father's things. I thought maybe you might want to have them."

She presented him with the box and for a moment Flip wasn't sure if he was meant to open it now or wait. His mother didn't look away, so he took off the top. The first thing he saw was a tie.

There was a watch that wound by hand, its crystal cloudy and cuff links and a few photographs of Flip as a child, and of his mother and his father together when she was much younger. Flip noticed for the first time how much alike he and his father looked. Perhaps it only took time.

Most of the things were worthless. A clip to go with the tie. Some papers for a car his mother didn't own anymore. At the bottom was a folding knife with a carved handle. The image was of a deer with a full rack of antlers standing on a hillock with a stream flowing beside it. Flip found the deer mesmerizing and he forgot everything else when he lifted the knife from the box. He opened the blade. It was as long as his middle finger.

"Your father used to whittle with that," Flip's mother said.

"He whittled?"

"He was always a country boy."

Flip slipped the knife into his front pocket. "Thank you," he said.

"I'm sorry there's not more."

"It's plenty."

Flip's mother hugged him again and kissed him on the cheek. "I'll make something for you to eat," she said.

"Okay."

She left him with the box. Flip took it to his room and sorted out the things he wanted from the things he didn't. The photographs went on top of his chest of drawers. Maybe he would buy frames for them. The tie was ugly, but he decided to keep it. The same with the cufflinks and tie clip. The rest he put in the trash can. He would throw it out later, when his mother wouldn't see.

An engine rumbled on the street. Flip looked out his window and saw Alfredo parking in front of the house. All at once the warm feeling he'd had drained away and he was cold. His skin prickled as if he was standing in the open door of the refrigerator.

He got to the front door before Alfredo had a chance to ring the bell. Alfredo stopped short when he saw Flip.

"I'm here for your mother," Alfredo said.

"I know."

"I don't have nothing to say to you."

"I got something I need to say to you."

"Say it out here, then. I don't want Silvia to hear."

Flip moved out onto the front step and to his credit Alfredo did not retreat. There may have been the slightest of twitches in the man's cheek, but he did not show fear. When Flip looked into his eyes, he found only anger. Flip did not blame him.

"You want me to meet with your boss again?" Alfredo asked.

"No. You don't have to see him again."

"Then what?"

Flip gave Alfredo the offer just as José told him to. When he got to the payment, Alfredo made a face as if he was going to spit in Flip's eye. He didn't, and when Flip was done he was very quiet. "So?" Flip asked.

"When is this going to happen?"

"I don't know. Soon."

"Then you don't need to talk to me anymore."

"I guess not."

"You still going to work?"

"For now."

"Until you can make better money dealing drugs," Alfredo said.

Flip dropped his gaze. "I'll tell Mamá you're here."

"Thank you," Alfredo said, and it sounded like a curse.

SEVEN

MATÍAS WAITED IN THE HALLWAY WITH Galvan while Sosa did his work. It seemed they were always together, the three of them, in the damp hallway outside the interview rooms, and always under the same circumstances. Someday, Matías thought, he would have to invite them for lunch. Anything to get them out in the clean daylight, away from the smell of concrete, urine and blood.

This was not a place for small talk, so Matías and Galvan stood silently, each staring at the door to the first interview room, willing it open. Matías hoped he would not have to send in Galvan at all, that Sosa would be able to apply the pressure he needed to make things happen.

A few minutes later, the door opened and Sosa came out. He was sweating heavily and there were large circles of dark wetness under his arms. He patted his forehead with his tie. When the door fell shut behind him, he said, "It's done."

"Thank you, my friend," Matías said.

He went in. Víctor Barrios was stripped to the waist and his heavily tattooed chest was blotched with purplish, fresh bruises. The man sagged in his chair and might have been dead except for a slow, barely visible rise and fall of his shoulders. Víctor didn't even react when the door closed again.

Matías had no notebooks this time, no files. None of the things with which he would make theater for the *entrevistado*. He had lost track of the number of men he had broken in here, or had broken for him. The number of confessions must have topped a hundred. Matías could have played his role tonight, but he didn't have the patience for it.

"Wake up," he said. "I know you're not unconscious."

Víctor stirred. He cracked an eye and regarded Matías suspiciously. "What do you want?" he asked.

"Your life," Matías said. "I'm going to have you killed tonight."

The man opened both eyes now and a visible shudder passed through his body, though the shackles that held him to the table kept him from falling from his chair. "You wouldn't," he said.

Matías stood across from Víctor. The odor of urine hit him again and he realized there was a pool of it coming from underneath the table, starting at Víctor's feet. He wrinkled his nose and tried to breathe through it. "The record of your arrest has already been destroyed," Matías said. "No one knows you're here except myself and two other officers. The guards won't remember you after a couple of hours. It will be as if you never existed."

"Who the hell are you?"

"That's not important. What is important is you cooperating with me in every way you can. If I'm satisfied, then you live. If not, then you disappear. One more body on the pile in Juárez. Except I'll do one better than you Aztecas: I'll let you keep your arms and legs on. The head will have to go."

"I don't know how I can help you. The other one, he wouldn't answer anything. I asked him why and he kept on..."

"You think you're being treated badly," Matías said.

Víctor kept his silence. At least he had learned that much.

"Tell me now why you have been meeting with Gonzalo Flores."

"Gonzalo Flores?"

"Don't tell me you don't know him," Matías said. "If you lie to me—"

"No! I know him. He's the manager of a shipping depot. He deals with fresh produce trucks."

"Fresh produce trucks headed where?"

"To the United States."

"And what does Julio Guerra want with them?"

Víctor shrank into his chair.

Matías stepped forward and slammed his hand on the table. "*What does Julio Guerra want with them?*"

"It's not Guerra! It's an American. José Martinez."

"I'm not interested in him, I'm interested in Guerra!"

"Guerra's trading drugs for guns with José Martinez!"

"Drugs from where?"

"I'll tell you exactly where! I'll tell you anything you want to know!"

Matías eased back from the table and let his voice relax. "You're going to do better than that. You're going to take police to the places where the drugs are stored and point them out. You're going to tell us when those drugs are going to be shipped through Gonzalo Flores' depot. And you're going to be *happy* about doing it."

"Please…"

"Spare me. I had some of you Azteca *cabrones* try to kill me and my wife. If you think I'm going to sit back and take that kind of treatment, you're out of your mind."

"I had nothing to do with that. I don't even know who you are!"

"And you're not going to find out! If you hear my name, it's because I whispered it to you before blowing your goddamned brains out."

Víctor began to cry, great tears rolling down his face. His hair was mussed, standing straight up in places, and his body was streaked with perspiration. Matías thought the puddle of piss grew larger.

"Shut up! Shut up or I'll kill you right here, right now!" Matías said. He drew his pistol and held it at his side so that Víctor could see it.

"*¡Por favor, no!*"

"You will do what you've been asked to do, yes?"

"Yes."

"You'll inform on your own people when you are asked to, yes?"

"Yes!"

"Do I have to send my friend in here again to make sure? He'll step on your balls until they break."

"No, no, I'll do anything you ask! Please, don't kill me."

Matías holstered his weapon. Almost unconsciously he adjusted his tie at his throat. "I'm tired of playing games with you sons of bitches," he said. "It ends now."

EIGHT

CRISTINA LET FREDDIE PLAY HIS GAME. SHE returned to work for a few hours, but got nothing done. When she returned, she got him into bed on time, but she wasn't tired. She tried tranquilizing herself with a beer, sitting on the couch, a cooking program on the television. Every time headlights flashed in the street she tensed up all over again.

Again and again she had caught herself thinking about what she would do if José Martinez's men struck. Her route to work was straightforward and wouldn't take anyone watching long to figure out. Freddie's schedule was absolute and could not be tampered with; any deviation could set him into a tailspin and ruin his entire day. He had to be up at the same time, be put to bed at the same time and all things must happen in a regimental order, even walking to the bus.

She found that she wasn't concerned for herself. It wasn't as though she didn't care if some Azteca soldier found her on the street, but she didn't think of the eventuality as something that affected her and her alone. If she had to, she could take a bullet. She wasn't afraid of that. She feared only for Freddie.

If she was gone, Freddie had no one to look out for him. No grandparents, no aunts or uncles. His father might be tracked down, though it would take time. In the meanwhile he would pass into the foster system, one that was completely inadequate for his needs. Cristina was sure everyone would mean well and that they would try, but it would not be enough. It could never be enough. Freddie needed his mother.

Cristina was on her second bottle and was not soothed. She decided to put the lights out in the front room and stand in the dark, peering out onto the street through the parted curtains, watching for any sign. If they were keeping track of her already then they were better than she gave them credit for. That a bunch of overgrown hard-drinking, hard-partying children could make her so anxious gave her pride a twist. She had to remember that they were kids with guns.

She wasn't sure how Matías Segura managed it, living on the Juárez side of the border. When McPeek told her that he had been targeted there had been shock, but also a deeper understanding that this was what passed for normal in the city to the south. In America they called it a War on Drugs, but in Mexico it was literally war. How long could they keep it contained on the other side of the fence? It could start with her. With Freddie.

Freddie was deeply asleep when she went to his door, breathing loudly in his small bed. Soon he would outgrow it and need a full-sized mattress. Cristina was losing her little boy. For an instant she saw him in her arms, soaked in blood, and she covered her face reflexively to make the image go away. Things would not end that way.

For a while she sat down beside his bed, letting the big red numbers on his clock slip by. He didn't stir when she rested a hand on his chest. She could feel his heart beating. Once again, for the thousandth time, she wondered what he could be dreaming about. Was it elevators and Roblox, or did his intensely literal mind finally let go in sleep and take to the skies in fancy?

Cristina felt like she might cry and she retreated from the room, pulling the door just to. In her bedroom she used her phone to call Robinson. He answered right away. "Hey," she said.

"Hey, yourself. You're up late."

"You, too."

"I can't sleep. It happens sometimes. What's your excuse?"

"You know. All of this. Freddie. He doesn't deserve to be caught up in what's happening."

"There's nothing that says you have to stay there," Robinson said. "You could get a hotel room for a little while, change things up. You're practically on José's doorstep, living where you are. I worry, too."

"I can't leave here, Bob. Freddie wouldn't understand and he needs to have his things."

"What, then?"

Cristina sat on the edge of her bed and kicked off her shoes. Sleep was no closer than it had been before, but maybe the act of undressing and lying down would make her body react. It was worth a try.

"Cris? What do you want to do?"

"I think we should talk to McPeek about closing this out. The whole thing. We have enough to take down José and I'm sure they've got solid enough charges against his *soldados* to reel in a serious catch."

"You think she'll go for it?"

"Maybe. If I say we're going to pull Flip, she might be amenable to the change. Without him they don't have the warehouse, they don't have the Juárez killing… it takes a lot off the table."

Robinson was quiet, and then he said, "You know she'll just take over from us. She's got her hooks into Flip as much as we do. And he'll have to go along because otherwise she'll have him back at Coffield doing time for everything. He won't last a stretch inside if anyone guesses what he was up to."

"I'm running out of options to play," Cristina said.

"If you want to talk to her, then we'll talk," Robinson said. "Maybe she'll listen up when she hears José's thinking about green-lighting cops. It would make me pay attention."

"I don't know if that will be enough. It's just talk."

"José's cold enough to order one of his own men shot just because he *might* make a deal with the state. He's cold enough to take out a police officer. For my money, that's worth a trip to jail."

"She wants this warehouse deal," Cristina said.

"We can't always get what we want. When do you want to see her?"

"Tomorrow," Cristina said. "Let's do it tomorrow."

"All right. In the meantime, get some rest; you're no good to me fried."

"Yes, sir."

"Good night."

NINE

"LET ME GET THIS STRAIGHT," McPEEK SAID. "You want us to make our move now, when we still have a case to make? That's what you're saying, right?"

They sat in McPeek's office with the door closed and the atmosphere was close. An air vent over Cristina's head made noise, but nothing seemed to come out. Robinson stood over her with his arms crossed in front of him. McPeek's desk was in a kind of organized chaos, with photographs and paperwork and folders arranged in some system Cristina could not understand.

"José's talking about killing cops," Cristina said. "That's serious."

"I agree, which is why I don't want to see José go down on any charges that aren't going to keep him in prison for a very long time. If you're concerned about your safety, I'll arrange for protection. You can be relocated."

"She won't move," Robinson said.

"Why not?" McPeek asked.

"It's complicated," Cristina said.

"Uncomplicate it for me."

Cristina looked to Robinson. He said, "We're concerned about our informant, Felipe Morales, too."

"Flip's turning in good evidence, isn't he?"

"Yes, but—"

"Then he's not a major concern. You said he got José to admit, on tape, that he's going to use Flip's workplace as a destination for drug shipments, didn't you?"

"Yes, he did."

"Anything else he does at this point is just icing on the cake. He doesn't have to stick his neck out. Tell him to let things progress naturally, not to force it."

"I want to pull him," Cristina said.

McPeek looked at her hard. "That's not going to happen."

"You said yourself that he's just dotting the i's and crossing the t's now."

"Those things have to be done. The more we get from him, the better the case. You ought to know that better than anyone. What's going on here?"

Robinson pinched the bridge of his nose between thumb and forefinger. "We're both nervous about safety moving forward. This whole thing is close to the finish and we don't want bullets to start flying. Especially at us or the people working for us."

"It's taken care of," McPeek said. She pulled a piece of notepaper from a pad. "Give me your addresses and I'll have someone watching your homes 24/7."

"And Flip?" Cristina asked. "Who's watching out for him?"

"Flip's taking big chances, but that's what's going to keep him out of prison," McPeek said. "Now, are you going to give me those addresses or not?"

"Fine."

McPeek took down their information and then picked up the phone. "I'm going to arrange this right now," she said.

She talked on the phone for ten minutes while Cristina and Robinson could only watch. Cristina thought she might have felt a breath of air come from above, or it might have been her imagination. If the door was open it would be easier to breathe. Cristina felt tight across the chest. *Freddie*, she thought. Now someone would be watching him, but she did not stop worrying.

When she was done on the phone, McPeek said, "I hope that's good enough. You want me to have armed agents stationed in your house, Detective Salas?"

"No," Cristina said and she flushed. Whether from embarrassment or anger, she didn't know.

"Detective Robinson, are you satisfied?"

"I guess so."

McPeek steepled her fingers. "In the next few weeks we're going to roll up José Martinez's operation. I got word this morning that there's been a major break on the Mexican side. This is going to be big. The only thing everyone has to do is keep calm and stay the course. There will be enough credit for all of us to share. You brought us Flip and that's going to count for a lot, especially when he testifies. Now I don't want to be rude, but what else do you need from me?"

"Nothing," Cristina said and she stood up.

"And if you're concerned about Flip, don't be. José doesn't suspect a thing or he wouldn't open his mouth so wide when Flip's around. Flip's going to make it out of this okay."

Robinson opened the door. "Thanks for your time, Agent McPeek."

"I'm always available."

Cristina said her good-byes and let Robinson escort her from the building. They walked down a sun-washed sidewalk toward the parking lot. Robinson had a ball cap on. Cristina put on sunglasses. Summer in El Paso was punishing. "I guess that's it, then," she said.

"What else did you expect? I told you—"

"Yeah, you told me."

"Cris, you know I'll always stick by you when you're right."

Cristina smiled a half-smile and put out a hand for Robinson to shake. "Do you think I'm right about this?"

"I think you have cause to worry. And now things are being done."

"I want to talk to Flip," Cristina said.

"What about?"

"About keeping his head down."

"I think he knows that already."

"But he doesn't know how close we are. I want him up to speed so he can make the right decisions. He's putting it all out there for us. We owe him the truth."

"We can't have him crawl up into his shell," Robinson said. "Not right now. You heard McPeek. The better he does for us, the better he does for himself."

"Is it a crime to worry if a good kid gets himself killed?" Cristina asked.

"'Good kid'? Are we talking about the same Flip?"

"You looked over his records, you know what he went inside for. He's not like the rest of them. He's in over his head."

"Funny how that seems to happen to him."

"Now what are you trying to say?"

They reached the car. When Cristina opened the door, a wave of invisible fire came out. She took down the cardboard shield on the dashboard and tossed it in the back seat. The air conditioning could not come soon enough.

Robinson buckled in. "I'm saying it's not worth it to get too attached to this guy. He's got a job to do, the same as us. It's not our fault he ended up where he is."

"Then why would I feel responsible if he ended up dead?"

TEN

THEY LET HIM OUT AND VÍCTOR BARRIOS WENT back to his *hermanos*. Matías gave him a long lead, but he did not let Víctor out of his sight. He had Paco arrange for a tail everywhere Víctor went and listening devices were put in Víctor's apartment. The only thing Víctor would not do was wear a wire, and Matías did not press the issue; he was doing enough for them already.

Over eight days Víctor gave Matías and Paco and the other agents a tour of Julio Guerra's operation, one stash house at a time. Photographs were taken and teams were set to watching. By the end of those eight days, Matías had thirty men involved. Some nights Matías did not go home because he was with the men shadowing Víctor. His beard had started to grow out.

On this night Matías watched over Víctor from the back seat of a powerful black SUV, a hundred meters from the entrance of a club called *El Sombrero Rojo*. Paco sat next to him and they took turns looking through the high-powered lens of a digital camera as cars and people came and went at the entrance.

"I would give anything to be in there right now," Matías said.

"What do you think you'd see?" Paco asked. From the beginning he'd been pulled into the same warped schedule and he was no longer crisp in his jacket and tie. The driver idled the engine for a little while each hour to run the air conditioning and get the stickiness off the men inside the SUV, but now the engine was quiet and the air was stale.

"I don't know," Matías replied. "But it has to be better than sitting out here with you."

"Very funny. I didn't exactly volunteer for this."

"How long ago did Víctor go in there?"

"Three hours."

"He said Guerra might be there tonight."

It did not take much to summon the image of Julio Guerra to mind. The Azteca capo was slender and tall and he cultivated two thin mustaches as if he was an old-time matinee idol. He had been in prison three times and with his shirt off there was no mistaking him for anything but a member of Los Aztecas; their marks were all over him.

"How much do you trust Víctor Barrios?" Paco asked.

"Not at all. Why?"

"He could be telling them everything in there."

"If he'd told them anything, we would have heard from the other teams by now. They'd strip those stash houses to the bare walls. No, he's scared enough to do what he's told."

"More scared of you than he is of his own family?"

Matías paused with his eye to the camera. "Yes," he said finally. "Just enough. Someone's coming out."

The doors of the club parted, held by two doormen in sharp, red uniforms. For a moment all Matías could see was women: a pair of girls with teased out hair, one of them bleached a startling blonde. Then he saw the man. He clutched at Paco's arm. "What?" Paco said.

"Look," Matías said and handed over the camera.

Paco did look. "Guerra," he said.

Matías tapped the shoulder of the agent in the passenger seat. "Are you getting this?"

"All on video," said the man. The window was cracked to admit the lens of a high-definition camera.

"Be ready to move," Matías told the driver.

"What about Víctor?" Paco asked.

"Víctor can find his way home without an escort tonight. We finally have Guerra out in the open and I want to see where he goes."

The SUV's engine turned over and the air conditioner started to whir. Matías took the camera away from Paco and took a dozen stills of Julio Guerra waiting at the curb for his car to come around. Another man was with him, probably the driver. Matías' heart was beating faster.

The car came. It was a white Mercedes S-Class. The driver held the back door for Guerra and the girls, then went round to his side. In moments they were moving and so was the SUV, pulling away from the curb and falling into place in traffic, two cars back from Guerra's. The agent in the passenger's seat got on the radio and reported their movement.

"Don't lose him," Matías said.

"I won't," said the driver.

They passed through the center of the city. Matías' driver never edged too close, nor did he let Guerra get too far away. The balance was delicate, interwoven with vehicles that came and went along the way. Matías wondered if they would hit a roadblock and, if they did, what Guerra would do. Did he have drugs in the car? Perhaps. Guns? Almost certainly.

Matías did not notice the old Cadillac when it pulled up alongside Guerra's Mercedes at a red light. The white gleam of the Mercedes had all of Matías' attention. He did not even notice when the windows on the Cadillac went down and the gun barrels poked out.

Automatic weapons fire exploded on the street, tearing up the space between the Cadillac and the Mercedes. Matías saw the windows of the Mercedes burst, and paint stripped away as bullets tracked the metal. He was dimly aware of shouting at the agent to call out on the radio *now* and of drawing his weapon, throwing the door wide.

His feet hit the pavement and he was back in himself. The cars between the SUV and Guerra's Mercedes were jammed against one another in their haste to be away from the killing zone. Now their drivers and their passengers were ducked down, out of sight, and that was the smartest thing they could do.

Another burst of rounds buried themselves in the Mercedes and then the Cadillac gunned its engine. Matías dashed forward, firing his pistol at the car as it screeched away. Paco was there, too, but their weapons popped like firecrackers where once there'd been the roar of assault rifles.

"Go, go, go!" Matías shouted to the agent behind the wheel of the SUV. The driver drove up on the sidewalk and skirted the sea of shattered glass and broken metal, lights behind the grille flickering and an electronic siren blaring. In a second it was gone, after the Cadillac, its sound retreating quickly.

Matías approached the Mercedes with his gun up. One side of the car was peppered from nose to tail with bullet holes and both the tires on that side were blown. Blood painted the inside of the windshield where the driver took a round in the neck. Matías tried the rear door and found it unlocked.

Julio Guerra and the girls were slumped over one another in the back seat, their faces stained red, eyes still staring. Matías expected to see a gun in Guerra's hand, but they were both empty.

"*Jesucristo*," Paco said. "Matías, what happened?"

Matías holstered his weapon. "Julio Guerra was just eliminated from our investigation."

ELEVEN

"**Y**OU SHOULDN'T BE AT MY HOME," VÍCTOR SAID.

They stood in the shadowed front room of Víctor's apartment – Matías, Paco and Víctor – with the door firmly closed. A PFM vehicle sat down on the street, watching the ways to and from. If the agents inside saw anything, they would call Matías on the radio he wore on his waist.

"Are you telling me what to do?" Matías asked sharply. "I hope that's not what you're doing, Víctor."

The man flinched as if slapped. "No, no," he said. "It's just that somebody might see you."

"No one saw us. We were never here," Matías said.

Víctor was still dressed for a night out, in a fancy shirt and slacks. He was barefoot, though, and for some reason this struck Matías as funny. Barefoot on his threadbare carpet in a tiny apartment. It made him seem pathetic.

"What do you want with me?" Víctor asked.

"You heard about what happened to Guerra tonight?"

"Yes. We all know."

"Then tell me."

"It was the Sinaloenses."

"You know this for sure?"

"It has to be! We've had trouble with the Mexicles lately. Maybe it was them. The pressure is on in Juárez, man! It's not safe to be an Azteca anymore."

Matías barked a laugh. "When was it ever safe?"

"I'm telling you all I know."

Matías took one step toward Víctor and the man shrank back. It was dark, but Matías could read Víctor's face well enough. "Who takes over for Guerra?"

"R-Renato, probably. He's been doing a lot for Julio lately."

"Renato Durán?" Paco asked.

"It makes sense," Matías said. "He's one of Guerra's lieutenants. I just didn't know how close."

"Real close," Víctor volunteered. "Renato does everything Julio says."

"Does that include the shipping deal?" Matías asked. "Does it?"

"I don't know! Renato was there a few times when I talked to Julio about meeting with José. I think he knows what's going on. Julio never told me I had to keep my mouth shut."

Matías looked around the room at the bare walls, the slumping couch, the little television and stereo. There were no windows here. He imagined the whole apartment penned up without a ray of outside light. A cell for Víctor Barrios.

He thought. If the plan with the shipping depot died with Julio Guerra, then the Americans would be unhappy. But there was still Renato Durán. Renato could save everything.

Matías pointed at Víctor. "I want you to go to Renato as soon as you can and find out if the deal with the trucks is still on. Tell him that José Martinez wants to know. And when you find out the answer, you contact me right away. No bullshit from you, do you understand? I can't have Julio Guerra, but I'm still going to make my case."

"I'll do it," Víctor said quickly.

"After this you better think about someplace to take a vacation," Paco said.

"What does that mean?"

"It means if you keep coming through for us, you get a walk," Matías said, "but staying in Juárez is no good for your health. If you want my advice, you leave just as soon as we're done."

"When will that be?"

"Soon. Find out about those trucks. Then I'll let you know."

Matías went to the door, cracked it first and peered out into the hallway. There was no one there. He let Paco out first and followed close behind. As soon as they hit the street they piled into the back seat of the waiting PFM sedan. "Go," Paco said.

"Goddamned Mexicles," Matías said. "They couldn't keep it in their pants."

"You think Víctor is telling the truth, then?"

"Why not? It makes sense. The Sinaloa cartel is cleaning house all through the city. Of all the goddamned bad timing! If this goes to hell before the Aztecas can send even one truck over the border there are going to be some very unhappy Americans."

Streetlights slid by. It was well past midnight.

"What should we do?" Paco asked.

"We wait for Víctor to find out if it's still on. Then we do what we planned to do all along: let them make their delivery and sweep up behind them. Julio Guerra might be dead, but his family is still alive to do his bidding. I'm not going to let that *cabrón* buy the rest of them out of jail by dying on me."

"Okay, Matías. We'll keep on."

"What other choice do we have?"

TWELVE

Flip saw José's Lexus as soon as Clayton's truck turned the corner onto Flip's street. It was parked in front of his mother's house, looking something out of place along the curb where older model cars usually sat. Flip could not see if José was inside.

Clayton came up behind the Lexus and stopped. "See you tomorrow," he told Flip.

"Yeah. See you. Thanks, Clayton."

"No problem."

So far Clayton hadn't asked why Flip no longer rode with Alfredo, even though Alfredo was okay behind the wheel again. Flip offered to pitch in for Clayton's gas and the man was happy to accept. Flip hoped the arrangement would last long enough for him to make a better one; he wouldn't be riding with Alfredo again.

The Lexus' engine wasn't running. Flip stooped down to look through the tinted windows of the car, half-expecting to see José's profile, but the front seats were empty.

He went up the walk slowly, his mind working. The house looked the same and he heard no sounds from inside. When he reached the door he used his key and stepped into the air conditioning.

A murmur of voices carried from the kitchen, and then Flip heard his mother call him. "Felipe! We're in here!"

Flip went to the kitchen and saw his mother there at the table. Across from her sat José, dressed down like he had been when he met Alfredo. He wasn't even wearing his big watch. When he laid eyes on Flip he smiled and the smile was relaxed and open. "Hey, Flip," he said, "we've been waiting for you."

"Mamá, is everything all right?" Flip asked.

"Everything's fine. I was talking to your friend José. Why haven't you introduced us before?"

"I never thought about it," Flip said. Then to José he asked, "What are you doing here?"

"I came by to see you, but I was early," José said. "Silvia was kind enough to let me in."

"Sit down, Felipe. You want something to drink? I made *limonada*. Have some."

Flip took a seat at the table between his mother and José. His brain felt airy, as if he wasn't quite there with them, but when he looked at José that sensation went away. Flip's mother poured him a glass of *limonada* from a pitcher. Slices of lemon floated on the ice.

"José says he might have a job for you," Flip's mother said.

"What kind of job?"

"Carpenter's work, of course. José says his company builds houses."

"Good, solid houses," José said.

"More *limonada*, José?"

"Yes, thank you."

"Felipe, you look tired. Are you tired?"

"I'm okay, Mamá," Flip said, but he kept his eyes on José. "I just didn't expect visitors, is all. When is Alfredo coming over?"

"Not tonight. He says his arm is hurting him."

José frowned. "That's too bad. I would have liked to meet Alfredo. Flip talks about him. He sounds like a great guy."

"He asked me to marry him. This is the ring."

"It's beautiful!"

Flip cleared his throat. "Mamá, I think maybe I'll go out with José for a while. Is that okay? You don't have to fix dinner for me."

"I'll make sure he eats," José told Flip's mother.

"Okay, but make sure you change out of those smelly work clothes. You have fresh shirts in your closet. I ironed them."

"Thanks, Mamá."

He got up from the table and left José with his mother. Back in his room he changed clothes quickly. The sudden sound of his mother's laughter passed through the walls. José laughed, too.

On impulse, Flip brought out the thin wire and the recording device from where he hid it in his chest of drawers. It took a moment to fix the wire to his belly and chest and it was invisible once he pulled his undershirt over it. Anyone who noticed the digital recorder's outline in his pocket would think it was a pack of smokes.

Flip got back to them in just a few minutes. Nothing seemed to have changed at the table. José sat there and Flip's mother was there, the pitcher of *limonada* between them. José looked at him and for a moment Flip had no voice. Then he said, "I'm ready. You ready, José?"

"I think so," José said and he drained his glass. "Silvia, thank you so much for the *limonada*. It was nice to finally meet you."

Flip's mother clasped hands briefly with José. "It's good to meet friends of Flip's. He doesn't have very many. He's always been shy."

"Shy? Well, I guess so. Come on, Flip."

They went outside and Flip's mother locked the front door behind them. José led the way to his car, spinning his keychain on one finger and for a second whistling some fragment of a tune Flip didn't recognize.

Flip got in the Lexus with José. The engine turned over and the air conditioner started to blast along with the radio. José turned it down so it was only a whisper.

"Why did you come to my house?" Flip asked.

"Is it a problem? Your mother's a very nice woman. Too bad her fiancé's such a fucking *puto*."

José drove. Flip could not guess where they were going. He only hoped it would not be Juárez. He did not want to go back to Juárez again.

"Why did you tell her you wanted to hire me to be a carpenter?" Flip asked.

"You want me to tell her the truth? In my experience, mothers don't handle that news very well."

"She'll know when she tells Alfredo."

"I think he'll keep his mouth shut. He hasn't told her so far."

A few turns later and Flip thought they were headed back to José's house, but then they headed the opposite direction down a long street until they reached an apartment building painted sky blue with black railings. The building was shaped like a U and in the center of it was a pool. José parked in the lot.

"What is this place?" Flip asked.

"Come on."

Flip followed José out of the car and through the gate onto the property. They passed the manager's office and caught a flight of steps to the second floor. A few people were down by the pool, including a mother with her young child. The little boy wore yellow floaties on his arms.

José skipped a handful of doors until he came to one marked 212. He dug into his pocket and produced a key. The key unlocked the apartment. "Inside," he said.

All of a sudden Flip was back at Emilio's apartment, sitting on the couch in the darkened living room with the other Indians, passing judgment on him. The party feeling that came after was just a shadow of the rest. He only saw Emilio, pleading his case, pleading for life. And then he died in Juárez anyway.

"You coming in?"

Flip was unfrozen. He passed through the door into the apartment and smelled the odors of air fresheners and carpet cleaner. The blinds were open, allowing brilliant sunlight into the front room where new-looking furniture stood around. José closed the door after him.

"What is this place?" Flip asked.

"Your place," José said. He moved beside Flip and pressed the key into his hand the way he'd pressed the pistol into it. "Fully furnished. The rent's paid for the first three months. After that it's up to you."

"José—"

"Don't thank me right away. I know you have to get used to it."

The apartment wasn't large, but it was palatial by the standards of Graciela's one room, or Flip's space at his mother's house. There were two bedrooms and a good-sized kitchen. Everything was made up and there was even art on the walls, as if this were a showplace. Flip did not know what to say.

Flip found his voice: "What do I do for this?"

"I told you before: you work for me. Somebody has to take Emilio's place. You got to get your ink, fly the flag, represent for your family. And I know you won't fuck up like Emilio because you've already been on the inside and you don't want to go back. That makes you smarter."

"José, I don't know nothing about selling drugs."

"What's to know? You'll have *tiendas* working for you, moving the stuff. You just got to learn how to break down the shipments. You're like a distributor. Like wholesale, you know what I mean? Let the other Indians handle the retail."

"They busted Emilio."

José put a finger to his head and poked his temple. "That's because Emilio was stupid. He didn't take care of things. I know you aren't going to make the same mistakes. Enrique wouldn't vouch for somebody undependable. And you already showed me you're down for the cause. I'm not going to forget Juárez."

Flip wanted to forget Juárez. The images kept coming unabated. He tried to blink them away. "What about my job?"

"You can keep it. Your PO wants you working and I need you to make sure your boss does what he's supposed to do. What you do for me here, you do on the side. Like I said: you'll have help. And when you're not on parole anymore, we'll talk about stepping you up in the organization. You can do it full-time." José took a step forward. "Are you all right, Flip?"

"Yeah, sure," Flip said, though he felt that lightheadedness again, the same sense of unreality that seized him at his mother's table. He went for the couch and sat down. "It's just a lot all at once, you know?"

"I wouldn't bring you in if I didn't think you could handle it, Flip."

Flip just nodded. If he hung his head down he could catch his breath and he no longer felt suffocated. Every time José spoke it was like a weight pressing on him until he weighed a thousand pounds.

"You down, Flip?"

"Yeah," Flip said. "Yeah, I'm down."

"You're gonna need this place anyway, Flip. You have a family now."

Flip jerked his head up. "What?" he said.

"You and Graciela. I heard there are congratulations in order."

"Where did you hear that?"

José made a vague gesture with his hands. "Around. You see, I always have my eye on you, Flip. That's why I know I can believe in you. You're not a snitch or a bitch. You understand me?"

"I understand."

"Anyway, tell your mamá that you got a raise at work or whatever and move your shit in here. A *sargento* shouldn't be living at home."

"I don't know what to tell you, José."

"You don't have to tell me anything. Just say 'thank you' and we're square."

"Thank you."

José smiled at Flip and sat down beside him on the couch, lounging with his arms out along the back. "It's all about what you can do for the family. I have high hopes for you, Flip. You're my investment. Together we're going to be big. No limits."

"No limits," Flip repeated.

"Go ahead and call Graciela," José urged. "Tell her to come around and see the place. She's going to go nuts for it."

"I'll call her in a minute," Flip said, and he rose from the couch. Once again he wandered the rooms, smelling their artificial clean smells and seeing the perfect way it was all laid out for him. The lightheadedness hadn't gone.

"You going to be okay, Flip?" José called.

"Yeah, sure," Flip said. Unconsciously he touched the wire running up his body. Was it getting everything? "I just got to decide which room is going to be ours."

"Let Graciela pick," José said. "Always better to let the woman pick."

THIRTEEN

José was gone by the time Graciela arrived. She knocked on the door quietly, with hesitation, and stood on the threshold biting her lip when Flip opened up.

"Hi," she said.

"Hi. Come in."

Flip let her walk from room to room just the way he had and did not bother her until she came back to him and let him put his arms around her. "It's great," she said, though her voice was hollow.

"You don't like it?"

"I like it fine," Graciela said. She stepped away from him and Flip thought she looked very small in the broad front room. "I just…"

"If you don't want to live here, that's okay," Flip said. "I'll understand."

"It's not that."

Graciela went to one of the chairs and sat down. Flip wondered when she would start to show. Right now she was still slender and gave no hint of what was going on inside her body. He couldn't imagine her living in her little apartment after months had gone by; it was not enough for her.

"What's wrong?" Flip asked.

"José really wants you," Graciela said. "He wouldn't do this for just anybody."

"I guess so."

"Flip…" Graciela started and then trailed off.

He came to her and knelt down by the chair. When he held her hand, it seemed cold. "What?" he asked.

"I thought you had plans. Things you wanted to do."

"I *do*. I got lots of plans."

"How are you gonna do them if you're running around for José? When are you going to get a job as a carpenter? That's what you want to do, right?"

"Yeah."

Graciela looked him in the eyes and Flip saw they were dark and filled with an emotion he couldn't put a name to. She closed her fingers around his and held them tightly. "If you wanna do those things, you got to be your own man," she said.

Flip was quiet for a while, just holding her hand. After a while he took a deep breath and said, "I'm doing what I can do. I don't have a lot of choices right now, but it's going to get better. I promise."

"I don't want to end up like Emilio's girl, Alicia. He's run off to Juárez and he ain't coming back. You got responsibilities, Flip."

"I know. I didn't forget."

He thought she might cry and so he gripped her hand more fiercely. Graciela took a long, ragged breath and let it out slowly. She was on the edge. Only he could hold her there.

"I've made a lot of mistakes," Flip said.

"I know."

"No, you don't know. I never told you what I went to Coffield for."

"You don't have to."

"I want to," Flip said.

"Okay."

Flip told her about his friends, Roberto and Manuel. They were all in the same grade together growing up and their houses were close by one another. When Roberto started stealing, they all started stealing. Little things to start with, then bigger and bigger.

Once, when they were seventeen, they stole a car and drove it until the gas tank went dry. Then they broke out all the windows and jumped up and down on the roof until it caved in. That was fun.

After high school they weren't so close, but they still got together. Roberto did some time in county jail. Manuel got a job doing concrete on construction jobs. Flip lived off his mother because he could and she let him. They partied with some of the neighborhood girls. Roberto liked the ones still in school.

It seemed like a good thing when Roberto came to them with his idea. He knew a man on the South Side who kept a lot of money from his liquor store business in his home safe. Flip said he didn't know anything about breaking open safes. Roberto said he wouldn't have to.

They wore bandanas over their faces and Flip kicked in the front door. The guy was home with his wife and his kids. Roberto had a gun from somewhere and he herded everyone into one of the bedrooms. When they were all down, he told the guy to open his safe.

At first the guy said there was no safe and Roberto beat him. After that the guy was a lot more cooperative. He showed them the safe under a tile in the kitchen floor. He opened it for them.

Roberto promised lots of money. Hundreds, maybe thousands. The guy had five hundred dollars in the safe, plus a bunch of papers that weren't worth anything. Roberto took the money and he beat the guy again. Flip said they should go; he could hear the guy's wife and kids crying in the other room.

After it was all over, Flip could not say when Roberto pulled the trigger or why. The gun made a loud popping noise and the guy was on the floor of the kitchen bleeding from his head and ear. Roberto was in a hurry to go then and they ran for it. Everybody went a separate way. Only Roberto had a car.

The police found Flip a mile away, walking for home. They saw he was sweating and the sweat didn't stop when they brought him to the station. A detective showed Flip how his shoe left a clear print on the dead guy's door. After that Flip told them the truth.

They charged Roberto with manslaughter and Flip and Manuel as accessories. The judge gave Flip sixteen years. His mother cried in court that day. Flip felt shame.

Roberto went to a different unit in the system and Manuel to another. They sent Flip to Coffield, and that's when everything changed. Flip became an Indian.

When he was finished with the story he searched Graciela's face for a response. He did not know what to expect, but she didn't take her hand from him and she didn't look away. "You didn't kill nobody yourself?" she asked finally.

"No, I didn't. I swear."

"Are you gonna kill people now?"

"No. I wouldn't do that. Not for anybody."

"What if José said to?"

"Not even if José said to."

"I can't be married to no killer, Flip."

"I swear on my baby's life, I won't."

"But you still got to do what José says."

"For now, but things can change."

"How?" Graciela asked.

Flip felt the digital recorder in his pocket. All of this was being recorded. The detectives would hear it. The FBI agent would hear it. But he was not ashamed of this. Of what he had done, of what he let Roberto do, yes, but not this.

"If I had to go away," Flip said, "would you come with me?"

"Go away? Like where?"

"Just somewhere. Away from El Paso. Maybe to California or something."

"Why would you go to California?"

"Just tell me," Flip said. "If I had to go, would you come with me?"

Graciela looked at him and Flip feared the answer. She said,

"Yes, I would. You're my baby's father. How could I let you go away without me?"

Flip rose and gently pulled her from the chair. He kissed her on the lips, held her in his arms and enjoyed the warmth and pressure of her body against his. She put her hands on his hips and then tugged his shirt free of his jeans. Her fingers touched the skin of his waist.

He went rigid and pushed away from her. Graciela nearly fell back into the chair. "What?" she asked. "What did I do?"

"It's nothing," Flip said, and he felt the heat of burgeoning sweat on his face. Had she felt the wire? He stepped back a pace and then another, his heart beating hard. "I just got to use the bathroom, that's all."

"You scared the shit out of me, jumping like that."

"Sorry," Flip said. He retreated into the bathroom, closed and locked the door behind him, and stood with his back to it trying to catch a breath that did not want to be caught. His chest hurt.

He stripped off his shirt and undershirt and stood looking at himself in the mirror. The wire snaked up his body, white and thin. Peeling the tape was like pulling a Band-Aid.

Graciela spoke through the door. "Are you okay in there?"

"I'm fine. Just a minute."

The recorder and the wire went into his pocket. The skin where the tape had been was pink, but it could have been anything. Graciela would not suspect. He put his clothes back on and flushed the toilet and noisily washed his hands in the sink.

She waited for him in the hall outside the door, her expression displeased. "What was that all about?" she demanded.

"Sorry. I got some bad food with José. It's okay now."

He tried to hold her again, but the spell was broken. Flip felt like a stranger in this apartment that was supposed to be his. Graciela was already gathering up her things. "I can drop you somewhere," she said.

The pool was empty when they left the apartment and the manager's office was closed. The sun lay heavily in the west, though it would be a long time setting. At least now there was a breath of wind, even though it was hot.

At first Graciela did not want to talk and Flip waited until he felt the time was right before he asked, "When do you want to move in?"

"I got two months left on my lease," Graciela says. "It'll cost me if I break it."

"So I just stay there on my own?" Flip asked.

"Yeah, I guess you do."

"It won't be the same without you."

"You'll survive."

She brought him back to his mother's house and stopped in front. Flip reached across to touch Graciela's hand, but she did not take his. She stared out the windshield, her jaw set. The Hyundai idled unevenly.

"Graciela…" Flip said.

"What?"

"Thank you."

"For what?"

"For everything."

The hard line of her profile softened and Graciela turned toward him. This time she reached for him and he was glad to take her hand. He wanted to bring her inside with him, put her on his bed and make love to her, but that was impossible. Maybe she would take him to her place if he asked. He did not ask.

"I don't know how to figure you out sometimes, Flip," Graciela said.

"I know. I'm sorry."

"You don't have to be sorry. Just don't be weird."

"I won't next time. I promise."

"Do you want to go out tomorrow night?"

"Where do you want to go?"

"I don't know. We haven't been dancing in a while. Maybe the club?"

"You can't drink. The baby."

"I won't," Graciela said. She leaned across to kiss him and Flip tasted her. Her arms twined up around his neck. His hand touched her breast. Slowly they came apart.

"Hey," Flip said.

"Next time," she said.

"Okay."

Flip got out of the car and waved good-bye to Graciela from the curb. She left him in a slowly swirling cloud of exhaust and vanished down the street into the lowering sun.

He went up to the house and let himself in. His mother was watching television in the living room. "Was that Graciela?" she asked.

"Yes, Mamá."

"You should have asked her to come in! I have some carrot cake I made and there's plenty to share."

"She's busy tonight, Mamá. Maybe next time."

"You want to watch *Wheel of Fortune* with me?" Flip's mother asked.

"In a little while, Mamá."

He went to his room and closed the door. The recorder and the wire went back into their hiding place. Flip slipped his father's knife from his pocket and flicked open the blade. His face was reflected in the steel. It felt sharp enough to draw blood when he tested the edge. "What would you do, Papá?" he asked out loud.

Flip put the knife away. It had no answers for him.

FOURTEEN

WHEN CRISTINA CAME DOWN HER STREET she spotted the FBI detail immediately. Their car was new and shiny and did not fit in on a dusty street in Segundo Barrio. Two agents were inside and Cristina caught a glimpse of them as she drove past: a pair of nondescript men in jackets and sunglasses.

She parked and looked back to where they were. She raised a hand. A second later one of them waved back.

If they were obvious to her, they would be obvious for anyone coming down the street with intent to do her harm. Cristina felt awkward about the arrangement; she hoped that El Paso police officers would handle the duty of watching out for a fellow officer. In the end it was probably better this way, because with the feds doing the mundane jobs, the local cops could concentrate on handling the situation on the ground. Still, she would have liked to know the names of the people watching her.

Ashlee was in the kitchen when Cristina came through the front door, cleaning up plates from dinner. She came into the living room wiping wet hands on a simple apron. "Hi," she said. "You're early, aren't you?"

"A little bit," Cristina said.

Freddie was at his place at the computer, fully engrossed in his game. When Cristina spoke, he didn't react at all. He kept his eyes on the screen when Cristina came for a kiss, and she was forced to leave one on his cheek. Only then did he speak: "Mom, you're home."

"I am. How are you?"

"I'm kind of busy right now. I'm playing my game."

"You play your game. I'm going to talk to Ashlee."

Ashlee put the apron on a peg in the kitchen. Cristina went to join her. "What's up?" Ashlee asked.

"Anything unusual happen today?"

"No, I don't think so."

"Anybody try to talk to you or Freddie?"

"No. Why?"

"I'm just checking," Cristina said. She hadn't shared with Ashlee the news about the FBI and if the girl hadn't picked them out in their car that was okay. Telling Ashlee would open up a whole area of questioning Cristina wasn't ready to deal with. Would Ashlee be safe going home or coming to the house? Did she need protection, too? And on and on.

"I guess since you're here, I can go," Ashlee said.

"Sure. I can take it from here."

Ashlee gathered her things and gave Freddie a hug good-bye. "See you tomorrow, buddy," she told him, but he had nothing to say.

"Be careful on the road," Cristina told Ashlee, and when the girl had gone Cristina locked the door behind her. In their car the FBI agents would make note of Ashlee's departure and the time, maybe even logging it into a book. Everything about Cristina's house was subject to observation and report now. Again she felt discomfited.

"Hey, peanut," Cristina said to Freddie, "how about you watch a video with me tonight? Okay?"

"Okay. Let me play first."

"I'll give you another thirty minutes."

Ashlee had left no plate for Cristina tonight. The freezer was full of microwaveable meals and Cristina cooked one of those. She ate by the sink and tossed the flimsy tray in the trash when she was done. While Freddie played, she picked out a DVD of cartoons that were not too long. Anything past a few minutes tested Freddie's ability to concentrate. In the words of the people at his school, watching a video with his mother was "not a preferred activity."

They watched the cartoons and afterward it was time for bed. She came into his room after he had undressed, and she sat on the edge of his bed. The ceiling fan turned slowly above them, stirring the air. With the air conditioning on, the fan could make it uncomfortably cool in the room, but Freddie liked to bundle himself in blankets and did not mind.

"Hey," Cristina said to him. "Can I talk to you about something?"

"What?"

"I want to talk to you. Can you show me your eyes, please? Over here. Look at my eyes."

It was hard for him to focus on her for more than a second or two. Conversations were conducted at odd angles, as if Freddie and Cristina were displaced and no straight line could be drawn between them. When she asked to see his eyes he could barely maintain the contact, but she did it anyway because it was her way of telling him to pay close attention.

"Freddie, you know Mom does dangerous work sometimes, right?"

"Very *dangerous*," Freddie said.

"That's right. Mom deals with a lot of bad people and they do not nice things. But you know I'm very careful so I can always come home to you."

"Are you careful?" Freddie asked. He looked at a hand-drawn picture on the wall of an elevator. The brand name of the elevator, Otis, was scrawled in his uneven hand.

"I am. And Uncle Bob is careful and all the people Mom works with are careful."

Cristina wasn't sure what she wanted to say, what she could say that would make sense to Freddie and stay in his mind. Many times she would speak and he would forget. It took long repetition for most things to sink in. Tonight she wanted him to remember.

"Are we going to have a story?"

"Yes. Listen, Freddie: sometimes the bad people try to hurt Mom because she puts their friends in jail. But they're not going to get Mom and they're not going to get you. We have people watching over us to make sure that doesn't happen. Do you understand?"

"I understand," Freddie said.

Now she didn't know if she was saying these things for Freddie or for herself. "I don't want you to worry about Mom, okay? Mom is going to be all right and she'll always come home to you. I promise."

"I promise," Freddie echoed, and then he made an oinking sound and giggled. "I'm a pig!"

A tear struggled in the corner of her eye and Cristina quashed it with a fingertip. "Okay," she said. "Story time."

FIFTEEN

MATÍAS OVERSLEPT AND DRAGGED HIMSELF
to the bathroom to regard an unshaven face that had begun to look
too ragged to be presentable. He showered and took a razor to it
until he was happy with what he saw. Paco called while he was in
the bathroom, but left no message. Matías called back.

"Paco, ¿qué necesitas?"

"A call came in from Víctor Barrios. He got to speak with Renato
Durán."

"And?"

"The deal is still on. José's people are sending over the payment
for the drugs tonight: a dozen assault weapons, plus ammunition.
I have the time and place for delivery."

Matías held the phone in the crook of his shoulder as he tied his
tie in the mirror. The bed was unmade, the room generally messier
than it had been when Elvira was around. The whole apartment
was starting to slip. "Does he know what to do?" Matías asked.

"Yes. He tracks the distribution of the weapons and reports
back to us. He says they'll probably hold the guns in one of their
stash houses first and then parcel them out when they can be sure
no one's paying attention anymore."

"Those poor dumb bastards," Matías said. "I almost feel sorry
for them."

"When are you coming in?"

"Soon. I got a late start today."

"The FBI woman also called. McPeek? She wants to meet with us, with *you*. I told her we could do it in the afternoon. Is that okay?"

"That's fine. She probably heard about Guerra from someone and now she's going to be in a panic. We have to keep control of this thing, Paco, for all our sakes. Those drugs have to ship. Víctor didn't say anything about when they would go?"

"Nothing."

Matías jerked his head in frustration. "I want you to call Felix Rivera and make sure he's ready to move when we tell him. Everyone to the front lines. We hit all of Guerra's old stash houses, the ones Víctor pointed out to us, just as soon as the shipment's en route. We'll cripple Los Aztecas, Paco. I know it."

"And what we don't do the Mexicles will handle?" Paco asked.

"Something like that."

"Listen, Matías, there's been some talking going on that maybe you ought to know about."

In the kitchen Matías boiled water for coffee. He was already late, so there was no reason not to take the time. He grunted into the phone. "What kind of talking?"

"Los Aztecas have already targeted you once…"

"If they want to take another stab at it, they know where to find me," Matías said. "But I think they have bigger problems to worry about. The Mexicles just killed one of their leading capos and they aren't likely to stop there. I'm not going to let them scare me out of doing what needs to be done."

"I didn't say you were a coward, Matías."

"When it comes to this, don't worry about me," Matías said. "Soon we'll come down on Los Aztecas like the hand of God. Then we'll all be on their list. You, too."

"I don't much like the idea of that."

"This is Juárez, Paco. Everyone's a target. Let me drink my coffee and then I'll be in. We can talk then."

"See you, Matías."

Matías ended the call and put the phone in his pocket. Now he had time to reflect on what Paco had told him and what it all meant. He hadn't lied when he said he was not afraid. In Juárez there could be no fear because the moment a policeman started to worry about such things he was useless. People died in the city for no reason other than being in the wrong neighborhood when a firefight broke out. Bombs were going off. Citizens vanished off the streets and turned up on the side of the road missing limbs or heads. Matías could not afford fear in a place like this.

Once the water boiled he poured it into a French press over fresh-ground coffee to brew. He found himself eager for the taste of it, that first indicator that the day was begun, even though he was already falling behind. If Elvira was here, he wouldn't be so sloppy; she kept him on schedule and focused. Waiting for his coffee, he realized again how much he missed her.

He wondered what she was doing right at that moment. The idle days had to be driving her mad, but despite calls and coaxing she had not relented in her decision. The last time they spoke, she offered Matías the name of a private security firm operating out of Monterrey. According to her, the firm was founded by an agent of the old AFI and there were people he might know working there. He hadn't recognized any of the names she gave him.

Matías did not say yes to Elvira because he felt compelled to say no. Like a policeman did not show fear on the streets of Ciudad Juárez, Matías did not see himself stepping back from this, and it would be stepping back. She didn't press further that time. Maybe she knew without Matías having to say anything, or maybe she was just waiting until the next time. He wished it could be next time right now, but he couldn't be distracted by calling now. Maybe tonight. Maybe then.

SIXTEEN

THE WEEKEND CAME AND WENT. FLIP TOOK Graciela dancing at a new club, one José and the Indians did not frequent. It was a good time and afterward they went back to the new apartment for the night. In the dark he thought about asking Graciela how José had known she was pregnant, but the moment did not seem right and by the time the thought occurred to him again it was morning.

Flip hadn't told his mother he was moving. Eventually he would have to, but he did not look forward to the reaction the news would bring. He was not a boy anymore, but to his mamá he would always be. Maybe leaving was a good thing.

Flip was on his lunch break at the warehouse when the call came. No one noticed when he stepped away from the picnic tables, or remarked when he turned his back to the others to speak. Flip was still ill at ease.

"Flip, it's José."

"José. What do you want?"

"Hey, I'm sorry I called you at work, okay? I just thought you might want to know: our first truck is coming through on Wednesday. I want you to tell that boss of yours which one to look out for. You got a pen?"

"Yeah, I got a pen."

"Write this down." José gave Flip an identifying number that Flip scrawled on the palm of his hand. "You know what the truck looks like, right? When you see it, you call me. And make sure your boss puts it somewhere out of the way. Nobody touches that truck until our people come to unload the stuff."

"People are gonna ask why's that truck just sitting there," Flip said.

"Tell them you don't know. Tell them it's none of their business. It's your boss that has to worry about that kind of thing. So long as he keeps up his end of the deal, I don't care what he says to them. Remind him that I'm paying him a thousand bucks to do nothing. He'll take it and like it or he'll get another ass-whipping."

Flip looked at the ground. "I'll tell him," he mumbled.

"Now listen to me, Flip. Listen carefully. I don't want you around when the truck gets unloaded, all right? You leave that to the people I send. You're my lookout, my man on the inside. That's what you do."

"Okay, José, I won't stick around."

"Good boy. Hey, how's the new place working out?"

"It's great, José, thanks."

"You don't need to thank me. I told you before, you're my investment. You got to have nice things when you work for me. It means you'll do good work. Anyway, I'll talk to you later. Say hello to Graciela for me."

"I will. Good-bye."

Flip shut his phone and glanced back over his shoulder at the picnic tables. Not one curious eye was turned his way. He put the phone away and walked back toward the warehouse on heavy feet.

Since he came back to work, Alfredo had stopped taking his meals outside with the other workers. Instead he lurked in his office, filling out paperwork with one hand while eating with the other. He used to come out more often and talk to the guys on the job, but that had ended, too. Flip thought maybe it was because Alfredo did not want to see him.

He knocked on the office door. Alfredo looked up, saw him through the window, and looked back down at his work. Flip opened the door and came in.

"What the hell do you want?" Alfredo asked.

"José just called me."

"The great José," Alfredo remarked. "What the hell does *he* want?"

"The first truck is coming Wednesday. I don't know what time. José wants to make sure you have an eye out for it. Here's the registration number." Flip wrote the number from his palm on a piece of notepaper and passed it to Alfredo.

Alfredo finally lifted his gaze to glare at Flip. "You people are really going to go through with it, aren't you? This stupid plan to ship drugs into the country? All it would take is one phone call from me and the police would be all over this place just *waiting* for the chance to throw your worthless ass in jail."

Flip thought he should be tough, but instead he wanted to throw himself down and beg Alfredo for forgiveness. He didn't care how it would look, or anything about his pride. What he wanted was for things to be good again. Finally he said, "You wouldn't snitch on José. You can't."

"What do you mean by that?"

"If you tell the cops, you'll never be safe. José would put a green light out on you. Every Azteca in the city would have your name. You'd be a dead man."

Alfredo said nothing for a long time, though his eyes were flinty. "You really are some piece of work. If I didn't know better, I'd say there was no way Silvia could have raised a piece of shit like you. Your father would disown you."

"Don't talk about my father."

"Why not? You going to kill me yourself?"

"Just don't talk about him. You want to be mad, then be mad at me."

Alfredo paused. Flip saw he was gripping a pencil tightly. He was almost curious to see if it would snap. "You need to get the hell out of my sight," Alfredo said. "Get out. Take the rest of the day off. Just go away."

"I'll finish my shift," Flip said.

"What's that supposed to be? You being responsible? Don't make me laugh."

"I'll finish my shift," Flip repeated.

"Then finish your goddamned shift. See if I care. If you won't go away, then get out of my office. I don't like the smell."

Flip let himself out and did not slam the door. Walking away he could feel Alfredo watching him. He was glad to be outside again.

SEVENTEEN

It was the first time Cristina had seen the whole group together since the first day she and Robinson were brought in on the operation. Everyone was there around the conference table and McPeek was at the head with her remote in her hand and a PowerPoint slide already displayed on the big screen. She waited until the room had settled and then she cleared her throat. "Welcome back," she said. "We're about to see everything come together."

Cristina sat elbow to elbow with Robinson. When she glanced at him his attention was on McPeek. Where she was tense, he was relaxed. It was always that way between them.

"D-Day is *tomorrow*," McPeek continued. "Yesterday we got confirmation through two sources that José Martinez and his crew are going to receive a shipment of narcotics from Mexico sometime Wednesday evening. You all got the packet I emailed about the target site, but here it is again: a food-shipping warehouse on the east side. José's people will be on that site, collecting the goods, after they close for work at five o'clock.

"Representatives of the FBI, DEA and local law enforcement will be on hand for the bust. Meanwhile other elements of the operation will stand ready to execute arrest warrants for forty-three suspected Aztecas, including José Martinez. We expect to haul in more dope and more guns when we make the arrests. Special Agent Muir of the ATF can give us some information about that."

The man spoke up from his spot at the table: "We know that last week José Martinez's outfit shipped twenty-four brand new AK-47s, purchased from one of our agents, into Juárez. The Mexican police have the serial numbers of the weapons and, upon seizure, will be able to confirm the transaction. They also sent a thousand rounds of 7.62mm ammunition down south. Clearly they don't plan on letting those guns sit around picking up rust."

"How do we know those guns haven't already disappeared?" Cristina asked.

"I received word at a meeting with my opposite number in Juárez that the weapon situation was under control," McPeek said.

"What does that mean?"

"It means it's *under control*," McPeek said more firmly. "The Mexican authorities now know who receives weapons and where they're kept after they make the crossing. It's a real coup, and on this side of the border we get to stack gun charges on top of every-thing else José's people are on the hook for."

"Our agents have sold the Aztecas a pretty sizable arsenal of arms," Muir said. "Pistols, shotguns, semiautomatic rifles. I want everyone here to know that they could be looking down the barrels of these guns when it comes time to put people in handcuffs. Every entry is considered high-risk."

Robinson nudged Cristina's arm and leaned in close. "When isn't it?" he asked.

"We don't want a shootout or a standoff on our hands when we go in," McPeek said, "so our agents and officers on the ground are going to execute these warrants hard and fast. Are there any questions? Then let's move on."

There was more, but Cristina had heard all she needed to hear. At her level, they would be responsible for executing warrants, cleaning up the trash. She hadn't expected any more than that and was not disappointed. The questions she had could not be asked in an open room. McPeek never mentioned Flip by name, but all of them knew that there was someone on the inside and that someone had given up José's secrets.

The slides came and went. Cristina pretended to take notes. When finally it was over, she lingered to shake hands with a few people she knew. She saw McPeek deflecting invitations for more talk, and once when their eyes met, McPeek nodded to her.

It took fifteen minutes for the room to clear. McPeek took her time stripping the cables from her laptop. The big screen had gone blue. Robinson closed the conference room door.

"Excited?" McPeek asked.

"Of course," Cristina said.

"All right. This is a good operation for everybody. Everyone will look great."

Robinson stood beside Cristina, waiting for her to speak first. His arms were crossed in front of his chest.

"We wanted to talk to you about Flip," Cristina said.

"What about him?"

"Well, we want to know how he's going to be handled. If everything happens the way you say, he's going to be swept up with the rest of the Aztecas. Then what?"

"He's an informant. He'll be taken care of."

"We were hoping for something a little more concrete," Robinson said.

McPeek packed her laptop into a slim case. She stopped and looked at both of them. "Why are you always coming to me worrying about your CI?"

"Flip gave us good information. He's been loyal from the get-go. I want to know that if he sticks his neck out even further to testify, he's not going to get it chopped off," Cristina said. "Didn't you just listen to your presentation? José Martinez is a criminal in two countries, dealing in drugs, guns and murder. I think we have a right to be concerned about Flip's welfare."

"Fine," McPeek said. "What do you want?"

"If he testifies against the Aztecas, he has to disappear," Robinson said.

"We can relocate him."

"What about his family? If the Aztecas can't get to him, they'll go after his mother, the people he's closest to."

"Arrangements can be made," McPeek said.

"Are you sure?" Cristina asked.

"I'm sure. Listen, I don't know what you think about how the FBI does its business, but we're not in the habit of using informants up and then letting them burn. I promise you we'll take good care of Flip, whether he turns himself in voluntarily or he gets picked up in the sweep. Is that good enough for you?"

Cristina looked to Robinson and then to McPeek. "It's good enough for me."

EIGHTEEN

THE SHIPMENT LEFT THE DEPOT IN THE middle of the day with Matías and a squad of Felix Rivera's men watching. Matías got on the radio: "Paco, the truck is headed your way. Follow it to the bridge and make sure it makes no stops along the way."

"You got it," Paco replied.

Their black panel van was hot and Matías wiped a trickle of sweat from his forehead. There was nothing to be done about the perspiration gathering underneath his clothes and the vest he wore. When this was over he would feel dirty and itchy. He was already beginning to feel that way.

Matías changed channels. "All units, move in."

The driver turned the engine over and the van leaped forward. At the same time Matías heard the sudden wail of sirens and up ahead local and federal police vehicles screeched up to the gates of the depot. The panel van shot through the heart into the open area before the building, surrounded on all sides by trucks loading and unloading. One of Felix's men opened the side cargo door and Matías jumped out into the blazing sun with the others behind him.

Loaders and drivers already had their hands up as more vehicles poured in through the gates. Black-armored forms swarmed out onto the asphalt brandishing weapons. Matías climbed the steps up to the building's entrance with his gun out. He pointed at a man.

"Gonzalo Flores. Where is he?"

The man indicated the door without lowering his hands. Matías was aware of two PF agents at his back as he passed through the entrance. It was much darker inside and Matías' sun-dazzled eyes had to adjust. He saw an office through a broad glass window. Inside there were women and men, their hands going up at the sight of weapons.

Matías tried the door. It was locked. "Open it!" he commanded.

An electric lock buzzed and Matías was through. "Gonzalo Flores," he said.

A man emerged from another door. Matías recognized him immediately. "I am Gonzalo Flores," he said.

"Get down on the ground!" Matías commanded.

Flores obeyed immediately and Matías crouched over him to bind his wrists with plastic cuffs. The PF agents were into the connecting rooms now, herding out bodies, gathering everyone in one corner of the front office.

"Secure the files," Matías told the agents. "The rest of you sit down on the ground with your hands on your heads."

"What have I done?" Flores asked.

"You be quiet," Matías replied. "You'll have time to talk later."

It took less then ten minutes to secure the entire depot. More than twenty employees and eleven truck drivers were detained, lined up on the concrete platform outside the loading docks. Everywhere there were police. An armored truck stood in the middle of the yard, squatting like an enormous black beetle.

Matías saw Felix Rivera, carrying a shotgun and armored like the rest of his men. They shook hands. "Nice and smooth," Felix said.

"We'll pull their records apart," Matías said. "The Aztecas' contact here has been taking cash payments for months. This isn't the first time they've shipped from this place."

"What about the truck with the goods?"

"On its way to America."

"A good day. We're executing raids on the stash houses as we speak."

Matías' phone rang. He parted from Felix and answered. "*Bueno.*"

"Matías, it's me."

"Elvira! Now's not a good time."

"What are you doing?"

Matías looked along the line of detainees, cross-legged with their hands cuffed behind their backs. Almost all of them would be released, but first they would be questioned and the fear of God put into each and every one of them. The worst off would be Gonzalo Flores. Matías expected he would not even need Sosa and Galvan for him.

"Matías?"

"I'm in the middle of something. Can I call you back?"

"No, I'm getting on a plane."

"A plane? To where?"

"To Juárez."

"*Elvira…* why didn't you tell me?"

"I thought you'd be glad."

"I am glad. It's just that I won't be home until late tonight."

"I can wait for you."

Matías' lip trembled and for a moment he thought he might cry, but it would do no good for anyone to see him that way. He put his hand over his face. "I'm happy you decided to come back," he said.

"I'll see you tonight. I love you."

"I love you, too."

There were many things to do and clearing up the shipping depot was only one of them. The detainees were rounded into wagons and transported to the local command center where they could be processed. Tattooed Aztecas were kept separate from the civilians. Agents were in and out of interview rooms. The sheer amount of paperwork was enough to bury Matías for two weeks.

Paco returned from the border with news that the truck had crossed over without incident. He dived into the sea of forms alongside Matías and there was much coffee and takeout food consumed. Every time Matías looked up, another hour had vanished.

Finally he'd had enough. He straightened up in his chair at a borrowed desk and stretched until his back popped. "That's it," he said. "I'm finished."

"It doesn't look like you're finished."

"I can't look at another page. We'll go at it again tomorrow."

"What about Flores? Did you want to interview him tonight?"

Matías shook his head. "Let him sweat it out in a cell for now. He can wait."

"I don't understand. I figured you'd want to work all night."

"Elvira came home," Matías said.

"What? That's terrific!"

"I'd like to get home before midnight," Matías said. "And before I'm useless. You should go home, too. Daniela will be surprised."

"Maybe I will. And listen, Matías…"

"Yes?"

"Good job today."

"It was a team effort. You were with me all the way. I just did what I had to do. Good-night, Paco."

He left the building and found his car. The lot was still crowded. Many police would work through the night. A part of him felt guilty for leaving them for this, but he knew mostly they would understand.

It was too late to find a florist open, but an all-night *farmacia* had cheap bouquets for sale by the register. Matías picked one with yellow and red flowers. The clerk complimented his choice.

The block was crowded near the apartment and he was forced

to park a ways from the building. The street was quiet and the city was calm. He did not hear the crackle of gunfire from some faraway place.

He was curious to know how things had gone on the American side. Tomorrow he would call Jamie McPeek and she would tell him everything. Matías almost skipped to the door.

In the vestibule he paused to check the mail, but there was none. Elvira must have collected it. He put his keys in the lock of the inner door when the outer door swung wide.

Matías couldn't turn before the first bullets struck him. The noise was thunderous in the confined space and he went deaf in the instant he was torn apart. He dropped the bouquet and it fell into blood. His feet slipped. He could not stand. The shooter kept on until his gun was empty, then let the door close. Matías imagined the sound of running footsteps down the sidewalk.

He was stained with red and more was coming all the time. Matías tasted copper in his mouth. When he slumped over he saw his keys were still dangling from the lock.

Elvira, he thought. There was more, but it clouded over and he was borne away.

NINETEEN

CRISTINA SAW FLIP LEAVE THE WAREHOUSE in his girlfriend's car and one by one the other employees headed on their way. Alfredo Rodriguez was the last to go, pausing at his truck for a long time, casting his gaze back toward the building as if he was considering going back inside. Cristina wished him away. "Come on," she said under her breath. "Don't be stupid."

"There he goes," Robinson said.

Space was at premium on the road outside the warehouse gate and the car Cristina and Robinson rode in was one of only three lined up along the face of a vacant lot facing the building. One held a quartet of DEA agents, the other a like number of El Paso police. Any more and they risked tipping off the Aztecas when they came for their truck. The truck that idled on the west side of the warehouse, the driver still behind the wheel. Cristina tried to imagine how much they were paying the man to take this risk. Probably not much.

More police waited a block away in the parking lot of a closed-down fast-food restaurant. They would swing into place once Cristina, Robinson and the others moved. No one knew how many Aztecas to expect, but they were ready to handle the situation however it played out.

They waited nearly an hour before another vehicle came up the road. Cristina spotted them in the side mirror coming closer: a dark blue pick-up truck with a cherry shine, followed by a green sedan. The pick-up passed them and left-handed through the gates. There were at least three in the king cab. The sedan was full.

Cristina drew her weapon, checked it. Beside her, Robinson did the same. "Five or six guys," Cristina said. "Easy."

"Just watch yourself," Robinson said.

"I'm always careful."

The pick-up and sedan pulled alongside the Mexican truck and disgorged their passengers. There were eight Aztecas altogether and they fanned out in the empty yard, forming a loose perimeter around the trucks. At this distance Cristina could not see if they were armed. She had to assume they would be.

The Mexican driver got down from his seat and came around the back to unlock the cargo area. The truck had an extendable ramp. He put that down and walked up inside with one of the Aztecas.

The radio beside Cristina squawked. "Salas, we're waiting on your go." That was Hanning, one of the DEA agents.

Cristina took up the radio. "Give it a minute. I want to see the stuff coming out."

As if on command the Mexican truck driver and the Azteca reappeared, carrying square bundles that looked heavy. An Azteca put down the tailgate of the pick-up and lifted the plastic shell that covered the bed. The men moved toward it.

"Okay, let's go. Everybody go," Cristina said.

Cristina hit the siren and peeled away from the curb, leaving rubber trails behind. The car jounced as it crossed the threshold of the warehouse gate. Behind her the other cars had their lights and sirens going. They came up alongside quickly and all three screeched to a halt a dozen yards from the pick-up.

She bailed out of the driver's seat with the engine still running, vaguely aware of Robinson doing the same. Cristina saw Aztecas breaking for the far end of the warehouse, but others stood where they were as if frozen. The nearest Azteca had his back to her and did not move.

"Police! Everybody get down on the ground!" Robinson bellowed.

Cristina came out from behind the shield of the driver's side door, weapon out and leveled on the closest Azteca. He still had not moved. "Get down on the ground *now*!" she shouted.

He turned. The movement was so casual that Cristina could only look at him as he faced her. She saw him clearly: a young man in his early twenties, a tattoo on his neck, a t-shirt worn beneath an open short-sleeved shirt. His jeans rode too low on his hips.

The gun in his fist caught the angled sunlight. It was a ridiculous weapon, one of the heavy, oversized .44 automatics that looked good being carried around. A gun to be seen. Cristina saw the barrel pointed directly at her and then the flash.

Robinson was yelling, the DEA agents were yelling. A crippling blow crashed into her chest, crushing the wind out of her lungs, spiking pain. She was hurled back against the open car door and the side mirror struck her on the back of the head. Cristina saw bright light. Then she was down and she could not breathe.

Weapons fired on both sides of her, but Cristina did not see the Azteca go down. She could only picture it as she stared up into the sky, struggling to take a breath. There was the dimmest awareness of her pistol resting in her right hand, but she couldn't move her limbs. The asphalt beneath her was flat and hot.

Suddenly Robinson was above her, filling her vision and blocking out the sky. Her head was buzzing from lack of oxygen. Robinson touched her cheek and called her name. His words filtered through to her slowly. *Breathe, goddamn it. Breathe!*

Cristina struggled to fill her lungs and then at all once she was able to suck down air. Her whole chest was on fire, as if her ribs were cracked. Robinson supported her head, still telling her to breathe, breathe.

"Freddie…" she managed to say.

"You're all right," Robinson said. "It didn't go through. Your vest stopped it. You're all right."

She reached for Robinson's arm and gripped it. Now she felt heady, on the verge of passing out. There were still sparkling flecks in her vision. "Freddie," she said again.

"You're going to see Freddie," Robinson said.

Mom is going to be all right and she'll always come home to you. I promise.

"I promise," Cristina said.

TWENTY

He sat in Graciela's little apartment on the undersized couch, listening to the rattle of the air conditioner and the babble of the television. Graciela worked in the compact kitchen making something, he didn't know what. When his phone rang, Flip saw it was José.

"That son of a bitch," José said to Flip. "That *hijo de puta!*"

Flip was still. It had been hard to leave the warehouse and harder still to come home with Graciela knowing what happened next. They told him not to worry. They told him José would be taken with all the others. But he had known, he had *known*, and now José was on the phone. "What's happening?"

"That bastard boss of yours sold us out!"

"Alfredo?"

"Yes, Alfredo! That shit-sucking bastard told the cops. They were all over the warehouse when we came to get the stuff! Who knows what else they know! I can't get through to anybody."

"Where are you now?" Flip asked.

"I'm on the road with Angel and Fernando. Where are you?"

"At Graciela's," Flip said, and immediately regretted it.

"Meet me at the apartment. Ten minutes. Meet me right now. We have to figure out how to work this."

"I don't know what I can do," Flip said.

"Just meet me!" José said and killed the call.

Flip felt the tremors threatening. His stomach was cold. He sat woodenly on the couch hearing nothing but his own heartbeat. Then he called the detectives. Their phones both went to voice mail.

"Who was that?" Graciela asked from the kitchen.

"José. I have to meet him."

"Now?"

Flip nodded stiffly. "Now."

"But I almost have dinner ready."

He got up from the couch and went to Graciela. He put his arms around her and held her tightly for as long as he dared, because if he held on too long he would not let go. "I'll be back," he said.

"How long?"

"I don't know. I'll be back. I need to borrow your car."

"You don't have a license."

"I know how to drive. Just let me borrow it."

Graciela left the two-burner stove reluctantly and found her keys in her purse. "Don't wreck it."

"I won't."

Flip went down to the street and got into the car. It felt strange to have a steering wheel under his hands. For a seemingly endless moment he just sat, afraid to turn the key, afraid to go. He started the car.

José's Lexus was in the parking lot when he got there. He saw no one in the pool, but a floating lounge kicked around at the edge, abandoned and caught in the circulating current. He held the keys to the apartment in his hand, the sharp edges digging into his skin. Every step to the second floor was an effort. At the door time expanded again and it seemed a long while before he put key to lock and let himself in.

The three of them were in the living room. José was pacing. "It's about fucking time," José said. "I thought they got you, too."

"I'm here," Flip said.

"Angel, Fernando, wait outside," José commanded the two big

men. "If you see anything, you holler out. Go."

Flip stood aside to let them out and shut the door behind them. José was pacing again.

"That motherfucker Alfredo must have told them everything," José said. "Now they're all over the family. Nobody's answering their phones. It's just you and me now, Flip."

"If the cops know everything, then they know about this place," Flip said.

"Yeah, yeah, yeah, but maybe not. I didn't see anybody when we came."

José threw himself down into a chair and ran a hand through his hair. He was sweating badly and it showed through his shirt. A vein stood out prominently in his forehead.

"What do you want me to do?" Flip asked.

"You're gonna help me deal with the situation," José said. "We're gonna start with your boss. They might come to get us, but we're gonna let them know what happens when they fuck with the Indians."

Flip came closer to José. Already he was breathing shallowly and too fast and he worried that he might faint if he kept on. He wished he was wearing his wire, but there had been no time for that. The only ones who would know what was said were him and José, and maybe it was better that way.

"I'm putting a green light out on Alfredo," José said. "You understand? And you're gonna do it."

Slowly, Flip told himself. He forced himself to keep from hyperventilating. Now he was within an arm's length of José in the chair. "I don't have a gun," Flip said.

"I have one. Or you can borrow Fernando's. Yeah, you can borrow Fernando's. Just walk up to that motherfucker and *pop!*"

"Alfredo's my mother's fiancé," Flip said.

"Fuck that!" José exclaimed. "I don't care who he is! He's *dead.*"

"I can't do it," Flip said. He put his hand in his pocket.

"What do you mean, you can't do it? I just *told* you to do it. And when I tell you to do something, it gets done. You understand?"

"I won't go against my family."

"Flip, you stupid bastard, I *made* you!" José rose from the chair and speared the air with his hands. "You have a family right here and I'm telling you to do a green light!"

"I can't," Flip said.

"I gave you everything! This place? Mine! Graciela? Mine! Opportunities? All mine! You belong to me!"

Flip had the knife out and open before José could see. Flip stabbed him twice quickly, low in the body, beneath the ribs. José made a sharp exhaling sound and then Flip stabbed him again in the side of the neck.

José fell back in the chair and Flip was on him, stabbing over and over. He did not stop when José scrabbled at him with weakening hands, or when a shower of misting blood sprayed in his face. José was masked in it, drenched in blood, and Flip's right hand was covered to the wrist. A gurgling sound came from José's throat.

Now Flip stepped away, his shoulders heaving with great, sucking breaths. He was filthy with José's blood, his jeans soaked and the front of his shirt smeared where José tried to fight him off. Flip looked at the knife and saw that crimson had sunk into the deep lines of the carved handle. The blade was spotted. He wiped it on his leg and put it away.

Angel and Fernando were still outside. Flip lifted the edge of the blinds and peeked out at them. They were watching the courtyard. He went to the front door and turned the deadbolt.

Immediately there was a knock. "José? José, what's going on? José!"

Flip retreated to one of the bedrooms. One of them, either Angel or Fernando, was kicking the front door now. Flip went to the window. Iron bars crossed the pane.

He remembered something about his keychain and he fumbled

with it, his hand blood-slicked and already growing tacky. A small key to go with the door key. Flip threw open the window and fitted the small key to a lock on the bars. They came open.

The front door crashed open as he snaked through the open window. He fell onto a walkway that traversed the back of the building, linking one apartment to the next. Flip left a bloody smear on the concrete as he scrambled to his feet and ran for the far staircase just as quickly as he could.

"Stop!" someone shouted from behind. Flip did not stop.

He flew down the steps two at a time and dashed for the open street at the end of the lot. Then he was around the corner of the building. José's Lexus waited and, beside it, Graciela's car.

Flip had her keys in his hand. He crossed the nose of the Hyundai when a shot rang out. A stinging, burning pain sprang up in the back of his leg and suddenly he could not put weight on that foot. Another shot turned the Hyundai's windshield into a field of spider webs.

Fresh blood poured down his leg as he got behind the wheel. Flip could feel it dripping into his sock and the spreading warmth beneath him told him it was soaking into the seat. He turned over the engine, crashed the shift into reverse and laid twin rails of black rubber out of the parking lot and into the street. A passing car clipped the bumper and went skidding out of control.

Another bullet struck the side of the car and then another. Flip put the Hyundai into drive and stomped the accelerator with his good foot, skirting the other car. In the rear view mirror he saw Fernando in the street with a gun, but no more shots came.

He knew where he was going and how to get there and he did not let up on the gas. Stop signs and lights streaked past, but he didn't slow for them. By the time he saw Graciela's building he felt dizzy. The floor mat was thick with his blood.

Flip hopped the curb on the right-hand side and brought the car to a stop. He stumbled out of the driver's seat into the street and then dragged himself to the sidewalk. The entrance to the building seemed a mile away. He levered himself up on the leg that would hold him and half-walked the rest of the way until he could fall against the door. His fingers were going numb as he sorted out the right key and inside there were stairs to navigate. He was leaving a trail behind him, wet and wine-colored.

When he made it to the second floor he had just enough strength to knock. He collapsed with his forehead against the cool wooden floor. The door opened and Graciela was screaming, pulling him onto his back, touching his face.

Flip tried to push himself across the threshold, but there was no more left. A ringing started in his ears and blackness played at the edges of his vision. "Graciela," he whispered.

Graciela was bawling into the phone. It was too late for that, Flip wanted to tell her. He'd left too much of himself along the way. *Just be with me now*, he thought.

"Graciela."

"They're coming, baby. You're going to be all right."

"Graciela, I'm sorry," Flip murmured. More black now, closing over him. He couldn't feel his pulse beat in his leg anymore.

Graciela held his head in her lap. "Don't talk, Flip."

"Take care…" he said.

"Flip, don't talk."

"Take…"

"Flip? Flip! *Flip!*"

He heard her yelling as from far away. He couldn't see at all. Her touch faded. Flip tried to form a thought, but it wouldn't happen. He felt his heart beat slower and slower.

Flip didn't know why he'd been afraid. Dying was easy after all.

TWENTY-ONE

THEY WERE STILL IN PLACE WHEN CRISTINA got home, the FBI agents in their car, watching. More than likely they would stay there a while, at least until things settled down, though the crisis was past. José Martinez was dead. He wasn't going to be green-lighting anybody.

It still hurt where the bullet had struck the vest in the middle of her chest. Afterwards, when she took off her shirt in the ladies' room to check herself, she saw a quarter-sized black bruise between her breasts with livid colors branching out from it. Over time it would probably spread, even as it faded. Hopefully it would stop hurting so much; it pained her just to move her arms or breathe.

The lights were on in her house. Cristina had asked Ashlee to stay late to cover for her. It was well past Freddie's bedtime. She took an uncomfortable breath and let it out, repeated that, and then she was ready to get out of the car.

Tonight she didn't wave to the FBI men. She was just too tired. Fatigue wore heavily around her shoulders and weight of a different kind, as well. Cristina thought of Flip.

Ashlee was on the couch watching television. "Oh, you're here," she said.

"All done," Cristina said. "Sorry you had to wait so long."

"It's no problem."

"Did you get Freddie to bed all right?"

"Yeah, he was great."

"Good. I guess I'll take over from here."

She waited while Ashlee gathered up her things and then they said good-bye at the front door. Cristina watched from the window until Ashlee got into her car, though she needn't have bothered. There were others watching, after all.

On another night she might have gone for the refrigerator and a cold beer, but tonight she went straight down the hall to Freddie's room. The door stood ajar, the room dark inside. Cristina listened and heard Freddie's sonorous breathing.

She slipped in. Freddie seemed so small in his bed, covered by a blanket, his head canted to one side, his mouth open. Cristina sat on the edge of the mattress and lay her hand on his belly. In with breath, out with breath, slow and steady.

Her first thought was to wake him, but she did not. Then, unbidden, he stirred under her hand and she saw his eyes open, the lids heavy with sleep. "Mom?" he asked.

"I'm here, peanut."

"I was dreaming."

"What were you dreaming about?"

Freddie stretched, his skinny arms over his head, and he yawned. "I was dreaming about elevators. *Glass* elevators."

"Was it a good dream?"

"Yeah." He closed his eyes and didn't speak for a while. Cristina thought he might have fallen asleep again. She was about to lift her hand from his body when he said, "Are you home?"

"I'm home."

"You weren't here for bedtime."

"I'm sorry. Mom had to work."

"Were there bad people?"

"Yes."

Freddie turned on his side and nuzzled his pillow. "Will you stay with me?"

"I'll stay with you until you fall asleep," Cristina said.

"Okay."

"I love you, peanut."

"I love you, too."

TWENTY-TWO

HE WAS AWARE OF PRESSURE ON HIS LEG, LIKE a thick rubber band wrapped too tightly around his thigh. Beneath the pressure was pain, lurking and subdued. The room was dim.

"There he is," said someone.

The light came up slowly against Flip's eyelids and then it was bright. It hurt for him to open his eyes. They felt gummed shut.

First he saw the nurse and then he saw the detectives. They stood near the door to the room, watching him. He could see out into the hallway beyond and there was a uniformed cop there, sitting in a straight-backed chair.

"Give him a minute," the nurse said. "The drip has to wear off."

"Thanks," said Detective Salas.

The nurse left. Flip become aware of the tubes running from the backs of his hands, the gentle clamp on the tip of his index finger and the machines that monitored him, all lights and numbers.

"Welcome back, Flip," Detective Salas said.

Flip's throat was terribly dry and when he tried to speak he failed. He licked his lips and swallowed and tried again. "I thought I was dead," he said.

"You were."

"Clinically dead," Detective Robinson added.

"How do you feel?"

"Not good."

"It's the drugs. It'll pass."

"Graciela…"

"Your girlfriend? She's here," Detective Salas said.

"Can I see her?"

"Sure. Your mother's here, too."

"Good," Flip said and he closed his eyes again.

The detectives didn't leave. "Flip, there are going to be lots of questions. José…"

Flip opened his eyes. "I killed him."

"You have to answer for that."

"I will."

"I'll get your people," Cristina said. "Rest up."

They slipped out the door and left Flip alone. He waited for Graciela and his mother. He wondered what he would tell them, what they had already been told. He tried to imagine what the police would do to him, the prison he would go to.

Flip found he didn't care much for any of the answers. They would come and he would deal with them. He had already died. There was nothing left to do.